WHEN THE SNOW GUMS DANCE

ANNE RENNIE

Anne Rennie is one of Australia's bestselling authors. Born in Cambridge, England, Anne studied at the Royal College of Music in London and the Akademie fur Musik, Vienna. She went on to become secretary and concert manager of the Royal Philharmonic Orchestra in London before meeting her Australian husband on the ski slopes of Austria, marrying and moving to Australia. There she raised a family, taught Suzuki piano and fell in love with the country.

Her first novel *Reach for the Dream* became an instant bestseller and was quickly followed by *Ride with the Wind* and *Song of the Bellbirds*. After conquering crippling arthritis Anne wrote *Pain-Free Living, a Cookbook for Arthritis Sufferers* that continues to help sufferers worldwide. Her short stories and articles have been published in anthologies, and leading magazines and newspapers.

Anne was described in *Dymocks Monthly Review* as '... fast becoming an Australian literary voice to be reckoned with', and was featured in ABC TV's *Australian Story*. She is a keen glider pilot and in 1998, with husband Jim, won the NSW Two-Seater Gliding Championship. Anne wants to continue to write stories that are 'a darn good read' and to encourage others to reach for their dreams. She is currently working on her next novel.

Also by Anne Rennie

Fiction
Reach for the Dream
Ride with the Wind
Song of the Bellbirds

Nonfiction
Pain-Free Living, a Cookbook for
 Arthritis Sufferers

Critical acclaim for Anne Rennie

'Anne Rennie is fast becoming an Australian literary voice to be reckoned with.'
DYMOCKS MONTHLY BOOK REVIEW

'You can smell the smells, hear the birds, and taste the grit in your mouth.'
THE LAND

'The Australian Outback has provided inspiration for some of the most outstanding and memorable pieces of Australian literature – and to that list can now be added Anne Rennie's story *Reach for the Dream*.'
NEW IDEA

'A story of endless twists and turns, soaring success and bitter tragedy ... Anne Rennie again delivers a thrilling saga.'
TURF MONTHLY

What readers say about Anne's novels:

'Wonderful! ... filled with emotions. I cried yet again but also smiled.' Karen Moore, Sydney Australia

'One of the most heartwrenching stories I have ever read.' Delia Connor, Massachusett, USA

'Adrenalin pumping, high romance, fast action – Anne's got them all! ... a ripping good yarn.' Robyn Pearce, Auckland, New Zealand

'Unputdownable' Molly Balaban, Islington, UK

'Anne has always kept me enthralled with her pages ...' Catherine Bird, Sydney, Australia

'I am hooked ... my Mum hasn't been able to put it down either and is suffering from lack of sleep!' Belinda Battersby, Scott Creek, South Australia

WHEN THE SNOW GUMS
DANCE

ANNE RENNIE

POCKET BOOKS

SYDNEY • NEW YORK • LONDON • TORONTO

If you wish to write to anne rennie she can be contacted via her website www.annerennie.com

WHEN THE SNOW GUMS DANCE

First published in Australia by Pocket Books in 2002
An imprint of Simon & Schuster Australia
20 Barcoo Street, East Roseville NSW 2069

A Viacom Company
Sydney New York London Toronto Singapore

© Anne Rennie 2002

All rights reserved. No part of this publication may be reproduced, stored in a retrieval system, or transmitted, in any form or by any means, electronic, mechanical, photocopying, recording or otherwise, without the prior permission of the publisher in writing.

National Library of Australia
Cataloguing-in-Publication data

Rennie, Anne
  When the snow gums dance

ISBN 0 7318 1019 8

1. Skiers – Victoria – Fiction. 2. Man-woman relationships – Victoria – Fiction. 3. Australian Alps (N.S.W. and Vic.) – Fiction. I. Title.

A 823.3

Cover design: Michael Killalea
Cover image: Michael Killalea
Set in 11/14 pt Sabon
Typeset by Asset Typesetting, Moruya, NSW
Printed in Australia by Griffin Press

10 9 8 7 6 5 4 3 2 1

To Jim, Patsy and Ellie with all my love

Acknowledgments

As always when writing a novel there are many people to thank. Once again thank you all for your patience, understanding and willingness to share your knowledge.

In particular I would like to thank the following: Dr Gordon Foulde, Dr Paul Preisz, Dr Martin Duffy, Trish Hendry, from St Vincent's Hospital Emergency Centre, Darlinghurst, Sydney; Dr Ian Cameron, Professor of Rehabilitation, Royal Rehabilitation Centre, Sydney; Therese Hannah, researcher for *All Saints,* Channel 7; my friends from Whistler Resort, Canada, and Heavenly Inn, Lake Tahoe, USA; Perisher Valley, Australia; John Menyhart for our wonderful stay at Smiggin Holes, Australia; James Nichols from Community Aid Abroad, Emergency Relief; NSW State Emergency Services; Australian Volunteers International; and my nephew Clinton Duncan.

Thank you to Jody Lee and the team at Simon & Schuster for so warmly embracing *When the Snow Gums Dance*. Heartfelt thanks to my dear friend and agent Selwa Anthony with her wealth of ideas and knowledge, who is always there to guide and encourage; to Julia Stiles who tirelessly edits my novels in the kindest possible way. Most of all thank you to my wonderful husband Jim and my two gorgeous girls, Patsy and Ellie. *When the Snow Gums Dance* would never have been written without your endless patience, encouragement and humour. Thank you, Jim, for teaching me the joy of skiing.

Legend of the Snow Gums

There is a legend that if two people kiss beneath the snowgum, arms entwined under branches heavy with snow, the love that results will be more potent and more passionate than any other on the face of the earth. Yet in adversity that love can freeze over in an instant, like the crystal-clear icicles that hang from the snow gums' branches, or melt into nothing with the coming of the spring warmth. To be kissed beneath the snow gums is to receive love at its most pure and its most devilish, and only immeasurable sacrifice can bring peace to the lovers.

PART ONE

Chapter One

Seventeen-year-old Kylie Harris knew she didn't really have time to ski the slalom course before the school bus arrived that crisp winter morning. She also knew that if her mother found out she was risking being late for one of her final-year trial exams, she would almost certainly be banned from competing in the Lyrebird Cup tomorrow, a race she desperately wanted to win. But in her mind she had no choice. Three times now she had fallen on Murphy's Turn, the last steep bend of the course. She needed a couple more goes at it.

The sun was just peeping over the snow-capped ridges of Victoria's Snowy Mountains as Kylie crept from the drying room of Sunburst Lodge and out into the snow, clutching her skis and stocks and school bag. Shivering, she zipped up her purple and white ski jacket, a hand-me-down from her elder sister Gwyneth. She adjusted the tight-fitting black ski pants she had saved six months to buy, and which her mother heartily disapproved of, and crunched quietly down the road. Heart pounding guiltily, she stepped into her skis and pulled on her gloves. She pulled the headband up around her wild, flaming red hair, and slung her school bag over one shoulder, glancing quickly behind her to check the house was still sleeping. Grabbing her poles, she pushed off towards the express quad chairlift that would take her up to Koala Bowl and the slalom course.

Kylie had stepped into her first pair of skis when she was two, but it was not until Geoff and Susan Harris bought Sunburst Lodge in the heart of Lyrebird Falls ski resort eight years ago that Kylie's passion for skiing really started to blossom. Encouraged by her parents, both good skiers themselves, she discovered she was a natural and she quickly started winning trophies. The prestigious Lyrebird Cup was the only junior trophy in the district she hadn't won. This year was Kylie's last chance to compete, and she was convinced that if she could add this internationally recognised award to her collection, she had a far greater chance of being accepted into one of the overseas ski hire clinics. She intended to apply as soon as she could afford the airfare. For passionate, uninhibited Kylie, the Lyrebird Cup was the start of her dream to become a ski instructor to the rich and famous.

By the time Kylie had covered the distance between Sunburst Lodge and the chairlift, she had convinced herself if the worst happened and she missed the bus she could get around her dad. Not only had she inherited his adventurous spirit and fearlessness on the slopes, she knew how proud he was of her skiing achievements and that he understood how much winning the Lyrebird Cup meant to her. She had also learned from him that there were times in life when you took risks. This was one of those times. Besides, her mother was far too occupied organising Gwyneth's wedding to take her usual notice of Kylie's activities. Last night there had been talk of nothing else, her dad trying to work out how they were going to accommodate all the cars, while Gwyn and Susan went over and over the plans with such controlled precision and boring detail that Kylie had wanted to scream out, 'What happened to romance and fun?' But she had kept quiet, partly because she wanted her sister to be happy, and partly because she was hoping that they would all stay up so late, immersed in the wedding, that they would be too tired to hear her slink off before school. Kylie had been right about slinking off. There had been no sign of movement as she had slipped past her parents' bedroom door this morning.

Tom Wickham, the resort engineer, was already on his daily rounds, checking the chairlifts for ice and any mechanical problems. He greeted Kylie with a cheery grin. 'Bit early for the milk run,' he laughed.

'I know. I was hoping ... Please, Tom, can I get an earlier ride? I wanted to have another go at the slalom course and I don't know if I can make it this afternoon, with exams and everything.' She turned her melting green eyes on him.

Tom thought for a moment. He knew how desperately Kylie wanted to win the Lyrebird Cup. 'Go on then,' he smiled. He radioed to his mate at the top of the slope, then pressed the button so the chairs slowly ground into motion. 'Just you be careful up there today, there's still quite a bit of ice about.'

'You're tops!' grinned Kylie. Quickly she slid her bag off her shoulder and handed it to Tom with a grateful smile. She skied through the automatic bars and onto the quad chair. 'I'll love you forever,' she shouted, pulling the safety bar down in front of her.

Kylie's mood changed from guilt to excitement as the chair sped her up the mountainside. She glanced at her watch. It'd take her ten minutes to get to the top; if she went flat out, she'd just have time for two runs and still make it to the bus. She looked around her, as always filled with awe at the beauty of the snowfields. Behind and above her stood the main restaurant of Lyrebird Falls, the ski racks empty, the buildings silent. Beneath her and to either side, clouded in a faint mist, stunted gumtrees lined the wide pistes, a faint dusting of snow on their frosted branches. They sent long shadowy blue fingers across the pristine slopes which were broken by the occasional rock starting to break through. Snowmakers dotted the bottom of the slope, ready to spew out snow with the flick of a switch. Kylie's eyes glowed with delight as the quad chair reached the peak; here the snow was tinged a pinky gold by the early morning sun. This was the magic of Lyrebird Falls: the silence, the empty world, the crisp breeze stinging her cheeks, the challenge of the slopes.

Kylie adjusted her sunglasses then skied across to Koala Bowl and the top of the slalom course. Sheltered from the wind, with the sun on the slope for most of the day, the run was both delightful and challenging, with sheltered spots that could get icy as soft snow refroze. Today it was groomed to perfection but the freezing overnight temperatures had left a hard crusty surface and icy patches. A young man clad in the purple and green resort gear was placing the slalom poles in position. He waved to her. Kylie waved back and then skied across to the start gate, a built-up mound of snow. Perched on the steep slope, she glanced down the mountain and her heart started to pound. She set her watch and pushed off. Knees bent, skis parallel, she zigzagged down the slope, carving the first tracks of the day. The cold wind brushed her cheeks and made her eyes water. She sped up, digging her ski edges in harder as she went, exulting in the pure rhythmic freedom.

The first two corners were easy, the snow crisp and firm under her skis. At the next turn she almost lost her balance as her skis slipped over ice. Jolted, she took the next bit slightly more slowly, then covered a steep but fairly easy run across a wider piste, slid comfortably round the next curve and headed towards Murphy's Turn. Her stomach muscles tightened as she neared the dreaded spot. Forcing herself to relax, she rapidly recited her instructions to herself, shifting her weight, bending her knees. She was almost around. Heart pounding, totally focused, she felt a rush of exhilaration. She was going to do it! Just as she thought she was clear, her outside ski slipped and she lost her balance. She toppled sideways and slewed round on the icy surface, losing her left ski as she skidded downhill at an alarming rate. Frantically she tried to grab onto snow, the side of the track, anything, her gloved hands grasping and scrabbling as she slid faster and faster down the slope. Her other ski was wrenched from her boot, her poles snatched from her wrists as she fell.

She started to panic. There was nothing she could do to stop herself. For what seemed a lifetime she careered downhill. Then finally she was on softer snow. Just as she realised she wasn't going to die she slammed into a large pile of snow, just missing the base of a tall gumtree. A searing pain shot through her right knee. For a few moments she lay still, shaking with relief. Gingerly she tried to stand up, but then abruptly collapsed, overwhelmed with pain. She rubbed her knee and tried standing again. This time the pain was less severe. Fighting back tears of anger and disappointment, she brushed the snow from her jacket and looked up the hill. Her skis and stocks were dark patches on the slope. Slowly and painfully she trudged uphill and collected her gear, angrily dashing the tears away. If she skied as badly tomorrow, she might as well not even enter — if she could even ski, she berated herself as she stepped back into her skis and picked up her stocks. But it was more than that. The fall had really frightened her. Never before had she felt so out of control, and her confidence was badly shaken. She wove her way carefully along a track through the trees back towards the chairlift, wondering if she really wanted to ski the run a second time. At least the pain in her knee was easing. Realising time was running out, she sped up through a short narrow track between the trees, her weight on her good leg. The dappled light painted blue shadows on the snow, and the flash of sand and orange bark on the gnarled branches cheered and soothed her. She was just turning into the final downhill run when another skier shot noisily out from one side, almost clipping her skis and sending snow shooting over her.

'Watch out, you idiot!' she shouted, swerving.

'How's the Queen of the Mountain today?' called a voice.

Kylie's heart missed a beat. She turned around and stared into the warm blue eyes of Danno O'Keefe, the twenty-three-year-old son of Norman and Molly, owners of the biggest lodge in Lyrebird Falls, as well as two others in perfect locations in the valley and a flourishing hotel at a popular seaside resort down south.

'Are you trying to ski into me, Danno?' Kylie shot at him, blushing crimson, praying he hadn't seen her fall.

'Just paying you back.' Danno grinned, referring to two days ago when she had ploughed into him and a group of friends standing in the queue at the bottom of one of the chairlifts.

Kylie blushed even deeper. 'I didn't do it on purpose. Anyway, I thought I was rather spectacular,' she retorted. Her heart was still doing somersaults, and she wished she didn't always feel like a kid sister around Danno. 'I wouldn't hang around me today, though. I just wiped myself out on the slalom.' She looked up at him, torn between wanting to stay with Danno and knowing that if she didn't get a move on she'd never make it in time for the school bus.

'I've just got time for one more run. Feel like joining me?' she asked, starting to move off. She immediately regretted her impulsiveness — Danno might be the best-looking bloke on the mountain as far as she was concerned, but she didn't want him to see a repeat of her recent performance.

'Love to, but I'm supposed to be on the other side of the hill,' replied Danno. 'Race you to the chairlift, though.'

'You're on!' Kylie sped down the slope, the wind and Danno's company filling her with a fierce joy. She could hear Danno's skis scraping against the icy crust right behind her.

Determined to keep in front, she bent her knees, ignoring the pain, and sped downhill. As she flew over moguls, twisting and turning, she could almost hear his breath in her ear. She caught sight of him out of the corner of her eye as he shot past her. Then the race was on, the two of them neck and neck, passing and falling back, one in front, then the other. Kylie bent further into her skis, picking out the steepest paths where she could gain speed. The bottom of the chair was in sight. At the last minute, almost catching one ski on a jutting rock, she veered to the right, ducked past some overhanging branches and zipped through a small clump of trees. She shot out the other side convinced she was leading, only to find Danno was almost at the bottom of the chair. Laughing at the sheer exhilaration of the race, Kylie skied down, slewed round and stopped centimetres from his skis, showering his legs with snow.

'That was great!' she grinned, cheeks flushed pink, green eyes shining.

'Not bad! Keep that up and you'll definitely be Queen of the Mountain tomorrow,' laughed Danno, equally flushed.

Kylie stuck her tongue out at him and gave him a shove.

'Hey! I meant it!' shouted Danno, almost losing his balance. For a moment his eyes held hers, his expression suddenly serious, and he wondered if she made everyone she met feel as good about life as she did him. He glanced at his watch. 'I'd better shoot off before they fire me. See you tomorrow.' Then with a wave he was gone.

Kylie watched him disappear across the snow. She suddenly realised her legs were quivering. She grinned at the empty slope, a whole lot more determined not to let the mountain beat her.

The hill was waking up now. People were walking around; the chairlift was ferrying supplies up to the restaurants; and skidoos with their orange trailers packed with supplies raced across the snow. Tom was nowhere in sight but the lift operator knew Kylie and let her slip on after loading a pallet of bread. Settling into the seat, she tried to concentrate on her skiing, but her mind kept slipping back to Danno.

Danno had been in fifth grade when nine-year-old Kylie moved to Lyrebird Falls and their paths had never really crossed until two summers ago. She had been out walking. He had been chopping fallen trees and branches for firewood. She would never forget the way his midsummer blue eyes had held hers, the way they had fleetingly today. Their effect on her had taken her by surprise, sending tiny ripples of pleasure through her, turning her insides into jelly. He had grinned at her and in that moment she would have done anything for him. She still remembered how good it had felt sitting on the old tree stump watching him swing his axe, chest bare, muscles rippling as he split the fat logs. She had helped him heave the logs into the back of his ute and he had complimented her on her skiing. To Kylie the afternoon had felt like an intimate rendezvous. She had always despised her classmates who got crushes on local blokes a lot older than them, but with that one glance she was lost.

She still cringed at how she had spent that whole summer and autumn besottedly grabbing every opportunity to be near Danno, finding little things to do for him, wishing he would show the tiniest glimmer that he felt the same way about her as she did about him. Convinced her feelings for him must scream out to the whole community, Kylie was amazed when her friends not only didn't tease her about him, but didn't even appear to notice. The shock came when Danno started dating Gwyneth, petite, blonde, conservative Gwyneth who seemed to attract the most devastatingly handsome men. Kylie had been sure she would die of misery and jealousy, but she never told a soul. To her intense relief Gwyn and Danno broke up three months later and Kylie started going out with one of the local boys closer to her own age. But the attraction she felt towards Danno wouldn't fade. Eventually she simply refused to think about him.

Amazingly the relationship between Gwyn and Danno had never hurt Kylie's relationship with her sister. Firstly because she wasn't all that close to Gwyn, and secondly because Kylie was enough of a realist to know she had never been in the running with Danno. He had never given her any reason to believe that he thought of her as anything other than a good skier and Gwyn's little sister. In fact, if it hadn't been for Kylie's skiing accomplishments, she doubted he would have noticed her existence at all.

Danno had a smile that could light up the world. He'd also had a string of girlfriends, most of whom he managed to stay friends with. The saying around the resort was that if you weren't Danno's girlfriend, you belonged to his ex-girlfriends' fan club.

'Not me, buddy,' Kylie muttered ferociously, raising the safety bar as she reached the top of the ride. She pushed Danno from her mind and decided that if she took the slalom course slightly more slowly this time she'd be fine. Her knee was giving her only occasional twinges now.

Crossing her earlier tracks, Kylie slipped in

amongst the trees, feeling a lot less nervous about trying the course again. Then she stopped, unable to resist the beauty of the frozen world around her. The gumtrees cocooned her; dappled sunlight filtered through their leaves and played on the snow beneath. She gazed up at two gnarled old trees arched above her, their branches gently touching. As she listened to the silence she was caught up for an instant in the magical stillness. Gently she stroked her gloved hand along the silky brilliance of a thick branch, vividly reminded of the legend of the snow gums her grandmother had told her as a little girl. It was nonsense of course, according to her mother. Even so, Kylie tried to imagine what it would be like to be kissed under the branches of these ancient trees, to be loved and to love so deeply and so passionately that you would be prepared to do anything for someone ... A shiver ran through her body as she imagined what it would be like to kiss Danno. She felt a lump rise in her throat.

'Trees don't dance,' she said firmly, shaking herself out of her reverie, ashamed of her blatant sentimentality. She was wasting precious time when she could be practising the run. Yet the longing remained as she skied back out into the sunlight towards the course.

After an initial burst out of the starting gate,

Kylie steadied herself, brought her pace right down, taking the turns much more slowly, always on the lookout for ice, slowing down where before she would have sped up, her goal to get down the run without falling. By now the sun had started to warm the surface, softening some of the ice, and with each turn her confidence slowly grew. She had a nice little run on the wide piste and this time made it round Murphy's Turn without incident, and while she was trembling all over when she reached the bottom, she was happy she had proved to herself she could ski the run without toppling. But she felt far less confident about the Lyrebird Cup. Her knee had started bothering her again and her timing had been atrocious. She checked her watch and gave a gasp. It was far later than she'd realised. Streaking across the remaining distance to the chair, she hurriedly stepped out of her skis, scrambled out of her ski clothes and pulled her school jumper over her tunic. Leaving her gear in the usual spot in the maintenance hut, she raced as fast as her knee would allow towards the car park. The late bus was just pulling out. Waving and shouting, she managed to jump on. Red in the face, clutching her bag, her flaming hair a tangled mess, she sat down with a sigh of relief, suddenly overheated.

Chapter Two

Saturday dawned sunny and cold. By ten o'clock lowering snow-filled clouds had rolled in over the mountain peaks and the wind had picked up. The unexpected warmth of the day before had melted the snow, turning it slushy in places, and it had then refrozen overnight, leaving a crusty hard-packed surface. The slopes were treacherous in spots, with unexpected icy patches over a thinning base and exposed rocks. The slalom course was going to be an even greater challenge today.

Kylie climbed into her ski gear in the warmth of the lodge drying room, her knee burning from the deepheat she had recently rubbed in, her stomach fluttering nervously. Stepping outside her heart sank as she was met by an icy blast. These were not the conditions she wanted for this race. Still, at least she was able to compete. After a hot bath, more heat-balm and a good night's rest her knee was a lot less painful. Bowing her head against the wind she set off to warm up on one of the gentler slopes, glad to be outside and away from the tension in the house. With Gwyn's wedding day coming up at an alarming rate, her mother was increasingly unapproachable, and although nothing had been said, Kylie had a sneaking suspicion Susan knew that she'd arrived twenty minutes late for her first exam yesterday.

The Lyrebird Cup was scheduled to start at midday. By eleven o'clock fifty contestants from all over the district were waiting in the icy wind, faces blue, their cloth racing numbers flapping on their backs. Kylie was contestant 48. Staring straight at her was Dave Jenson, the only contestant she considered a serious rival. Tough, fiercely competitive and the winner of the Lyrebird Cup for the last three years, Dave had lost other junior trophies to her, but never the cup. Even a badly sprained knee last season had hardly changed the margin by which he had won. She waved cheerfully to hide her nervousness. The churning in her stomach increased as she tried to ignore the voice in her head that screamed at her to turn and run, that she was a fool to race with her knee throbbing and yesterday's terrifying fall so fresh. Resolutely she kept telling herself she could do this as, one by one, the competitors raced down the slopes, churning up the piste.

'How're you going, kiddo. How's the knee?' Kylie jumped as her father walked up to her, a walkie-talkie in his hand.

'Fine,' she lied bravely. She smiled at him. 'Thanks for being here today, Dad.'

'Wouldn't have missed it for quids. Your mum really wanted to be here too, but she had to sort out a crisis over bookings.' Geoff gave her arm a quick squeeze. He talked into the radio for a moment, taking in the fleeting disappointment on Kylie's bright nervous face at the mention of her mother. He wished Susan had made the effort to join them, and tried not to think of the fight they had had over Kylie entering the race. Susan was so overwrought about Gwyn and this bloody wedding that she had been furious when she inadvertently discovered Kylie had been late for her exam. It had taken all Geoff's powers of persuasion to stop her from forbidding the girl to compete. He watched Kylie now with pride. He was glad he had persisted with Susan, though this was another argument they didn't need.

There had been too many over the last few months and Sunburst was the cause of most of them. He loved the lodge as much as Kylie did, but he knew buying it had been a financial gamble, and now they were going backwards at an alarming rate. With the added expense of Gwyn's wedding, he was starting to worry about how they were going to dig themselves out of debt.

'Nope, I wouldn't miss it for quids,' he repeated, dragging his thoughts back to his daughter. 'Go for it, kiddo. You can win.' He smiled lovingly at Kylie, then moved on back to his work as one of the race coordinators.

Kylie bent to adjust her ski boots for the final time, wishing she felt as confident. She straightened, the knots in her stomach increasing. To add the final touch, competitor number 44 had been carted away in the banana boat with a suspected broken collarbone. It had started snowing. Visibility was deteriorating rapidly and the race officials were muttering about cancellations. Number 45 leaped out of the starting gate. Kylie's legs felt like jelly. All her tenuous confidence oozed away. Adjusting her goggles she narrowly missed hitting her head on the underside of Danno O'Keefe's clipboard.

'Sorry,' she stumbled, glancing up, wishing she didn't blush every time he came near her.

'Number 48 — Kylie Harris. Ah there you are!' he teased, lifting his clipboard and checking it for damage. 'Good luck!' he added quietly. 'Go easy, there are some nasty icy patches.'

Kylie nodded tensely, her focus back on the

race. She clutched her poles with shaking fingers as he ticked her name off his list. Dry-mouthed she took her place at the start gate as 46 shot down the hill. The start looked impossibly steep. They must have built the mound a good metre higher since yesterday. Number 47 moved into position and was gone. She could hear the blood pounding in her ears. Then it was her turn. The starter shouted 'Go!' and she leaped off, hurtling down the hillside, edging her skis, swerving past the poles, racing against the clock. She almost missed the second poles, losing precious seconds. Visibility was worsening; a steady stream of snow spattered her goggles, and by the third turn there was a complete whiteout. She had no idea what she was skiing on and only the bright orange of the poles and her memory of the course kept her on track. The wind was buffeting her, slowing her down. Leaning forwards, fingertips frozen inside her gloves, she charged onwards. Because she was favouring one leg she was unbalanced. Suddenly her ski slipped, forcing her to put all her weight on her bad knee. Biting her lip against the pain, she managed to right herself as she curved towards Murphy's Turn. Fearful of falling again, she slowed her pace. Convinced she had lost the seconds needed to beat Dave Jenson, she carved through the snow.

Suddenly she was in the shelter of the hill, the wind stopped and for a few seconds she fell into the magical rhythm of skiing. She wanted to laugh out loud. This was crazy, the weather, the conditions, charging down the mountain in a blizzard. What the heck, she had lost anyway, so why not enjoy herself? Back in the groove, skis parallel, she sped up, turning, twisting, letting her hips and knees flow, her skis following as though they were an extension of herself. She was round the dreaded turn before she knew it. Turning into the final straight she pointed her skis downhill, then ran up a small mogul created by the previous skiers, leaped into the air and did a scissor action with her skis, landing perfectly to the delighted roar of the spectators who had braved the elements. She raced to the finish and slid to a halt. Panting, she quickly moved out of the fenced-off area and took off her skis.

'That was quite a stunt!' called a friend.

Kylie nodded. She had lost, she knew that, but she hadn't felt that good skiing in ages. She turned to see contestant 49 do a spectacular fall just before the finish. Then, heart sinking, she watched Dave Jenson wedel his way confidently down the final slope.

'Conceited creep,' she muttered under her breath. She would so like to have beaten him, to have won for her dad. Second place was not where she wanted to be, and now when they least needed it, it had stopped snowing and visibility was improving.

Everyone crowded around for the race results. Kylie didn't hear her name at first. Then finally, in amazed disbelief, she heard herself announced as the winner of the Lyrebird Cup. Somehow, miraculously, she had won. She had won by half a second. Once she had relaxed and just gone for it, she had caught up the time she needed. Grinning from ear to ear she stepped up and accepted the huge silver cup from Norman O'Keefe. She held the silver challis over her head for all to see. The crowd cheered, and she felt a lump in her throat as she saw the pride in her dad's eyes, the pain in her knee forgotten. This was a moment she would remember forever.

The minute she stepped down from the podium she was engulfed in a bear hug from her dad. 'Well done, kiddo. I always knew you could do it!'

She hugged him back, realising in amazement that there were tears in his eyes. Her dad never cried. 'Dad!' she exclaimed, then her own eyes filled with tears. 'I so wanted to win for you,' she mumbled into his jacket.

'Well, you did that,' said Geoff briskly to cover his emotions.

Danno walked up. 'Congratulations. I guess now you really are Queen of the Mountain.' There was genuine admiration in his eyes.

'I guess I am,' she replied, eyes shining.

'You deserve it. How's the knee?'

'How did you know?' she asked, surprised.

'You looked as if you were favouring one side when we were racing yesterday. Was I right?'

Kylie nodded. 'I fell at Murphy's Turn before you turned up. I honestly thought I'd stuffed up everything and I'd have to withdraw.'

'She's a pretty special little skier,' interrupted Geoff, beaming at Kylie.

'She certainly is, sir,' replied Danno.

To hide her confusion, Kylie gave her dad a shove then grinned back at Danno.

'I'd better get back to your mother,' said Geoff. 'Don't drink too much lemonade!'

Kylie threw her arms around him again and kissed him on the cheek. 'Thanks for being here, Dad.'

'He's pretty proud of you,' remarked Danno as Geoff hurried off.

'I know!' cried Kylie. She felt on top of the world. Suddenly all her friends were flocking around congratulating her, and complete strangers too. It started to snow again. Big soft flakes landed on her hair and eyelashes. This was good skiing snow. Kylie looked around for

Danno but he had vanished. Quashing a flicker of disappointment, she allowed herself to be carted off to the Lyrebird Restaurant where, smiling brilliantly at everyone, she immersed herself in celebrations. Toasted noisily in champagne and beer, Kylie revelled in her triumph. Even Dave Jenson came up and congratulated her. Feeling slightly tipsy, clutching her precious cup, she finally headed home to get changed and join the celebrations planned for later that evening.

Bubbling with excitement, Kylie flung off her ski gear and raced barefoot into the sitting room. She stopped, feeling as though she had been doused with cold water. Her mother was sitting grey-faced, rocking a sobbing Gwyn in her arms.

'How did you go, darling?' Susan asked, trying to smile. Then she saw the cup. 'Oh, you won. Well done!' But even to her ears, her response sounded lame.

'What's the matter?' cried Kylie, putting down the cup and hurrying over.

'Your sister ...' Susan started, brushing away tears that slid down her cheeks, her arm tightening around Gwyn.

Gwyn lifted her head. Her face was blotchy, her hair messed up. Kylie stared at her — Gwyn was always so neat and tidy, and she never showed extremes of emotions. 'It's off,' Gwyn wailed. 'My wedding's off.' Shoulders heaving, she buried her head back in her mother's breast. Two seconds later she raised her head, her eyes momentarily flashing with anger. 'He's having an affair. How could you have an affair with your fiancée's best friend a month before your wedding? How could you do that to someone?' She hiccuped, shaking with misery.

Susan held the sobbing girl close, her mouth set in a grim line. Finally she pulled away, forcing Gwyn to sit up. 'Darling, you're going to have to be incredibly brave and be thankful you found out before and not after you got married.' She wiped her eyes and gave a huge sigh. Was there no end to the disasters surrounding this family? The only bright spark for weeks was Kylie winning the cup, and not only had she not been there to see it, she had been so furious at her being late for the exam, she had very nearly put a stop to it. Now she bitterly regretted having missed seeing her race.

'Do you get your name engraved on it, darling?' she asked, standing up and examining the cup, her attention momentarily off Gwyn.

'Yes,' Kylie replied quietly.

'I think I'll go and have a bath,' said Gwyn with a sniff. She wiped her cornflower blue eyes, huge in her pretty, fragile face. Petite with short wavy blonde hair, even in her unhappy state she managed to look beautiful. Her pale blue figure-hugging sweater accentuated the colour of her eyes, and her tight jeans flattered her neat figure. Kylie suddenly felt fat and ugly.

'I don't know,' Susan sighed again after Gwyn had left the room. Then she turned to Kylie. 'Tell me all about the race.'

Finally allowed to share her victory uninhibited, Kylie poured out her excitement to her mother. Sheepishly she even admitted having been late for her exam. 'You knew, didn't you?' she finished.

Susan nodded. There wasn't much she didn't know about this family, only now she was really glad Kylie had been allowed to have her moment of glory. The girl positively glowed. 'Why don't you see if you can go and cheer your sister up? You never know, maybe if she came out with you she might forget all this for a few hours.'

Once Kylie had skipped out of the room, Susan picked up the cup again. She envied her daughter's carefree optimism and felt thoroughly mean that she hadn't had the energy to say more. She ran her fingers over the engraved names, thinking of all the work involved in cancelling the wedding and wondering how on earth she had been so frivolous as to allow Geoff to talk her into agreeing to buy Sunburst.

The lodge had been eight years of nonstop struggle. She couldn't take any more of it.

Kylie walked into Gwyn's room and sat down at the pretty dressing table. She started fiddling with the powder puff, carefully rearranging the lipsticks out of their neat rows into a circle. Gwyn was lying face down on the bed. She didn't move. Finally when it was obvious her sister wouldn't go away, she sat up.

'I'm glad,' said Kylie, staring boldly at Gwyn. 'Paul is a boring, small-minded, mean little dweeb and he doesn't deserve you.' Gwyn first went red and then white. 'Well he is, Gwynny. He's mean and rotten.' She walked over to the window and stared out at the softly falling snow. Tomorrow there would be ten to twelve centimetres cover of wonderful soft snow to ski on. 'When was the last time you had any fun? You work at that boring bank job you pretend to like, you spend boring evenings with Paul talking about banks and banking, you never go out anywhere interesting ...'

'Don't mention his name,' choked Gwyn, starting to cry again. 'How can you say that? How can you be so mean and horrible?'

'Gwynny, I love you but you ... Are you ... were you happy before all this?' She went over and put her arm around her sister. 'Remember when we climbed to the top of the mountain and declared what sort of men we would marry? You with your perfect knight in shining armour, me with my hero a bit rusty around the edges.' She gave a short laugh. They had been nine and twelve and they had made daisy chains together. It had been one of the few times Kylie had seen her sister really laugh. They had a closeness then which had dwindled as they grew up.

Kylie talked on, trying to ease her sister's pain, and invited her to the party. 'You never know, you might even enjoy it,' she finished lamely. It seemed strange and wrong that she should be the one in charge. Gwyn must have suddenly felt so too because she wiped her eyes, walked over to the dressing table and started brushing her hair.

'Thanks for being so sweet, but this is my problem. I'll work it out. I didn't mean to spoil your day. I know what winning the Lyrebird Cup means to you. I'd just be a drag if I came along. But thanks anyway.' She rearranged the lipsticks back in their straight lines.

Watching the fight gradually coming back into Gwyn's face, Kylie wondered how any man could be so blind as to let Gwyn go. 'BP — Before Paul — you were fighting off half the men in the valley. Come with me, Gwynny. Don't let one dropkick ruin your life.'

'No, really, I'll be fine.' Gwyn gave a wan smile and shooed her out the door.

Twenty minutes later Kylie raced out of the house, her mother's voice reminding her of the midnight curfew ringing in her ears.

The party was already well underway, noise spilling out into the night. Everyone wanted to dance with the Lyrebird Cup winner or buy a drink for the Queen of the Mountain. After the emotionally draining chaos at home, it was exactly what Kylie needed. Gratefully she soaked it up. She flirted outrageously, drinking champagne and dancing with most of the young men in the room. To her amazement, halfway through a dance with Glen, a friend she had dated a few times in the last three months, Danno butted in, declaring he was staking his claim to the evening's prize. Smiling apologetically at Glen, Kylie allowed herself to be whisked away in Danno's arms.

She felt her cheeks burn as they were bumped together in the crush. The music was so loud it was impossible to talk, so after a couple of attempts Kylie gave up and just enjoyed dancing, the champagne relaxing her.

Even in the strobe lighting Danno was good looking. It was hardly surprising all the girls fell for him. As they danced she wondered what really made him tick. Sure there were all the jokes and stories about and his string of girlfriends, and his life was already mapped out with his dad owning the lodges at Lyrebird Falls and the seaside place, but Kylie had caught a thoughtfulness in his eyes when he wasn't aware he was being watched, a wistfulness even, and she wondered whether there was more to Danno than the playboy image he was so eager for everyone to see.

'Fancy something more energetic?' Danno shouted in her ear as the music changed and the beat sped up.

'Sure!' Kylie shouted back, and Danno twisted her around, pushing her away then pulling her to him, twirling her around again in the fast new dance movements that were sweeping the country. Eyes shining, Kylie kept up, following his every move, burning off her energy, hardly having to think as he led her so well. She was enjoying herself enormously, though she was fully aware that dancing with him meant nothing more than an evening's fun. Suddenly she was conscious others were watching. Tossing her head, she danced more vigorously, grinning broadly. So he was a playboy. For an evening, why not enjoy the feeling?

Finally, the music stopped. Immediately Danno released her from his grasp and everyone clapped them. Breathless, Kylie grinned up at Danno then bowed to the onlookers in the hall as someone went to change the CD.

Danno's hand was still in the small of her back. 'I give you the Queen of the Mountain,' he shouted and everyone cheered.

Kylie smiled back at the crowd then up at Danno, hovering, uncertain what to do next. He looked so handsome, with his tanned face and thick black hair. How she longed for him to see her in a different way.

They stood in the middle of the dance floor, chatting with a group of his friends who had gathered around. The music started up again in a slow rhythm. Danno pulled her gently back into his arms and they moved together in time to the beat. Kylie's heart raced wildly. Gradually Danno drew her to him until they were dancing close, her cheek millimetres from his. Kylie could hardly breathe. The heat of his body burned into her and her body responded, throbbing with yearning. His cheek brushed hers and her legs turned to jelly. Then she was jolted out of her euphoria as Sophie Wickham, Danno's latest, tapped her on the shoulder. Feeling like an interloper, Kylie blushed to her ears in the dimness.

'Sorry I couldn't get here sooner, Danno. Hate

to break up the party but we've got to go.' She looked straight at Danno.

'Sophie! I didn't realise it was that late. I'm sorry, I've got to go,' stumbled Danno, turning to Kylie and releasing her, at the same time glancing at his watch. 'Sorry! Another time maybe. Thanks, it was fun. Congratulations, Mountain Queen!' He leaned over and gave her a quick peck on the cheek. 'I really enjoyed our dance,' he whispered, and Kylie wondered if she had imagined the fleeting longing in his eyes.

Suddenly Kylie felt foolish. Everyone in the resort knew that Danno was out of her league. The whole dance thing was just part of the game, even the kiss. Like he said, she was just the prize for the night.

Glen grabbed her. 'Now Mr Big has gone, you can stop looking so damned happy and we can continue where we left off.'

Kylie shook off her sudden gloom and grinned at Glen. He was fun and uncomplicated and he kissed nicely. Firmly putting Danno out of her mind, she spent the rest of the evening wrapped around Glen, returning with equal fervour his long kiss goodnight in the frosty night air. Creeping into Sunburst at five minutes after midnight, she fell into bed filled with a sense of wellbeing, having promised, in her tipsy state, to ski the milk run with him the following day.

Chapter Three

Kylie woke to bright winter sunshine at midday. Staggering downstairs in her pyjamas, feeling fragile, she was greeted by her mother and father and Gwyn, who was still pale and wan but neatly dressed and calm. They were all sitting around over brunch at the kitchen table.

'How's the Queen of the Mountain this morning?' Geoff asked, sounding a bit too jovial. He took a long sip from his ice-cold glass of beer.

'For the first time ever I think I might pass on skiing this morning,' said Kylie with a half-laugh as she opened the cupboard and fumbled for the cereal. She stopped her hand halfway to the cereal packet and turned round. 'Am I missing something?' she asked, suddenly aware of the heavy atmosphere in the room.

Susan stood up and fetched some more milk from the fridge. Gwyn moved the magazine she had been reading from Kylie's place setting.

'We've got something we need to discuss with the whole family,' began Geoff deliberately.

Kylie helped herself to milk and sugar and sat down, feeling progressively sicker.

'We're selling the lodge and moving away from Lyrebird Falls,' blurted out Gwyn, unable to stand the tension.

Kylie looked blankly first at Gwyn then at her parents, trying to digest what she had just heard. Then she burst out laughing. 'This is a joke. You're not serious? Dad? Mum?'

'You explain, Geoff,' said Susan weakly. She didn't think she could stand one of Kylie's temper tantrums right now. She and Geoff had been up half the night, going over and over the whole issue. This was the only answer.

'I think you both know your mother and I have been very concerned at the way bookings have dropped off over the last couple of seasons. We haven't had the money to do what we hoped with the place and, well, we've decided to cut our losses and sell up.

'It will solve a lot of problems for us and in the end we will all benefit. I've been offered the job of resort manager on Dunk Island up near Cairns and I've decided to take it. We're moving up there just as soon as we can get this place sorted out.' He looked at each of his daughters in turn, seeing the bland interest in

Gwyn's eyes, hating to see Kylie's look of utter disbelief.

'You mean you're going to sell our home and move away from here forever?' cried Kylie.

'Forever's a bit dramatic,' said Susan swiftly.

'Well that's what it'll be,' retorted Kylie, letting her spoon clatter into her bowl. She was suddenly furious at her mother for making these decisions without discussing them with her. 'Did you tell Gwyn before you decided all this?'

'I may have mentioned it. Gwyn and I discuss a lot of things. Now look, Kylie, before you go getting all upset, your father and I have thought this through very carefully. We know how much you love the snow, but you can't always choose in life, and this is an opportunity we had to take for the whole family.'

'Oh, and I'm glad you included the whole family when you made the decision. Obviously I don't count!' Kylie pushed away her cereal bowl and stood up.

'Of course you count. Sit down and don't be so melodramatic,' said Susan crossly. She glanced despairingly at Geoff.

Kylie turned on her mother. 'No I don't, otherwise you'd have told me! And don't roll your eyes at Dad like I'm just in the way! You don't care about what I might want. You never have. You didn't want me to enter the Lyrebird

Cup. You're not interested that I'm the only girl for ten years to win all the prizes on the mountain. You couldn't even be bothered to be there, and now you're telling me —' She faltered, choked by a mixture of anger and hurt.

'You don't have to give up your skiing, darling.' Susan was determined not to lose her temper or let Kylie upset her further.

'Like they've got snow on Dunk Island! I can't believe you could do this to me! And you go and tell Gwyn everything.' Tears of rage and frustration started in her eyes and tumbled down her cheeks. 'Do I sit my HSC or do I throw that away as well?' Her hangover and lack of sleep weren't helping her powers of logic.

'Kylie, that is quite enough,' said her father, his voice raised. 'You will stop escalating this into a full-blown pantomime. Just calm down and we can work everything out. We still have to sell the place, and you have to finish your HSC.'

'Calm down?' shrieked Kylie. 'No, I won't calm down. It's always calm down, Kylie, be patient, Kylie. Why didn't you ask me, Dad? Just when I do something special, just when I think you're going to be really proud of me, you knock it all down. I love skiing, I live for it. This is what I want to do with my life and you ... you want to move us to some island in Queensland.

Why d'you have to take away the one thing I really love? I hate you! I hate you both, and I hate you, Gwyn, for not talking to me when you knew all along what was going on.' Stumbling away from the table, she ran from the room, tears streaming down her cheeks, Sunburst and all her dreams strewn in tatters around her.

Gwyn found Kylie standing on the stone bridge a kilometre or so from the lodge. She was throwing sticks into the freezing water below. Gwyn stood beside her and started throwing sticks as well, watching them float down the narrow torrent butting up against frozen layers of overhanging snow. She loved this place too, with its chocolate-box winters and shady summers.

Kylie threw another stick. 'I didn't mean to say I hated you,' she said without looking at her sister.

'It's okay,' said Gwyn.

Kylie turned on her. 'It's not okay. Why didn't you tell me? Why didn't you even mention it?'

'I don't know. I guess I didn't think they were that serious. I was so caught up in my wedding and stuff ...' Her voice trailed off. She stared back at the stream, the sunlight dancing on the ripples, thinking how she and Paul had stood here not so long ago, talking about how happy they were and the life they would have together. Gwyn's throat constricted. Her eyes filled with tears. 'Mum didn't mean to leave you out ...' she started. She couldn't go on. She turned away.

'Gwyn?' Then Kylie saw the tears. 'Oh Gwynny, I never meant to be so selfish. Oh Gwynny, I love you ...' She put her arms around her and Gwyn promptly burst into tears. Kylie blinked back tears of anger at her parents' actions but also at her own selfishness.

'I'm sorry,' said Gwyn, wiping her eyes and sniffing. She looked across at her sister's anxious face and gave a choked laugh. 'I'm the one supposed to be sorting you out!' They started talking then, all the emotion of the last few days passing between them.

Finally Kylie took a deep breath and looked around her. How she loved this place. She turned back to face her sister. 'Why don't we take off abroad together for a year? I mean, there's nothing keeping you here, and I don't think I could bear to see someone else living in our home. We could head off to Canada for the ski season and see a bit of the world while we're at it.' She started talking about jobs they could get and about some of her friends who had already done the season in Whistler-Blackcomb, one of Canada's bigger resorts. The more she talked about it the more excited she got.

'I reckon we just pack up and go, sis. What d'you think?'

'It certainly beats moping around here, that's for sure,' commented a thoughtful Gwyn.

'Absolutely!' cried Kylie, linking arms with her sister.

Two hours later Susan walked into the sitting room to find the girls giggling and exclaiming at some of the more ghastly wedding presents as they packed them back in their boxes and ticked them off on the list. Shaking her head in amazement, Susan walked out again, wondering if she would ever understand her younger daughter.

Chapter Four

Once decided, Kylie was determined to ski the following season in Canada. Her desire was fuelled partly in defiance of her mother who was very much against Kylie working a job when she should be studying hard for her exams. Undaunted, Kylie started discussing her plans over dinner one even-ing, causing yet another clash between her and her mother.

'There will be plenty of time next year to go tripping around the world and it would be much more sensible,' Susan responded crossly. 'We will be settled in our new home by then, and it gives you a whole year to save up.'

Kylie scowled at her mother and started arguing. Determinedly Susan changed the subject, which only maddened Kylie further. Throwing the remains of her dinner in the bin, she declared that she was going to study and slammed out of the room.

'I really wish we could persuade Kylie to see sense, darling,' said Susan when she and Geoff were in bed later that night.

'Leave her be, Susie. The more we go on at her, the harder she digs in her heels. She still has to get the money together, don't forget, and nagging at her isn't going to make her study harder. Personally I'd rather see her ploughing her energy into something positive than taking out her frustrations over us selling Sunburst on you.' He kissed a rather disgruntled Susan and rolled over.

Susan lay awake, trying not to worry about the girls. Gwyn was still miserable, and Susan couldn't deny her hurt at the way Kylie blamed her entirely for their decision to move. How she wished her younger daughter wasn't so stubborn and difficult. Firmly Susan turned her thoughts to the latest prospective buyers who had tramped through their home earlier that week. They had sounded very keen and Sunburst was definitely a bargain if you had the cash to improve it. Maybe things would be settled sooner than they knew.

As Geoff had predicted, Susan's attitude to Kylie's plans simply made the girl more determined. Unable to get her regular job in ski hire, she took any job she could get, serving at the various mountain restaurants at the weekends, working odd shifts as a lifty when someone fell sick, or helping out as a casual when the ski-hire place got really busy. Gradually she saw her savings increase. At the end of September when the ski season officially closed, she managed to score a part-time job in the local chemist shop, and by the time she sat for the HSC she had enough money saved for her airfare, a season's lift pass and living expenses for a couple of weeks.

Once her exams were safely out of the way, she started planning in earnest, finally deciding on Whistler. The glossy brochures had sold it to her, along with the fact that she knew several people who had worked at the ski school and said it was one of the best. The only thing stopping her from actually picking a date and booking her flight was Gwyn, who was still dithering about whether to go with her.

'It's not as if you need to save up like me, Gwynny,' announced Kylie, jolting her sister out of her sombre reverie one Sunday afternoon as they sat lazing in the sunny backyard, brochures and discarded lists scattered around them. 'You're loaded, and with all the money you've saved, all you have to do is hand over your credit card and your plane ticket's booked. Do come with me, pleeeease, Gwynny. It'd be really great to go together. We could have so much fun. We haven't done anything together for ages,' pleaded Kylie

Gwyn grinned weakly. 'We've never done anything like this together!'

'All the more reason to come. You deserve to do something really special after the horrible time with you-know-who. Be adventurous, Gwynny.' Kylie stuffed a brochure over the novel Gwyn had been pretending to read.

Gwyn couldn't help laughing at Kylie's earnest face and eager attempts at persuasion. She could now manage to talk about the whole wedding fiasco without starting to cry, but she still found it hard to whip up enthusiasm for anything. Getting through the routine of work and hiding at home was more than enough for her at present. However, as Kylie rattled on about ski resorts and places to stay, joking about glamorous suntanned ski instructors, she couldn't help getting caught up in some of her sister's enthusiasm. She had been a keen skier herself until she'd got involved with Paul, and she had to agree it sounded enticing.

She mentioned it to her mother in a quiet moment, casually picking up an apple and starting to peel it. Watching her daughter's face, Susan started to look at the trip in a whole different light. There was no stopping Kylie. She was resigned to that fact. But maybe in the light of Gwyn's reaction it wasn't such a bad idea after all. For the first time since her break-up with Paul, Gwyn was showing a genuine spark of interest.

The more Susan thought about it, the more she became convinced the trip could be the very thing Gwyn needed. Besides, she was worried about Kylie's maturity travelling overseas. With the girls going together she felt much more comfortable. Gwyn would keep Kylie on the right track.

When Kylie announced triumphantly that Gwyn had given in her notice at the bank and that they were planning to fly out of Melbourne in ten days time, Susan, who had learned of Gwyn's decision half an hour before, merely smiled and asked if they were going to take their own skis with them.

Kylie felt suddenly flat. Quickly she threw her arms around her sister. 'This is going to be the biggest adventure of our entire life,' she squealed.

Gwyn hugged her back. 'It might just be,' she said.

The next day an offer was made for Sunburst Lodge and immediately accepted. The sale threw the whole household into chaos. With Susan trying to organise removalists and the girls organising tickets and buying last-minute items and everyone making endless lists and tripping over boxes and clothing unable to find anything, it was bedlam. Yet Susan realised she hadn't seen the family this happy since she could remember. Pouring herself a large glass of wine, she drank down a gulp, silently toasting the success of the next year. Perhaps this really was all going to turn out for the best. Although she knew she'd miss both the girls when they were gone, she had to admit she could do without the sulky presence of Kylie around the place for a while. She let her mind wander over images of long white beaches and palm trees on Dunk Island. Yes, maybe this was a very good idea after all.

Chapter Five

Kylie and Gwyn arrived in Whistler late on a mid-November afternoon. One of two big modern ski resorts nestling at the foot of the huge Whistler and Blackcomb mountains, Whistler was the brightest star in Canada's winter playground. Despite their tiredness the two girls peered eagerly out of the coach window at what would be their home for the next six months. The heavy falls were yet to come, but the whole place was covered with a light dusting of snow. Kylie gasped in delight at the wide elegant streets and well laid out houses and shops. Tiny white fairy lights hung from the eaves, twinkling in the fading light, giving the place an air of Christmas.

Dropping off holiday-makers who had ridden the same coach, they were driven another ten minutes from the centre of town, the houses becoming progressively less attractive and the roads narrower. The coach finally stopped outside a dingy cabin in a small backstreet. Rickety steps led up to a dark unimpressive doorway. Clambering from the bus and shivering in the cold, the girls retrieved their bags and scrambled gratefully into the warmth of their lodgings. The house was as dingy inside as out. Dimly lit, it smelt musty and of stale food. The landlady, in her early forties, greeted them in battered bedroom slippers and too much rouge, rubbing her hands on a dirty apron. At her side was a small boy whom she clipped around the ear and sent scurrying back behind the paint-chipped door

Kylie's heart sank. She glanced briefly across at Gwyn whose expression was frozen in a polite smile. Determined to let nothing spoil their adventure, Kylie smiled at the landlady, introduced herself and started commenting on their journey and the prettiness of Whistler. Once inside their room with its yellowing walls and faded brown and olive curtains, she hugged her sister tight. 'We made it!' she cried. Then she heaved her bag onto one of the narrow beds and looked around.

Gwyn peered through the grubby window out into the fading light, her heart sinking too. The view was onto a narrow back alley. Piles of dirty snow lay against the kerb and some animal was scrounging around a group of garbage bins. She drew the curtains closed and gave a shudder. 'More snow'd be good,' she announced, unable to keep the disappointment from her voice, feeling suddenly overwhelmed with tiredness.

'It'll come. It's still early in the season,' Kylie replied, trying to summon up enthusiasm she suddenly no longer felt. 'We've arrived, Gwynny! We're actually here. Now the real adventure begins! We'll feel better after we've had a good night's sleep,' she added hopefully.

Kylie was the first up the next morning, peering through the window. Everything did in fact look less depressing today. Despite being seedy and far less than they had hoped for, their room was warm, and Kylie could make out a bus stop a short walk down the hill. Even the piles of dirty snow at the edge of the road looked less depressing in the morning sunlight. Despite the lack of snow on the roads, some was still caught on the branches of towering fir trees, and dripping icicles hung from the eaves of the cabins nearby.

Excitement started to bubble up inside Kylie. Opening the window a crack she gasped at the cold, and then decided Gwyn had slept enough. She shook her awake. 'Wakey, wakey, rise and shine. Day's begun! Must get on!' she chanted, using one of the family's favourite sayings.

Gwyn opened one eye, groaned and turned over. Two minutes later, after a severe badgering from her sister, she stumbled off in search of the bathroom. Once she was dressed and fully awake, Gwyn too started to feel more cheerful. Over breakfast she started mapping out the day, deciding that the first thing they had to do was find jobs.

'Boring! Boring!' interrupted Kylie, grinning at her sister's serious expression. 'The first thing we're going to do is to spend Dad's money. Remember, we're here to have fun!' Despite the tight finances, Geoff had insisted on giving both girls a present of money, making them promise to spend it on the best new skis and boots they could find.

Kylie found a bus timetable and got some directions from the landlady, then she shooed Gwyn out the door and onto a bus. Realising she had lost the battle, Gwyn too started to get excited as they travelled towards Whistler Village and the impressive-looking slopes.

The two sisters wandered along one of the village's redbrick pedestrian 'strolls', and suddenly Gwyn disappeared inside a shop with a cry of delight. She reappeared almost immediately. 'Kylie! You have to come in,' she cried, her blue eyes shining.

Laughing, Kylie let herself be dragged into the warmth, then she gave a little gasp of understanding at the glittering beauty confronting her. The whole store sold only Christmas decorations. Fake Christmas trees heavily decorated with gold and cream ribbons and balls reached to the ceiling; gold and white angels sat on shelves alongside Santa's elves and every other conceivable Christmas bauble. The decorations were arranged in blocks of colour throughout the shop, red here, blue there, gold and cream in the corner. Hearts, trumpeters, tiny glass birds, Christmas wreaths — all gleamed back at the girls from floor-to-ceiling shelves. It was like stepping into a children's paradise.

Gwyn was examining some tiny red and gold figurines. 'Aren't they exquisite?' she exclaimed. 'I'd like to buy you one. It can be my special arriving present to you. Which one do you like?'

Kylie stared at the myriad tiny figures, feeling a lurch of happiness. She moved from one shelf to another and back again, looking and comparing, unable to decide.

'Ooh! You're so hopeless at making up your mind — I'll choose,' laughed Gwyn.

'I am not,' protested Kylie, still unable to decide.

Finally, after fifteen minutes, they emerged back into the crisp cold sunlight, each clutching a special package — an angel blowing a trumpet for Gwyn, and a heart with a dove inside it for Kylie.

Buying the boots and skis took another hour and a half; then, armed with the latest and best equipment, they set off in search of lift passes and the ski slopes. They walked past huge condominiums and hotels which looked like fairy castles against the backdrop of snow and fir trees. With their lift passes flapping against their ski jackets, their walking boots and precious parcels safely stored in a locker nearby, they headed for the big quad chair at the foot of Whistler Mountain.

The lack of snow cover had not deterred the skiers and the slopes were teeming with activity. At the top of the first slope Kylie looked out across a picture-postcard world. The slopes were lined with huge fir trees and the mountain seemed to go on forever. Signposts marked each run and sloped off in all directions. Kylie almost had to pinch herself to believe she was really there. The only strangeness was the pines and larchs instead of the familiar gumtrees.

'How about this?' Kylie suggested to Gwyn, pulling out a pocket-sized map of the mountain and tracing her finger along the paper. Starting with a nearby green run, the easiest of the three levels, they could catch another chairlift at the bottom of that run, ski down a slightly harder blue run, then take another lift across the valley, ski down a beautiful tree-lined run and arrive back where they stood now.

Gwyn nodded in approval, feeling only slightly nervous. It had been a while since she had done a lot of skiing. She let Kylie lead, then she pushed off down the first run after her. It only took one run for her to regain her confidence. Soon the girls were racing each other down the slopes, laughing and shouting, falling and pulling each other up. Half an hour and two great runs later, flushed and sweating, they were back at the top of the Express chair.

'What a blast!' cried Kylie, skiing down to Gwyn and stopping with a flourish, snow shooting out from the back of her skis.

Gwyn's glow said it all.

'Come on, I'm starving!' she declared and together the girls headed off towards a nearby restaurant nestling in the curve of the hill.

As she sipped hot soup and gazed across the mountainside, Kylie gave a huge sigh of contentment. This was beyond anything she had hoped for.

Kylie had missed the October ski-hire clinic and the next one was not scheduled until mid-

December, so she was resigned to taking any work going, confident she would eventually get into the ski school. She was more anxious about Gwyn finding work. The first three days they drew a blank, finding only waitressing jobs or bar work, neither of which Gwyn was prepared to do — she was convinced she could use her bookkeeping skills to earn some decent money. Each evening they returned to their dingy lodgings, their spirits flagging.

On the fourth day Kylie woke to find it had been snowing all night and a thick layer of snow lay across everything. 'Hey, look at this!' she cried, her spirits soaring.

Grumbling, Gwyn staggered to the window and gave a cry of delight. After a hurried breakfast they scrunched out onto pristine snow and caught the bus across town, stopping at a chalet they had rung the previous day.

The girls fell in love with Bear's Paw Lodge immediately. Set back from the road, nestling in amongst the fir trees, the pretty dove-grey lodge was just a five-minute walk from the bottom of the ski slopes. Someone had cleared a path from the driveway to the verandah steps, which were already covered in a layer of snow. Huge icicles hung from the steep roof, which was covered in places with a good twenty centimetres of snow.

Kylie was the first to react. She turned to Gwyn and hugged her. 'Isn't it magic? Keep your fingers crossed!'

Inside was as charming as outside. The warm rustic theme had been taken through the whole lodge. Little toy bears and pictures of bears were dotted through the main entrance, embroidered on the cushions that lay on the chairs and in the carpets. The whole place smelt faintly of lavender and potpourri.

Trying not to show her nervousness, Gwyn told the receptionist who they were and that Mrs Vernon, the owner, was expecting her. Mrs Vernon appeared a few moments later and ushered Gwyn into her office. Whilst her sister was being interviewed, Kylie wandered around the foyer, checking everything out, and finally sat down next to the cosy gas fire set in a big moulded stone fireplace guarded by roughly carved wooden bears. She was just wondering how much longer her sister was going to be when Gwyn reappeared, her face wreathed in smiles. Unable to contain her excitement, she hurried over to Kylie and squeezed her arm.

'They want me to start tomorrow!' she whispered, eyes shining; then she collected herself and introduced Kylie to Mrs Vernon.

'We could really use Gwyn's talents here,' said Mrs Vernon pleasantly. 'It gets pretty busy here all through the season, so we need someone we can rely on. Gwyn says you are after work too. We might be able to offer you something part-time if you are interested.' She seemed a nice, homely sort of woman and both girls warmed to her immediately.

Ten minutes later they danced down the steps, Gwyn grinning triumphantly at her success and Kylie happy to have scored a job helping run the sauna and hot tub and cleaning some of the rooms. Racing to the nearest phone they spent some of their precious savings calling home. Gwyn was full of exuberance, chattering excitedly about her new job. But Kylie, still angry with her mother, was more subdued. She replaced the receiver and started walking down the street, her hands thrust deep into her ski jacket pockets, a scowl on her face. She suddenly felt empty.

'Mum sounds so happy,' cried Gwyn, hurrying beside her. Kylie sped up.

'Don't stay mad at Mum. They didn't sell up just to annoy us,' said Gwyn quietly as they sat in a small cafe drinking hot chocolate.

'She could have discussed it with me too.' Kylie glared an instant at her sister then relaxed. She gave a shrug. It was done. She was not going to let her mother's behaviour spoil her life. 'Let's check out some of the shops,' she said.

Gwyn sighed inwardly helplessly. She knew when her sister was changing the subject.

Gwyn loved working at Bear's Paw. The lodge was run by the whole Vernon family, which consisted of Mum, Dad, Granddad, and two girls aged nine and eleven. There was an older daughter, but she was travelling overseas. Working with a local girl called Joslyn, Gwyn looked after the Lodge accounts and helped out with bookings and general office duties when things got very busy, which they frequently did.

The work was not exactly what Kylie wanted, but it was easy money and it gave her plenty of free time to ski the slopes. Over the next few weeks, while she waited impatiently to try out for the ski-hire clinic, she got to know the mountains, teaming up with some of the local instructors and getting the inside information about Whistler-Blackcomb. When she finally tried out for the ski-hire clinic she was accepted into the Whistler school and, at her request, given the tiny tots' classes.

She would never forget her first week with her little band of six, their big eyes peeping out from under huge helmets, tiny hands encased in bright-coloured mittens, their cheeks rosy from the cold. They were both a delight and a constant challenge. They were minute against the background of fir trees and vast pistes and Kylie was constantly counting to make sure she had all her little ducklings with her. Little Laura needed to have her ski pants hitched up at the end of each downhill run, and five-year-old Vivette was so rugged up she looked like a tiny Michelin man. Then there was four-year-old Jonathan who for the first two days struggled to fight back the tears and by the end of the week was fighting to be allowed to be first on the chair. Kylie fussed around them, amazed at their lack of fear. When one class moved on and another arrived, she loved getting to know her new little ones and seeing them progress.

The place was inundated with Australians, both on and off the slopes, making Kylie and Gwyn feel at home. Kylie bumped into several skiing friends from Lyrebird Falls and the two sisters teamed up with a group of young Aussies, meeting up in the evening to sample the nightlife around Whistler Village. The weather was improving too. Every few days brought a new dump of snow, so by Christmas the slopes were deep and soft with a solid base. Every day as Kylie skied the wide-open pistes she rejoiced at her good fortune. On her days off Gwyn frequently joined her and they cavorted together, responsibilities forgotten for a few hours. To cap it all, Kylie managed to wangle Gwyn into the ski lodge where the instructors stayed, which was not only closer but also cleaner and more sociable.

Christmas was a massive party including a large contingent of Australians, banishing any chance of feeling homesick, and that was followed by Australia Day, when it seemed the whole mountain celebrated. Every time Kylie skied her group onto the lifts someone shouted out 'Happy Australia Day!' or 'Good on you, cobber!' and in the evening everyone congregated in the local pub for Aussie meat pies and Foster's lager. They sang raucous drunken renditions of 'Waltzing Matilda', 'On the Road to Gundagai' and 'Danny Boy' until they were hoarse, and Kylie fell into bed exhausted, wondering if life could get any better.

Chapter Six

'I really didn't think it would be this good,' Kylie admitted to Gwyn one afternoon as they were shopping in one of the huge supermarkets. Gwyn, engrossed in deciding whether they could afford to add a piece of delicious Canadian cheese to the already groaning trolley, grunted cheerfully and wandered down the aisle.

That was another thing, Kylie thought. Gwyn was so happy. Since the job at Bear's Paw she had come right out of her shell, and the two of them had become very close. It was as if Kylie had discovered the sister she had always wanted. She felt she could talk about anything and everything, well almost — she hadn't had the courage to mention Danno, except in the most casual of ways, though she sometimes thought her sister knew how she felt anyway. The two of them always seemed to be giggling and joking together or sharing girlie heart-to-hearts.

'Have a good day on the slopes?' asked a voice in her ear.

Kylie turned to see a pretty redhead about the same age as herself whom she had helped a couple of times on the slopes. The Canadian girl's unzipped multicoloured ski jacket displayed a neat figure squeezed into dark blue bib and braces.

'Fantastic, how about you?' replied Kylie. She leaned over to speak to the woman behind the bakery counter, making a chatty comment about the variety of buns.

'Say that again,' insisted the girl. 'I just love your accent.'

Kylie laughed. 'What, about the buns?' The girl nodded and Kylie repeated the order, confusing the saleslady. Everyone started laughing. Gwyn came over and the three started talking. The girl's name was Samantha Gates.

'Everyone calls me Sam — no relation to Bill,' she laughed. 'Listen, I'm heading off to meet some friends for a spa and a swim at my condo after I've dumped this lot. The guys've just gone to get some beer. Why don't you join us? It's on the second floor.' She gave the name of the condominium.

'We'd love to,' replied Kylie quickly. A hot spa sounded just what she needed after today's efforts on the slopes.

The temperature was dropping rapidly as they

hurried back to their lodgings, the cold stinging their ears. They shivered as they waited in the wooden shelter for the Whistler Village shuttle bus, which delivered them to Sam's condo. Stepping gratefully into the warmth they made their way up to the second floor and down the long passage to the spa, their feet muffled by thick carpet. Popping her head round the spa door, Kylie looked about for Sam. The spa was taken up by an assorted group of men and women, but there was no sign of their new friend.

'Are you with Sam Gates?' she asked the group shyly.

'Sure are!' grinned one of the young men, raising his beer bottle with a grin, clearly disregarding the notices that said drinking in the spa was forbidden. 'Come and join us. There's plenty of room.'

'Thanks,' nodded Kylie more confidently. Quickly she and Gwyn withdrew to the nearby change room, slipped into their swimsuits and, dropping their towels on a bench, walked back to the spa.

'The idea is you warm up in here, then if you're brave enough you go for a swim out there. It's only −8 degrees in the pool at the moment. Watch the ice!' grinned the man who had spoken first. He moved over to make space for the two girls.

'What d'you reckon, Gwynny, shall we give it a go?' laughed Kylie, then she gasped as she edged slowly into the scalding water. Waiting a few seconds till her legs could stand the heat, she sank down into the bubbles till her shoulders were beneath the surface, the warmth spreading through her body. She could feel every nerve tingling. She let herself relax as the jets of bubbles thumped pleasantly at her back and legs. Some time later, once she was thoroughly warmed up, she glanced through the floor-length windows. She could just make out the pool through the steamed-up glass.

'I'm going to give the pool a whirl,' she called across to Gwyn. She stepped out of the spa and opened the door, then gasped as an icy blast caught her. The tiles around the pool were covered with a thick layer of snow, half-melted where people had trodden, ice already re-forming. Heads bobbed above the steam that rose from the blue-green water. Gingerly Kylie walked to the ladder at the edge of the pool and tested the water with a toe. It was warm. Feeling a soft tickling sensation she looked up. It was snowing. With a laugh she slipped into the water and swam a length. The effort warmed her up and she turned and lay on her back watching the snowflakes float gently down, feeling them settle on her face, her eyelashes, her nose. She held out her arms and watched the soft crystals melt against the warmth of her skin.

Gwyn appeared at the edge of the pool. She dived in and swam over to her sister.

'It's snowing! This is crazy!' exclaimed Kylie. She hugged Gwyn then swam to the edge of the pool. She leaned against the tiled wall, the water lapping just above her shoulders, her face tingling from the snow.

Gwyn followed. 'This is so much fun!' she cried, treading water beside Kylie. She leaned over and whispered, 'I've got a surprise for you.'

'What sort of surprise?'

'I'll tell you as long as you promise to stop being picky about every bloke you meet,' Gwyn retorted, then swam away.

'Me? Picky! How rude!' cried Kylie in mock outrage. She lunged playfully at her sister. Reaching out she tried to dunk Gwyn, failed and instead got dunked herself. Coming up spluttering for air she tried again and Gwyn once more dunked her. For the next few minutes the two laughed and splashed around, pushing one another under the water until Kylie finally gasped, 'I surrender! I surrender!'

'Promise,' demanded Gwyn, a satisfied grin on her face.

'Promise,' panted Kylie. 'Now go on, tell me what the surprise is.'

'Guess who showed up ten minutes ago?' Gwyn whispered. She swam closer. 'You know Kit, the guy I met at the disco, the one we both agreed was the sexiest guy alive? Well, he walked in two seconds after you came out here. He's got a mate who's equally gorgeous and I've just got us a dinner date!' Triumphant, she swam off down the pool, delighted by the effect of her announcement.

Kylie swam after her. 'Both of us? How did you manage that?'

'I told him I never go out without my sister. And guess what — he owns a Ferrari and he flew down in his dad's plane.' Her cornflower eyes were huge with excitement.

Kylie started giggling, but Gwyn interrupted her with a dig in the ribs, at the same time grinning up at a bronzed broad-shouldered hunk in tight bathers. Kylie just had time to register muscles tight from regular workouts before the young man dived into the pool and swam across to them.

'Hi, Kit. You remember Kylie?' said Gwyn blushing.

'G'day, Kylie.'

The Australian greeting sounded strange with the Canadian accent. Kit gave Kylie a dazzling smile, but his eyes wandered quickly back towards Gwyn.

Kylie felt a sudden twinge of envy at her sister, followed by a rush of admiration. Gwyn was so beautiful. No man could resist her.

'Meet my buddy Kevin,' sang Kit as another equally good-looking young man joined them. He started chatting, asking her if she'd skied the glacier yet.

Kylie looked at Kevin and had to agree he and Kit were both very attractive. It was just that neither of them matched up to ... She felt the familiar thud in her stomach, then felt angry at herself. She started swimming slowly down the pool on her side, trying to concentrate on what Kevin was saying. Gwyn's comments about being picky rang in her head. She was being ridiculous pining for a love that had never existed.

She and Kevin swam around for a few more minutes then stepped out of the pool. Shaking the water from her hair, Kylie pulled her costume down under her neat buttocks and hurried across the freezing deck, already shivering again as she dived inside. Slipping back into the hot spa with a grateful sigh, she turned her full attention on Kevin. The other two joined them and they all started talking, the girls vying with tales of Sunburst and

Lyrebird Falls, the boys talking of heli-skiing and shooting down some of the more difficult black runs at Blackcomb. Kevin really did have the most beguiling smile, Kylie thought as they chatted, and a beguiling smile was surely better than impossible dreams and old memories.

Chapter Seven

Over the next few weeks Kylie and Gwyn saw a lot of the two Ks, as they quickly nicknamed Kit and Kevin. Sometimes the four of them went out together, sometimes they went out in pairs. Kylie was happy to go out with Kevin, flirting and larking about, but she kept the relationship casual. Gwyn got far more intense.

'You really like Kit, don't you?' Kylie asked one evening as the two girls were getting ready to go out.

Gwyn looked up happily. 'He's nice. We get on well together, that's all,' she said evasively, but as the weeks went by it was obvious she was getting more and more involved. On her afternoons off, instead of skiing with Kylie she met up with Kit; when the four went out together there was less swapping of partners on the dance floor, and more often than not Gwyn and Kit would disappear halfway through the evening. While Kylie missed her sister's company, she was happy to see her enjoying herself, glad she was coming out of her shell and willing to get into another relationship. Kylie had told Kevin at the outset that she was not interested in a serious relationship herself, and he rubbed along easily with that.

Kylie was so engrossed in her job and her little ones that at first she didn't notice the change in Gwyn. Then early one afternoon she returned to their lodgings to find Gwyn unexpectedly home from work. Kylie could see immediately that she had been crying but when she tried to discover what was wrong, Gwyn clammed up. Kylie let her be and curled up with a book in front of the big log fire in the communal sitting room.

Over the following few weeks Gwyn's work hours became more erratic, her cheerfulness more forced. Often still in bed as Kylie left for the ski slopes, sometimes not arriving home until well after midnight, Gwyn brushed away Kylie's concerns, assuring her everything was fine and intimating that her work hours had changed. However, as Gwyn's appetite diminished and her new vitality evaporated, Kylie started getting worried.

'Why don't you ask for a few days off? I'm sure Mrs Vernon won't mind. You work hard enough for her,' she suggested one morning, noticing Gwyn's watery eyes and slightly flushed cheeks.

'You fuss too much,' declared Gwyn, her eyes filling with tears. She reached for the tissue box and sneezed three times in quick succession. 'Go and enjoy your day. In just over seven weeks we'll be wending our way back home to good old Oz and none of this'll matter.' Her voice was muffled through the tissues.

'That was something I wanted to talk about,' started Kylie. She glanced at her watch and gave a gasp. If she didn't hurry she'd be late for her class. 'We'll talk about it tonight before we meet the two Ks,' she shouted as she raced out of the door.

Returning late that afternoon it was quite obvious to Kylie that Gwyn wasn't interested in talking about anything. Bundled up in her pyjamas and jumpers, eyes streaming, smelling strongly of Vicks, she croaked that she wouldn't be going anywhere that evening except to bed.

'Tell Kit I'm really sorry and that I don't want to give him my cold. I'd be no company anyway,' she coughed, blowing her sore, reddened nose.

'Don't worry. I'm sure Kit'll understand. I'll look after them both. Give me two guys to flirt with,' she joked, trying to jolly Gwyn along. 'It might help Kevin cool off a bit. He's been getting a bit too keen lately. See you later.' She closed the door and hurried to the bus shelter.

As she waited in the biting subzero air she thought about how close she and Gwyn had grown since the beginning of their trip, but still she had the niggling feeling Gwyn wasn't telling her everything. She stepped onto the bus, grateful for its warmth, and sat gazing out of the window. The resort looked like a Christmas party, its pretty fairy lights strung from the buildings, the snow caught in the gleam of the street lamps. It really was an enchanting place. She had no desire to return home, in fact quite the opposite. As the season raced to its close she had begun racking her brains as to how to persuade Gwyn to stay on for the following season. Whistler was reputed to be beautiful in the summer and there were so many places to see. She felt a pricking at the back of her nose and hoped she wasn't coming down with Gwyn's cold.

The pub was crammed to overflowing, loud music blaring across the room. Kylie couldn't see Kit or Kevin anywhere. Fighting her way towards the bar, she felt a pair of arms slide round her waist and a warm mouth plant a kiss on her cheek. Jerking round she looked into Kit's dark brown eyes. 'Hi, Kit! Better not let Gwynny see us,' she joked, grinning cheerfully.

'Where is she?' asked Kit looking past her. Kylie explained, and for her the evening deteriorated from then on. Kevin turned up shortly afterwards but, bored with trying to coax Kylie into kissing him, soon got distracted by a blonde with an inviting cleavage. Partly insulted, partly relieved, Kylie turned to Kit and started chatting about the day.

But Kit had other ideas. After making understanding noises about Gwyn, he started flirting with Kylie in earnest, occasionally running one finger along her arm. Feeling extremely uncomfortable, Kylie knocked back her drink, and accepted another one. Kit sensed her discomfort and slid his hand around her waist.

Kylie felt horribly disloyal to Gwyn. She kept up a banter of conversation at the top of her lungs, accepting more drinks while trying to work out how best to shake off Kit without offending him. Wishing she hadn't decided to come on her own, Kylie drank too much, joked too much and flirted too much. When she was well and truly drunk, she suddenly found Kit kissing her. It wasn't just a friendly kiss. It was passionate, intimate and arousing. His whole body pressed against hers. She could feel his erection against her thigh. Sobered she tried to pull away, but Kit was enjoying kissing her far too much to let her go. Finally managing to push him off, she screamed at him that he was going out with Gwyn and then tried to storm off.

Grabbing her arm, Kit forced her to him, face flushed. 'Hey, it was only a bit of fun. No need to get so worked up! Anyhow, your sister and I were never serious.' He let her go, arms flung wide, eyes glittering from too many drinks. The two stood staring at one another. Kylie's eyes flashed dangerously.

'You know, you're really attractive when you're angry,' Kit said, attempting to pull her back into his arms again.

Rejecting the idea of rushing out of the pub where it would be just her and Kit on the freezing street, Kylie forced herself to control the outrage that bubbled up inside her. 'I did overreact a bit,' she replied, smiling sweetly into his hungry eyes. Before he could kiss her again she quickly entwined her fingers through his and, inwardly shaking with rage, dragged him towards a group of Aussie mates that were gathered around the pool table. The blokes were exchanging skiing stories, each trying to better the last, the girls chipping in as loudly as the rest. Paul, whom Kylie had known since she was a kid and who was now thoroughly plastered, immediately put his arm around her and kissed her resoundingly on the mouth.

'Don't mind me, mate,' he said, squinting at Kit who was forced in the crush to let go of Kylie's hand. 'You remember that race?' slurred Ryan, his arm crooked round her neck, his cheek next to hers.

Kylie glanced over at Kit and rolled her eyes, as though this were none of her doing. He shrugged and wandered off. Only half listening to the chatter, still fuming that Kit would come on to her like that, Kylie's heart missed a beat at the mention of Danno. Suddenly she felt as though she couldn't breathe. Her heart started racing crazily as Ryan recounted a story she had heard a million times.

Kylie felt her cheeks scalding. 'I'm not feeling so good,' she shouted in Ryan's ear. It was true, the mixture of alcohol, belting music and stuffy atmosphere was making her feel extremely queasy, but it was Danno's name jolting through her that made her want to escape. Ryan started protesting, but Kylie hurried out onto the street and into a taxi. When she arrived at her lodgings she dashed into the staff entrance and wove her way unsteadily upstairs, stomach churning. She fumbled with the key and finally stumbled clumsily into the room.

Gwyn was still awake. 'You look awful,' she croaked.

'I'm fine.' Kylie kicked off her boots and anorak and climbed, fully dressed, into the big double bed they shared. 'No I'm not, I've had a revolting evening.' She threw back the covers and sat up, her hand to her mouth. Racing to the bathroom, she threw up twice then crawled back onto the bed, groaning. After two more dashes to the bathroom, her stomach gradually settled and she lay back, eyes closed, trying not to think about the evening or how much Kit's disgusting behaviour would hurt Gwyn. She was afraid she might have led him on. Gwyn had gone back to sleep, so Kylie lay curled up, head thumping. She felt more and more miserable and guilty by the second as she listened to Gwyn's gentle snoring. Tossing and turning, unable to sleep, Danno protruding into her jumbled thoughts, she finally helped herself to some painkillers and nudged Gwyn awake.

'Go to sleep,' mumbled Gwyn.

'Gwynny, wake up, please. I can't sleep, I feel awful, I need to talk to you,' she insisted, shaking her sister.

Gwyn rolled over and opened her eyes. She sat up reluctantly and listened unhappily as Kylie told her about her evening.

'Men can be such bastards,' Kylie finished

with a sob. What does Kit think I am — a complete rat who'd go after my sister's date? I'm so sorry, Gwynny, I didn't mean to do anything to make him think …'

Gwyn had that shut look on her face. 'I didn't think that, silly. It doesn't matter anyhow. I wasn't all that taken with him,' she lied and rolled over.

Kylie watched her a moment. 'What was it like kissing Danno?' she asked softly to Gwyn's back.

Gwyn's eyes shot open. 'What? Where did that come from?'

Kylie looked slightly sheepish. 'They were talking about him at the pub tonight and … well, was it, you know, really … good?'

'Oh go to sleep!' snapped Gwyn, falling back on the pillow and throwing one arm over her face. Kylie's revelation about Kit had dug deep. She had been trying to kid herself that she wasn't falling for him and that it was only a holiday romance. She had failed miserably. Half of her couldn't wait to get out of the place, the other dreaded the thought of leaving Kit.

'But was it?' Kylie persisted. Somehow she had to know.

Gwyn glared at her sister. 'It's three o'clock in the morning, I'm on early shift in the morning, I've got a stinking cold, and you've just told me my boyfriend's a complete twerp. I'm not going to tell you the intimate details of my love life. I went out with Danno for a few weeks. We kissed. I know you had a crush on him. It was years ago! Why the heck do you need to rake all that up now?' She turned her back on Kylie, pulled the covers up to her neck and burst into tears.

'Oh Gwynny, I'm sorry, I'm really sorry,' cried Kylie miserably. She tried to hug her.

Gwyn shook her off. Then she rolled over to face her sister, tears streaming down her face. 'I got the sack from Bear's Paw three weeks ago. I've been working in one of the local restaurants. Oh Kylie! I didn't want to spoil everything for you, I really didn't.' She covered her face with her hands and sobbed, her shoulders heaving.

'What?' cried Kylie reeling with shock. 'Three weeks ago? Why didn't you tell me?'

'I couldn't!' sobbed Gwyn. 'How could I? You were having such a great time. Everything was going so well. I couldn't ruin it all for you.'

'I knew something was wrong,' said Kylie, cross with herself. 'I kept wondering what I had done. You wouldn't let me near you. It felt like there was an invisible wall around you. I couldn't reach you and I didn't know why.' She gathered Gwyn into her arms. 'Don't ever do that to me again. Don't ever shut me out like that.' She shook her none too gently, then held her close again, an unusual firmness in her voice. 'Why?' she asked when Gwyn had finally calmed down.

'Mrs Vernon's daughter came home and I was told my services weren't needed any longer,' hiccuped Gwyn. 'Mrs Vernon was very nice about it and gave me a couple of places to try, but they didn't have anything available. Then I thought, oh well, it's just over two months before we're going home so I'll get any old job. I thought I could handle it but I can't. It's so boring.' She blew her nose.

'I hate this place. I hate my job. I work my butt off. I never get out on the slopes any more, at least hardly ever. I'm so angry and disappointed. Working at Bear's Paw was so fabulous ... then ... nothing. After I got the sack the two things that kept me going were seeing you happy and Kit. I really thought he felt the same about me as I did about him. Tonight's the final bloody straw. I ... This is not what we wanted, Kylie. Where's the glamour, the excitement we talked about?' She wiped her reddened eyes with a corner of the sheet.

'What's making this trip work is us — you and me together,' Kylie replied firmly. She got up and made them each a cup of hot chocolate.

'How could you be such an idiot?' she said, handing the steaming mug to Gwyn.

Gwyn shook her head as she accepted the drink. 'I don't know. I just didn't want to spoil everything for you,' she repeated. 'You're right, the best thing about this trip is you and me.' She smiled for the first time that evening. 'We've got to know each other so much better. It's like having a girlfriend to confide in, only better ...'

'And then you don't confide in me!' accused Kylie, more relaxed now she understood what had been going on for the past weeks. 'Gwynny, you can be so dumb sometimes! You wouldn't have spoilt everything. We could have hunted for another job together, and as for tonight's little episode ... to tell the truth, I think I'm off men!'

'Me too,' laughed Gwyn. 'What was it that you wanted to talk about?"

Kylie took a deep breath. 'Look, I know you haven't been happy ...'

'Don't pussyfoot around. Remember we're best friends and we can tell each other everything,' smiled Gwyn.

Kylie bit into a stale biscuit and pulled a face. 'Okay then, here I go, boots and all!' She told Gwyn that she had been thinking what a waste it was to go home without seeing more of Canada and America and how she longed to do some travelling and then come back and do another ski season. 'The skiing here's just fantastic. We don't have to come back to Whistler, we could go somewhere else.' She rattled off several other Canadian resorts and some American ones. Watching Gwyn's face carefully, she talked on, 'There's got to be other places for you like Bear's Paw.'

Gwyn listened, chewing on her biscuit and vacillating. Part of her longed for the safety of home, but she had to admit there was nothing special waiting for her back there. She wasn't sure she could cope with another ski season, but they didn't have to decide that right now. Kylie had a point. It did seem a shame to waste this opportunity. As for Kit, she knew she'd been desperately trying to replace Paul.

Kylie lay back in the comfortable silence. Gwyn seemed so vulnerable where men were concerned. She was so quick to fall in love, trying to make each relationship 'The One' before she had sussed the person out, believe every flattering comment made to her. It seemed to her that Gwyn was always desperately searching to be loved when she didn't need to.

Gwyn sighed. 'I love you, sis,' she said into the darkness. Then added more softly, 'It was good … you know, Danno.' Kylie wasn't sure she wanted to know any more.

❄ ❄ ❄

It snowed all night and kept up throughout the following day. Huge soft snowflakes were still falling three days later as Kylie trudged off to work, the sky heavy with snow. Yet despite the chill wind and the promise of bad weather, Kylie's heart gave a happy twist at the sight of the tiny tots waiting excitedly to begin their lesson. Well rugged up, helmets and goggles hiding their pixyish faces, cheeks bright red in the cold, they held their mittens out in delight to catch the snowflakes.

Kylie checked their skis and boots, then marshalled her twelve little ducklings up the rope tow to the top of the nursery slope. She played a few warm-up games, then she got them to snake their way slowly down behind her. Flapping her arms and calling out to them to copy, she made sure they stayed close together and kept their ski tips touching in the snowplough. At every turn she demonstrated encouragingly, bending to one side and then the other. The children copied, shifting their weight from one ski to the other, their faces beaming with her constant praise.

Kylie kept one eye on the weather which was closing in rapidly. Twenty minutes into the lesson visibility was down to a few metres. The wind was picking up, and the children were struggling against its strength. When a gust knocked over little Tammy, the smallest and normally one of the most courageous children in the group, and she started to cry, refusing to stand up, Kylie decided to call it a day. Getting the children to make a daisy chain and shouting to them to hold hands and not let go, she raced over to Tammy. By now it was blizzarding hard, and Kylie wished she had stopped earlier. She scooped the little girl in her arms, placed her squarely between her own skis, then, holding her tight, led the group as fast as she dared down the hill straight to the entrance of the hotel that towered close to the nursery slopes. There she gathered the group together, helped them quickly out of their skis and shooed them inside.

She was greeted by a welcome blast of heat. Clattering into the big lobby, she got everyone to take off their boots, dripping anoraks and trousers. Puddles of water formed on the tiles. The children's little cheeks were purple with cold. Kylie hurried over to the concierge, ignoring his surprised expression, and requested that he ring the ski school to say her kindy class was safe, before they sent out a search party. Then she trooped her tiny tots into the spacious dining room and across the soft carpet to the big open fire. She sat them down in a circle and reassured them that their parents would not be lost in the snow and that they would soon come to collect them. Then she started teaching them to ski on the carpet.

Engrossed in her games, delighted at how quickly the children caught on, Kylie lost track of time. Suddenly little Bethany leaped to her feet and ran across the carpet crying, 'Mommy! Mommy!'

Kylie looked up to find a ring of parents watching in fascination. 'Well, that's it for today! Tomorrow when the sun is shining we'll do it all again in the snow,' cried Kylie, clapping her hands and grinning at everyone. She sat back on her heels, smiling and waving as the children were collected and led away. Her heart twisted again as the last little one was gathered into his parent's arms and vanished outside. The sight made her all the more determined to persuade Gwyn to stay for a second season. She gave a sigh and stretched her legs, touching her toes with her fingertips. When she straightened she realised she was starving hungry.

'Excuse me,' came a voice. 'I've been sitting watching you for the last half-hour mesmerised. Can you tell me exactly what you were doing?'

Kylie glanced up to see a well-dressed man in his midforties looking down at her with friendly grey eyes. His thick dark hair was tinged with grey; he wore a large gold signet ring on the chubby little finger of his left hand.

Kylie blushed and stood up. She had been so involved with the children she had completely forgotten she was in the middle of a hotel dining room. 'Teaching them to ski,' she replied, trying to smother the sound of her stomach rumbling.

'On carpet?' exclaimed the man.

'It's the way I learned. We don't have such a long snow season in Australia so sometimes you have to improvise. My teacher taught me most of what I know off the snow!'

'Amazing!' The man looked at her thoughtfully for a moment. 'You're with the Whistler ski school for the season.' It was more a statement than a question. 'Mmm. You're very good with the little ones. Not easy to keep them amused for long stretches of time.' He held out his hand. 'Michael Klein.'

'Kylie Harris. I like challenges,' she replied, smiling and shaking hands. They chatted for a while about the weather and how the children coped on the slopes and Kylie felt herself blushing again as his eyes washed over her. Michael Klein was very attractive and courteous, but there was something about him she didn't quite trust.

She caught sight of him two days later

watching her with her class and waved cheerfully. He came over to her after her class had finished and invited her for a drink. As she was intending to get something to eat anyway, she accepted his invitation and chatted casually as they skied the short distance to a nearby hotel.

'You must be wondering why I have been taking an unusual interest in your skiing classes,' announced Michael as Kylie tucked gratefully into a bowl of hot soup. He heaped two spoonfuls of sugar into his huge cappuccino, stirred his cup and then sat back, looking straight at her.

Kylie noticed the charismatic warmth in his grey eyes but still couldn't dismiss her original reaction. If he's out to pick me up, he's wasting his time, she thought as she dipped a large piece of crusty roll into her soup and bit into it with satisfaction. Skiing was hungry work.

'I have a proposition to offer you, Miss Harris,' Michael was saying. 'A far better prospect, I can assure you, than working at Whistler, not that I have anything against that fine ski school. To put it bluntly, Miss Harris, I want to poach you from here and move you to Aspen.'

Kylie's head shot up in disbelief. 'Oh yes?' she said cautiously, her spoon halfway to her mouth. It seemed in the short time since meeting her, Michael Klein had wasted no time in finding out all about Kylie, checking her credentials and her background. He even knew she had a sister. It made her feel slightly uncomfortable.

'I have three children, aged four, seven and nine. I want you to teach them to ski. I can make the job very attractive.' Michael was suddenly very businesslike. 'I own one of the largest hotels in Aspen and the children are at the perfect age to learn to ski. Marie — that's my wife — is very keen for them to have private tuition.' He paused for a moment. 'Naturally, I would organise all the sponsorship for you to work in the US.' Michael was attending a bi-annual trade conference, he had not been actively searching for a tutor for his family but seeing Kylie work had made this task doubly delightful. To have stumbled on such an accomplished, attractive young woman was a bonus. He watched Kylie closely, having played his trump card, then waited with slight puzzlement on his face when she didn't immediately react. 'You are aware how hard it is to get sponsorship to work in America?'

'Absolutely, and I really appreciate your offer, Mr Klein ... It's just that it's, well, all a bit unexpected.' Kylie was suddenly flustered.

Michael leaned back in his chair, his hands in his big ski jacket, watching Kylie with satisfaction. 'Of course, of course, how silly of me. Some complete stranger starts digging into your background and then charges up to you and offers you a job out of the blue. I would be worried if you didn't want to check me out. Look ...' He handed her his card and then pulled out a battered ski map of the district, scribbling down two names on the back. 'Go and talk to these guys. They'll answer any concerns you have.' He handed the map to Kylie. 'Seriously, ask them as many questions as you like. They've known me for years.'

Kylie glanced at the names — the head of the Whistler ski school and another top instructor. 'When would you need an answer?' Kylie asked, feeling more at ease. 'The thing is, my sister and I are about to go off travelling and everything's a bit vague. We don't even know if we're staying for the next season, although I'd like to.' The words slipped out before she could stop them.

'Take your time,' said Michael expansively. 'You've got my card. Have a chat to these two guys and when you're ready give me a call. I believe your sister — Gwyn? — was working at Bear's Paw for a while? Whistler's a small town. I know the owners,' he explained when he saw Kylie's odd expression. 'Ed Vernan had mentioned Gwyn and her talents over a beer. I'm sure we could accommodate her as well.'

Kylie nodded politely and pocketed the card. 'Thank you, but I'm not sure we'll be staying for a second season. My sister hasn't made her mind up yet.' She stood up, about to say something, not sure why she was hesitating — it seemed like a tragedy to let such an opportunity slip by.

'That's a pity,' said Michael, standing up with her. 'If you change your mind you've got my card.'

They shook hands and Kylie hurried back to her lodgings, half regretting she had made her answer seem so final. She'd make enquiries about Michael Klein anyway, just to find out what he was all about.

All thoughts of Michael and Aspen were swept from Kylie's mind as she stepped inside to find Gwyn on the payphone in tears.

'Who?' mouthed Kylie.

'Mum,' gulped Gwyn. Still fragile from the past few miserable weeks, hearing her mother's voice had brought feelings of homesickness flooding over Gwyn.

Kylie grabbed the phone and spoke cheerfully into it, reassuring her mother that they were both fine but that Gwyn had been having a bit of a rough time. After several conversations back and forth, they finally hung up.

Back in their room Kylie slumped down on

the bed. 'If you really want to go home, we'll go, Gwynny, of course we will.' She tried to sound convincing, but the thought of missing out on their travel pulled at her. Soon she was starting to talk Gwyn around — it was only a few more weeks and an opportunity like this wasn't likely to come again.

'Mum said the same, that I ought to stretch my wings while I could,' admitted Gwyn, her shoulders sagging. She wiped her eyes and sniffed. 'You're right. You're both right. Mum even said she'd send us money if we needed it. I'm just having an off-day. Maybe I shouldn't have rung. I just needed to hear her voice. They sound as if they're having such a good time on Dunk Island.' She gave a huge sigh. 'I miss Mum so much.' She gave a wobbly smile, then reached for the pile of brochures on a nearby chair. 'Let's have a look at those photos of the Grand Canyon again.'

As the two pored over the glossy pictures Kylie wondered whether she would ever understand Gwyn's ability to change her mind so much. Soon, however, they were arguing amiably about how long to stay in each place. Three weeks later they packed their bags and waved goodbye to Whistler.

tantalising to be so close and yet so far away. She pulled out the card and glanced down at it. *Michael Klein*. It took her a moment to register who he was. About to crumple it up and toss it in the nearby bin, instead she flicked it back and forth in her fingers, her mind working. What if …?

'Got any ideas for lunch? I'm starved. Then we'd better check our flights.' Gwyn stopped, seeing the expression on Kylie's face. 'What?' she cried, snatching the card. 'Who's Michael Klein?' she asked, intrigued.

'Remember the day we had that really bad blizzard? This man was watching in the hotel when I was teaching my littlies. After I'd finished he came up and asked me if I'd be interested in teaching his kids to ski next season. That was Michael Klein.' She retrieved the card, bent it into quarters and stuffed it back in her pocket. 'He lives in Aspen.'

'Aspen? Really?' interrupted Gwyn, suddenly interested. 'So why didn't you mention this Michael Klein to me before?'

'I forgot,' replied Kylie truthfully. Then she told Gwyn how she had discovered Michael Klein was one of the richest men in Aspen, with resort hotels all over the place and a guest list that read like a who's who of Hollywood.

'Apparently he owns the biggest hotel in

Aspen, so why on earth he would want to ask me to teach his kids skiing ... He was going to find you a job as well and get us green cards and everything. It all sounded too good to be true.' She stopped at the look on her sister's face, torn between sticking to the plan to fly home and trying one last time to persuade Gwyn to stay on for the season.

'Why don't I call his bluff?' she said lightly. 'I'd bet any money he won't have the faintest notion who either of us are, but it might be a bit of a giggle.'

'And if he did remember?' asked Gwyn, her eyes clouding.

'He won't, not in a million years. Look, I meant it as a joke. That's all.'

'And if he doesn't see it that way?' persisted Gwyn.

'I could stay and you could fly home?'

'Absolutely not. Leave you on your own with a wildly handsome *married* American. Mum'd kill me! She told me to look after you.'

'Then you'll just have to stay with me,' giggled Kylie.

'Aspen's a very posh ski resort. I wouldn't mind a quick peek,' retorted Gwyn, the faintest glimmer of longing in her voice. 'Let's see the card again. Definitely upmarket,' she said, straightening it out and running her finger over the slightly raised dark blue writing. She looked across at Kylie, her eyes twinkling. 'Nothing ventured, nothing gained, as Mum's always reminding us. Give him a call. If he'll pay our airfare there as well and organise a limo to collect us from the airport, I'm in,' she announced, giving Kylie a playful nudge.

Before her sister could change her mind, Kylie piled into a nearby telephone booth and dialled, Gwyn squashed up next to her. Michael's secretary answered. Her extremely cool response nearly had Kylie slam the receiver straight down. Giggling like schoolgirls, the two waited as they were put through and Michael came on the phone.

'Kelly! How lovely to hear from you. How can I help you?' he said, his deep voice cheerful and friendly.

'Kylie actually, Kylie Harris,' she corrected him boldly, and quickly reminded him where they had met and of his offer. 'See, I told you he wouldn't know me from a bar of soap,' she whispered, hand cupped over the mouthpiece. Gwyn's cheek was pressed close to hers as she struggled to hear the whole conversation. Both of them shook with suppressed laughter, waiting for the swift dismissal. It never happened. Before they knew it, Michael had talked them both into accepting jobs, organised to pay their flight to Aspen and have one of his hotel staff collect them from the airport, and had arranged for them to call his secretary collect to discuss flight times. After he'd hung up Kylie and Gwyn stared at one another.

'What do we do now?' cried Kylie.

'Catch a flight to Aspen,' replied Gwyn casually.

'But I thought you wanted to go home?'

'How can I say no to Aspen, the ritzy playground of the megarich?'

Kylie goggled at her sister, speechless. Then they both burst out laughing.

Gondola Lodge was even grander and more opulent than either Kylie or Gwyn could have imagined. Still recovering from the whole excitement of travelling business class and being chauffeured from the airport in one of the hotel's staff cars, they followed the porter into the elegant Victorian-style hotel. They were greeted by the general manager, a solid, slightly fussy woman who explained that Mr Klein was busy with one of his private little dinners for two hundred guests in the grand ballroom. She then gave them a brief description of the layout of the hotel and where the staff would eat.

The manager showed the girls to their rooms

and informed them that Michael would see them in the morning, then she hurried off. Kylie and Gwyn stared at one another in amazement. Separated by a wide corridor, their rooms were enormous, each with its own ensuite. They were identical except for colouring, with Kylie's decorated in blues and yellows, and Gwyn's in greens and deep magenta.

'Pinch me so I know this is real!' squealed Kylie. Dropping her bag carefully on a prettily upholstered chair, she started exploring, opening cupboards and drawers and checking the view from the window, which turned out to be onto the back of another part of the hotel.

'Oh well, I guess you can't have everything,' Kylie grinned and started unpacking.

Half an hour later they went in search of food. Accidentally taking the wrong lift, they ended up on the same floor as the reception. Unable to resist taking a peek into the grand ballroom, while Gwyn hovered nervously by the lift hissing for her to come back, Kylie watched hidden in the shadows as the doors swung open and closed and staff walked in and out carrying large silver platters of mouth-watering food and flutes of champagne.

'I swear I saw Pierce Brosnan,' whispered Kylie, finally hurrying back to Gwyn who quickly shoved her into the lift and pressed the button.

'We'll get the sack before we've even started if you go snooping around like that,' whispered Gwyn crossly, but her eyes twinkled with expectation.

'You're enjoying this, aren't you?' cried Kylie.

'And you're not?' retorted Gwyn.

The next morning the girls were summoned to Michael's opulent office. He walked round from behind his leather-topped desk and greeted them expansively, shaking them both by the hand. Gwyn smiled shyly. Kylie's heart started thumping with a mixture of excitement and concern that they might have got themselves into something more than she had bargained for. She dismissed her uneasy thoughts as Michael apologised for his unavailability the previous night and asked about their journey, clearly at pains to put them at their ease.

'I really didn't think you were serious,' Kylie blurted out, then clammed up, cheeks flaming, wishing she hadn't sounded so childish. She threw Gwyn a grateful glance as she quickly filled the awkward gap, graciously thanking Michael for organising the plane tickets and then chatting about their travels. Given the breathing space, Kyle recovered and joined in the conversation, asking more sensible questions about their work at Gondola Lodge. The ski season didn't officially start for another three weeks, and while the snowmachines were already hard at work, the ground cover was still thin. Besides, the children were still in Boston with their mother.

'We split our lives between Aspen and Boston. Marie's family are from Boston and the children go to school there. It makes everything a lot easier,' he explained. 'In the winter I spend virtually all my time here in Aspen. I have organised for you, Kylie, to attend a private clinic this Wednesday to try out for the ski school. It's merely a formality. I have no doubt as to your abilities, but you need to be officially accepted. You'll want to get to know the area before Marie brings the children down too, which I'm sure you won't find a chore.' He gave a short laugh then turned to Gwyn, his eyes lingering a moment on her face, making her blush. 'Miss Harris, we can use your services immediately. One of my most valued staff is about to go on maternity leave and we are already incredibly busy.

'We are a big family here at Gondola Lodge and I hope you both enjoy your time with us,' he finished. Gwyn blushed deeper.

Kylie glanced out of the window at the slopes with their sparse snow cover, and then back at

Gwyn. Excited at the prospect of skiing again, she pushed her sense of misgiving from her mind.

Gwyn quickly began to blossom in her job in the hotel's accounts department, and Kylie passed the ski-hire clinic test, taking her first class the following day. Despite the thin snow cover, she revelled in discovering the slopes. But at the end of the third week in November, with the season's first good dump of snow, she came down to earth with a rush.

Summoned into Mrs Klein's massive sitting room, Kylie felt as though she had walked onto a film set. Her long legs crossed, Marie Klein sat centre stage on one of two huge cream overstuffed lounges sunk in thick cream pile carpet. Around her, plump cushions lay scattered with papers and magazines. Her perfect heart-shaped face was framed by burnished hair swept up in the latest style. Long pink fingernails that exactly matched her lipstick tapped impatiently on a smoky-grey glass tabletop on which rested two packets of cigarettes and a gold lighter. The rest of the room was furnished with a mixture of ebony and gold dressers, expensive vases and more smoked glass tables. A fortune in original artworks adorned the walls, and thick velvet maroon and gold curtains framed the big picture windows that looked out onto the ski slopes to one side of the hotel, cleverly secluded from prying eyes. Kylie couldn't stop herself from staring in awe at the pure blatant extravagance before her.

Marie Klein, Michael's second wife, was a beautiful, spoilt, hard-faced woman in her late thirties, dripping with gold and diamonds that she somehow managed to carry off with her tall elegance. A lover of designer clothes and jewellery, always wearing the latest ski gear, she was seen in all the most exclusive homes and hotels in Aspen but never went near the snow. Dressed today in a flawlessly elegant pair of long white pants and a casually expensive pink cashmere top, Marie shook out a menthol cigarette from one of the packets and lit it with the gold lighter. She motioned for Kylie to sit down in the cream armchair in front of her.

'Michael tells me you are very good at teaching children to ski,' she announced in her attractive Boston drawl. She blew a cloud of cigarette smoke towards the ceiling, a pink rim clearly visible around the tip of the cigarette. Her eyes were as icily grey as her husband's were warm and her smile never came near them.

Sinking too deep into the creamy soft cushions, Kylie reddened as she almost lost her balance. She quickly pulled herself onto the very edge of the chair and smiled bravely at Mrs

Klein. 'I love working with kids. They're so full of life. We had a heap of fun at Whistler.'

'My children learn very quickly,' Marie continued as though Kylie hadn't spoken. She then explained in great detail everything she required Kylie to do when teaching the children — how to be fair, to be sure never to allow Hillary to become too upset as she was the youngest and very highly strung, and to give Brad the respect and room he needed as Michael's only son. She squashed her second half-smoked menthol cigarette in the heavy glass ashtray then picked up a third, hovering with it and the lighter near her lips. Just then the double doors opened and the children burst in with their nanny, a prim young Englishwoman in her late twenties.

Dropping the cigarette and lighter with a clatter on the tabletop, Marie leaped up with a cry of joy. She bent down and opened her arms as Brad, Lisa-Jane and Hillary raced towards her. She gathered the two older children up in a huge hug and kissed each profusely in turn; then she stopped abruptly, frowning at Nanny who, red-faced, quickly removed the lollypop Hillary was sucking and gave her fingers a quick wipe. Her clothes safe from her daughter's sticky grasp, Marie hugged Hillary too, and the little four-year-old immediately started jumping up and down demanding to know what presents her mother had brought her.

Seeing Hillary receiving most of the attention, Brad and Lisa-Jane quickly started jumping on the lounge, clamouring to be noticed. Hillary twirled around and around, showing off to her mother, and getting thoroughly overexcited and out of control. Then she lost her balance and fell, catching her chin against the glass table. Letting out a bellow of pain she fell to the floor where she lay motionless. Panicking, shouting at the nanny, Marie gathered Hillary up in her arms, pushing the hair off the little girl's tear-streaked face, coaxing her to sit up. Then she smothered her in kisses, ineffectually ordering the other two to behave and be more careful of their sister. Hillary continued to play up to her mother's attention, sobbing loudly and clinging to her, which in turn escalated Brad and Lisa-Jane's protestations. Kylie had never before seen peace turned so fast into such uncontrolled chaos.

'There there, Mummy's special baby girl,' cried Marie, continuing to fuss over Hillary, who was still sobbing, her little shoulders shaking pitifully. 'Nanny will take you on a sleigh ride, my darling. Shh, shh, darling. Organise it, Nanny! I promised them they could go today and they are so excited.' She turned, her cold grey eyes on the nanny as she rocked

Hillary back and forth. With a loud hiccup the little girl wriggled free, and Marie reached for the cigarette pack.

Lips pursed, the nanny silently gathered up the three children and led them out of the room.

In the ensuing silence Kylie was not sure whether she too had been dismissed. Her heart sank at the thought of trying to control, let alone teach these thoroughly spoilt children, and she watched in wonder as Marie sat down and lit another cigarette, apparently oblivious to the fact that she had initiated the whole chaotic scene.

'You can start their lessons this afternoon. Hillary will only ski in the red outfit with the rabbit's fur hat. As you see, she is very sensitive. Nanny will show you their clothes and new skis and boots.' Marie dismissed her with a wave of her hand, hardly bothering to glance in Kylie's direction.

Kylie gratefully made her escape, wondering just what she had walked into, and went in search of Gwyn, only to learn she had gone out on an errand. She spent the rest of the morning washing her clothes, reading listlessly and trying to stay positive. She met Nanny and the children after lunch on their way to the drying room where all the ski gear was kept.

'They're not bad once you give them a few

home rules to go by. They're just revoltingly spoilt with a mum and dad who've got too much money and almost no time for them. All they really want is lots of attention and love. It's sad really,' commented Nanny, whose name was Jillian Hart-Smith, as she helped a thoroughly uncooperative and tearful Lisa-Jane struggle into her new ski boots. Brad was kicking his new ski helmet around the wooden floor and Hillary was whinging at him to stop.

With the children finally dressed in their mini designer outfits, Jillian straightened and grinned at Kylie. 'They're all yours. Have fun. Don't hurry back,' she said and disappeared back inside.

'We're going to have lots of fun in the snow,' smiled Kylie, feeling suddenly very alone.

The children were obviously tired from the morning's activity and Lisa-Jane was now wailing that her mother had said she didn't have to ski if she didn't want to. Taking the belligerent girl's hand, Kylie found it was shaking. She crouched down and talked to her gently, gradually calming her and promising they wouldn't do anything scary. Then she picked Hillary up off the floor, narrowly averting a crying spell by promising fries and their favourite drinks after class, and clasped the little girl's hand firmly in hers. Complimenting Brad on his smart helmet, and with three sets of skis and stocks tucked under her free arm, she led them out onto the snow.

The first lesson was a huge test of endurance. It took twenty minutes to get them all into their skis, goggles straight, gloves on, and then Hillary wanted to go to the toilet. Finally on the slopes, Kylie spent the afternoon alternately stopping Brad, who quickly got his balance, from belting off downhill, comforting Lisa-Jane who froze with terror over everything, and dealing with Hillary who kept throwing temper tantrums when she wasn't the centre of attention. Determinedly cheerful but with her patience stretched to the limit, Kylie gave a sigh of relief as she finally bundled them into the warmth and thrust them back into Jillian's care.

The next few days proved equally trying. Despite getting out on the slopes a little more quickly, each child demanded Kylie's attention all the time. Seeing how fast Brad was learning, Kylie made the mistake of suggesting to Michael in front of Marie that he might be better off in his own class at the ski school, with kids closer to his ability. The reaction she got made her wish she had never said a thing. Both parents were adamant that Brad continue his private lessons. Michael became extremely abrupt while Marie made veiled comments about Kylie's competence. Kylie thought she was about to be fired on the spot. She was greatly relieved when Michael calmed Marie down, and she made a mental note to talk to Michael separately next time about anything to do with the children's progress.

Out on the slopes, with the children's safety foremost, she ran a kind but tight ship. One morning she finally ran out of patience with Brad after he refused to stay with the girls yet again, and shocked him by threatening no more hot dogs if he didn't do what he was told. Knowing that Marie would be horrified if she ever found out, she gave him a sound talking-to and then asked him to help be the teacher with her.

'You're getting very good, Brad, and I need your help,' she explained. From then on Brad slowly started to cooperate, encouraging Lisa-Jane when he thought Kylie wasn't watching, where before he had teased her unmercifully. It gave Kylie the breathing space she needed.

By the end of the week they were ready to take their first ride on a chairlift to one of the easiest runs. Hillary was round-eyed with awe. Lisa-Jane stayed glued to Kylie, repeatedly saying, 'You won't let me fall off, will you?' Brad was first off the chair at the top. Over-confident, tired of being good, he set off too fast downhill, lost his balance and tumbled unhurt into the snow, losing both skis and most of his pride. To Kylie's relief, he ceased to be so much of a troublemaker after that and life on the slopes became somewhat easier.

In the evenings Kylie and Gwyn escaped into town to explore the social life. Sometimes they went out with Gwyn's work mates who introduced them to their friends and took them to the local dives and discos; sometimes the two of them just wandered around, soaking up the expensively casual atmosphere, full of giggling excitement when they caught a glimpse of a well-known face. Each day as she walked in and out of the Gondola, as the hotel was fondly called, Kylie got a buzz at seeing famous people casually drifting past or sitting drinking endless cups of coffee in the elegant lounges overlooking the slopes.

As Christmas drew near, with the Klein children's skills and confidence growing daily, everyone started having fun. The children laughed and cavorted with Kylie, only reverting to their revolting behaviour when Marie appeared. Since the discussion over Brad's lessons, Kylie had thankfully had very little to do with Marie, who spent her time flitting to and from Boston. However, Michael regularly enquired how the children were going in their lessons and by Christmas Eve Kylie was able to report that all three children were skiing really quite well.

'And what's Santa going to bring my special little snow bunny?' asked Michael, sweeping Hillary up in his arms and whirling her around, making her squeal with delight. When he set her down she clung onto his leg adoringly, beating her little fists against him for more while he patted the other two children's heads absent mindedly.

Just then Marie appeared, looking stunning in her latest elegant outfit and accompanied by a cloud of Opium. She was puffing on the inevitable menthol cigarette, which she quickly stubbed out half smoked at a frown from Michael, and enquired in a loud voice which celebrities they were dining with that evening. Kylie marvelled at the chaos Marie caused in the children, and wondered how Michael could allow it, or if he was even aware of it.

'I s'pose he must love her,' she said later to Gwyn as the girls wrapped up their Christmas presents in Kylie's room. 'It's his second marriage and the kids are both of theirs, but she's hardly ever here. It seems such a strange set-up.'

'He's so sweet and kind and she's such a bitch,' sighed Gwyn. 'The kids adore him too. I feel so sorry for him. It's such a waste!'

Kylie gave her sister a long stare. 'He's married, Gwyn.'

'What's that supposed to mean?'

'Only that sometimes you're too good-natured,' she replied quietly.

Christmas could only be described as controlled chaos. Descended on by both Marie's and Michael's relatives, including Michael's three girls from his first marriage, the hotel was overrun with children, their doting parents and desperate nannies. Despite the bedlam, Kylie and Gwyn managed to squeeze in a call to Australia which made them both feel calmer and a little bit homesick. On Boxing Day, having managed to squeeze in a quick call home, Kylie took Lisa-Jane and Brad onto the slopes, leaving Hillary curled up fast asleep on one of the huge sofas with Jillian. Kylie and the two older kids had the best fun yet. The snow was stunning, the weather crisp but sunny, and Lisa-Jane was filled with unusual confidence as she paraded in her new ermine-trimmed ski outfit. New Year with few Aussies around made Kylie and Gwyn feel very homesick for Canada as well as Australia. Then Jillian, having fallen madly in love with one of the ski instructors, talked Kylie into looking after the kids several nights in a row and Kylie took pity on her, knowing she would be travelling with the kids back to Boston within a few days, though they would be returning for the weekends. When it finally came time for them to leave, Kylie found herself unexpectedly looking forward to their return. One person she was not sad to see go, however, was Marie who, she was delighted to learn, would be away for most of the next two months.

Alternating between instructing at the Aspen ski school and weekends on the slopes with the Klein children, and generally living it up at night, the weeks flew by. The only slight irritation was Jillian, who was now openly dumping the kids on Kylie at every opportunity.

'I wish she'd stop doing it to me all the time. She makes it so hard for me to refuse her,' Kylie grumbled to Gwyn, having yet again allowed herself to be talked into babysitting.

'Tell her you're busy. Tell her you don't want to, that it's her job,' replied Gwyn cheerfully as she hurried towards her office. She didn't like Jillian — she considered her stuck up and selfish and thought she took ruthless advantage of Kylie's generosity. They had already argued about her.

'You know what she's like,' went on Kylie, knowing she was being weak.

Gwyn stopped at the door that led to the accounts office. 'Tell her you're in love, that'll stop her!' she called in a stage whisper then disappeared.

Kylie was still smiling at Gwyn's comment when she arrived at the ski school to take her class. It was so great to have a big sister who was her best friend as well. They shared everything.

One Saturday in early February, Kylie hurried down the back stairs of the hotel after a full morning on the slopes with the Klein children. She was aching all over and angry at herself for having been so stupid as to let Jillian persuade her to babysit yet again. This morning Hillary had demanded to be carried off the slopes, screaming for her mother. Short of dragging her all the way back to the hotel, Kylie had had no choice but to carry her. Kylie sighed. She had just over half an hour before she had agreed to take over from Jillian.

Slipping through the door into the hot tub room, Kylie sent a short silent message of thanks to Michael who had said she could use the room whenever there were no guests booked in. She had to admit her first, slightly uneasy impressions of Michael had been way off the mark. He really had been amazingly generous to both of them and Kylie had managed to stash away quite a tidy sum from her extra work with the ski school. She pulled back the heavy plastic cover on the hot tub and pressed the button to start the spa bubbles. Quickly washed off in the shower, liberally spraying around eucalyptus from a bottle on a shelf in the shower recess. She breathed in the soothing perfume, then happily she climbed up the few steps at the edge and sank down naked in the hot water, the heat already steaming up the big mirror on the wall. She swam around, enjoying the freedom and the sensation of the heat and bubbles on her naked skin, then lay back against the side and closed her eyes.

The children really weren't that bad any more. Lisa-Jane was willing to be more daring, and she could see the pride in Brad when he thought she wasn't looking. She really must persuade Michael to let him join a class. With Marie out of the way, maybe now she had more of a chance of being heard. And Hillary, well, with a mother like that ... Her thoughts drifted to her own parents and the love and time they had lavished on her and Gwyn, and she was suddenly overcome with a longing to be with them. She wanted to talk to them, to hug them close and thank them for all they had given her, and to apologise to her mother for being so angry when she and Gwyn had flown out. She was so lucky. She wiped away a tear. Why was she crying? Life was fun. But there was one thing that was missing. She stretched out her fingers, enjoying the light touch of the bubbles hitting them. All she needed now was for Mr Right to walk in. Only Mr Right wasn't going to walk in because he was on the other side of the world and he didn't even know he was her Mr Right.

She closed her eyes, visualising Danno, seeing his clear blue eyes, his brilliant smile, remembering the amazing sensations he'd aroused in her as they whirled around the dance floor. Suddenly she sat up with a jerk as she heard the door click shut. Shocked, she peered though the steam at the back of a perfectly shaped male body. Broad bronzed shoulders tapered down a muscled back to a neat waist and red bathers encasing a taut bum. The stranger turned around and automatically Kylie brought her hands up to cover her bare breasts and sank deeper into the steaming tub. Dark eyes stared at her from under thick curling lashes, and there was a look of surprised apology on the young man's face. He had that lean, good-looking confidence that would melt the toughest heart. Except mine's not available, Kylie thought decisively.

'Er, excuse me, this is occupied,' she called, her mouth suddenly inexplicably dry.

'Oh! Sorry, I thought this was my tub,'

replied the stranger, his eyes travelling from her face to her shoulders and then across the top of her breasts just showing above the waterline, and back again to her face. If it had been possible to feel any hotter, Kylie would have done so. Cheeks burning, she sank even lower in the water.

'It probably is. Michael ... that is, the hotel owner, lets me come in and have a quick dip when there's no one here.'

The young man nodded. 'I wasn't expected till tomorrow but I caught an earlier flight.' He took a couple of steps towards Kylie.

'I'm really sorry. I'll get out,' stuttered Kylie, swimming to one side, then realising her towel was on the other side of the room. Not only was he good-looking, he had the most amazingly sexy voice.

'No, really, don't let me spoil your fun. You look as if you're enjoying yourself. Anyway, if you feel like it, you're welcome to stay. I mean, the tub's big enough for ten people. D'you mind if I share it with you? I could do with some company. I seem to have been sitting in airports and hotels on my own forever.' He gave her a heart-stopping smile and, before she could reply, disappeared into the shower.

Contemplating whether she could or even wanted to make a dash for her towel before he reappeared, Kylie had just made up her mind to hop out when he stepped back into the room, running his hands through his thick black hair. Hesitating a moment, he tested the water with one hand. 'Boy, this is hot! I'm Tom Cooper, by the way. May I?' he asked, starting to climb up the steps.

'Sure,' replied Kylie and introduced herself, casually checking the bubbles really did hide her and wondering how she was going to get herself gracefully out of this predicament.

'Wow! This feels good. So what are you doing for Michael?' asked Tom, sinking down into the water.

'I'm teaching his kids to ski.'

Tom's expression changed to one of admiration. 'You're game. How did you get talked into that one?' he asked. 'Don't worry, my family's known Michael's since I was a kid. We nicknamed him the Tyrant, but his kids changed everything. I feel quite sorry for him. Marie's something else.' He stopped, realising he was being far too personal with a total stranger.

Kylie grinned. 'They're okay, they're just kids. Give them lots to do and plenty of attention and they're fine.'

'Seriously? You'd be the first.'

'Weee-ll, they were bit of a handful to start with,' Kylie admitted slightly breathlessly, feeling his eyes on her again. 'What are you doing here?'

'Me? I come up here as often as I can,' replied Tom. He started talking about Aspen and the social life and how he'd always wanted to visit Australia. Kylie talked animatedly about Lyrebird Falls and her family, unable to ignore his attraction. She glanced up at the clock on the wall, suddenly realising she was ten minutes late for Jillian. Forgetting she was naked, she almost stood up. Her towel glared at her white and fluffy from the other side of the room.

'It's been great talking to you, Tom, but I've got to go,' she said, more abruptly than she intended. She hesitated an instant, then blushing furiously said, 'You're going to have to close your eyes while I hop out 'cos I'm not wearing anything.'

Tom's eyes washed over her, sending hot waves of embarrassment and arousal through her. 'What, and miss out on an invitation like that?' he grinned, his eyes dancing.

'I'm not getting out till you shut your eyes,' she repeated. His eyes were still on her. 'Please, I have to go to work.'

'Looks like you're going to be late,' Tom teased.

'You seriously want those three monsters to come tearing in here to join us?' threatened

Kylie, starting to enjoy the game as much as Tom, the danger of not quite knowing where it would end heightening her flirtation. Then she suddenly remembered she had told Jillian she would be in the hot tub. 'Look, do me a favour, just close your eyes,' she said urgently.

'Only if you promise to go out with me for a drink later,' replied Tom, sensing her mood change. He closed his eyes. Kylie hopped out and darted across to her towel, wrapping it tightly around herself.

'I can't. I've got the kids all evening,' she said, silently cursing Jillian. 'Thanks anyway, and thanks for the company. I enjoyed myself. Maybe some other time …' She opened the door then stopped as his next words hit her.

'I don't know why you wanted me to close my eyes — you've got a great body.'

Kylie whirled round, picked up a nearby towel and hurled it at him. He caught it with a laugh. 'Next time I promise I'll keep my eyes closed.'

Chapter Nine

Kylie didn't hear from Tom for the rest of the week. Irritated that she couldn't get him out of her head, she kept hoping she might run into him in the hotel. Then she learned from one of the maids that his room had been unused for the last five days. Irrationally she felt a whole lot better. The following Tuesday, having finally managed to stop thinking about him. She was in the drying room dressing Hillary after her lesson when Gwyn came racing down to report that Tom had rung her room by mistake and was waiting for Kylie in reception.

Kylie's heart missed a beat. Her fingers started to shake as she tried to button up Hillary's cardigan. 'Tell him I'm not here, that I've gone out for the evening. Tell him … anything, just make something up,' she said, panicking. She glanced down at her tatty old jumper over her oldest pair of ski pants. She looked an absolute fright.

'Too late — I told him you'd be right down,' squealed Gwyn, having nipped down to reception, unable to resist the temptation to check him out. 'Here, let me do that! Did you have a great day, sweetie?' Gwyn asked Hillary, kneeling down, taking over from her sister.

'You didn't?' groaned Kylie, sitting back on her heels.

'He's absolutely gorgeous! I'm madly jealous.' Gwyn stood up and retied Hillary's hair ribbon. 'Be nice — he just promised to take us both skidooing. His mate owns the skidoo hire place. It'll be a blast. I've been dying to try it. I shouldn't tell you, but he's carrying this absolutely enormous bunch of flowers.'

'You're so hopeless,' laughed Kylie as they hurried the children back upstairs to Jillian. She ran her fingers through her tangled red mane and then relaxed. 'Hell, if he doesn't like me as I am, I'm not interested,' she said decisively. She was blowing this whole thing up into something it wasn't, doing the very thing she had inwardly criticised Gwyn for. He hadn't even asked her out yet

'Think skidooing,' Gwyn whispered provocatively.

'Skidooing,' repeated Kylie. 'You owe me big time,' she said, pointing a finger at Gwyn; then she walked out of the room and down the stairs, her sister's laughter ringing in her ears.

Tom saw her immediately. 'Hi!' he grinned, striding across to her. With a beaming smile he thrust a huge bouquet of flowers into Kylie's arms.

Kylie blushed deeply, suddenly awkward. He looked even more appealing dressed in his open-necked shirt and trousers, his seductive aftershave fighting the deliciously perfumed flowers. She buried her face in the flowers, trying to think of something sensible to say, but she couldn't.

'Are you free tonight? I was wondering if you'd like to go for a drink somewhere,' Tom asked almost hesitantly.

Kylie felt her blush spreading down her face and neck. 'Well I had planned ...' Before she could get any further Gwyn burst into the foyer and raced over to them, still clutching a pile of children's clothes.

'Yes she is and she'd love to. We were planning to go to dinner at one of the pubs then on to a disco! Feel like joining us?' she panted, ignoring Kylie's embarrassment. 'If you can handle more than one female, that is.'

'My sister Gwyn,' Kylie grimaced comically and then started to laugh. 'I'd love to come for a drink if you can cope with us both.'

'Sounds fine by me,' replied Tom, grinning

back. 'Shall I meet you both back here, say, eight o'clock?'

'See you then,' waved Gwyn as Tom walked away. She slipped her hand through Kylie's arm. 'You were going to say something dumb like "I was thinking of having a nice quiet evening" weren't you?' she accused.

'Certainly not!' lied Kylie. 'Well, maybe I was. Stop matchmaking!' she added, trying to sound cross and failing miserably.

'Don't need to, you're in love already,' retorted Gwyn cheekily.

'I most certainly am not,' shot back Kylie, but she had to admit she was glad Gwyn had forced the issue. Tom really was very attractive.

Shortly after eight, Kylie and Gwyn were sitting in one of Aspen's more popular pubs chatting amiably with Tom and two of his mates. They'd been joined by Mary, a friend of Gwyn's from work, and another girl Kylie hadn't met before but who seemed to know everyone. Kylie felt considerably more confident having changed into a clean pair of jeans and one of her favourite T-shirts. Gwyn, as always, was turning heads in hip-hugging jeans and a casually elegant top Kylie hadn't seen before which set off her petite figure to perfection. The group were having so much fun that they naturally gravitated to a restaurant for dinner and more laughter, agreeing to take in a club later on.

'You don't mind if I don't come to the disco with you,' said Gwyn to Kylie in the ladies' powder room as they were freshening up after dinner. It was more a statement than a question. 'I sort of made an arrangement with Mary. Sorry, I forgot to tell you.'

'What arrangement?' asked Kylie, surprised.

'It's pretty boring really. Mary's been invited to a private party with the "beautiful people". She's asked me to go for moral support.' Her wide cornflower eyes couldn't hide her excitement. 'I couldn't say no. Anyway, now I can find out if the beautiful people are really as bitchy as everyone says. I did try to get you in, but Mary said it was hard enough squeezing the extra invite for me. You won't miss anything. Besides, you're having such a great time with Tom. It's pretty obvious he likes you.' She winked then hurried back into the restaurant.

'We're just chatting and then going dancing, that's all. Stop making it more than it is,' called Kylie after her sister, annoyed and confused that Gwyn hadn't even mentioned the party she had obviously known about for several days. They shared everything. It was so out of character. 'Be careful,' she said, suddenly concerned, as they joined the others. Rumour had it that some of these parties could get pretty wild.

'Of what? We'll have a few drinks, dance a bit and leave,' laughed Gwyn, then smiled softly at her sister. 'You're such a worrywart! I'll probably be in bed way before you. Wake me when you get in. That's an order!' She gave Kylie a peck on the cheek, then grabbed her bag and jacket and left with Mary.

Shaking off her misgivings, Kylie smiled at Tom, who was holding her coat. He was turning out to be good company and she loved dancing. She piled into his car with the rest of the group and was soon laughing and joking again as they set off for the nightclub.

The place was packed. Strobe lighting swept the dimness. Loud music blared through huge speakers, making conversation virtually impossible. Armed with drinks, the group found a table and then Tom asked Kylie to dance. She accepted eagerly and they joined the throng on the dance floor.

Buffeted by the crush, trying to shout against the noise, Tom leaned towards her ear to say something; his cheek brushed hers and she found she didn't mind the sensation. Feeling the same frustration as Kylie at not being able to carry on a conversation, Tom suggested they sit the next one out. Gratefully she agreed and he led her to a table that had just been vacated further away from the loudspeakers. Once they were settled he ordered a bottle of Dom Perignon, then asked her how her week had been with the Klein children.

'Busy and chaotic!' she replied, grinning. 'But I'm still employed, much to my amazement!'

'Sorry I didn't get in touch before. I meant to, but my work hours are a bit erratic.' Tom handed her a glass of champagne.

'What do you do?' asked Kylie, taking a sip. The champagne was delicious and it made her feel incredibly decadent.

'I'm a stuntman. Actually, I've taken a year off study. I'm working on this latest James Bond movie. I'm Pierce Brosnan's stuntman. Trouble is, they need you at all hours of the day and night and you never know how long the takes are going to be, and I didn't just want to leave a message at the hotel.'

'I thought I saw Pierce Brosnan the evening we arrived here!' exclaimed Kylie, leaning towards him. 'Now I know I did! How did you get to be a stuntman? Isn't it dangerous?' Suddenly the evening was getting very interesting and so was Tom.

'I like living dangerously!' grinned Tom. He then explained his father was a plastic surgeon in Beverly Hills, working with Hollywood stars, and that he himself had just finished his intern year in one of the big hospitals there but had decided he needed a break. 'Dad wasn't all that keen at first, but he came round eventually. I've pretty well made up my mind to go back to medicine after my year off, but I just wanted some excitement in my life instead of endless study. Then a friend of Dad's suggested my being a stuntman, so I went for a couple of interviews and got offered a job. It was luck more than anything, although it helped that our family has known the Kleins for years. Michael gets around. He's very well respected by people in the film industry.' He leaned over and refilled her glass.

Kylie glanced at her watch, her head buzzing pleasantly with champagne, and gave a horrified gasp. 'I didn't realise it was so late! I'm going to have to get back or I'll never get out of bed in the morning.' She dreaded the thought of coping with the kids after only a few hours sleep.

'Me too. I'd love to drag you around the dance floor again, but I've got an early start as well.' Tom drained the last drops of his Dom Perignon from his glass.

When they stepped out into the sharp cold, Kylie had to admit she had had a far better evening than she had anticipated and that she would really like to get to know Tom more. She glanced up at the white fairy lights adorning the buildings and thought how strange it was to be standing in Aspen in the middle of the night with Pierce Brosnan's stuntman. Watching him as they chatted in the car on the way back to the hotel, she found herself wondering what it would be like to be kissed by him. As they walked up from the hotel car park their fingers brushed occasionally and she felt a tingle run through her body.

'I've really had a great time. Perhaps we could do this again?' asked Tom as they stood in the deserted foyer.

'I'd like that,' replied Kylie, suddenly shy.

They stood chatting a moment longer then, wishing him goodnight, Kylie hurried up to her quarters, dying to tell Gwyn everything. Using her spare key she crept into her sister's room. Gwyn was propped up in bed half asleep, a magazine fallen open in front of her. Kylie shook her gently.

Gwyn immediately opened her eyes. 'Well, tell me all,' she said, sitting up.

'All of what?' teased Kylie, flopping down on the bed and stretching languorously. 'I had a such a good time!' Her green eyes were sparkling. 'Tom's so nice. He didn't come on to me once, although I almost wish he had! And get this — he's Pierce Brosnan's stuntman! That is, when he's not studying to be one of the world's leading surgeons.'

'See, I told you, you are in love!' cried Gwyn, now wide awake. She demanded every last detail of the evening, what they'd talked about and if Tom had asked her out again.

'He might have,' teased Kylie.

'He has! Your eyes are a dead giveaway. Did you ask him about skidooing?'

'I clean forgot,' cried Kylie, her hand flying to her mouth. 'There was so much to talk about ... I'll ask him when I see him next.'

'Oh, so there is a next time!' cried Gwyn in mock surprise. 'My evening wasn't a complete failure either,' she went on proudly, not giving Kylie a chance to reply. She told her briefly about meeting some of the beautiful people and of being slightly disappointed that there were no really high-profile stars there.

'But take a look at this,' she said and reached into her purse, pulling out a card and handing it to Kylie. It read *Chuck's Colorado Skidoo Adventures*.

'Ohh!' Kylie's eyes lit up. 'Is this Tom's friend you were talking about?'

Gwyn nodded, smothering a huge yawn. 'I met him tonight. I thought you'd probably blow it with loverboy so I organised a backup plan.

He said to pick a day, so make a date with Tom and we'll go.'

'Sounds a heap of fun. I will,' grinned Kylie, starting to yawn herself. She stood up. 'Thanks for being awake. Tom is nice.' She gave her sister a hug. 'I love you,' she said and went to bed.

'I love you too,' Gwyn murmured to the closed door.

Three days later Kylie searched in her purse for some money and found it was empty. Cursing under her breath, she went looking for Gwyn. 'You don't suppose one of the maids took it, do you? I hate to sound so suspicious but they're the only ones who go into our rooms apart from us. I've searched everywhere for it. I only just got paid.'

Gwyn's hand flew to her mouth. 'Oops! Sorry, Kylie, I meant to tell you. It was me. I was desperate. I had to get something to wear and I'd run out of money. I didn't think you'd mind. I'll pay you back. I bought this gorgeous top. You'll love it. You can borrow it if you like. You were out skiing or with Tom or something, otherwise I'd have asked. Here …' She fumbled in her purse and emptied out a few one-dollar notes and some coins. 'Oh heck. I thought I had more. I must have spent more than I thought.

Oh dear. I'll pay you back from my next pay packet, I promise.'

'That's two weeks away. You might have asked, Gwyn. What am I supposed to do till then? Starve? Stay in?' snapped Kylie, further annoyed at Gwyn's offer for her to borrow the top when she knew Gwyn was two sizes smaller than her.

Gwyn's eyes went all misty. 'Please don't be cross, Kylie. Get Tom to take you out. You told me he always insists on paying for everything, so what's the worry?' She gave a sheepish grin. 'If that's too hard, you could always offer to babysit for Jillian and get her to pay you.'

'Like she would! And stop pushing me at Tom. Anyway, he's away all week.' Kylie glared at her sister, then her expression softened. She shouldn't be mean. She'd asked for Gwyn's help before, just not for money, and it wasn't as though she was totally strapped for cash. She gave a sigh. Gwyn wasn't normally so extravagant when it came to clothes. 'He must be someone very special. Have I met him?' she asked.

'Be patient. You will,' replied Gwyn.

'Is it Chuck? Well, show me this creation my hard-earned money bought.' Kylie knew from experience she would get nothing more out of her sister right now. The top suited Gwyn perfectly. An exquisitely cut soft turquoise, it clung to her trim figure and brought out the colour of her eyes. Agreeing it was a great buy, telling her she didn't need to lose any more weight, Kylie went in search of Jillian and the kids, who had just flown in from Boston for the weekend. She tried to suppress her irritation at Gwyn. Now she would have to dip into her savings.

Chapter Ten

Two weeks later Kylie woke to brilliant sunshine. Leaping out of bed, she ran to the window. Today she and Gwyn were going skidooing with Tom and Chuck, having finally managed to arrange a day when all four of them were available. A crisp breeze blew across the valley, and the clouds still covering the mountain tops were being rapidly blown away.

As soon as the children's lesson was over, Kylie raced off to find Tom. He was waiting by his car, ready to drive them the thirty-minute stretch out of town to Chuck's Colorado Skidoo Adventures where they had arranged to meet up with Gwyn and Chuck. Kylie chattered away excitedly as the road wound its way around the foot of the mountains, its banks covered with snow, boulders and tufts of dry grass starting to show through in some of the sunnier spots.

She reached over and squeezed Tom's hand,

thanking him for organising the trip, and he squeezed back, turning his head briefly and giving her a dazzling smile. Kylie was excited at the prospect of skidooing and she was also determined not to let the recent fight she had had with Gwyn spoil the day. It had been about money again, but at least they had made up, and she knew Gwyn was looking forward to today as much as she was. Gwyn was so unpredictable these days. Lately she'd been uncharacteristically distant and secretive. It alternately irritated and worried her.

Ten minutes later they turned sharply off the road and drove into the snowmobile hire resort. Chuck saw them drive in and hurried over, leaving one of his staff members to organise the group of people standing by twelve snowmobiles neatly lined up, one behind the other.

'No sign of your sister yet,' he said after introducing himself to Kylie. He glanced at his watch and then at the blue sky, snow-laden clouds hovering over the distant mountain peaks. The weather looked pretty stable but they were forecasting more snow and mountain weather could be changeable.

'She'll be here soon,' said Kylie confidently. Her excitement mounted as she watched the group of eager novice riders receive last-minute instructions then climb on their allotted bikes, the sun catching the sleek black metal bellies.

'Are we riding those?' she exclaimed as, with a roar, the group started their machines and then moved off down the track.

Tom shook his head. 'Those are just for the tourists. Wait till you see what Chuck's got hidden in his shed.' He grinned tantalisingly. 'C'mon then, let's get you set up.'

Pulse quickening, Kylie followed the two young men into a nearby building where Chuck fitted them out with helmets; then, while Chuck waited for Gwyn, Tom and Kylie marched over to a shed that housed several other privately owned snowmobiles.

'This is what we'll be riding,' announced Tom, sliding the door open, then standing aside.

'Wow!' cried Kylie, eyes widening at the sight of two black and green snowmobiles in mint condition, with huge jagged yellow streaks painted down their sides. They looked almost too perfect to touch.

'This one's mine, Chuck houses it for me,' explained Tom, lovingly stroking the nearer of the two.

At his instructions Kylie helped him roll the two vehicles out of the shed and then watched as he stuffed a packet of biscuits, bars of chocolate and a thermos of coffee in the saddlebags.

'I don't know where Gwyn can have got to,' she said apologetically, glancing anxiously around her. 'I hope nothing's happened.'

Chuck came over and the three waited for another twenty minutes until a call came through on Chuck's radio. It was one of the girls from Gwyn's office full of apologies, saying Gwyn had asked her to call and explain she couldn't make it because of work.

Kylie felt herself redden with embarrassment. 'I'm so sorry ...' she started.

'That's cool,' interrupted Chuck quickly, hiding his disappointment. 'You two go and I'll take a raincheck. There's a heap of stuff I've got to catch up with in the office. Now I don't have any excuses.'

Smothering her annoyance at her sister, Kylie smiled at Chuck for his good-natured understanding. It'd have to be a major crisis at work to have Gwyn cancel this late. She looked around her at the other skidoos disappearing up the mountain and decided she wasn't going to worry any more. Anyway, she really didn't mind the idea of just her and Tom setting off on an adventure into this vast white world.

Tom pushed the second bike back into the shed then helped Kylie onto his. After packing away her small backpack in the saddlebags, he pointed out the steadying strap and explained that she needed to lean with him as they went around the corners to stop the snowmobile from skidding off the tracks, then he got on also.

'Just think of it as a bike on skis. Hang onto the strap — or me if you feel safer. You ready? Let's go!' he shouted, starting the engine then revving it up.

Adjusting her helmet and sunglasses Kylie clasped her fingers around the strap in front of her, then they were off, roaring their way across the snow. At first the snowmobile's skis bumped over slushy snow, but they glided onto deep thick cover. They sped across two meadows wove through the trees, the dappled sunlight splashing across their faces, the noise of other snowmobiles a hum in the distance. Slithering around corners and tearing up hillsides, they passed half-frozen ponds with great mounds of snow perched beside, ready to drop through the thin covering of ice at any second. Then they were on the top of a crest. Kylie gasped with delight at the spectacular view across the valley to the white-topped mountains beyond. The sky was a brilliant blue, and the dark green pines were clear against the dazzling white. Kylie's spirit soared as they flew along, her body pressed close to Tom's, the breeze on her cheeks, the throb of the machine beneath her.

They slithered to a halt at a small kiosk at one

of the routine stops used by the snowmobile guides. Kylie shook her hair free of her helmet as she stepped off, her boots crunching into shin-high snow. Together they drank down scalding hot chocolate and stretched their legs. Back on the bike, Tom shot them up a steep incline, the skidoo bouncing and grinding as they reached the top of the hillock, then slipped and slid rapidly down the other side. Now they were well off the main route.

'D'you know where you're going?' shouted Kylie cheerfully. She was having the time of her life.

Tom nodded vigorously and they bounced along for another twenty minutes. They slowed down and Tom made a right-hand turn across soft snow, ducking between two low branches, then emerged into a clearing, stopped and switched off the engine. Kylie stepped off into deep snow and looked around her in awe, drinking in the exquisite stillness of the crisp cold world around her. It was like walking into a fairytale.

'It's so beautiful,' she whispered.

'This is one of my favourite spots. I only bring very special people here,' murmured Tom, walking up behind her and slipping his arms around her.

Kylie was reminded of Lyrebird Falls on one

of the more remote runs. It was as though the rest of the world had vanished and all that was left was beauty and pure white silence. She noticed animal tracks marking the pristine white and pointed to them wordlessly. Tom nodded, holding her close. For a moment she leaned into him then, with a little gasp of delight, she ran across the dazzling untouched snow, her boots sinking in up to her calves. She stopped and purposely fell backwards into the thick snow, moving her widespread arms and legs up and down in a scissor motion. Carefully she stood up and turned to inspect her imprint.

'There! A perfect snow angel. I've always wanted to make one of those.' She ran to the bike and retrieved her camera from one of the bags, then took a photo of the angel. 'Let's make one together!' she called out to Tom. Choosing a clear patch of snow she held out her hand and together they fell backwards in the snow, making more angels.

Kylie rolled over. 'Oh Tom, this is such an amazing experience,' she cried, her eyes shining. Before he could stop her she had run to grab the camera again.

'Hey, slow down for two secs!' said Tom, catching her and gently pulling her so she fell laughing on top of him. 'You know you are my snow angel,' he murmured then kissed her.

It happened so swiftly Kylie was taken by surprise, but she made no move to pull away. His lips were warm and inviting against hers and their effect slowed her right down. Surrendering to his embrace, she slid her arms around his neck and kissed him back. Finally they drew apart and Kylie looked up at him shyly. 'I like you,' she whispered. Then she broke away, snapping photos and dancing around, needing to break the mood.

Tom watched her from where he was sitting, longing to take her back into his arms but content to see how happy she was. 'You're only the second person I've ever brought here,' he said, his eyes smiling into hers as she stopped, ready to fall back into the snow again. He caught her and they fell into the soft snow together, laughing at how they were ruining the angels. He kissed her again and she smiled up into his eyes.

'And the first person was ...?' she asked, breathless, sitting back on her heels.

'Rosa. She was the first girl I ever loved. We were both fifteen.'

'That makes me feel so special.' She stroked his cheek tenderly. Then she picked up a handful of snow in her gloved hand and threw it at him playfully. He leaped up and she tried to dodge his snowballs, which landed on her collar, the soft snow dribbling down her jacket next to her skin. Then they were in a full-scale snowfight.

Finally, panting and begging for mercy, Kylie held up her hands in surrender. 'It is a magical place. I'll never forget it.'

They sat together, contentedly eating their packed sandwiches which Kylie had had the forethought to bring and drinking hot coffee from Tom's thermos. Then, after one last look around, they climbed back onto their skidoo and meandered along the white countryside through the trees, the throb of the motor the only sound breaking the silence. Kylie felt extraordinarily peaceful. Then it gently started snowing. Shouting for Tom to stop, Kylie leaped off the bike and held her arms out, wide-eyed with delight, watching as the huge crystals collected on her arms. She danced around in a circle trying to catch the snowflakes on her tongue, childishly unable to get enough of this fairytale place. Twirling round and round she nearly fell and Tom caught her and kissed her again. Kylie looked into his eyes, suddenly feeling constrained. He was such a nice person and great fun, but did she feel anything deeper for him, and by having fun was she leading him on?

'We'd better be heading back. Looks as

though the weather's closing in,' said Tom, breaking the awkward silence that had suddenly sprung up between them.

Kylie looked up at heavy grey clouds where moments ago there had been blue skies. Quickly they remounted the skidoo. Soon it was snowing hard. As they wove their way back along the track, visibility decreased rapidly.

'You're sure you know where we are?' shouted Kylie anxiously.

'Relax! I know this mountain like the back of my hand. I've ridden here since I was a kid. My dad used to bring me up here almost before I could ski,' Tom shouted back confidently, easing some of Kylie's fears.

But as the weather deteriorated further she started feeling very afraid. Heads bent, unable to see more than centimetres in front, they were forced to keep wiping the snow from their sunglasses. The snow stung their flesh; the cold bit into them despite their thick ski gear. Then the skidoo started slithering and sliding, Tom struggling to keep it heading forwards, hampered by the newly fallen snow.

'Hold on!' he shouted, turning his head briefly, his words snatched by the wind. Speeding up as much as he dared, he suddenly veered off the main path and careered up a steep slope.

'What are you doing? This wasn't the way we came!' cried Kylie, now extremely alarmed. They were miles from anywhere, and she realised that in the excitement of the adventure she had forgotten her father's golden rule — 'Don't rely on others, make sure you let someone know where you are heading.' She had no idea whether Tom had let anyone know where he was planning to go. She swore inwardly at her own stupidity. Her heart began beating crazily at the thought of being lost in the snow. She clung to Tom as they slithered up the unbeaten track, and peered through her smeared glasses at the wall of white broken by ghostlike tree trunks. The skidoo lurched again, Kylie clung on tighter as Tom forced it groaning and grinding through the deepening snow. The exhaust was starting to make her queasy.

'That's what I was looking for!' shouted Tom. He urged the snowmobile up one final bump then skidded to an undignified halt. Kylie wiped the snow from her goggles then gave a cry of amazement as she spied a little log cabin. Half buried in snow, with tiny windows and a steep roof laden with snow, it looked like a traditional gingerbread house.

'You knew this was here?' she cried, relief flooding through her.

'I was pretty sure I was in the right place. Had

me worried a couple of times!' Tom turned off the machine. The ensuing silence seeming to swallow them up.

'We'd better get this machine under some shelter before we and it get buried alive,' pronounced Tom, quickly helping Kylie off the skidoo.

Together the two shunted the snowmobile into what shelter they could find at the rear entrance of the cabin. Then, using a small shovel and a crowbar retrieved from one of the saddlebags, they started digging a path to the door. When they finally reached the door, Tom stretched up and felt around the framework to find an old rusty key. He turned it in the lock and pushed open the door. A large lump of snow slid from the roof, narrowly missing Kylie, who leaped back with a yelp and started laughing, partly out of fright.

'There aren't any bears around at this time of year, are there?' she asked, looking anxiously around.

'Nope, all fast asleep,' grinned Tom. 'Gimme a hand to get the bike undercover. We don't want to have to dig that out in the morning.'

'What d'you mean, in the morning?' asked Kylie with a panicked start.

'This lot's set in for the rest of the day,' Tom replied. 'But we're safe here. Truly.' He reached out and stroked her bright pink cheek with the dry part of his glove to reassure her.

Kylie wasn't so sure. Tom was a nice guy, but a night alone in a hut in the snow ... She took a deep breath and told herself she had no choice. She stepped into the little cottage and gave a cry of pleasure. 'What a quaint little place! You almost expect the seven dwarfs to come charging out demanding who has woken them up!'

'It is rather like that, isn't it,' replied Tom. He hunted in a cupboard and pulled out two snow shovels. He handed one to Kylie. 'We need to get the skidoo into better shelter. If we clear to the right of the back door we can leave the old girl under the eaves.'

Kylie grinned at him, suddenly enjoying the adventure. The brief respite from the blizzard and Tom's confidence had helped hers return. Eyes watering as a sharp blast of icy snow caught her unawares, she bent her head and followed Tom outside. Soon they had the snowmobile safely parked under the eaves and had accidentally uncovered the woodpile. Kylie stretched her aching back and looked around. The weather had closed right in. Unless there was a miracle, even she could see it would be crazy to attempt the journey back. She rubbed her hands together inside her gloves and helped Tom carry in armfuls of soaking wet logs, wondering how on earth they were going to dry them out. It was dusk, and now she had slowed down, the sweat inside her clothes was cooling and making her shiver.

'I wonder whether the dwarfs left another means of warming the place,' she mused hopefully, stamping off the snow from her boots. But they had no need to worry about staying warm. Beside the dusty fireplace was a neat pile of dry logs and kindling, some yellowing newspaper and a box of matches. Kylie quickly dumped her armful of logs and lit the fire. Then she stood, hands held up to the heat, gradually thawing out as Tom attempted unsuccessfully to radio back to base. The place was bare except for a small table and two rickety chairs.

Tom came over to her and rubbed her arms, warming her further. 'I'll have another crack at the radio later, though even if we got through, no one's going to try to get up through this tonight.' He looked at Kylie, his eyes soft. 'Maybe that's not such a bad thing.'

He stared down at her face, her cheeks glowing, eyes bright. 'You are very beautiful,' he murmured.

'Thanks, but it's not going to make us a meal!' laughed Kylie, slightly breathless. She moved away, feeling suddenly vulnerable. 'I'll have a look around and see what I can find.'

She poked into the tiny kitchen. There was a battered old kettle and a small stove with a gas cylinder in the cupboard beneath, a drawer of assorted utensils and pots and crockery in the other cupboard. It reminded her of a child's cubbyhouse. There was no food except for one rusty can of baked beans. Investigating further afield, Kylie discovered blankets in a wooden chest in a corner of the main room, four of which she pulled out and dumped on a chair to air by the fireplace. Then, unable to resist, she tramped up the stairs to the tiny loft. The last of the daylight was seeping through the tiny snow-covered windows. She could almost see the seven little beds stretched out before her in the dimness. Shaking herself back to reality, she saw there were several old mattresses in a pile in one corner. Whoever owned the hut had it rigged up for emergencies. She called out to Tom and they dragged two of the mattresses downstairs, laying them out near the fire. The room was starting to warm up.

The other thing missing apart from food was water, Kylie discovered when she turned the tap on and nothing came out. Guessing the pipes must be frozen solid, she selected the largest saucepan, wiped it out with a clean tissue from her pocket, then, braving the swirling snow outside the back door, broke off several large icicles from the roof. She dropped them in the pot and slammed the door on the blizzard, shivering as slivers of snow melted down her neck. Next she placed the pot on the stove and attempted to turn the lever. It was jammed solid. Undefeated, she opened the can of baked beans. They smelt okay. Gingerly she tried one. It tasted fine.

'We have food and drink,' she announced to Tom, walking back into the main room with the opened can of baked beans and the saucepan from which two rapidly melting icicles protruded. Tom burst out laughing then relieved her of the saucepan and placed it in amongst the glowing logs.

Ten minutes later they happily shared teaspoonfuls of scalding-hot baked beans and stale biscuits. Then they polished off the chocolate, washing it down with steaming, rather watery coffee, Kylie having added some of the boiled icicles to what remained in Tom's thermos.

'Could have done a lot worse,' said Kylie, licking the last of the chocolate from her fingers. She felt surprisingly revived. She pulled a blanket around her and held her hands out to the fire. The fire was belting out heat, sending shadows darting up the wall behind them, but a draught still whistled around their backs. 'Who owns this place?'

'No idea. It's been used as a mountain rescue hut for years,' replied Tom, moving closer to the fire. 'I guess no one's used it for a while, although someone must have brought in all this wood.' He slid his arm around her. 'I have to admit this wasn't exactly how I'd planned the day.'

'Me neither.' Kylie's heart started beating frantically then slowed again as Tom made no move to do anything further.

For a while they chatted about the day, reliving the magic of the ride, the fabulous scenery, the hilarious bumps as they had slewed round corners.

'I've had the best time ever,' said Tom. 'You're such fun to be with. I've never met anyone like you. I feel so ... so comfortable.'

'Mmm, me too,' sighed Kylie. It had certainly been an amazing day. The heat from the fire was making her sleepy. She let herself relax, leaning on Tom and enjoying the lazy sensation as he stroked her shoulder and played with the ends of her hair. The warmth and cosiness enveloped them. Outside, the wind continued to howl around the hut and the snow lashed at the windows.

'We will be able to get out tomorrow, won't we?' asked Kylie.

'With a bit more digging,' nodded Tom. He stroked her hair, sweeping it off her face, then he kissed her gently. Kylie kissed him back. He was nice, uncomplicated. She let him kiss her, but when his hand sought out her breast, she pushed him away and sat up.

'Tom ... I ...'

Tom took her hands and gazed into her eyes. 'I think I'm falling in love with you, Kylie,' he said huskily.

''Tis the flickering of the fire and the romance of this cottage,' said Kylie, putting on an Irish accent to lighten the atmosphere.

Tom attempted to pull her back into his arms but she moved away, not sure she wanted the conversation to take this turn.

'Look, Tom,' she said eventually, 'I think you're really nice and I'm really flattered that you feel like that but I'm no good at lying.' She paused, distracted by his crestfallen expression, then ploughed on. 'I'm not sure I can give you what you want.'

'Is there someone else?' asked Tom, anxiety clouding his brown eyes.

Kylie looked into his kind face, fighting off images of Danno. Why couldn't she just fall in love with Tom? He was such a decent, handsome bloke, and he cared about her. She had to forget Danno. She knew in her heart he was just a stupid teenage crush she had blown out of all proportion. A few glances, a downhill race, a dance ... A tiny pulse started to throb at the memory of her in his arms.

'No, no, there's no one else,' she said firmly, looking straight at Tom. She threw her arms around him and kissed him again, releasing him just as quickly. 'You are one of the nicest blokes I've met. We have fun. We get on so well. It's just that I'm not ready to go ... you know ... the whole way with anyone right now.'

'Would you be happy just to sit by the fire for a while?' asked Tom.

'Love to!' replied Kylie, happily cuddling up to him, willing to trust him. *See, he's nice, really nice,* she told herself when he made no attempt to start seducing her again. They sat staring at the firelight, the conversation safely back to life and skiing and Tom's job.

'You know that Gwyn and I are going back home to Australia at the end of the season, don't you?' said Kylie, purposely casual. She suddenly wanted to make sure she wasn't giving him any false hopes. *Oh, how she wished she felt more for him!* 'Gwyn has only stayed on for this long because she knows how much I want to finish the season.'

'I wouldn't be too sure of that,' murmured

Tom into her neck. 'You smell delicious. Kiss me again. Kissing's allowed. Kiss me again.'

Kylie stopped. 'What d'you mean, not be too sure? It was me that pushed for us to come here in the first place. It was me that contacted Michael and got us the jobs.'

It was Tom's turn to sit up. 'I realise. I wasn't talking about you. I was talking about Gwyn.'

'What about her?' asked Kylie sharply, a thin trickle of anxiety running through her veins.

Tom stared at her. 'You're not serious? I love your innocence! You said she's been behaving strangely recently, won't talk to you, disappears for nights at a time — surely you've guessed why? The whole of Aspen knows.'

Kylie stood up abruptly, her eyes bright with irritation. 'Knows what?' She was almost shouting.

'That she's having an affair with Michael.'

'Michael Klein?'

Tom nodded. 'Surely you can't not have heard!'

'Liar!' Kylie screamed and slapped him hard across the face before she could stop herself. Then she immediately crumpled. 'I'm sorry, Tom, I'm sorry, I really am,' she said, fighting back tears, stroking his cheek where red welts the shape of her fingers were forming. She was shaking like a leaf. Suddenly everything was falling into place. The expensive clothes, the money, the secrecy, Gwyn's eagerness to work so hard for Michael. She could smell his choking cigars. Why hadn't she put two and two together? Why hadn't Gwyn told her? And today of course, Gwyn having to stay back ... Surely after all she'd been through, Gwyn couldn't be that stupid?

Tom caught her trembling fingers and kissed them. 'Sshh sshh! It's okay, it's okay,' he crooned, wrapping her in his arms.

Kylie burst into tears. 'I just can't believe it. Gwyn's not that stupid,' she sobbed, her voice muffled against his chest. She pulled away. 'Does the whole of Aspen really know?' she whispered.

'Just about. I hate to sound callous but this is pretty typical of Michael. Young girl, attractive, dazzled by the lifestyle ...' Tom shrugged, and for the first time Kylie saw a hardness in him.

She got up and put another log on the fire, then pulled her blanket around her and started pacing the room. She peered out into the night. All she could see was blackness. The wind had eased off a bit.

'Here, come and sit down and we can talk about it,' Tom said gently.

Kylie slumped down beside him. 'I think you've got it wrong. Gwyn wouldn't be that stupid,' she said firmly, trying to convince herself.

'I didn't mean to upset you. I honestly thought you knew.'

Kylie looked up at him. 'You really did, didn't you?' She reached up and stroked the fading red marks on his cheek.

He caught her hand and kissed the palm, then stood up with a sigh. 'I think we'd better go to bed before I do something I regret,' he said, his eyes filled with longing.

'Good idea,' said Kylie. Tom's revelation had ruined any romance created by the cosy atmosphere, and suddenly she wanted to be down the mountain. She pulled the two mattresses closer to the fire, whilst Tom stoked it up, then she snuggled under the blankets. 'Thank you for ... you know.'

Tom reached over and patted her shoulder .'Don't worry, I'm sure it'll all sort itself out,' he said gently in the flickering light.

Kylie gave a sigh. He was really nice. If only he would be a bit less understanding. She lay listening to the creaking of the little hut and the blizzard outside, trying to convince herself he was wrong about Gwyn. As she drifted off to sleep, through her jumbled thoughts Danno kept flitting in and out of her mind.

❉ ❉ ❉

Kylie woke as the first rays of dawn peeped into the little hut. Stiffly she got up. She shivered. The fire was out and the room was freezing. Clutching her blanket, she walked to the window and blinked, blinded by what she saw, her breath white clouds melting Jack Frost on the windowpane. The blizzard had abated and she was staring out at oceans of fresh snow, all signs of yesterday's tracks buried in the metre-deep dump.

'Pretty amazing sight, isn't it?' said Tom, yawning and joining her.

'Can we get out?' Kylie asked anxiously.

'We'll need to take it slowly, but the way back from here's pretty simple.'

Neither of them made any reference to Gwyn or the night before, but their mood was more sombre.

The journey back to Aspen was almost more dazzling than the day before. Everything was covered in a metre of snow, and the branches of the huge fir trees were weighted down by the white covering. Tom ploughed the skidoo carefully along the hidden tracks, several times nearly veering off into a snowdrift. They finally reached Chuck's place just as the world was waking up, the smell of frying bacon making them hurry inside in search of breakfast.

Chapter Eleven

'Where on earth were you?' Kylie demanded as soon as she got back to Gondola Lodge and tracked down her sister.

'Work. I told you,' Gwyn said shortly, avoiding her sister's gaze.

'You're not having an affair with Michael, are you?' Kylie blurted out.

Gwyn's eyes shot to her sister's face. 'What? Don't be absurd! He's my boss and he's married!' She started laughing uproariously, then stopped abruptly. 'Whatever gave you that idea?' She stared at Kylie, eyes narrowed. 'Tom, it was Tom, wasn't it?'

Kylie looked away.

'It was Tom, wasn't it?' repeated Gwyn

'Tell me it's not true,' whispered Kylie.

Gwyn glared at her. 'D'you really think I'd be that stupid? Of course it's not true, and if that's the sort of nasty lies Tom's spreading, I'd ditch him pretty quick. Next time I try and choose your boyfriends, kick me in the shins.' She laughed again more naturally, throwing her arms around Kylie and hugging her close.

Kylie hugged her back, then wiped away the tears of relief that spilled down her cheek. 'I'm really sorry to be so mean,' she said, and blamed her emotionally confused state for even considering there might be some truth in what Tom had said. But despite Gwyn's hot denial, Kylie couldn't shake off a feeling of unease. There was something different about Gwyn, something she was holding back.

Kylie's sense of unease increased as the weeks went by. Their sisterly chats became less frequent and they saw less and less of each other as Gwyn either worked late or rushed off to endless parties, glamorous and smiling. Kylie bit her tongue, wanting her to be happy. Neither of them mentioned Kylie's accusation about Michael.

During this time Kylie saw more of Tom, which should have made her happy. He took her to glamorous haunts, bought her thoughtful little presents and made no move to force their relationship further, which only made Kylie feel even more guilty. She felt she was leading him on unfairly and she started looking forward to his return to his filming. It depressed her that she couldn't feel more for this incredibly thoughtful and loving man. Yet selfishly, with the distance between her and Gwyn growing, she was loath to break off with the one person she felt she could talk to. Kylie missed her sister's company badly and longed to get back to their intimate chats, and she finally realised that while Gwyn seemed to be thriving on it, the whole Aspen glamour thing was over for her.

The only place she felt really happy was on the slopes. She divided her time between the Klein kids' ski lessons at weekends and coaching lessons during the week. Although the spring weather was melting the snow in the village, the higher slopes were still in excellent shape and there were wonderful unexpectedly hot days when Kylie skied in only a T-shirt and ski pants, even removing her gloves. Sometimes she and Tom skied together, recapturing some of the easy happiness Kylie had felt earlier. Tom always delighted at being in Kylie's company, but for Kylie their closeness always vanished once they were off the mountain.

One night in late March, seeing a light under Gwyn's door and longing for a chat, Kylie was about to barge in, when she heard giggles and then a man's voice. Shaken, she retreated to her own room. In the morning she poked her head round Gwyn's door but she was nowhere to be seen, her bed neatly made. The room smelt faintly of expensive cigars.

Worried, lonely, longing to believe none of this was happening, Kylie donned her skis on her next free morning and went in search of Meg, one of her ski instructor friends. Together the two girls took off, exploring the backblocks, diving down steep ravines and leaping over moguls, chasing one another across wide clear runs, and laughing and playing in the snow. Kylie felt revived and refreshed.

At lunchtime Tom surprised her by joining them, and a tight knot gripped Kylie's stomach.

'I'll leave you two to it then,' said Meg tactfully.

Kylie gave her a grateful smile. 'Today I have to do it,' she muttered under her breath as she and Tom raced down a slope. Breathless, she stopped at the bottom, snow spurting from her skis. Tom skied right up to her, his skis outside hers, and clasped her in a bear hug.

'I love you more and more each time I see you. I hate being away from you even for a second,' he said, grinning happily.

Kylie felt her gut twist again. She pulled off her gloves. 'Tom, I think you're a wonderful man,' she started.

Tom's face took on a wariness. 'I know I'm pushy. I promised myself I wouldn't be. Where to now?' He turned to move off. Kylie grabbed his sleeve.

'This isn't working, Tom,' she said baldly.

'What, the run? It's a bit slushy ...'

'Us, Tom. Please don't dodge the topic, it's hard enough for me as it is. Can we at least talk about it?'

Tom's expression hardened. 'What is there to talk about?' He was suddenly angry. 'I love you. You don't love me. That's it. Finished.' He pushed off down the slope.

With an exasperated sigh Kylie chased after him, skiing in front of him so he was forced to stop. She didn't want it to be a messy ending. 'Don't let's do it this way. I really like you. You're such good fun to be with. It's just that ...'

'You don't love me,' he shouted, hurt and angry. 'I guess if you tell a guy for long enough, eventually he gets the message.' They stared miserably at one another across the snow.

'I don't deserve you,' Kylie said finally in an effort to alleviate some of the pain she was inflicting.

'Don't give it a second thought. It was nice knowing you. Enjoy the rest of your stay. Have a great trip home,' said Tom shortly and then shot off down the slope.

Kylie stood and watched him go. Could she have done it any less hurtfully? She'd tried to tell him their relationship was going nowhere that night at the gingerbread hut. Part of her felt as though two great boulders had just rolled off her shoulders, the other part felt suddenly lonely that she had lost a good friend. Perhaps if she had given it a bit longer ... She pulled on her gloves. What was she talking about? She didn't want to give it any longer. She didn't love him. She had never intended to fall in love with anyone in Aspen. She had come for the skiing. With a sudden lurch she realised she wanted desperately to go home.

Kylie finally caught up with Gwyn three days later after a blustery day on the slopes. Kylie gave her sister a quick hug and then collapsed onto her bed. 'Nice to see you, stranger! Aren't you going to tell me who this person is who makes you ignore your poor sister?' she asked, half teasing, half serious.

Gwyn hesitated a moment, a hint of wariness in her eyes. 'His name's Jerry,' she replied brightly, 'and he's megarich! A crowd of us are going for a drink tonight at the Rocky Mountain Pub. Why don't you and Tom join us?'

The mention of Tom gave Kylie a jolt. She hadn't even told Gwyn. 'We broke it off two days ago,' she said. 'He was getting too serious.

I felt as though I was stringing him along and it wasn't fair.' She paused. 'I sometimes wonder if I'll ever fall in love with anyone, I mean really fall in love, so you just know this is it for keeps.'

'You're not still pining after Danno, are you? Oh Kylie. Forget him. Move on. There's so much fun to be had in life. Come out tonight. I'm sure I can line you up with a date for the evening.'

'No, thanks, I just dumped one,' said Kylie, starting to laugh and giving Gwyn a playful punch. Things felt almost normal again. 'I will come tonight, though,' she said, cheered by how open and happy Gwyn seemed. She was happier than Kylie had seen her for ages. In fact she looked positively radiant.

Kylie was just about to ask more about this Jerry fellow when Gwyn said sheepishly, 'Promise you won't get the wrong idea, but Michael might be joining the party.'

Kylie felt as though she had been slugged in the stomach. Determined not to restart the whole argument when they had just begun to get close again, Kylie mumbled something and hurried off. A couple of hours later, after Kylie had had a long shower and changed her clothes, she went in search of Gwyn, only to find she had already left. Smothering her disappointment and irritation, Kylie headed off to the pub.

The group had clearly been there a while. Gwyn, already tipsy, hurried over to Kylie and introduced her to Jerry. Kylie shook hands politely and tried to look happy for Gwyn, but the more she watched, the less impressed she was. Loud and vulgar, with shifty eyes, Jerry splashed money about, dropped names and treated Gwyn more like a decoration to be exhibited than a girlfriend.

'Does he always treat you like this?' whispered Kylie when Jerry was getting another round of drinks.

'I like him. When I'm with his crowd I feel expensive,' replied Gwyn, tossing her head defensively. Her eyes were glittery and she was slurring her words slightly. She started giggling, telling Kylie about the amazing parties Jerry and his mates put on.

Kylie felt dull and out of it, worried that Gwyn was getting far too involved with a group who spent money like water and whose only ambition was to have a good time. She thought of her empty purse and wondered secretly if she would ever see her money again. Immediately she dismissed the thought as mean and disloyal. Gwyn was just out to have a bit of fun and where was the harm in that?

Two days later Kylie found her purse empty yet again. Roaring over to Gwyn's room she banged open the door, flinging into the room just her as her sister was getting dressed for work. Gwyn burst into tears.

'I'll pay it back, I promise.' She seemed very agitated. She had dark shadows under her eyes and her hands shook as she applied her mascara.

'Why couldn't you have asked me if you're that strapped for cash? What did you buy this time?' Kylie accused. She paused, suddenly concerned. Gwyn didn't look at all well. 'You don't need all this stuff,' she said, flipping her hand across the countless little tops, pants and dresses neatly hung in her sister's wardrobe.

Gwyn turned on her sister. 'Why can't you stop bugging me? What if I happen to like having heaps of clothes? What's it to you? Why can't I look nice? It's not my fault you scare all your boyfriends away.' She was shrieking now. 'Why do you have to go on at me all the time?' She pulled a face, mimicking her sister, her voice whiny. "Why d'you do this, Gwyn, why d'you do that?" Get off my back, will you? I'm the elder sister, not you. I said I'd pay you back. Now let me finish dressing or I'll be late for work.'

Kylie was so shocked by the unexpected attack, she retreated from the room speechless. Staring at the closed door, she hesitated then cautiously opened it a crack. 'Are you okay, Gwynny,' she called. 'Have I missed something?'

Gwyn was finishing a drink of water. 'I'm sorry. I just need a bit of time out. I've been going it a bit hard. I'll get you your money tonight.' Gwyn sounded almost normal.

Kylie walked away even more worried. Gwyn had never turned on her like that. Something had happened that she wasn't talking about. Silently Kylie swore at Jerry and his mates, wishing Gwyn would leave that crowd. The old bogy of Michael and Gwyn raised its head again and she immediately dismissed it. She and Gwyn had always been so honest and open with each other. She set off for the slopes, but the unsettled feeling stayed.

On her way back to her room later that day, Kylie knocked on Gwyn's door. There was no answer. Feeling like a thief, she unlocked the door and slipped inside. The room was neat and tidy, everything in its proper place, almost too tidy. Kylie walked around, wondering what she was doing spying on her sister. Cautiously she examined Gwyn's dressing table, lifting the lid of her jewellery box, checking through her clothes, noticing the half-empty bottle of vodka. She pulled open the drawer to the bedside table, not quite sure what she was looking for, and rummaged around. About to close it, she caught sight of a tiny plastic packet containing fine white powder right at the very back. Her heart gave a horrible lurch as she picked it up. The door swung open and Gwyn walked in.

'Spying on me now, are you?' she shouted. She stormed across to Kylie and snatched away the package. 'What the hell do you think you're doing, poking around in my stuff?'

Kylie stared back at her sister, momentarily stunned. 'Tell me it's not what I think it is, Gwynny,' she whispered. She suddenly felt very sick.

'What isn't what?' demanded Gwyn, shoving the package deep in her jeans pocket, her eyes darting accusingly at Kylie's face.

'Not drugs. Please, Gwynny, not drugs. You know what that stuff does to people.' Kylie was horrified. 'If you get caught with that stuff, we could lose our jobs, go to jail.'

Gwyn gave a harsh laugh. 'You're such an innocent, Kylie. Everyone here does coke. Don't tell me you haven't been offered some.' She pulled out the packet, took a pinch, laid it on the back of her hand and sniffed it in. Her eyes watered for a moment. 'Here,' she said, offering some to Kylie.

Kylie backed away. Gwyn started giggling, trying playfully to force Kylie to take a sniff. Failing, she fell back onto the bed and began talking about everything and nothing, about Jerry and parties and how she was having the best time. Kylie stared at her with increasing alarm. She had no idea what to do.

Gwyn sat up. 'Don't worry so much, silly. It's just a bit of fun! Oh, come on, sis! I just wanted to try some, to see what it does.' She sounded almost like the old Gwyn Kylie loved so much. 'Look, I'll get rid of it. It's totally overrated anyway.' She walked into the bathroom, shook the sachet contents into the toilet bowl and pressed the button.

Kylie watched the powder flush away, her shoulders sagging with relief. She turned and hugged her sister. 'Oh Gwyn, you scared me. Promise me you'll never do that ever again!' Her eyes were filled with tears.

Gwyn held her close. 'You're such a worry wart.' She paused, her eyes on Kylie's face, her expression tense. 'I lied to you,' she said quietly. 'Jerry's not the one, never was. It is Michael. We're in love. We just have to be a bit careful at the moment.

'Don't get mad at me,' she added quickly, watching Kylie's face. 'I know I should have told you straightaway but I couldn't. We'd sworn each other to secrecy. I s'pose because it's so special, so just him and me. I guess also I didn't want the usual homily about married men. I love him so much.' Her lips parted in a gentle smile. 'He's such a wonderful man, Kylie. He's so tender and thoughtful. It's just a matter of time organising the divorce from that bitch Marie. He says once Hillary's birthday's out of the way, he'll start the whole thing rolling. Then we can finally be open about our love. Oh Kylie! I'm amazed it all happened so quickly. I'm so incredibly happy!' She danced over to Kylie who was staring back at her, rooted to the floor in disbelief. 'Well, aren't you happy for us?'

Kylie was shaking with rage, rage at Michael for abusing Gwyn's vulnerability, rage that Gwyn could be so taken in, rage that she had allowed herself to believe Gwyn's lies. Her whole world was reeling; the truth she had tried to ignore was finally out.

'Surely you don't believe all that, Gwynny! Can't you see what he's doing? He's using you. He does this all the time, you know. Hillary's birthday is just an excuse!'

'I knew you'd be like this! That's the very reason I didn't tell you before.' Gwyn hugged her arms to her thin body. 'I don't care what you or anyone says. Michael really loves me. People do get divorced, you know.' She paused, purposely calming herself. 'Michael's really thrilled with the job you've done with the kids.' Then she burst out, 'Oh Kylie, I've so longed to tell you but we'd agreed …'

Kylie melted. She so wanted to be happy for Gwyn, for this to work out for her. 'Oh Gwynny, I miss talking to you. I've got so much to tell you. Let's do something tonight, go and see a movie or something, just you and me.' She thought that if they could only spend a little bit of time together she might be able to make her sister see sense.

'I'd love to, Kylie, but I'm meeting Michael in town in half an hour.'

'Oh,' said Kylie deflated. She had to curb the lecture that bubbled to her lips as Gwyn chatted on about Michael's virtues.

After her sister had left, dressed up to the nines, Kylie went in search of something to eat at a nearby cafe. Staring into her soup she wondered how she could have been so blind as not to see it. Why had she been so unwilling to accept the truth from Tom?

She was still thinking about it a few days later as she zigzagged her way down one of the intermediate runs, and she stared glumly out across the snow in her lunchbreak as the other instructors compared notes about the celebrity status of their students. Gwyn had been morose and strange again. It hadn't helped that Marie had arrived unannounced with the children. Nor that Kylie and Gwyn had had another argument, this time about pills Gwyn claimed were prescribed antidepressants.

'What's up with you? You look as miserable as all get-out,' asked Meg. 'Let me guess, man trouble again?'

Before Kylie could reply, a group of giggling kids chattering away in Russian was ushered to a table in the sunshine.

'They're having a happy time,' Kylie said quickly, not wanting to delve into her own troubles.

'They're a great bunch. They're the charity group from Chernobyl,' explained Meg. 'They learn quickly. This is a special treat laid on for them, a week's skiing before they fly home after treatment. Most of them have some kind of problem from radiation fallout. It's pretty grim. Half of them won't live past twenty'

Kylie shook her head, blinking back the tears. Glitz, glamour, money and fantasy. That was how it was here. Kylie was staring at reality. These kids were going back to … nothing.

She caught sight of the Russian kids again late that afternoon. As they laughed and cavorted in the snow, she felt her resolve harden. She would have one last go at talking to Gwyn, to try and get her to see reason. One last go … She felt sick in the stomach at the thought. Struggling with a desperate feeling of isolation, she longed for someone to turn to. She toyed with ringing her parents, then dismissed the notion. All it would do was terrify them. Gwyn would see reason, Kylie told herself firmly. They had always worked things out together in the past.

Suddenly Kylie remembered she had agreed to go to yet another party with Gwyn. Damn, she'd have to leave the slopes now if she was going to make it on time.

'Hey, sis, how ya going?' shouted Gwyn from the dance floor of one of Aspen's exclusive hotels. She was wrapped around Jerry and she looked ravishing in a new evening gown.

Kylie immediately wondered how she had paid for it. She marched over to her sister. 'We need to talk — now!' she said matter-of-factly, ignoring Jerry.

'Oh dear, this sounds serious! Jerry, I'll be right back.' She fluttered her thick eyelashes at him. 'Don't look so ferocious, this is a party!' she whispered to Kylie.

'Gwynny, can we get out of here?' asked Kylie urgently,

'No! I invited you to a party —'

'Good evening, ladies. Off duty and enjoying yourselves, I see. Lovely to see you both.'

Kylie felt a chill run down her spine. She turned and looked up into Michael Klein's eyes and suddenly she wanted to slap the arrogant artificial smile off his face. What was he playing at? Did he think she was a complete idiot or did he just not care? Gwyn beamed at him and her face confirmed all Kylie's worst fears.

'As always you two young ladies look stunning. Can I buy you both a drink?' continued Michael smoothly.

Fists clenched, seething inside, Kylie nodded politely, ordering a Campari and soda. For the next fifteen agonising minutes the three made small talk, Gwyn continuing to smile radiantly and irritatingly up at Michael.

'I thought maybe you might like to join my private party upstairs. Have a nice relaxed evening free of work and children,' invited Michael. 'Marie unfortunately couldn't join me tonight.' His eyes swept over them both, lingering a second on Gwyn. Jerry seemed to have disappeared. Gwyn was already agreeing eagerly.

Desperate to keep her eye on her sister, Kylie allowed herself to be escorted upstairs. The party was being held in the hotel's most extravagant rooms. Huge chandeliers and the heavy gold and green brocade curtains and velvet chaise longues added a Victorian elegance to the room. The polished wood bar with gleaming glass goblets, equipped to supply every conceivable cocktail, took up the whole of one wall and waiters hovered with trays of morsels, others ready to take the guests' orders. Michael introduced Kylie to a small group of his friends and then swept Gwyn away. Kylie smiled woodenly at the conversation — the latest Aspen gossip about a movie star who had left his wife and family for a rising starlet. Kylie escaped as soon as she could and poked her head into one of the adjoining rooms, quickly retreating when she noticed someone snorting cocaine.

The evening continued in an agony of misery for her as she watched her sister openly flirting with Michael, careless of who was watching. They danced cheek to cheek, kissing, and at one point disappeared from the room, returning giggling and obviously high as kites. Kylie wanted to scream at her sister, to shake her to her senses. Instead, she danced with every man who asked her, batted her eyelids at them and, when she could stand it no longer, excused herself and caught a taxi back to the hotel.

Back in her room, she tossed her evening bag on the chair and burst into tears. What was she going to do? This was a nightmare. Kylie searched through her purse for enough change to ring home. Then she threw the purse down. What could she say — that her sister was on drugs and having an affair with her boss? What could they do? God, where did she go from here?

She crawled onto the bed, curled her legs up to her stomach and sobbed, her whole body shaking, until she could sob no more.

Early the next morning Kylie walked into Gwyn's room to try and talk some sense into her. Her bed was unslept in. Careless of the consequences, Kylie went looking for her at work. She wasn't there either. Finally she tracked her down in a coffee shop. She was staring into space.

'You have to break it off with Michael!' Kylie said without preamble.

Gwyn looked blankly at her and pulled out a cigarette, lighting it with a gold lighter.

'Gwyn! When did you take up smoking? What's wrong with you? We always used to share everything.'

Gwyn pulled silently on the cigarette, tapping the lighter round and round on the table till Kylie could bear it no longer. 'For heaven's sake, Gwynny, talk to me. I'm your sister — you know, the one who laughs and giggles with you.'

'I need some cash,' Gwyn said tightly.

Kylie glared at Gwyn, her first instinct to refuse. If Gwyn was using drugs, giving her money was the worst thing Kylie could do. But she looked so desperate. She hesitated a moment as love fought commonsense, then rummaged through her bag and pulled out a couple of bills and handed them to her sister. 'Gwynny, what is it? What's going on? Please let me help you. Please,' begged Kylie.

'Thanks.' Gwyn stubbed out her cigarette and stuffed the notes in her pocket.

Kylie clasped her hands over Gwyn's shaking fingers, forcing her to look at her. 'How can I help you, Gwynny?' she whispered and her heart turned over in pain. She had never before seen such bleak hopelessness in anyone's eyes.

Just for a moment Gwyn smiled. She patted Kylie's hand. 'Don't worry. She'll be jake. Isn't that what Dad always says?' Tears began sliding down her cheeks.

Kylie put her coat around her, paid the bill and helped her into a cab back to the hotel. Unresisting, Gwyn let her tuck her into bed with a hot drink. Kylie then rang down to say Gwyn had a migraine and wouldn't be returning to work that day. Terrified of her sister's state of mind, she cancelled her ski class and stayed with her for the rest of the day, organised dinner, which they hardly touched, and finally climbed into bed and fell asleep with her arms wrapped protectively around Gwyn.

The next morning Gwyn seemed more cheerful and chatty, yet she still refused to discuss Michael, or her behaviour the day before. Reassuring Kylie she was fit for work, she agreed to meet her for lunch at one o'clock. She didn't show up.

Kylie couldn't forgive herself for being so stupid as to have let Gwyn out of her sight knowing her state of mind. When she didn't come back to the hotel that evening Kylie started to panic. She was almost tempted to go to Michael, but then she thought better of it. Instead she rang one of the girls who worked with Gwyn, but she had no idea where her sister might be.

After that she walked the streets of Aspen for hours, checking all Gwyn's normal haunts and many others without success, becoming more desperate as the evening progressed.

The pubs were starting to close now, late-night revellers wending their noisy way home. Kylie leaned against a wall, fighting back tears. She racked her brains for somewhere she might have missed, then set off towards the poorer end of town. In desperation she walked into a thoroughly sleazy bar in the worst part of Aspen, convinced Gwyn would never dream of coming to a dump like this. The bar gave her the creeps. Dark and dingy, it was filled with dim booths, their faded velvet scratched and torn. Smoke curled up in the thick atmosphere, and the sickly sweet smell of marijuana was unmistakable. In one of the booths two unkempt individuals were openly doing coke lines, one of them tapping the white powder onto the table, breaking it up and shaping it into lines with a credit card. The man behind the bar was casually drying glasses. Feeling sickened and scared, Kylie walked over to ask if he had seen anyone fitting her sister's description. He shook his head. She glanced down into the dimness with relief, about to turn away, then she froze as she stared into Gwyn's eyes. She blinked, unable at first to believe what she was seeing.

'Gwynny!' she called, running over. 'Are you all right? Thank goodness I've found you!' With a sickening thud she saw the lines of white powder spread out on the booth table, the bottles of vodka and tequila, the row of empty glasses. There were three of them with Gwyn, another girl and two men, one reasonably well dressed, tie removed, collar open, eyes distracted. He rolled up what looked like a hundred-dollar bill and snorted some coke up his nostril. Then he took a slug of vodka and sat back with a sigh. The other girl giggled and knocked back a shot of tequila. Gwyn snorted some coke.

'Gwyn, Gwyn,' Kylie almost shouted, 'you don't want to do that. Let's get out of here.' She tried to get Gwyn to stand up. Wordlessly, Gwyn shook her off.

'Hey, lady, piss off! This chick's with us.'

The man without the tie stood up and took a menacing step towards her. The other man, obviously out of it, simply stared at her like an idiot.

'Would you like a drink? Would you all like a drink?' cried Kylie desperately, trying to think of a way to get Gwyn away. The tieless man scared her. He had sat back down but he was looking at Gwyn as if he owned her.

'What? Have you come to laugh in my face now?' shouted Gwyn, finally acknowledging Kylie. 'Do you always have to be so damned right? You who can't even accept that someone could love you, really love you with every fibre ...' She started crying. 'He was going to leave the bitch, he promised. It was only a matter of time ...'

Kylie tried to put her arm around Gwyn but she shook her off, shouting that Michael had said he loved her and it was only a matter of time before Marie took her hooks out of him and disappeared off the end of the earth and there would be just her and Michael and the kids.

'The kids really love me, Michael really loves me,' she blubbered. 'If that bitch hadn't shown up …'

Someone started a jukebox. Kylie nearly jumped out of her skin. She forced herself to smile at Gwyn, trying to stay calm, trying to make her mind work, to think of some way to get her away from these people.

'Let's go and have something to eat, Gwynny. I'm starved.'

Gwyn reached for the vodka bottle in the middle of the booth table and took a slug. 'He said it was over with us. She made him do it. He'd never have done it on his own.' Her eyes glittered; her voice was gravelly, almost unrecognisable. How had beautiful, ethereal Gwyn been replaced by this thin wreck of a girl?

'Who gives a shit! We all know the truth,' Gwyn said, suddenly lucid. She pulled a small bottle of pills out of her bag, shook four into her hand and tossed them in her mouth, washing them down with more vodka. 'They're supposed to make me happy.'

The vacant man came momentarily out of his trance and helped himself from the bottle.

Kylie's heart leaped to her throat. 'No, Gwynny! No! You don't need those! I'll help you, you'll be all right.' Panic rose in her throat.

Gwyn gave an ugly laugh. Staggering to her feet, she pushed her sister away. 'What would you know? I love him. He loves me. We have great sex.' She turned around and started to shout, 'It was that fucking stupid bitch that made him say it was over.'

Gwyn grabbed the vodka again and took another swig. 'Over! We'll see what's over.' She waved the bottle in Kylie's face, swaying dangerously. 'You see, my darling sister, it *can't* be over. I'm pregnant and it's his fucking baby.' She scrabbled at the table, reaching for a bill to snort up some more cocaine, anything to numb her piercing misery.

Kylie slammed her hand on top of Gwyn's, sending some of the powder flying. Enraged, Gwyn turned and took a swipe at her, smashing her fist into her face, sending her sister reeling backwards.

'Fuck off! She doesn't want your help,' growled the tieless man, furious at the wasted coke. He raised his fist to thump Kylie who was now clutching at her nose. The barman was hurrying over with two mates. Suddenly Gwyn staggered. She started coughing. Her legs buckled under her and she collapsed to the floor. Her eyes rolled back in her head and she started convulsing.

'Gwyn!' shrieked Kylie. She knelt beside Gwyn, yelling for someone to get an ambulance. She felt as though she was watching herself and Gwyn in a strange horrible unreality. It was two o'clock in the morning.

'We can use his car.' It was the girl, waving car keys and gesturing to the idiot who sat staring blankly. The tieless man started shrieking abuse at them both, demanding they leave him money for the drinks. Hardly hearing him, Kylie and the girl carried Gwyn to the car. Even unconscious she was light as a feather.

Heart in her mouth, Kylie raced to the local hospital and charged up to the front desk screaming for help. A doctor and two male nurses rushed out with a trolley, wheels rattling noisily. They lifted Gwyn onto it then raced her back inside.

The doctor staccatoed out orders as Gwyn was thrust into an emergency bay, the curtains drawn around her by a black nurse. Kylie noticed irrelevantly that her crinkly black hair was dyed chestnut. Then suddenly Kylie was watching in slow motion as the curtains parted and the doctor reappeared.

'It's no good. She's gone. We didn't get to her quickly enough.' The doctor gave a weary sigh. 'Do you know this person?' he asked. He had

seen too many overdoses. They were such a waste of life.

'She's my sister,' Kylie replied, numb with shock. She stared at the doctor in disbelief as he explained gently how they had tried to save her, that they had done everything feasible. Gwyn couldn't be dead. She had so much to live for. She was her big sister. Suddenly she darted past the doctor towards the cubicle, tears pouring down her face. Gwyn wasn't dead. She couldn't be!

PART TWO

PART TWO

Chapter Twelve

Kylie checked all the dinghies were secured, the canoes safe on their racks, jetskis tethered on the beach, petrol turned off, and spare ropes and equipment stowed; then she locked the door to the resort boatshed. Wiping her arm across her forehead, she strolled idly down the long white beach. It was dusk. Her toes dug pleasurably into the soft sand still hot from the day; her thin cotton sarong tied around her bikini clung gently to her legs as she walked. Murmurs and clinking glasses wafted towards her as the few holiday-makers, nightly cocktails in hand, wended their way from their sea-view rooms to the long deckchairs set out unobtrusively at intervals along the edge of the beach to watch one of the famous Dunk Island sunsets. Kylie sat down on her favourite rock, cupped her chin in her hand and gazed across the rippling water as the great orange sun sank slowly towards the horizon, spreading its fiery tentacles across the sky and turning it glorious pinks and yellows. A lone fisherman stood at the water's edge, his body silhouetted against the sea as it changed to molten gold.

Sunsets on Dunk Island were truly spectacular and Kylie immersed herself in them in an effort to see beauty in her shattered world. It was almost three years since Gwyn's death, a time in which Kylie had wandered in a black hell, blaming herself, missing Gwyn desperately, wondering if there was any point to life. She wished she could turn back the clock, wished they had never gone to Aspen to chase the elusive glamour they'd thought they wanted. Her parents had flown out to Aspen as stunned by the tragedy as she, her mother repeatedly begging to know why Kylie hadn't contacted them earlier, hadn't screamed for their help. Susan kept asking Kylie what had gone wrong, how Gwyn could have changed so drastically, and her father was terrifyingly quiet and controlled. They flew Gwyn's body home and she was buried in Lyrebird Falls. The whole town had turned out, pouring out their love and sympathy to the shattered family. Kylie had only cried once, when her father spoke at the graveside, otherwise she had watched numbly through the entire proceedings, twisting round and round in her pocket the little Christmas decoration Gwyn had bought her that first day in Whistler.

Only when, a few weeks after they had returned from Lyrebird Falls to Dunk Island, her mother started on again about why Kylie hadn't phoned and what they as parents had missed, did Kylie finally turn on her, dark shadows under eyes huge with misery.

'Please, Mum, don't! Not any more! Gwyn's gone. Going over and over it like this won't ever bring her back.' Her hands were clenched, her grief-stricken face ashen. 'I loved her, I miss her so much ...' She thought then she would break in two with the guilt and misery that swamped her.

She was convinced that Susan and Geoff blamed her for Gwyn's death. Each day, as she saw her mother struggle to come to terms with the tragedy, she barricaded herself a little further behind her unbearable misery. Geoff said little, simply burying himself in his work, pushing himself harder, building the resort up so it grew to be more and more popular, if only for something to make his life seem once more to have a point. At night Kylie would hear her mother's muffled crying and each night she felt a little more shut out, accepting that it was what she deserved. Then when the pain became too great for Kylie, she packed a small bag, announced she was going to get a job on the mainland and flew to Mission Beach where she got work as a waitress in a seaside cafe.

But she couldn't settle. She kept moving from job to job, as if by keeping on the go she could rid herself of the pain and loss that haunted her. Sometimes she could hardly drag herself out of bed to face the day; at other times anger at the world, at God, at Gwyn, grew so intense she thought she might explode. These were often the days when she would fling herself into her work, purposely create an argument and get herself fired, or else hand in her notice and storm out. Then she would swing up for a while and cope, a tiny part of her knowing she was being irresponsible as she wandered endlessly around in this black hole.

Finally, emotionally exhausted, she returned to Dunk Island. That was twelve months ago. It had been a bumpy year in which Kylie and Susan had frequently clashed over silly things. Susan had insisted that she help around the resort — it was the only thing she could think of to get her daughter back on some kind of even keel. For her part, Kylie was always aware that she could never fill the space in Susan's heart, never have that bond that Gwyn and her mother had shared.

'I used to wish Gwyn would just disappear so

I could be the one you talked to,' Kylie admitted on one of her better days, some months after she had returned to the resort. She and Susan were tidying out some cupboards together. 'The thought keeps ringing in my head that by wishing she'd disappear, I actually made it happen. I didn't, did I?' she asked, her eyes desperate; then she dashed her arm across her eyes and reached into the cupboard, withdrawing a box of smelly old cloths covered with mildew. 'Phew, Mum! These are disgusting. How could you leave them to stink the place out?'

Susan bristled, biting back a retort even as her heart went out to her daughter. She longed to hug her, to stroke away some of the pain, but she had already tried that and had been rejected. She found it impossibly hard when Kylie went on the attack over petty nothings like some silly rags that had got damp.

'He was a smooth bastard,' Kylie went on. 'How could Gwyn have been so stupid as to fall in love with such a creep?'

'Don't talk about your sister like that!' snapped Susan, exhausted by her daughter's constant mood swings. 'Your sister made a mistake, one that cost her her life. Do you really think your continual sniping is going to make any of us feel better?' She started attacking the cupboards with her cloth.

Kylie slumped back, tears filling her eyes, her voice choked. 'Don't you think I feel bad enough about everything without you ramming it down my throat?'

Susan gave an inward sigh, bracing herself for another of Kylie's miserable rages. She understood anger was part of the healing process, but if only they could talk calmly for once …

'You and Dad hate me,' Kylie blurted out. There, she had said it. She had finally vocalised the misery and guilt she had held in for so long. Now her parents could say what they really thought, what they all knew to be the truth, that she was self-centred and thoughtless and that if she had tried harder Gwyn would still be alive.

Susan looked at her thunderstruck. 'Is that really what you think?' she asked, her voice almost a whisper.

'Well it's true, isn't it?' replied Kylie, arms clutched tightly around her body, pain spilling from her eyes. 'I'll just leave again. Then you and Dad can get on with your lives.'

'Don't be so utterly ridiculous! Now you are being selfish. Do you really think I want to lose both my girls?' Susan startled them both with her vehemence.

'I knew as soon as I met Michael not to trust him, but I ignored it,' went on Kylie, going over the same old ground. 'I wanted so badly to ski another season and Aspen offered everything we had ever talked about. If I hadn't been so determined to do what I wanted, we'd never have gone to Aspen. I should have gone with my first gut feelings. She was so happy ...'

Susan dropped her cloth into the pail nearby, wiped her hands on her old shirt and drew the shaking girl into her arms. For the first time Kylie made no move to shake her off.

'Going over and over this is doing nothing except making you ill. You're as thin as a rake. Anyway, you are talking absolute rubbish,' said Susan firmly, holding her daughter close. She smiled gently at her, feeling her daughter's pain. 'Darling girl, let it go. Gwyn is gone. We all loved her. Geoff and I know you did everything you could to help her, but ...' She stopped, unable to go on. How could she have been so blind as not to see Kylie would blame all this on herself? 'My darling, darling girl, I love you so much. We both love you so much ...' Her voice cracked.

'You and Gwyn, you were always so close, Mum. I know how much you miss her.' Kylie choked. Tears were streaming down her face. 'She was your best friend. She used to tell me. Oh Mum, I wish I had never persuaded her —'

'It's no good wishing, my love. We have to go

forwards now.' Gently Susan wiped away Kylie's tears with the edge of her shirt. She kissed her hair, breathing in its soft freshness, seeing her two precious girls as children running across the snow at Sunburst.

'There are things I have to tell you, Kylie,' Susan said, fighting back her tears. She explained that because Gwyn was the elder child she had naturally been the one she had talked to. Sometimes she had wondered if she had put too much of a burden on Gwyn, expected her to be more mature than she was. She had also seen signs of irrational behaviour in Gwyn as a child, the temptation to swing off the edge, but she had steadfastly ignored it. It had been easier that way, just as it had been easier to talk to Gwyn because Susan and Kylie were so alike that they clashed. She had always thought that if one of her two children were to go off the rails, it would be Kylie never Gwyn. How horribly wrong she had been.

Susan brushed away her tears. 'I blame myself for what happened, you know,' she confided. 'I knew Gwyn was emotionally fragile when you went off and I should have listened when she said she wanted to come home ... but it's time to move on now, to concentrate on the future, not the past.'

Kylie wriggled her toes further into the sand

now, brushing away the tears that were trickling down her cheeks as she remembered the love in her mother's eyes, the relief that had flooded over her. It had been a turning point for them both, a way back and the start of a new, closer relationship. Since then they talked of many things without blame or condemnation and some of the pain had faded. They had started laughing about little childhood incidents and Kylie was finally able to share some of the very special parts of their trip. Yet for Kylie, the growing closeness was always tinged with the thought that without Gwyn's death it might never have happened.

Staring across at the rapidly sinking sun, Kylie wondered if there would ever come a time when she would feel really happy and energetic again. Venus, star of the evening, blinked at her. Everything was so still and beautiful it was difficult to believe there was a world outside this magical island, and more difficult still to realise Cyclone Isla was headed towards Cairns, predicted to hit the coast at around two tomorrow morning. There was not a breath of wind.

Kylie wandered back along the cooling sand, the chairs and people now obscured in the darkness, hearing only voices murmuring across the stillness. She slipped past the beautiful palm trees that whispered around the tiled pool and hurried over to her father who was removing umbrellas from the tables in front of the almost empty restaurant. Geoff smiled at Kylie and quickly she helped him gather up the remaining umbrellas. Dunk Island was not directly in the cyclone's path, but they were still expecting gale-force winds, king tides and torrential rain. Over the past two days Geoff Harris had taken the precaution of boarding up windows with strips of timber and tying down anything that couldn't be moved to a safe place. The resort staff had already taken away chairs and tables from the open-air restaurant, securing tarpaulins and removing anything that might be ripped away by strong winds. Geoff checked the tables, their steel bases bolted to the concrete. Hopefully they would survive the onslaught.

The cyclone hit at ten past two, the eye of the storm flattening a small town one hundred kilometres north of Cairns. No one on Dunk Island could sleep. Half dozing, Kylie shot up in bed as howling winds and torrential rain battered at her boarded-up window. Teeth chattering, she grabbed a jumper and hurried into her parents' room where they waited and watched together as the storm crashed and banged around them. The sea whipped up into a boiling, frothing fury; huge waves crashed onto the mangrove-lined beach and raced up towards the buildings. Within half an hour the worst was over, and within an hour it was possible to walk outside without being swept away. Kylie and Geoff donned raincoats and hurried out with torches to check the damage. Two of their beautiful palms lay across the pool, tiles smashed. Three tables had been ripped from their steel stands and tossed across the pool deck. The main structure of the hotel, however, was fine, and apart from some roof leakage and several stone statues and pots smashed by falling branches, the resort was pretty much intact. The news from the mainland, on the other hand, was not good. The little country town that had copped the full brunt of the cyclone had thankfully been evacuated beforehand, but homes had been destroyed and people were devastated.

'I wish I could help!' announced Kylie after hearing on the morning news of people isolated by the disaster. Geoff and Susan looked up from their breakfast in surprise. It was the first time since Gwyn's death that they had heard real passion in Kylie's voice.

'Sure, love, we'd all like to,' said Susan, quickly pouring milk over her cereal. There was so much to be cleaned up, and with only a skeleton staff on the resort it would mean double the work for everyone.

'No, Mum, I mean I want to help.'

This time Susan heard the urgency in Kylie's

voice and saw the spark in her eyes, and her heart turned over. 'Why don't you ring up the local Red Cross and see if they need volunteers?' she suggested, hardly daring to breathe. 'Better still, why don't you take the midmorning plane to Cairns and go and see them. I'll come with you if you like.'

Kylie didn't need a second prod. She raced over to the phone, returning bursting with excitement as her mother was heading for the office. 'They need people to help run a soup kitchen and to distribute clothes and blankets and everything. It's okay, Mum, I'll be fine on my own, but thanks anyway.'

Susan wanted to cry. It was as though the cyclone had finally shaken Kylie from the numbness of the last miserable months. Maybe this would get her going forwards in her life again. After all, the girl couldn't hide on Dunk Island forever.

Kylie stood in the middle of an overcrowded school hall in the sticky tropical heat of Mackenvale one hundred kilometres north of Cairns. She was buttering mountains of bread and handing out soup to shocked families with frightened children, to the elderly and frail, and to tired and hungry rescue workers. She listened to heartbreaking stories of houses smashed like matchboxes, crops ruined and livelihoods swept away, and tried to think of something to cheer these people, to give them a sense of hope to start rebuilding their shattered lives. At the end of a long wet day she made one little boy with huge brown eyes laugh. He reminded her of one of the Chernobyl kids and she felt she had been given the greatest gift of her life.

Finding new energy as she helped people, some of whom had lost everything, Kylie's own misery was finally pushed into the background and that old spark rekindled. Everyone who met her was touched by her naïve enthusiasm and openness, and though she didn't realise it herself, her own healing journey had begun in earnest. After several phone calls back and forth to the resort, and assurances that her parents were able to manage without her, she remained on the mainland for several weeks. When she finally returned to Dunk Island she announced that she had joined the Australian Red Cross and had applied for a job as a volunteer working for humanitarian aid abroad.

'I don't know if I'll get anything because I haven't had any actual experience and they mostly need people with special skills, but Rachael, the girl I spoke to, was really nice and said to put my name down on the emergency list anyway and to keep searching the job ads. She got her job because she just kept on at everyone. I thought I might try it too!' Susan and Geoff wanted to cheer.

For the next three months, in amongst her regular commitments on Dunk Island, Kylie kept hounding away, ringing to see if any jobs had come up, trying to hide her disappointment when life seemed to have got stuck.

'What's a logistics assistant?' she asked with a sigh one hot Tuesday morning, having spent the last hour scanning the latest list of jobs.

'Shifting boxes, organising things, getting parts, fixing things, telling people what to do ... Have you checked that the next petrol delivery's confirmed?' asked Geoff.

Kylie's face lit up. 'That's what I've been doing for the last eighteen months, well nearly,' she cried, ignoring her father's question.

'Ye-es ... The petrol, Kylie?'

'Thursday, Dad. Don't stress!' Kylie circled the words *logistics assistant* with her green pen. 'I'm going to apply for that.' Rachael had also explained that the glamour jobs in the glamour places went first, and to get a foot in the door she needed to go for the less-exciting-sounding jobs. There was nothing glamorous in Kylie's eyes about counting and shifting boxes. She kept up her hopes.

Three frustrating months, four interviews, a mountain of forms and heaven only knew how many phone calls later, Kylie was finally notified that she had been accepted to train as a logistics assistant on a team preparing for overseas work, that she was to attend a two-week induction training course in Brisbane starting in six weeks time, and that she should get all her immunisation shots up to date.

Finally the day arrived. Her arm still sore from her cholera injection, malaria tablets packed in with her emergency medical kit, Kylie stood beside her bed, her things neatly laid out in front of her. She checked them off one by one for the fourth time, with her mother helping her. Satisfied she had everything, she squashed her belongings into her haversack. Susan checked Kylie had her passport, proof of all her inoculations and plenty of money, then she hugged her daughter and made her promise to ring regularly.

Downstairs, Geoff pressed a wad of notes into Kylie's hand. 'Just in case. You never know,' he said, slightly sheepishly. His eyes glistened as he drove her to the shelter by the island air strip and hugged her goodbye. 'Just come back safely to us,' he said, his voice husky. Susan was tearing a hibiscus flower into tiny shreds and crying unashamedly. Kylie hugged them both tight.

'I love you so much,' she said, her eyes alight with excitement. Finally she was going to do something to help others. Finally maybe her life would start to mean something again and the guilt that still swamped her would diminish.

She stepped out of the shelter and, with one last hug, stepped onto the small twin-engine plane. From eight thousand feet she watched Dunk Island shrink into the distance, the brilliant azure sea stretching out under her forever, sailing vessels turning into tiny white dots.

The induction training was held in a small brick building in the middle of Brisbane. Staying in the local youth hostel, Kylie rolled up excitedly on the first day and was met by a plump woman in her midforties clutching a wad of papers. The woman peered at her through glasses held by a gold-plated chain around her neck. She checked one of her lists then announced Kylie was part of a training team to be sent to East Timor.

Slightly startled, Kylie tentatively asked when this was happening.

'Oh I can't say, dear. We just get the teams ready and jump when the powers that be call,' she beamed as she ushered Kylie into the hall, already looking around for her next arrival.

Several teams were being trained over the

next two weeks and as Kylie met some of the others and listened as they confidently swapped stories of their experience 'in the field', she suddenly felt hopelessly daunted. Just as she was ready to admit she had made a dreadful mistake and make a run for it, a man in his late thirties, with brown hair and sharp features, strode over and shook hands with the group around her.

'I'm Craig Jarratt. I'm head of logistics and your team leader. You must be my assistant,' he said, his brown eyes smiling at Kylie out of his suntanned face. He had a firm handshake and a kind smile and her heart slowed down a bit.

Craig repeated what the plump lady had said, explaining that while they were one of the teams on standby for East Timor, they were not going anywhere in the immediate future. Teams were continually being trained to be ready for all kinds of emergencies and could be asked to work for a wide assortment of agencies.

Kylie was a bit disappointed to learn that the likelihood of her going overseas was very slim given her lack of experience and that she would probably be given a desk job. Swallowing her disappointment and remembering Rachael's advice about a foot in the door, she quickly discovered there was plenty she would be able to do from the Australian end, helping organise food and supplies and checking that they got to the right place on time.

Wondering just exactly how one got past the chicken-and-the-egg situation and actually gained experience, she worked as hard as she could over the next two weeks. She scribbled notes frantically all day and asked endless questions. She was sickened by some of the stories, but she squared her shoulders and tried to take it all in. At the end of each day she fell into a deep dreamless sleep and was up bright and early ready for more the next day. It really didn't sound that hard, shipping crates onto planes, following up orders, making lists and phone calls, hassling people, keeping track of things; but even if it was, at least she would be involved.

Two days before the induction training was due to end Kylie walked in to find her team huddled together around Craig, a new tension in the air. There had been a major disaster in Papua New Guinea north of the town of Rabaul. Kylie had heard bits of it on the news as she'd raced out of the hostel. It was all over the newspapers. A massive tidal wave measuring over ten metres had flattened whole villages. Those lucky enough to escape with their lives had been left with nothing. Reports were coming in of hundreds believed dead, and the death toll was expected to rise as people scrabbled to rescue loved ones trapped in the nearby mangrove swamps and under debris.

'A team is needed straightaway,' Craig explained urgently. 'One of the advance aid parties in Port Moresby has already been flown up to assess the damage, but as our team is well prepared, we have been assigned the task of setting up the aid. We'll be flying out tomorrow night. It's a three-month posting with the agency AustWorld.

'These tidal waves do colossal damage. Conditions could be anything when we get there. Anyone feels they aren't ready, now's the time to say so.' His eyes scanned the group. 'Kylie, I need your skills — d'you feel up to it?'

Kylie nodded, her hands starting to sweat, excitement leaping into her throat. Rachael at the Red Cross office had been right. Things did happen if you kept ploughing on.

Late the following evening the team, consisting of two doctors, two nurses, an engineer, a water and sanitation expert, and Craig and Kylie, piled into the back of an RAAF Hercules, crammed between boxes and sacks of food, medical supplies and water-purifying equipment. Her ears singing with all the things she would have to do, Kylie hugged herself as the huge transport plane roared off into the sky.

Chapter Thirteen

Too wound up even to doze, Kylie glanced around the plane cabin listening to the roar of the engines. Restlessly she shifted in her seat. They had been in the air for two and a half hours. Their ETA in Port Moresby was two am. She tried to imagine what it would be like walking into an area devastated by a tidal wave. She had seen a few blurred pictures in their briefing in Brisbane, showing people struggling to free their dead amidst the debris of flattened houses, and the media had reported casualties in the thousands. The whole aid assignment seemed to Kylie an overwhelming undertaking.

Craig came over and squeezed down beside her. 'Everything okay?'

Kylie nodded, grateful for his company. Despite her outward bravado, she felt under-confident, as though she had conned her way onto the team.

Craig started chatting about the latest reports of the situation on the ground, making no attempt to conceal his own nervousness and excitement. A wiry man, he was like a coiled spring, his eyes darting from one place to another around the cabin, his hands moving constantly as he reiterated the confidence he felt in his team. His energy had a surprisingly positive effect on Kylie, giving her a place to project her own energy, and he dissipated some of her nervousness by emphasising her role within the team. He reassured her that the others would support her and told her never to be afraid to ask if at any time she needed help. Craig was tough. Kylie had learned that pretty quickly. He was also a strong leader who was not always popular, but what she saw as they sat chatting quietly was a sincere person committed to helping others and someone who made her feel safe. By the time they landed in Port Moresby, she was starting to feel more confident.

The stopover at Port Moresby was just under four hours. During that time the team met two Papua New Guinea officials who were to accompany them to the disaster area and help with orientation, then had a short briefing to reassess the logistics of the whole exercise in light of new local information. They checked the aid workers expected to arrive in the next two weeks and voiced the need for local interpreters, given the hundreds of different dialects spoken, and Craig once again emphasised the importance of getting the local people involved in rebuilding their lives.

'Our job is to start the process with the locals, not to walk in there, interfere and then move on after a few weeks. They know a darned sight more about this country and how it works than we do. Remember that,' he said as the meeting broke up.

Back in the air, Kylie dozed off for a while, waking as they climbed over the impressive New Guinea highlands to see the dawn paint the clouds that dotted the tops of the mountains. Her eyes were glued to the tiny window as they began their descent over the lush green jungle to the small airfield. Her stomach started to flutter nervously as they touched down, the wheels scraping on the cracked bitumen in the early morning gloom. She could see some of the havoc wreaked not only by the tsunami but by the hundred and fifty knot winds that had hit the area the day before the disaster. Her stomach turned over. This was it. This was no summer camp. She was about to walk into something she had only skimmed through in charity brochures and caught glimpses of on TV.

Her eyes widened as she saw trees lying on their sides, vegetation tossed in ugly tangles along the edge of the air-strip, obviously hurriedly cleared to allow their plane to land. Part of the roof had been ripped off one of the two small buildings that made up the air-strip administration block. Kylie took a sharp breath, bracing herself for what was to come. Gwyn's face, peaceful in death, flitted before her, then came the desolation in her mother's face, and the numbing sense of inadequacy she couldn't shake off. If this aid work did nothing else it would force her to focus on other harsh realities of life. Hopefully she could contribute to making one person's life better.

The sticky tropical heat hit her like a wall as she stepped off the plane with the others, her haversack slung on her back. The sweet scent of hibiscus greeted her, reminding her of Dunk Island, the memory quickly spoilt by the sickly stench of overripe fruit, rotting vegetation and open drains that assailed her as she crossed from the plane to the administration block. The air-strip was about eight kilometres inland from the devastated area and a couple of hundred feet higher, but the high winds and torrential rain had still taken their toll. Now Kylie could see palm trees bent over at odd angles, dirt roads drowning in huge puddles. To one side of the airstrip stood a dilapidated hangar, miraculously still intact.

A small band of locals who looked after the air-strip dressed in long shorts and brightly coloured floral shirts strangely out of context with the mood of the place emerged from the building and were introduced. Stepping inside did nothing to relieve the sticky heat. Fans hung silent from the ceilings, the place dark and gloomy, power and water cut off. After more briefings, the team stepped back outside and Craig, who had remained calm throughout all the discussions, exploded in frustration. Having expected to use the building for their command base, he swore roundly at the local PNG aid team who had informed him they would be using the building as their command post and had made it clear that there was not enough room in it for any foreign aid workers.

'Just what we need, bloody-minded locals and nowhere to set up camp! Jesus!' Quickly he pulled himself together. At least the roads to the coast were passable, if boggy, and most of the vehicles had escaped the storm, so they would be able to move food and medical supplies without any major delays.

Grim and sodden with perspiration he scanned the airfield, and spied the hangar Kylie had noticed earlier and which had been allocated for supplies. 'We'll have to use it for our headquarters as well. Let's hope there's room for both us and the supplies. I don't know about you, but I don't fancy sleeping under the stars and being woken by a tropical rainstorm.' He grinned at his team in an effort to make up for his earlier outburst. He was well aware he had a short fuse.

'Well, let's go and check out this hangar,' he said, striding towards an open baggage cart in the hope that it would start. To his amazement it did. Five minutes later they were across the airfield and pulling open the heavy doors.

Kylie reeled back as the stench hit her. Rotting fruit in crumbling cardboard boxes lay strewn across the hangar alongside unidentifiable decaying carcasses. The remaining space was taken up by old broken equipment, barbed wire, bent steel poles and a rusty truck with no wheels. Rubbish lay everywhere. The only bonus was that it was relatively cool inside.

Craig swore again. Scowling, he lifted his cap and wiped the sweat from his forehead. It'd take a good half-day to clear this lot out, the pace slowed by the risk of the deadly snakes and spiders lurking in all the muck and the lack of water to wash out the filth.

Pressing her shirt across her face, Kylie stepped gingerly inside. 'At least everything's pretty dry,' she said, wrinkling her nose. Her cheery voice snapped Craig out of his inertia. Quickly detailing Bill the engineer and Frank the sanitation expert to restore power and water, or at least to get their generator working, he turned back to find Kylie had already organised the two nurses, Beth and Miriam, protective gloves donned, into a process line, shifting the boxes of rotting food and heaving them outside. Next, Chung Li, one of the team doctors, drove up in a ute which he had enterprisingly hijacked. Cheering, everyone started hurling the boxes on the back.

'Watch out for the local wildlife,' Craig called out, impressed at Kylie's show of initiative and secretly relieved. He had gone with gut feeling in including her on the team, but she had been a risk. What he saw here was confirmation that he had made the right choice. Grabbing a stinking box, he started to help.

It was filthy, gruelling work and Kylie was soaked with sweat within the first five minutes, but finally the hangar was cleared and they were able to start loading supplies inside. Bill had managed to set up their generator and they now had power in short bursts. Tomorrow Bill would help the guys at the administration block fix their ancient power plant and hopefully reinstall running water.

Exhausted but exhilarated, after checking and marking off the final box as the light faded, Kylie helped set up a sleeping area with Miriam and Mike, the other doctor, while Beth rustled up some sandwiches. Sinking onto a bench, realising she was starving as well as aching all over, Kylie sank her teeth grateful into the slightly soggy bread. Washing their frugal meal down with sweet cups of tea made from their precious supply of drinking water, they looked around at their handiwork, congratulating each other and cracking a few jokes, then set about the serious task of mapping out the next few days. Two planeloads of supplies were expected to arrive tomorrow. Kylie, with the help of one of the local men, would organise their off-loading, storage and ultimate delivery to the different regions while the rest of the team, with the exception of Bill, would drive to the stricken area to check it out and decide the best way to proceed.

Lying on her camp bed on top of her sleeping bag, hot and aching, mosquito net over her, Kylie was overwhelmed by a the sense of unreality. Only yesterday morning she had been standing in Brisbane. Now she was in charge of setting up the unloading and delivery of huge numbers of supplies, organising trucks and drivers into places she had no idea how to get to, and keeping track of it all in a strange country where she didn't speak a word of the language. It had all the hallmarks of a tropical movie adventure, except that just over eight kilometres away hundreds of people had lost their homes and many their lives. She rolled over, her eyes refusing to stay open and was asleep in seconds.

Shaken awake by Beth just before dawn, Kylie rubbed her eyes and stretched, taking a few seconds to realise where she was. It was real. She was an emergency aid worker in Papua New Guinea. Hurriedly she got dressed, longing for a shower.

The first thing Craig did was assign her two local guards. 'I need to know you are safe; besides, a lot of pilfering and looting can go on in situations like this. These guys'll handle that. They'll help you with the drivers too. They know everyone around here.'

Kylie gave Craig a quick nod, which she hoped looked confident. As Craig walked off she smiled cautiously up at her bodyguards. Unlike the Papua New Guineans she had come across so far, these two towered alarmingly above her. Chocolate brown with dark curly hair, their handguns bulging from bulky holsters slung around thick waists, she decided not to get into an argument with either. Then she noticed their eyes, glazed over with shock. She held out her hand and shook each of theirs in turn, her hand lost in theirs.

For the first two days the two huge men followed her around silently, doing everything she asked. First she set up rosters for the local truck drivers and organised the locations they would deliver supplies to. Gradually Kylie got to know each driver by name and heard their heartbreaking stories. One had lost almost his entire family, others were still looking, others again were simply struggling to come to terms with the whole shocking disaster. The drivers wore the same dazed look as the guards.

By the fourth day the atmosphere had started to change. Kylie's bodyguards were more in command, although she saw their softness when they broke into a smile at her pidgin English. Their growing confidence made Kylie feel safe to leave the hangar for longer periods while she sorted out spare parts for trucks and ventured over to the admin building to liaise with the airport staff. There a man in his early fifties, by the name of Mumaki, was particularly helpful. In charge of ground procedures, he had been one of the luckier ones, his family having escaped the worst of the disaster by having been visiting his sister in a village up in the hills. While their house and most of their possessions were gone, his spirit was intact. To Kylie's intense relief he offered to take over the responsibility of loading the supplies into the hangar and enlisting other locals to work under him, leaving her more time to check the supplies and fix up the trucks. Checking with Craig that this was in order, she happily agreed.

By the second week Kylie had organised everyone into a routine. Trucks arrived in the late afternoon, drivers stopped for a meal, slept and the following day loaded up and were gone at first light. Aid workers flooded in from Japan, Australia, America and New Zealand, and Kylie quickly dispersed them to their allocated villages up and down the coast. At the same time Craig moved the base camp from the hangar to the relocated village.

The air drops had slowed, with planes now scheduled to arrive only once or sometimes twice a week. Impressed by the job Kylie had done in getting the locals to take charge of the shipments, and desperate for every ounce of human labour, Craig announced he was moving her to the village as well. From there she would make her runs back along the eight-kilometre dirt track to the air-strip each afternoon, remaining for a few hours to oversee the loading of the supply trucks and sort out any pressing problems and paperwork. She would sleep over when there was an air drop, otherwise return to help in the village.

Happy to be once more in the centre of the team's action, and with the last truck gone by early morning, Kylie left the air-strip just after ten, her spirits buoyed. She drove the jeep she had recently 'acquired' down the bumpy dirt track and stopped, amazed, when she reached the place where the village had stood, the sweat trickling down between her breasts and under her arms. She might have been in a tropical island resort. The tidal wave had simply wiped out the whole area. Where there had been a village was now an inlet. Brilliant white sands stretched along the coast; the sun danced on the azure sea turned indigo in the deeper parts; the sea frothed up at the shore where once small wooden houses had stood, women cooked and children played. Behind her, bizarrely, two small fishing boats sat between huge coconut palms metres from the water's edge. Rotting stinking seaweed tossed up from the ocean's depths littered the foreshore, dispelling the tropical paradise illusion. Climbing back into her jeep, Kylie drove on to the relocated village.

The stench of dead bodies and decaying animal carcasses hung heavily in the tropical heat. Kylie gagged. Flies buzzed in her face as she looked for the command base. All around her there was activity as people worked on rebuilding the village. Blue tarpaulins flapped against roughly cut poles, providing makeshift shelters to house the survivors. Villagers and aid workers worked side by side cutting trees from a nearby forest and dragging them back to the village, or covering roofs with big pandanus leaves. Stripped to the waist, sweat glistening from their bodies, some of them sunburned, they worked in the stifling heat and stench.

This was far worse than the hangar. Kylie walked towards the field clinic, a tent outside of which a long line of people stood or sat patiently waiting for their turn. Some sat staring, unseeing; others cradled their injured relatives. A gaunt-eyed mother clutched a baby that could not have been more than a few days old. A short way off an old man sat chewing betel nut and spitting the blood-red juice onto the ground. Women wept quietly. The lack of noise sent a shiver down Kylie's spine.

She jumped as she heard her name then caught sight of Craig and a man she guessed to be the village chief. Gratefully she hurried over to where they sat in the shade of two huge trees.

'No dramas finding your way here?' asked Craig briskly, introducing her to his companion. After he had finished his discussion, which to Kylie seemed interminable as they seemingly went round and round in circles, Craig stood up, bowed as the headman left, then turned to Kylie. 'I need you to help locate the families of the wounded and dead,' he said briskly. 'Most of the dead have been buried, but we're still pulling bodies from the swamps. I need you to find out their names, which family they belong to, crosscheck against those still missing, and make sure all the buried have been accounted for.' He wiped his arm wearily across his sweating brow. It was a miserable business.

Kylie gulped and nodded, feeling suddenly terribly inadequate.

'Come and meet Ruhana, Mumaki's wife, she's in charge of the District Council of Women and knows everyone from this village and many from neighbouring ones. She'll give you a hand.' Craig set off towards the field clinic, Kylie hurrying beside him.

Ruhana was an attractive woman in her late forties with a big head of tight black curls and smile lines around her mouth and eyes. She was consoling a weeping woman who was clutching a young baby, two other frightened children clinging to their mother's skirts.

'She lost her husband, son and parents,' Ruhana explained after they had been introduced.

Kylie shook her head, blinking away tears. She

liked the older woman immediately. Buxom and motherly in her bright floral dress, somehow Ruhana brought compassion and efficiency together in an easy combination. The two sat down and started drawing up a list.

Later they walked to the newly dug graves. A man was leaning on his shovel, weeping; others stood around, staring vacantly.

'We'll get the names down and the graves marked. I remember most of them,' said Ruhana quietly. Kylie nodded, holding tight to her emotions.

After they had marked as many graves as they could, the two women moved about the village, listing their dead and missing, Kylie taking notes, the elder woman comforting where she could. There were still some hopeful that their loved ones would be found. They stopped to talk to a father whose young son who had had his leg amputated. Kylie's efforts to communicate in a mixture of bad pidgeon English and wild gesticulations quickly had the boy grinning up at his dad. The sight almost broke Kylie's heart.

The next day was no easier as Kylie continued to document the villagers. Ruhana was busy visiting some of the sick in the clinic, so Kylie struggled on her own, trying to get some sense from people who still searched, dazed and shocked, for their loved ones. She stopped groups who were sifting through the rubble of what had once been their homes, asking about their dead and missing. Struggling to understand their few words of pidgeon English, wishing she cold do more to comfort them in their misery. She had never experienced such numbing grief. Late in the afternoon, seeing two men trying to recover a dead pig caught high in a tree, she started laughing slightly hysterically, quickly controlling herself as she saw Craig come striding towards her. Nothing could have prepared her for what she was witnessing, nothing, and it showed on her face.

'How are you doing?' Craig asked, studying Kylie closely.

'Okay,' she replied quickly.

'If you feel you can't cope ...'

Kylie reached back and tightened the band around her flaming hair. This was it. He was going to send her back to the hangar to count boxes, or, worse still, have her shipped out. 'I'm okay really. I'm just a bit tired. I guess everyone is. Sorry if I don't always handle everything ...' She looked away, waiting for the inevitable.

'You're doing fine,' said Craig after a moment, giving her shoulder a friendly pat. He'd given her one of the grimmest tasks, he knew that, but it had to be done and he needed her help. 'How about we go and hassle for some tucker? I don't know about you, but I'm starving — and thirsty.'

Kylie blinked back tears, relief flooding through her as she followed him to the shade of the two big palm trees and the field kitchen.

Beth joined them, tired lines in her hot face. 'I'd kill for a cuppa,' she smiled wearily.

Balancing her meal on her knee, Kylie started chatting about some of the families she had met, what she had learned about the village. She talked rapidly, ignoring the misery stirring deep inside her. Beth brightened at her enthusiasm, sharing a couple of more light-hearted moments. It had been a grim day for her too. She'd had to help Chung amputate a young girl's arm. Patients had died; several were struggling with bad bouts of malaria. They were running out of essential medical supplies. Still, it was Kylie's first experience in the field and she didn't need anyone to add to her troubles. She looked a bit white about the gills. It wasn't easy. It never really got easy, but you did toughen up a bit.

Craig watched Kylie as she talked, seeing her beauty shine through her tired face, sensing her strength and her commitment. She was a hard worker; he'd seen that from day one. She was courageous too, and very attractive, he noted with a private smile.

The next day Kylie gratefully escaped back to

the hangar to await a planeload of supplies. She greeted her truck drivers cheerfully, sorted out the new delivery, finished her paperwork, then sat staring at the sun as it slowly slid behind the mountains, the sunset's beauty in stark contrast to the pain and suffering of the past few weeks. Suddenly tears started pouring down her face. She wiped them away but they wouldn't stop. She bent her head and covered her face with her hands, her shoulders shaking, as great sobs overtook her. Even when she felt a hand on her shoulder and a comforting murmur in her ear, she couldn't stop. Finally she looked up with a shudder. It was Mumaki. He smiled down gently at her and somehow she drew strength from his unspoken understanding. This was his country, the dead his people, yet he could still show compassion to her, an outsider — his courage was an inspiration.

The next day Kylie was back in the village trying to account for those still missing. She couldn't imagine ever getting used to the pain and misery on the faces of those left behind. A young woman close to collapse sat clutching her dead child, on the spot that had been her home, refusing to let the baby go. None of her family had been able to help her. She had refused to eat or drink for four days. Kylie was at a loss to know what to do. Then a deep voice behind her introduced himself as the local Catholic priest. He was a large man with a dark beard and eyes filled with compassion. He blessed the child and spoke gently to the mother, who finally allowed her baby to be taken from her and laid to rest. The father wept openly as they filled the tiny grave. Kylie watched dry-eyed.

Silently Ruhana came up and slipped her arm around Kylie. 'We must get the school built quickly, Kylie. The women need to think about a future for their children.' She spoke softly, but there was an urgency in her voice. Kylie turned and nodded. She needed that future too.

Later that afternoon, as she walked towards the edge of the mangrove swamps, helping to search for more injured or dead, Kylie stretched and mopped her brow, thinking about Ruhana's words. Getting the school back up and running was a project she could look forward to. The heat was oppressive, the humidity unbearable. She pulled her thin shirt from her wet skin, then stopped, straining her ears, wondering if she had imagined the faint cry. No! There it was again. Clambering over the twisting mangrove roots, she ventured a short way up one of the paths. Then she saw the owner of the sound. It was a young girl, her face covered with dried blood, hobbling painfully towards her, one foot dragging. She couldn't have been more than twelve. With a gasp Kylie raced towards her and slipped her arm around her shoulders. The girl was on the point of collapse, and as light as a feather. Supporting her, Kylie helped her slowly and painfully back down the path. Before they reached the main clearing another cry rang out, fearsome in its suffering, and an old woman ran to the young girl and threw her arms around her, tears pouring down her wrinkled face. Shouting and waving, the woman summoned an old man who came running towards them, tears streaming down his cheeks. Kylie couldn't stop her own tears at the joy she saw in these two people's faces as they hugged the girl. They had found their granddaughter, the only other survivor in their family. Helping them to the field hospital, Kylie handed the girl into Miriam's care, then went back to work, brushing away unashamed tears. Out of devastation had come a tiny spark of hope.

Chapter Fourteen

Kylie ticked off the list of drivers who had arrived back at the airfield and were scheduled to load up and leave the following day. A mixture of locals and foreign aid workers, there were five trucks going north and two going south. She smiled weakly as she put a tick beside the name Fred. A Danish aid worker with an unpronounceable surname and a great sense of humour, Fred constantly cracked unsuitable jokes at inappropriate times. She could have done with one of his bad jokes right now.

It had been another harrowing day. It had begun with the transportation of a very sick patient to the air-strip to be flown out to the nearest hospital. Neither Beth nor Miriam could be spared, so Kylie had had to cope on her own. It wasn't the first time she had driven emergency cases to the air-strip, but she hated it. Although she had been briefed on what to do should the patient suddenly deteriorate, the responsibility brought back the horror of Gwyn's death and her own helplessness in the face of her sister's collapse. Insisting one of the locals drive, Kylie had sat with the young patient, checking her every few minutes. To add further stress, it had poured with rain for the previous two days, hampering everyone's work and making the roads more dangerous. At one point the truck's nearside wheels had bounced clean in the air and she had thought they were about to roll. The poor woman had moaned in agony.

Kylie had heaved a sigh of relief when her patient was safely transferred into the hands of the paramedics. Then she had been told that half the supplies that were meant to have arrived on the plane had somehow got dropped off at an earlier stop. To top it all off, she had just learned that three of her drivers were late in, which always made her nervous. She was rechecking her list when a man's voice said, 'Excuse me, could you tell me who's in charge?'

Glancing up, she took in a man in his late twenties, a three-day stubble on his chin, dark rings under his amazingly blue eyes. Her mind only half on his question, she directed him to Mumaki who was working at the far end of the hangar. Craig had mentioned some more aid workers were expected to arrive in the next few days. She sucked her pen for a moment, watching as the young man strode off. He was good-looking in a sharp sort of way. She wasn't sure about the hair, curling dark tendrils stroking the back of his neck, and she preferred her men clean-shaven. He was too thin, his cheekbones jutting out in his darkly tanned face. She wouldn't forget those eyes, though. How could you? They reminded her of a midsummer sky. She froze suddenly and her heart turned over. Danno O'Keefe! It couldn't have been! At the same instant the young man turned and ran back to her.

'Kylie Harris! It is, isn't it? I didn't recognise you! What the heck are you doing out here?'

Kylie's heart started pounding crazily against her ribs. 'Danno! I might ask you the same question,' she shot back, suddenly aware of what a mess she must look, her dirty hair pulled off her face in a tatty scrunchy, her clothes sweat-soaked and streaked with mud. She laughed to hide her embarrassment.

'They transferred me over here halfway through my latest contract. Said they were desperate for engineers. It's fine by me. I don't care where I go. What about you? I didn't know you were doing aid work.'

'It's my first assignment,' Kylie admitted with a grin, realising he looked just as much of a mess as her, if not worse. 'It's great to see you. It's been a bugger of a day, 'scuse the French.' She started rattling on about truck drivers and supplies and the trip up from the village, then she suddenly stopped, embarrassed.

'You haven't changed one bit!' laughed Danno, running one hand through his hair. 'I never could keep up with the speed of your mind, or your skiing. How is your skiing by the way, and how's everyone back home? How's your mum and dad and Gwyn?'

Kylie's face went blank. 'Gwyn died,' she said baldly. She didn't want to talk about it or even think about it.

Danno looked shocked. 'I'm so sorry, I had no idea —'

'Where are they sending you?' she interrupted before he could ask any questions.

'Further north, unless they change their minds,' smiled Danno, sensing her discomfort. He explained that he was being sent to one of the larger villages about thirty kilometres north. 'Could end up doing anything from fixing up homemade hydro-electric schemes to digging wells and hammering nails into walls. You name it, I get to do it. They told me I'd be able to catch a lift with one of the truckies going that way.'

'You'd better come and meet Mumaki. He looks after the supplies. He's a really nice guy.'

Kylie walked quickly towards the hangar, glad he hadn't asked any more questions about Gwyn.

She glanced at her list. 'Tumi's doing the northern run. You could go with him,' she suggested. 'He's one of my favourites. Always smiling. Don't know how he does it. Lost half his family in the disaster. Knows every bump and curve in the road — if you can call it a road.' She laughed, partly to hide the distress she always felt when she saw Tumi, partly because being near Danno was making her jittery.

She left Danno with Mumaki and went back to her work, but even as she tracked down the missing drivers her mind kept wandering. She kept thinking of Danno and the amazing coincidence of him showing up here of all places. She had thought that if they ever ran into each other again she would feel something far more disturbing, tumultuous even, but it hadn't been like that at all. After the initial shock it had been more as though she was engulfed in a warm safety, that with him around nothing bad could happen. That, of course, was completely absurd, she told herself firmly as she checked the next day's schedule. She and Danno hadn't seen each other for years. She was completely over her teenage crush, and he had given her no reason to think he felt anything other than casual friendship towards her. Still, it was nice to see him again.

'How long have you been doing aid work?' she asked him later as they tucked into the big stew she had helped prepare for the truckies and workers.

'Must be nearly five years now. I've been all over the world. Seen some amazing stuff,' replied Danno between mouthfuls. He told her that his father hadn't been too excited at Danno's decision to become an aid worker. He had always hoped Danno would join him running the lodges. And it had always been Danno's intention to do so. He loved Lyrebird Falls and helping run the family properties, and even branching out on his own had appealed greatly. But as he explained when he finally got his father to listen, it had always been his plan to see more of the world first after he had finished his engineering degree. Aid work seemed like an exciting challenge. Grudgingly his father had accepted his point and in his own way was proud of his boy's contribution. Only now Danno was finding he was hooked on his work and thoughts of returning to Australia and Lyrebird Falls were far less enticing.

'What about yourself? Last time I saw you you were still at school.' Kylie winced at this comment then starting talking. Neither of them mentioned Gwyn again. Kylie watched Danno as they chatted. He had changed. There was a maturity about him, a hardness, no, a distance, as though his experiences over the last five years had forced him to create a protective wall around himself. Yet in his clear blue eyes she could still see the Danno she had adored as a teenager.

Danno stretched and pushed his plate away, then he ran his fingers through his hair, pushing the long locks back off his forehead. 'You're no good at cutting hair, are you?' he asked with a rueful grin. 'It's been driving me nuts, but it was either live with this or have some army sergeant shave it all off. I've had a couple of goes at it myself, but my pocket knife's pretty blunt. Beard's got to go too,' he added, rubbing his hand across his chin.

'I'm not shaving you but I could give your hair a go if you're willing to risk it,' Kylie offered, relieved that her heart had stopped giving those ridiculous lurches every time he looked in her direction.

Later that evening, as she hacked off Danno's curling locks in the fading light, she listened to his tales of running the gauntlet in war-torn countries, helping clean up after disasters like this one and setting up community projects. Kylie snipped off a last stray end then stood back to admire her handiwork. Even she had to admit she'd done a reasonable job. Then she fished in a bag and held up her tiny compact mirror to show him the results.

'Not bad,' Danno said with a lopsided grin, smoothing his short hair back at the sides. 'Not bad at all for a knife and fork.'

Kylie gave him a playful shove. 'Ungrateful monster! It's brilliant!' She put down the scissors and picked up a lock of Danno's hair, curling it around her fingers. 'I'll keep this to remind me of a very special night in a very strange world.'

That night, for the first time since arriving in PNG, Kylie slept dreamlessly, awaking the next morning remarkably refreshed. Two days later Danno headed up north with the supply convoy and Kylie couldn't deny her sudden sense of loss.

As Kylie continued her daily routine, she kept finding herself thinking about Danno, wondering where he was and what he was doing, if he ever thought of her. The outlying aid stations regularly put in requests for food and medical supplies, and she felt a rush of pleasure when one day a note from Danno arrived asking for extra supplies. After she returned his request with a note in a box marked for his attention, he started writing directly to her, giving little bits of information about what they had been up to. It became a little secret game between them, which took the edge off some of the raw reality of their job, and she waited eagerly for each note.

One day Danno drove the area supply truck up to the hangar, explaining to a surprised Kylie that he'd offered to take over from the regular driver who was sick. Delighted, Kylie hugged him then demanded to know in detail everything he had been doing. Suddenly embarrassed at being too forward, giving him no chance to reply, she started telling him how she and Ruhana had held their first class in the new school, admittedly with only half a roof. No one had cared. The building had been crammed to overflowing and it had been a joyous occasion in amongst so much sorrow and destruction. The women's and children's voices had floated across the camp as they sang their thanks to God.

'It was incredibly moving. So many of them have lost everything,' Kylie said, handing Danno a mug of tea.

'You really are making things happen here, aren't you?' he said softly, genuine admiration in his eyes. Kylie blushed and smiled at him.

After that Kylie stopped pretending and admitted to herself she was falling in love with Danno, not just a teenage crush but genuine, deep love. Every time a truck arrived from the north Kylie hoped Danno might have swapped again with the rostered driver, and when he hadn't she swallowed her disappointment and made up a special box for him, checking he had all the extra supplies he had requested and slipping in a few more. She bribed Beth to give her extra bandages and personal mosquito repellent, incurring a scowl from Miriam, and added her own ration of chocolate she had saved for him. While she was under no illusion that he felt anything more than friendship for her, doing these little things made her feel good.

Craig mopped his brow as he walked across to the field kitchen one evening. Stuffing his handkerchief back in his pocket, he gave a satisfied sigh. Finally the place was starting to look like a village again. Houses were shooting up, their thatched roofs giving a neatness to the place; the school Kylie had been into his ear about almost every day for weeks now had a complete roof and classes were being held regularly. There was now reasonable sanitation and the well was almost complete.

Craig could see Kylie chatting animatedly with Chung and Bill. She was good for the team. He forced himself to slow down, realising he was far too eager to join her. He had only once got personally involved with a fellow aid worker. He had wanted to marry the girl and had thought she felt the same about him, but when the contract had ended she had abruptly ended their relationship. He had been hurt far more than he liked to admit; he also knew he had transgressed the unspoken rule that you kept your private life out of aid work. After that he had not made the same mistake again. But his feelings for Kylie had crept up on him as he'd watched her confidence grow. He loved her freshness and energy and the effect it had on everyone, particularly himself; and on her down days, when she soberly soldiered on, he had to stop himself taking her in his arms and kissing her hurt away. He felt himself go hard just thinking of running his hands through her flaming red hair. Even hot and grubby as she was, she was hellishly attractive.

'Well, how have you put the world to rights this time?' he joked with her as he helped himself to a warm Coke.

Kylie blushed and then explained her plans for getting a school bus up and running. 'Ruhana and I have got it all worked out,' she announced.

'I'll bet you have,' grinned Craig.

'No, seriously! Ruhana was saying the women from the other villages —'

'I couldn't be more serious,' replied Craig, his grin widening.

'Well don't keep interrupting then!' Kylie shot back cheekily.

Craig downed his Coke, wishing, as she spoke excitedly of her plans, that he could whisk her away somewhere private. Maybe there was hope for the two of them. Stranger things had happened.

Two days later a truck came hurtling into the village as Kylie was walking across to the administration tent. Startled, she stepped back out of the road, then blanched as Danno staggered out of the passenger seat clutching his arm, which was wrapped in a grubby blood-soaked bandage.

'What happened?' she demanded, hurrying him over to the clinic.

'A pig gored me when I was trying to help the villagers catch it.' He pressed his fingers tighter around the bandage and winced. He had lost quite a bit of blood and was feeling decidedly woozy.

'It'll hurt for a few days and you're going to have to watch what you do with your arm for a while, but it's only a flesh wound,' said Beth briskly after she had examined the wound, cleaned it up and rebandaged it. He let out a yell as she quickly pulled down his shorts and plunged a hypodermic needle into the top of his right buttock. 'There you go, that's your tetanus shot.' She gave him a quick pat.

'Sadist! You enjoyed that.' Danno pulled up his shorts, sitting up too quickly, and nearly fell sideways.

'Ooh-ooh, a bit too clever, are we? You need to rest for a day or two. Get that wound cleaned every day and come back and see us in a week. Kylie'll give you what you need.' She looked across at Kylie who had been hovering, white-faced, close by. 'Men are such babies with needles. He'll be fine in no time. Go minister to him.' She winked at her. She had noticed Kylie's radiance and added energy and how it had coincided with Danno's arrival.

Cheeks flaming, mouthing for Beth to keep quiet, Kylie helped Danno off the bed. For the next few days she happily fussed over him. She took charge of changing his dressing, rinsed out his sweat-sodden shirt to make him more comfortable and made sure he was drinking enough in the stifling heat. When it was time for him to return up north, she slipped him an apple she had saved from dinner and gave him a long lecture on keeping his wound clean and not chasing pigs.

Danno grinned at her. 'Thank you, Mother Hen. I promise to do as you say.' But his eyes held no mockery. He leaned over and gave her a quick peck on the cheek.

Caught off guard Kylie was left standing speechless as the truck drove off. She waved as he vanished, choking back the sudden loneliness, her other hand to her burning cheek where his lips had touched her.

'How do you know him?' Beth asked Kylie when they both had a quiet moment.

Kylie told her. 'He doesn't know how I feel. He never has. I'm the little sister.' She gave a sigh. 'Still, you can love from afar, can't you?' She grinned, picking up a bandage from the muddle in the box in front of her and starting to roll it up.

She was glad when, back at the hangar two weeks later, a message from Danno arrived along with a small package hastily wrapped in brown paper. Curious, she unwrapped it and gave a little gasp. It was a tiny carved pig. She turned it over in the palm of her hand, feeling its smoothness, and then sniffed the musty perfume of the wood. Every detail of the pig's face was reproduced with delicacy and precision. Kylie opened the letter, her eyes drinking in Danno's scrawly handwriting as he wrote about how he was now hammering in nails again, his arm almost as good as new — but not chasing pigs, only carving them. He had been carving toys for some for the local kids, which made for great relaxation in the sticky heat of the evenings, and he loved to see the delight in their faces when he gave them the toys. In a postscript he wrote that he had added his name to the regular roster to drive the truck and that he'd see her soon at the air-strip and she should save him a warm Coke.

Kylie carefully folded the note and slipped it with her little pig into her pocket. She had no idea Danno could carve, let alone so exquisitely. She smiled at the image of him sitting scraping away on an old scrap of wood, surrounded by a bunch of eager big-eyed kids. He was full of surprises. It was one more thing about him to love. She gave a happy sigh, wishing she could believe Danno had joined the roster be nearer her. Whatever his motives, if he was now one of the regular drivers, it meant she'd see him every second week. She ran her finger down her roster, list and walked over to greet a driver who had just arrived. 'Where's Fred?' she asked as the local who usually drove in convoy with Fred stepped out of the vehicle. The Dane's run took in several villages to the south, and many of the roads were pretty treacherous, but this was the first time he hadn't shown up.

The driver shrugged, scratching his curly black hair. 'Him no drive wid me dis time.'

A frown wrinkled Kylie's smooth brow. To

add to her worries, phone communications still hadn't been re-established in that area and Fred had been having trouble with his radio.

When Fred had still not shown up on day three, Kylie started to get really anxious. Craig agreed they should send a scout on a motorbike to find out what had happened. The scout came back looking very sombre, reporting that the Dane's truck had run off the side of the road and toppled into a river taking a chunk of road with it. Fred had been taken back to one of the villages with a broken leg, two broken ribs and a dislocated shoulder. Luckily there was a clinic in the village run by a French nurse who had lived in Papua New Guinea for fifteen years. She and the villagers were doing all they could to keep him comfortable until they could get him more adequate medical attention. What supplies hadn't been ruined had floated off downstream.

Kylie's initial panic at learning of Fred's injuries subsided when she heard about the nurse, but there was still cause for concern. They had to get Fred out as quickly as possible, but all the trucks were away on delivery with no one expected to return until the next planeload of supplies in six days time. She swore roundly then stabbed at her list — yes there was. Danno! He was due in late tonight, having been held up by faulty electrics in his truck. She rang Craig and suggested she and Danno leave first thing in the morning and bring Fred back to the clinic. With the clinic staff still overworked, and knowing Kylie's level-headed approach, Craig agreed this was the only alternative. Danno was a very experienced aid worker with first-aid skills, so between the two of them they should manage. He tried to hide the hesitation in his voice as he wished Kylie luck.

Chapter Fifteen

At dawn, with a mixture of trepidation at the task in front of her and excitement at being with Danno, Kylie checked the stores in the truck one final time and climbed into the passenger seat. Her whole body ached — she had spent most of the previous evening with Danno loading boxes onto the truck and tying them down, having decided to take more supplies to replace some of those lost. However, they had limited the amount they carried as they were anxious not to make the truck too heavy, both knowing all too well the road conditions they could expect. Danno hopped up into the driver's seat, grinned at Kylie and turned the key in the ignition. The engine gave a few splutters and died.

'Come on, old girl,' encouraged Danno.

This time the engine started. Danno backed the truck out and turned and headed south along the narrow winding dirt road, the engine shouting so loud it made conversation virtually impossible. Kylie was shaken until her teeth chattered as they bumped over potholes and lurched across boulders on tracks just wide enough for a single vehicle. She held her breath as they navigated terrifying hairpin bends, the road getting progressively worse. The truck groaned as it climbed up into the hills. At one point they were forced to stop to let the engine cool down. They took the opportunity to have a drink and a couple of biscuits, then, refreshed, jumped back in. Once again the engine stalled. After two more attempts they both got out.

'It's sure to be something minor,' offered Kylie encouragingly to Danno, whose head was now under the bonnet. She didn't like the idea of being stuck in this godforsaken jungle with a truck about to die on them. She glanced thankfully at the box containing water-purifying equipment, and thought fondly of her battered jeep, reluctantly rejected because of lack of room for the supplies.

'She just needs a tweak,' agreed Danno hopefully, turning a grease-smeared cheek. He pulled at a few wires, cleaned a couple of spark plugs, fiddled around and then lifted his head up again. 'That should do the old girl,' he said, slamming the bonnet shut and wiping his hands on an oily rag. This time the engine roared into life. Revving her up alarmingly, he crunched her into gear and they were on their way again.

'Hope she doesn't die when we're up there,' shouted Kylie gloomily over the roar of the engine. She looked across with a certain trepidation at the dense mountainous country they would have to weave through before climbing back down to the coast.

'Have faith, my child,' Danno shouted back, grinning broadly.

'Thanks a lot!' Kylie yelled, but his confidence eased her tension. 'You'd wonder how anyone ever managed to even make a road through here,' she commented after a while.

'It's like being back home,' Danno replied.

'Different heat,' Kylie yelled, blowing a strand of hair from her hot face, trying not to think of the skidding wheels on the last muddy stretch, or the landslide they'd had to skirt round, driving perilously close to the edge that dropped dramatically away.

'The dust's much the same,' bantered Danno, feeling her concern. He grinned across at her, taking in her fresh khaki shirt and shorts, her arms tanned a delicious brown, the faint tang of baby talc, her slight frown. For an instant their eyes met.

A thrill rippled through Kylie. Quickly she looked away, folding her arms, trying not to make the glance something more than it was. 'I s'pose it is. Hey, look at those!' she cried, pointing as two brilliantly coloured birds darted across their path, looking like something from a David Attenborough documentary. For an instant she stopped thinking of the precipice to their left. Just as she was going to make a bad joke, Danno rounded another terrifying bend, brought the truck to a sudden halt and gave a low whistle. Kylie gave an involuntary gasp. Most of the road was missing, having slid away down the mountain on the passenger's side it was far wosrse than the scout's description. What was left was too risky to squeeze the truck across. Sheer rock to the right gave no chance to dig out a track.

'Doesn't look wonderful.' Danno was suddenly serious. He stepped carefully out of the truck, walked cautiously to the edge and peered over the side, Kylie following close behind. Her stomach clenched as she stared down the ravine. At the bottom Fred's truck lay on its side, the cabin almost submerged in the river.

Kylie gave a small cry and grabbed Danno as his foot slipped, sending dirt and small boulders racing down the hillside and into the muddy water. 'Don't do that again!' she cried.

'Thanks. I don't intend to. I'm not in a hurry to join that truck down there,' he replied unsmilingly. Then more cheerfully he added, 'Cup of coffee in a nice hotel sounds good right now.'

'You're not wrong,' shot back Kylie, wondering what they should do. Her stomach tightened at the thought of backing down the road, so she suggested they try and drag up some of the dead trees she'd noticed just before the last bend and make a sort of bridge.

Danno nodded. 'That could work.' He pointed to the section of road closest to the edge. 'If we could stretch them across that part then crisscross the smaller branches ...' He rubbed his chin. It was risky but the alternative was even riskier.

He backed the truck down the hill, its wheels slipping and sliding alarmingly, and together they tied a couple of logs to the towbar and heaved branches into the back. Engine groaning, they dragged their load back up the hill and stopped as near to the hole as they dared. The last few metres they had to shift the logs by hand. The first rolled straight over the side in a rumble of dust and small pebbles making Kylie jump with fright. Holding their breath, they watched the second slightly smaller log which, to their relief, stayed put. Carefully retracing their steps, they dragged up more logs. Then, sweating and panting in the thick humid heat, after much grunting and groaning and swearing, they heaved them next to the one in place and then managed to fill up part of the road, crisscrossing the smaller branches across the first big logs, tying them with rope to large boulders at the far side, creating a reasonable-looking mat.

Gingerly Danno took a step onto the temporary bridge to test their efforts, gradually allowing it to take his full weight.

'Careful!' Kylie bit her nails in worry as he took another step, then another, and finally, to her horror, he gave a small jump. 'Don't!' she cried, her heart in her mouth.

Two large strides and he was back on solid ground, dancing cheekily across to her. Kylie gave him a friendly punch and he caught her in his arms. She held her breath, swimming in the depths of his midsummer blue eyes as he stared down at her. Suddenly he gave her a slightly embarrassed brotherly hug and released her. 'I reckon we should try driving the old girl across,' he said, his voice slightly husky.

'I agree,' croaked Kylie, swamped by a mixture of longing and disappointment, her whole body tingling from his embrace.

'D'you reckon you could drive? You're lighter than me and every bit counts. I'll guide you.'

'Sure,' replied Kylie, trying to focus on the job

in hand. They were aid workers. Fred needed urgent medical attention and they had to get over this bridge. This was no time to be overcome by emotion. She gave Danno a nervous smile, got into the truck and started the engine.

'Rev her up as hard as you can, never mind the noise!' shouted Danno.

Kylie nodded and pressed the accelerator, the truck still out of gear. Her right leg wouldn't stop trembling.

'Ready when you are,' mouthed Danno from the other side of the bridge, giving her the thumbs-up and beckoning her slowly towards him.

Kylie gripped the steering wheel with sweating palms and gauged the best path. Carefully she ground the truck into low gear then inched forwards towards the temporary bridge, keeping well to the right. Her eyes flicked up to Danno as he directed her, then back to the track. She was so close to the rock face the truck was almost scraping it. Now she was on the branches. She felt the truck sink down a fraction and forced herself to stay calm. She was halfway across. Danno was still beckoning. There was an ominous crack. Automatically she wrenched the wheel around, jammed her foot on the accelerator and tore across the remaining track, her nearside wheels almost lifting off the ground. She jammed on the brakes and came to a stop a few metres away from the bridge, shaking from head to toe. She turned in her seat to see their hard labour slowly slide over the edge.

Danno opened the truck door and dragged her out. 'Are you okay?' Kylie nodded, but she looked very pale. 'You did it! You got us across, you brilliant, gorgeous, amazing girl!' He was shaking too. Grabbing her, he kissed her hard on the mouth. She was still shaking like a leaf in his arms. He hugged her to him. 'You're safe, you're okay.' He stroked her back and held her close till she stopped shaking, then he guided her to a rock and sat her down.

'I was bloody terrified and I wasn't even in the truck,' he said with a short laugh. He sat down beside her, resting his hands on his knees. Neither spoke for a moment, both caught up in what might have happened and the confusion of their kiss. 'I didn't know you were into stunt driving,' said Danno, breaking the tense silence.

Kylie looked at him quizzically, wishing he'd take her in his arms again, or at least give some kind of sign that he had actually kissed her. 'What're you talking about?'

'You came off those trees like a female 007! Did you know you were flying on only two wheels?'

'Was I?' laughed Kylie, basking in his admiration.

Danno hesitated a moment then stood up. Kylie followed, flapping her sweat-soaked shirt. She walked over to the hole and stared down.

'This place gives me the creeps. Let's get out of here,' she said and climbed back into the driver's seat.

'You sure you want to drive?' asked Danno, climbing in beside her.

'No worries! Couple of doughnuts around the next hairpin and a quick two-wheel skid down the next hill and I'll be ready to roar,' she grinned, her heart singing again. There had been no mistaking the admiration and it wasn't for any little sister. 'Seriously though,' she shouted as they bumped along the track, dodging rocks and automatically ducking as branches swept their windscreen, 'how the heck are we going to get back with Fred?'

Danno relaxed, leaning against the cabin, his right arm lying lightly across the back of the hard seat, fingers just short of her shoulder. 'Dunno!' he shrugged, watching her flushed face and bright eyes, longing to take her in his arms again. But what had he to offer her? A quick fling for the next few weeks, heavily frowned on by their co-workers, and then what? He couldn't do that. If he got involved with Kylie, it'd be for life, and in a few weeks he could be on the other side of the world. The thought of never seeing her again made him go cold inside.

'I've learned one thing,' he said, bringing his thoughts firmly back to the present, 'it's that there's usually a way round these problems when you finally get to them. Let's see what the locals have to say.' Maybe he should take his own advice, he thought wryly.

The two spoke only intermittently as they covered the remaining distance, the engine noise and their own thoughts stopping either from saying much. Every so often Kylie felt Danno's eyes on her, but when she glanced around he was either staring out at the road or would quickly point to a bird or an animal scampering back into the jungle.

They ate their lunch as they drove, then swapped drives on their descent to the coast. Finally they reached the village by mid-afternoon and were met by a band of villagers who came rushing out onto the road to greet them.

Fred was lying on a thin mattress in the clinic tent, pale and obviously in a lot of discomfort from his injuries. His broken ribs made talking and even breathing very painful. While Fred's was one of many shoulders she had had to fix, it was causing him a lot of distress, explained the French nurse.

'Will he be okay for another couple of days?' Kylie asked anxiously, relieved the nurse turned out to be so competent. 'The road we came down's impassable so we're going to have to find another way back — if it exists — and I can guarantee it won't be a comfy ride.'

'I can give him some more shots for the pain, but he really needs proper medical attention. His blood pressure's erratic and that leg needs to be X-rayed in a proper hospital. He's pretty resilient considering,' replied the nurse.

Kylie walked over to the patient. 'Hi, Fred, not feeling too great, I gather. Don't try to talk. We'll get you out of here and more comfortable as soon as we can,' she smiled. Fred lifted one hand in acknowledgment then let it fall back onto the sheet. It was hot and sticky inside the tent, but the nurse had lifted the flap behind Fred's bed so he got what breeze there was.

'You did a good job on that road, mate,' said Danno, walking up behind Kylie and grinning down at Fred. They'd met a couple of times over a beer after loading up at the airfield and Danno appreciated the Dane's sense of humour. 'We polished the job off for you good and proper. Now there's no road! Could be a couple more days before we get you out of here. I'm really sorry, mate.'

Fred grinned weakly and pointed feebly at a dark stocky villager sitting at the back of the tent. The man had rescued Fred from the truck and now felt it his duty to stay with him until he either died or was taken to hospital. The man explained in pidgin English that there was another route up further into the hills which they could take back to the main camp. Although it was twice the distance, the track had recently been driven on and, unless they had torrential rains in the next twenty-four hours, it should get them safely back to base.

Having helped unload the medical supplies they had brought, they left a dozing Fred and went to find the headman. Although damaged by ferocious winds, the village had largely escaped the destruction wreaked by the tsunami. Most of the huts were intact and smoke rose cheerily from small fires as the women prepared the evening meal. After they had explained their intention to take Fred back to base camp in the morning, Danno and Kylie were invited to share the evening meal with the headman and his family. Small children, some of them naked, clambered around them, asking questions and jabbering away in their own dialect, bringing back a certain sense of reality.

After their meal the two wandered down to the water's edge, enjoying the cool breeze after the stifling heat of the journey. Not wanting to break the peacefulness that surrounded them, they walked along the sand in companionable silence, stepping over clumps of seaweed thrown up onto the shore. Their hands accidentally touched from time to time, sending little thrills through Kylie. The moon turned their world into a shimmering tropical paradise, and Kylie took off her boots and socks and walked barefoot in the water, letting the waves lap gently over her toes.

'Isn't it beautiful?' she whispered, her eyes alight. She tilted her face to the moon, its light tinging her hair an ethereal silver, making her more nymph than human.

Unable to resist her, Danno came up behind and slid his arms around her waist. 'Mmm,' he murmured into her neck. Kylie shivered deliciously. He turned her to him and kissed her. She surrendered to his embrace, letting the waves of longing course through her veins.

Finally, he released her. 'I was wrong. You have changed,' he said, taking one of her hands in his, examining it, stroking his fingers across broken fingernails. They were strong, capable hands. 'You're a woman, a beautiful, brave, gutsy woman,' he said huskily. He gazed into her eyes, his expression soft, and she smiled back, swallowed up in those clear blue eyes.

Gently Danno drew her back into his arms and kissed her again. She floated in the delicious sensations that flooded over her.

'Tonight is like a tropical dream. It feels so unreal,' she said quietly when they finally broke apart. 'You, me, the moonlight, the beach, the beautiful, glistening ...'

'... smelly beach,' interjected Danno, indicating piles of seaweed and debris dotting the sand.

'It is a bit on the nose,' she giggled, aware once more of the ever-present stench of rotting vegetation. Danno bent and picked up a piece of driftwood. She watched as he turned it over, running his hands along it, strong hands roughened by hard work, hardly the sort that she would have imagined could produce delicate carvings.

'Where did you learn to carve?' she asked.

'I don't know. I've mucked about with a penknife and wood since I was a kid. What animal d'you think is hidden in this?' He examined the driftwood then handed it to her.

'No idea,' replied Kylie.

'Sounds weird, but I've always been able to "see" things in lumps of wood. I don't know how, but often when I start it's like I'm just chipping away the outer covering to reveal the carving inside.'

Her whole being overflowing with love for him, Kylie let the driftwood fall from her fingers, slid her arms around Danno's neck and kissed him. He stroked her hair and kissed her back long and hard, as if he couldn't get enough of her. Finally, he reluctantly released her, his eyes still feasting on her.

'I've only got a little while before I finish here and fly back to Australia,' sighed Kylie. 'It's gone so quickly. I've no idea what I'll be doing after that.' She paused. 'I wish whatever it is could be with you,' she finished shyly.

'Me too,' said Danno. He slipped his arm around her shoulder and hugged her, then he grabbed her hand. 'C'mon! We'd better get back before they send out a search party for us.'

The journey back to base was relatively easy. Pumped up with morphine, Fred was semiconscious for most of the time, only groaning when they bumped over particularly rocky stretches. He also took the pressure off the slight awkwardness that had developed between Danno and Kylie as they concentrated on keeping him as comfortable and still as possible. As soon as they were within radio distance Kylie called up Craig, reporting that they were on their way back and that while Fred wasn't in the best shape, he was not in imminent danger of dying. Craig replied that there was a supply plane due in four days time which could fly him out to Port Moresby hospital. Its arrival also meant Danno's departure up north with fresh supplies.

Once back at base camp, Kylie returned to her regular routine. With no supplies due in until Fred's transport plane arrived, there was little for her to do at the air-strip, so she spent most of her time in the village, glad that she could be close to Danno as the time ticked away before he would have to leave.

Craig watched the two of them closely and noticed how Danno glanced at Kylie tenderly or smiled at her when they were recounting their ordeal yet again. Suddenly Craig wanted this cool, capable Australian who managed to command respect from everyone, and who always seemed to be hanging around Kylie, to disappear into thin air.

'Amazing, the talents of my team!' Craig said with a short laugh the third night after their return. The team were meeting over a hot beer, and Kylie had just finished regaling them with more details of their adventures. 'While you've been cavorting across the countryside, I'll have you know we've been slaving away. Seriously though Kylie, your work with Ruhana has been such a success that the school is overflowing. She's due back tomorrow, by the way. You'd better go and have a chat with her first thing. She's got some new projects she wants you to be involved in.'

'Oh great!' grinned Kylie, pleased that Craig was taking such an interest in her work with Ruhana. 'Well that'll take care of my time, in between whizzing up to the air-strip to sort out the drivers. Danno, how about hotting up my little buggy?' she grinned.

'Don't you dare touch it, Danno,' said Craig jovially, controlling his growing irritation. 'That buggy's working just fine. Hot it up any more and I won't be able to work for worrying.'

'Go on, just a little,' wheedled Kylie, giving Craig a friendly pat. She stopped as she felt him tense suddenly. 'Okay, okay! You're right! She's fine as she is,' Kylie said quickly. 'You're very sweet to worry. Isn't it great to have a boss who cares?' she added, her glance taking in the whole group. She didn't see Danno's, and Craig's eyes locking for an instant or Craig looking away first to hide his building hatred.

Chapter Sixteen

Kylie stood by the truck window, a dull pain in her heart. If only she had been able to say goodbye to Danno properly ... She told herself she was being stupid — he'd be back in a few days when it was his turn to pick up supplies again. They had managed to slip away a couple of times on the pretext of checking the truck, but both of them had felt nervous, as though eyes were watching them, and their kisses had been hurried and unsatisfactory. How she longed to feel his mouth on hers, taste his kisses, kisses that were searching, demanding, yet unmistakably gentle and affectionate. Every day she found herself falling more and more in love with this man. Each time he had to leave she found the separation harder to bear. She hoped it didn't show too much on her face.

'Cheer up! The end of the world isn't for another couple of weeks,' laughed Danno, determinedly cheerful. He too hated the parting. He longed to take her in his arms and kiss away her sadness, but he didn't want Craig getting into her ear. He didn't trust that man.

He gave her a quick hug and climbed into the truck. 'I'll be back annoying the heck out of you before you know it.' He grinned and started the motor. The old girl groaned and spluttered into life.

Kylie put her hands over her ears as Danno revved up the truck. 'She's still as noisy as ever!' she yelled, jumping on the truck's running rail. 'You will keep writing me those silly notes, won't you?' she demanded, poking her head into the cabin.

'Of course, and you will keep sending me your quota of chocolate, won't you?' he asked cheekily, taking his foot off the accelerator and letting the engine idle.

'Maybe!' Kylie replied with a lopsided grin.

Craig drove up beside them in his Land Rover, Fred ensconced as comfortably as possible in the back, looked after by one of the local nurses. 'Ready then, Danno?' he shouted.

'Whenever you are!' waved Danno, leaning half out of the cabin, still grinning at Kylie who hurriedly stepped away from the truck.

A tiny muscle tightened in Craig's cheek. 'Ruhana's expecting you, Kylie. She was talking about visiting some of the villages in the hills. Take your time.'

'Thanks!' She waved at Fred. 'We'll miss you. Get better quickly.'

'He'll be fine after your sterling effort,' shouted Craig. 'See ya!'

'See ya!' Kylie shouted back, waving briefly, smothering her disappointment, for the first time thoroughly irritated by her boss. It would have been quite simple for her and Danno to drive Fred to the plane, which would have given them a few more precious hours together. They had, after all, brought him safely down the mountainside. Craig seemed to have conveniently forgotten that and insisted she needed some down time from such stressful situations. He had told her in the nicest possible way not to worry about anything, that as well as looking after Fred, he would look after her job of organising the incoming supplies and truck drivers for the next few days. While she had protested that she was fine, there had been no changing his mind.

She watched the two vehicles vanish down the bumpy track to the air-strip, tears glistening in her eyes. She walked back to the village, her anger at Craig increasing, and nearly ran into Beth who had come hurrying over to her carrying a pile of empty cardboard boxes.

'Hey, Kylie, got a minute?' she called

Kylie dashed the back of her hand across her eyes and gave Beth a shaky smile. 'Sure. What's the problem?'

'That last list of supplies I requested ... They've sent me heaps of what I don't need and none of what I do.' Beth gave an exasperated sigh. It was the third time this had happened.

Glad to have something to take her mind off Danno, Kylie followed Beth back into the clinic to sort out the muddle. He'd be back in two weeks and in between there'd be his funny little notes, so what was she weeping and wailing about, she kept asking herself as she checked the order against Beth's supplies.

Danno branched off to the loading area as Craig headed for the airfield administration building. He too was disappointed and annoyed at Craig's decision. Following the look he had caught Craig giving him the other evening this sudden change of plans for Kylie seemed to him just a bit too much of a coincidence. The man was up to something. He walked round the truck, kicking the tyres, checking they were still good, and then he lifted the bonnet and tested the electrical system. He'd had a couple of goes at it since the bridge incident, but it still wasn't a hundred percent reliable. When he got back to the village he'd spend longer on it, he promised himself.

Kylie filtered into his thoughts. He could still smell her soft warmth and feel the rush of pleasure as she returned his kiss on the mountain road, the sweet sensation of her body pressed to his as they stood on the beach in the moonlight. How he had longed to make love to her then and there. She was so beautiful, so different from any other girl he had ever met. But then he'd known that back in Lyrebird Falls. It was just that she had never shown the slightest interest in him. And now, her gentle surrender when he kissed her, the easy companionship that had sprung up between them ... It was so tantalising.

He shut the truck bonnet and felt a hand on his shoulder. It was Craig.

'I've been wanting to have a bit of a chat with you.'

'Right,' said Danno, immediately on his guard.

'Just a few bits and pieces, protocol and all that.' Craig paused for a second. 'These notes you've been sending Kylie, they have to stop, and the freebies.' He held his hand up as Danno started to speak. 'Look, I know it's only small bikkies but this stuff's very sensitive. If there is even the slightest suspicion that aid workers might be on the take, it could create a lot of problems for everyone. I know Kylie meant no harm slipping in the odd extra roll of bandage, but ...' His voice hardened. 'We're running a serious clean-up operation here, O'Keefe. It's been highly successful so far. We're nearly at the end of it and I don't want you stuffing up the rest of my team by doing the wrong thing.'

He put his arm around Danno, propelling him towards the hangar. 'From now on, no chatty notes, just the facts. No freebies, no asking for favours. In fact, you will send your requests through Mumaki. I'll tell Kylie that's what we've decided, that way there'll be no confusion. Mumaki!' he called, finally removing his hand from Danno's shoulder and beckoning.

Danno thought he was going to explode with rage. 'Now hang on a minute! Kylie and I have done nothing wrong.' He was only just managing to hold himself back from hitting Craig.

'You will do as I say.' Craig's voice was dangerously controlled. 'I will not be accused of turning a blind eye to improper behaviour.'

'Improper behaviour! That's bloody nonsense!' shouted Danno.

'Just do your job as I direct or I'll have you shipped out,' snapped Craig. 'Have I made myself clear?'

'Perfectly,' scowled Danno.

'Good man!' Craig slapped him congenially on the back. 'As I said, these are all minor things and we all get carried away from time to time. You understand, I'm sure.'

Danno understood only too well. The man was a conniving, scheming bastard. He stormed off to organise his supplies, barking out orders to the locals and loading the truck in double quick-time. How dare the man insinuate he was on the take! How dare he suggest he didn't take his work here seriously or that he was embroiling Kylie in something dishonest! But he knew he had to be careful. Craig was perfectly capable of carrying out his threat and ruining Danno's chances of further aid work.

Two days later, back in the village up north, Danno was ordered to take over as main engineer in a village even further up the coast and was told another man would take over his duties as driver. Danno swore lively then sat down, tears of rage and frustration momentarily blinding him. It had to be Craig. Blast the man to hell! This had nothing to do with his work and everything to do with Kylie.

Kylie's spirits rose as she waited in the hangar for the trucks to roll in from the north. Then she came thudding down to earth after everyone had arrived except for Danno.

'Him no do de trucks no more,' explained his replacement, a villager with hesitant English.

Swallowing her disappointment, Kylie decided to check with Craig. Surely the driver had made a mistake. Craig explained that Danno had been needed urgently to take over the engineering work up in another village, several hours north of where he had originally been working.

'He said he'd contact you. I gather you and he had a chat line open when he ordered supplies.' Craig laughed. 'Go and check the requests list. Just keep the treats to a minimum.'

'How did you know about those?' asked Kylie, blushing furiously.

'I'm not blind, you know.' He walked off, feeling highly satisfied.

Kylie hurried to the hangar and grabbed the request form. Her eyes scanned Danno's familiar scrawl then shot up to Mumaki's face. 'Is this it?' she exclaimed, shocked. There was nothing, just a 'Hi Kylie', then requests for supplies. No jokes, no funny little 'how are you's, or 'guess what's, nothing.

'News from the Great Danno?' grinned Mumaki coming up to her, his white teeth gleaming against his chocolate skin. Wordlessly Kylie handed over the list. 'Mebbe he bin busy busy or too much tired,' said Mumaki quickly, seeing Kylie's crestfallen face. 'Next time everything good for sure.' He felt as disappointed as Kylie. Listening to Kylie's translation of Danno's notes had been a bright spark amongst his often cheerless duties.

She choked back her disappointment, terrified this might be Danno's way of cooling things off between them. She scribbled back a note trying to sound chatty, saying she hoped Danno wasn't too rushed off his feet, and shoved it into Mumaki's hand.

All day she fought back tears as she thought of their walk on the moonlit beach, of Danno's arms around her, of his kisses. She was sure he had felt something towards her. She was sure of it. So why the sudden change?

The next note came back with a curt, *Everything's fine this end, working hard. Say hi to the team for me. Danno*. Kylie couldn't believe her eyes. She felt sick to her stomach. She blinked back her tears, wondering again why Danno's tone had changed so dramatically. She could only hope the next note would be back to Danno's usual chatty style, but it wasn't. The notes remained curt and to the point, containing only vital information and requests for essentials, and after the first few they were not even addressed to her.

Kylie felt more and more bewildered and miserable with the arrival of each shipment.

Once she wondered if Craig could have said something to Danno, then immediately dismissed the thought, feeling horribly disloyal. Craig had admitted knowing of the notes and had actively encouraged her. She started turning her misery inwards, convincing herself her time with Danno had been just a flash in the pan, romance snatched as a refuge against the continual trauma and suffering they had had to deal with. She had built it up to more than it was because she so desperately wanted it to be something. She had to face it. There was nothing in the relationship. They had kissed a few times, that was all. The moonlit stroll had been the emotional end to an emotional day. She cried herself to sleep silently every night.

Finally Beth, who had been watching Kylie become more and more withdrawn, crept into the tent after having worked the late shift, pulled back Kylie's mosquito net and gave her a shake. 'You and I need to talk — now.'

'What's the matter?' gulped Kylie, hiding her tear-streaked face with her arm.

'You are. Get up and have a cocoa with me.'

'I'm really exhausted,' pleaded Kylie.

'You're really miserable and I'm really worried about you,' whispered Beth, grabbing

Kylie's hand and squeezing it. It was too much for Kylie. She burst into tears, stuffing her sheet in her mouth to smother her sobs.

'C'mon, old silly,' whispered Beth, leading her out of the tent.

Sitting under one of the big old palm trees in the moonlight, surrounded by the strange night noises they had become so familiar with, it was an enormous relief to Kylie finally to talk to someone about Danno. As the two girls clutched cups of rapidly cooling cocoa, Kylie poured out her heart. 'I just don't know what I've done to make him not want to write to me any longer, and there's no way of finding out,' she hiccuped finally.

'Maybe you haven't done anything. Maybe there's some stupidly simple explanation, like he's exhausted or run off his feet,' murmured Beth, giving Kylie another hug.

'I wish I could believe it was that simple,' replied Kylie. She fell silent, watching the moonlight play on the trees. 'Oh Beth, it was so wonderful. We both knew we couldn't have a full-on affair while we were working together, but we were so close, I felt so needed.'

'You don't think it was just because he was available and this is a pretty grim place?' asked Beth, trying to inject some reality.

Kylie looked at her friend, raw emotion

spilling from her eyes. 'I've always loved him from the first day I saw him on the ski slopes. There's never been anyone else. I thought it was just a silly teenage crush but it's not, Beth, it really isn't. He's the only man I've ever loved, or could ever love.' Her voice was harsh in its intensity.

Beth felt a sudden lump in her throat that Kylie could feel such passion. Danno was a looker all right, the whole team had agreed on that, but this was no one-way affair. Beth had caught Danno watching Kylie and she'd seen the expression on his face, the softness and something else. It had made Beth go weak at the knees and for an instant feel a twinge of envy.

'Maybe this was all I was meant to have,' sighed Kylie with a forlorn shrug. She twiddled her finger around the rim of her mug, her lower lip trembling. 'He never actually said he loved me. Sometimes things just aren't meant to happen.'

'Blimey, you can be a misery when you want, Kylie Harris. Who're you trying to kid? Everyone in camp knows he's completely stupid over you.'

Kylie's head shot up. 'Really?'

'Really!' laughed Beth, nodding. She gave a huge yawn. 'Now finish that up before you drown half the mozzies around here.'

'Honestly, Beth? Do you think he really does love me? Then why doesn't he write?' she ended flatly.

'Like I said, maybe he doesn't have the time. You don't know what's going on up there. Be patient. This is not the best place in the world to be having a passionate affair.' She held out her hand. 'Things'll work out. Right now the team needs you. Mike got it in one hit the other night. He said it's like the light's been turned down to dim with you drooping around. Turn up the lights again, Kylie. Blind us all!'

Kylie burst out laughing. 'Did he really?' She threw away the remains of her cocoa. Beth was right. She couldn't change things or sort them out yet, and nothing could diminish her love for Danno, so why wear herself out with worry? Deciding Danno was just grossly overworked, she walked back to the tent feeling her energy return.

'Thanks for listening, Beth. You're such a dear friend,' she said, giving her a hug.

'Good night, sweet dreams,' grinned Beth and disappeared into the tent.

Kylie stopped a moment to stare up at the moon, wondering if somewhere out there Danno wasn't staring up at it right now as well. She ran her fingers lightly over her lips, remembering the soft touch of his mouth, imagining his strong arms around her, and gave a shudder of pleasure. With a sigh she blew a kiss to the moon, then crept back to bed. But on her next trip to the air-strip all her doubts resurfaced.

'Where's our sunny Kylie gone to?' asked Craig, sitting down next to her on her return. He clasped his hands together and let them droop between his knees.

'Didn't have a wonderful drive back,' admitted Kylie. It was true — the road to the village had been a river of mud and very scary in parts. With a huge effort she forced herself to be cheerful. 'Only another two weeks and we're out of here,' she said brightly.

'Which brings me to something I've been wanting to tell you for a while.'

Kylie's heart missed a beat, hoping it was something about Danno. It wasn't.

'You've been outstanding, Kylie. I took a risk bringing you onto the team, but I couldn't have asked for more from you.' Craig's admiration was obvious even to Kylie. 'You've handled everything that's been thrown at you. You've done a great job from the day we arrived.' He paused, pleased to see Kylie brighten at his words. 'I wanted to make sure you knew how extremely happy I've been with your work and to ask if you would consider being on my next team. Though I can't promise anything definite and I haven't a clue where we'll be sent.'

Kylie looked up with a start. 'Really?' she asked. It took a few seconds to absorb what he had asked; then, without thinking, she jumped up and threw her arms around Craig. He hugged her back as long as he dared. She felt so soft and warm, so inviting.

'That's one of the reasons I want you working with me,' he smiled. 'You're so full of life and energy. I've been at this game long enough to know how people tick and you've brought something special to this team.' His arms were still around her. 'People work well around you — you just have that knack of bringing out the best in others. Selfishly I want that for myself and my next team!'

Kylie grinned back, her cheeks flushed with pride. 'I'd love to,' she cried. Giving him a quick peck on the cheek, she skipped off to find Ruhana and to wrap up some of the details of their work. There was now a real possibility she would get more work in the field. Beth was right. She had to get on with her life. If Danno wanted to do something about their relationship, it was his call.

The last days of the assignment were filled with mixed emotions for Kylie. She felt miserable that

Danno was up north and she was about to fly out without a word between them, but against that the rest of the team was buoyed up by the work they had achieved and the thought of finally shifting out. The village was almost back to normal, the local women cooking again on their wood stoves, the aromas wafting invitingly with the smoke in the hot, still evenings. Children ran and played in the dirt streets, their cheerful cries in stark contrast to Kylie's arrival. Some of them clutched little cars and trains carved by Danno, adding a poignancy to the scene. A group of them raced up to Kylie and waved their toys in her face, their eyes filled with mischief. She gathered them to her, inspecting each carving in turn, touched by their outward happiness. It was the emotional wounds Kylie and the rest of Craig's team couldn't fix. They would take years to heal as families slowly rebuilt their shattered lives, but at least the work she and Ruhana had started was helping. Families from the different destroyed villages were learning to live together and the whole place was slowly beginning to function as a community. It was a good feeling to know she had helped with that.

Kylie took one last look around her as she and the others strode across the tarmac in the sticky heat to the RAAF Hercules. Somewhere out there Danno was still working, she thought with sadness, her eyes scanning the surrounding jungle.

She slept for most of the journey back to Australia, emotionally and physically drained. Waking, her heart gave a joyful leap as she stared down at the vast stretch of brown land below. Everyone cheered and started singing 'I Still Call Australia Home,' as they touched down at Brisbane Airport.

In the hotel Craig had organised for the team, she sank into a luxuriously hot bubble bath, sliding down in the water until only her face was left above surface, her long flaming hair spreading out around her like bronze seaweed. She swished her hair back and forth, her mind a lazy blank. It felt wonderful.

The following day Craig called a debriefing session, congratulating everyone again on their efforts in PNG and wishing them well, advising them he would be in touch as soon as news of a new assignment came through. Kylie spent the rest of the day shopping, stocking up on shirts and shorts, boots and socks, and treating herself to nonessentials like perfume, new lipstick and new swimmers. Then she checked on flights to Cairns and Dunk Island.

On her return to her hotel room there was a note from Craig. She picked up the phone and dialled his room. 'Are you serious?' she gasped after listening to what he had to say.

'Absolutely. Meet me in the bar for a drink in an hour.' Kylie put down the receiver and hurried into the shower.

'Sri Lanka is a bit more dangerous than PNG, but the work will be much the same,' Craig explained as they sipped on long cold Bacardi and Cokes. 'Go away and have a break and I'll see you for a briefing in two weeks. How does that sound?'

'Amazing!' replied Kylie, looking at him over the rim of her glass. Excitement was bubbling inside her. She had got work without even trying, and this time with no arguments, no pleading. She'd be going off as an experienced aid worker.

The two of them ate a companionable dinner with Beth, who had been unable to get an earlier flight home. Afterwards they strolled along the river in the balmy evening, watching the city lights. Kylie found it hard to believe she was really back in Australia. After three months in PNG the sights and sounds were too rich and bright, too opulent and fast, too much for her to take in.

Chapter Seventeen

Kylie saw her mother as soon as she stepped off the plane onto the tiny air-strip on Dunk Island. Her arms were full of pink and yellow hibiscus flowers and her floral dress was a bright splash of colour against the green of the palm trees. She was standing in the shade searching the tourists alighting in front of Kylie. Dropping her bags Kylie hurtled across the narrow stretch of tarmac and flung her arms around her mother, sending the huge brilliant flower heads flying. Their soft familiar fragrance mixed with her mother's warm perfume as they hugged and kissed, laughing and crying together.

'Kylie, darling, thank God you're home safe. Let's get a look at you,' gasped Susan. Brushing away tears of happiness she stepped back, her hands tightly clasping her daughter's. 'Well, whatever you've been up to, it hasn't done you any harm. You look very well, if a bit tired around the eyes.' She took in Kylie's sunburned face and trim figure.

'You always say that, Mum,' laughed Kylie, kissing her again. 'It's so good to be back.' She breathed in deeply, filling her lungs with the fresh salt sea air as she looked around her. 'It smells so clean!' she cried. Then she started chattering nineteen to the dozen, tripping over her words in her hurry to tell her mother everything that had happened to her in the past three months. She skirted over the parts she thought might worry Susan, and her mother interrupted from time to time to ask a question or demand an explanation.

'We've had our fair share of interesting incidents, too, while you've been away,' commented Susan. 'Oh yes, and we've bought a pup,' she announced as they reached the house, where Kylie's bags were already being carried inside by one of the resort staff. A young retriever-cross puppy bounded down the steps towards them, all tail and paws, and leaped up at Kylie's shorts.

Kylie gave a gasp of delight. 'Oh Mum, he's gorgeous! You lovely puppydog. I thought you swore you'd never get a dog! Does he have a name?' She gathered the squirming, wriggling bundle of soft yellow fur in her arms, from where he proceeded to lick her face and every other bit of her he could reach.

'Tiger,' replied her mother.

'Hey Tiger!' cried Kylie, laughing and pushing his wet nose away from her cheek. He started chewing her fingers with his sharp baby teeth. Extricating her finger with a yelp, Kylie hugged the pup then let him wriggle back down on the ground. 'What made you change your mind, Mum?' she asked, giving her mum another hug.

'We-ell, it was very quiet around here after you left,' Susan replied, suddenly looking away. She turned back smiling, not wanting to dampen Kylie's happy homecoming with reminders of Gwyn. 'I am so proud of you and what you do, you know that, don't you?'

Kylie felt a stab in her chest. She missed Gwyn too. Although it had been over four years since her death, as Kylie had stepped off the plane she had automatically looked around for her sister, expecting to hear her cheery voice and to see her come running up to greet her. 'Here, Tiger! C'mon! Good boy! Where's Dad?' Kylie pushed away her sad thoughts, playing with the pup again, laughing as his tail seemed to wag in complete circles. She didn't want to think about Gwyn. Not now.

'Fixing a burst pipe in one of the buildings by the archery area. He'll be over shortly. He missed you too,' replied Susan more brightly.

'I should hope so!' laughed Kylie, walking into the house and kicking off her shoes, enjoying the cool touch of marble under her bare feet. Tiger padded off in search of something to chew. 'You'll never guess who turned up in PNG,' Kylie went on.

'You're absolutely right!' said a deep voice behind her.

'Dad!' shrieked Kylie, whirling around. She threw her arms around her father and kissed him as he swung her in the air, hugging her tight. He set her down, then checked her out as Susan had done.

'They fed you at least. Good to have you home, pumpkin,' he smiled.

'Good to be home,' beamed Kylie.

Over dinner Kylie told Susan and Geoff of her adventures overseas, describing the great team she had worked for and what a fabulous boss Craig was, sharing her amazement at Danno's appearance in such an unlikely place, describing the shock of arriving in the area after the tsunami and the contrast when they flew out three months later.

'I love this work. It was so rewarding to think we had managed to help even a little.' She paused, pushing away the intrusive image of her and Danno. 'There was this wonderful woman called Ruhana ...' She launched into another tale, finishing by announcing that Craig had invited her to be on his next team.

'We'll be working in Sri Lanka doing the same sort of stuff.' She stuffed a forkful of salad in her mouth. 'I've got two weeks leave then we're off. I can't believe it. Everything's happened so fast ... I'm going to veg out while I'm here — sail, swim, sunbake ... do nothing.' She pushed her plate away, stretched and smiled across at her parents. Her mother had gone very still. Kylie sat up abruptly. 'What?'

'In your dreams, my girl,' interrupted her father jovially. 'Now you're home you can earn your keep.' Susan got up and silently cleared away the dishes.

Kylie leaned anxiously across to her father. 'What did I say? What's the matter with Mum? She's hardly said a word.'

'With you going at a hundred miles an hour, did she have a chance? I'm only joking! It's good to see you so enthusiastic.' Geoff paused. 'Give her time. She misses you dreadfully,' he explained quietly. 'She would never stop you but she was never keen on you going off to these places.' He gave a sigh. 'She's still struggling with Gwyn's death.'

'We all are, Dad.' Kylie's eyes filled with tears.

Geoff put his hand briefly on Kylie's shoulder. 'Take it easy, pumpkin. You're doing absolutely the right thing getting on with your life and I know it's taken a lot of pluck.' He refilled his wine glass and took a large sip. 'Spend some time with your mum. She needs you,' he murmured as Susan walked over with coffee and liqueurs.

Waking to the sound of waves breaking on the beach, and magpies and parrots calling from the trees, Kylie stretched deliciously in the cool of her spacious tiled bedroom, then pushed back the covers and dived into the shower. Taking her father's advice she had insisted on helping out with her old job of running the sailing activities whilst she was home. After a leisurely breakfast she and her mother strolled down the beach to the boatshed, the two chatting comfortably. The cool August breeze caressed their cheeks, and they laughed as Tiger ran between their legs then tore off across the sand, chasing shadows and stumbling over shells, occasionally frightening himself when a seagull swooped down low.

'I love you, Mum,' said Kylie, tucking her hand in her mother's arm and walking them around a large mangrove tree growing into the sea. The beach was so clean compared to the ones she had just left behind.

'I love you too, precious girl,' replied Susan.

They had arrived at the boatshed. Kylie let

out a gasp of surprise. 'Wow, you've spruced this place up a bit,' she exclaimed, inspecting the newly painted shed and the smart new tables and chairs with their colourful beach umbrellas. She walked into the boatshed and looked around. A young man Susan introduced as Guy, one of the staff hired to run the watersports, appeared and Kylie shook his hand.

'Your dad's been working pretty hard, we're really pleased with the look of the place now,' Susan said proudly as they moved back out into the sunshine.

'You really like it here, don't you, Mum?' smiled Kylie.

'I do, but that's not to say you have to love it too,' replied Susan quickly. 'We have talked about your aid work and if that is what you want to do, then you go and do it. We want you to be happy, darling.' She waved at a group of resort guests trudging up the sand towards the boats. She nudged Kylie. 'Go on, darling, take one of the boats out. I can see you're dying to. You can start working hard tomorrow!'

Kylie's face lit up. 'Are you sure?'

Susan nodded happily.

'You're on, Mum!' Without waiting for another prompt, Kylie gleefully snatched up a lifejacket then ran over to one of the small catamarans and dragged it down to the water's edge. Laughing and shouting as Tiger bounded around her, yapping and getting underfoot, she pushed the boat into the water and clambered onto the trampoline. Kylie pulled on the sail, grabbed the tiller and headed out into the little bay. In seconds her mother was a small bright dot on the beach, Tiger an even smaller dot darting back and forth, jumping and barking.

Kylie pulled harder on the sheet, letting the breeze fill the sail. The little boat sped up. Soon she was skimming the waves, one hull out of the water. She revelled in the rush of wind in her face, the spray splashing up over the bow, and drank in the brilliant blues and greens and purples of the sea. She felt the same exhilaration as she experienced downhill skiing. Throwing back her head, she laughed at the sheer joy of sailing.

She came about, then steered towards a far headland that marked the end of the bay. Danno'd love this. She had watched him on some of the downhill races and seen his face, felt his excitement and his energy mirror hers. Tears pricked her eyes. If only there was a way to recapture what had been between them when they kissed under the moon that night on that beach ... But she knew in her heart there was not.

Suddenly she spotted something in the water.

Slowing down she let the boat creep towards the dark object. Maybe it was a bottle or an empty can. One of the rules of the resort was to keep the bay clean. Then to her delight, she saw her 'can' was the head of a giant turtle that had popped above the surface and was now looking around. Normally shy animals, this turtle swam around seemingly unconcerned at her presence, then it dipped and disappeared. Kylie waited. There it was again, only this time closer to the boat. She could almost touch its hard shell, see the pretty markings on its back. For a few moments the giant turtle played around her, dipping and bobbing, rising to greet her then diving back down again as she changed course.

Finally it sank underwater, its oval shape shimmering as it dived deeper and vanished.

Kylie felt her eyes prick with tears again. This time they were tears of thanks, thanks that nature had given her the gift of this beautiful creature swimming alongside her.

For the rest of the morning Kylie played on the sea, letting the wind carry her up and down the bay, searching in vain for more turtles. She finally headed into shore when she could no longer ignore the rumblings of hunger from her stomach. Her arms and face were hot from the sun. After a vast salad roll washed down with a can of icy-cold Coke, she spent the rest of the day helping Guy organise the canoes and skidoos, chatting to the resort guests and mending the rigging on one of the catamarans, the turtle's visit haunting her pleasantly.

The days on Dunk Island raced past as Kylie got caught up in the resort's sailing activities. It was almost as though she had never left. She took her father's advice and spent as much time as she could with her mother, enjoying the closeness they had built up before she had left for PNG. Most evenings the three of them took their drinks down to the water's edge and watched the sun set. On one particular evening, as she and Susan sat by themselves, watching the sun disappear behind the hills and turn the world pink and gold, Kylie finally told her mother about Danno.

'I guess we're just not meant to be,' she ended, trying to sound convincing. She poked at the sand with a stick, determined not to cry.

Susan put her arm around Kylie's shoulders and hugged her tight, tears starting in her own eyes. Surreptitiously she wiped them away.

'What is it, Mum?' asked Kylie, sensing her mother's distress.

Susan gave a little choke. She shook her head, unable to reply for a moment. 'I love you, Kylie, and I want you to have the best life. I just don't want to lose you too.' Her voice was barely a whisper. 'I miss Gwynny so much.'

Kylie felt a pain stab her heart.

The guilt over Gwyn's death, which had never quite left her, threatened to swamp her. 'I miss her too, Mum,' she whispered. 'I've never had a friend like her.' Her voice tailed off. She wiped her eyes and looked across at her mother. 'Every time I got depressed or overwhelmed in PNG, and there were plenty of times, Mum, Beth would say, "What you can't fix, you let go of and get on with what you can fix." And you know what? I kept thinking of you and the way you just keep going — with Sunburst and the family and now here.' She gave her mother an abrupt hug, knowing how inadequate her words were.

Susan shrugged. 'What else can you do? You know, there may be a perfectly reasonable explanation for Danno's behaviour. I always liked the boy.'

Before Kylie knew it her two weeks were almost up. A few days before she was due to depart, partly excited, partly nervous, she sat on the tiled floor of the sitting room, near the open French windows, mending one of the straps of her rucksack in the fading light. Susan was busy in the adjacent office finishing up the day's paperwork; Geoff was still out in the resort somewhere. Kylie's back and shoulders tingled from the sun and wind. It had been the best day yet out on the water, she thought as the phone rang. Her heart gave a hopeful lurch, something she had not managed to cure herself of despite the many calls to the resort.

'Kylie, phone,' called her mother.

Kylie's head shot up in surprise and she jabbed herself with the huge sailmaker's needle. 'Ouch!' she cried and leaped up. Her legs started to shake. Racing into her mother's office, she mouthed, 'Who is it?' as she grabbed the receiver. It was Craig. Kylie suddenly felt terribly let down. To compensate she sounded the exact opposite, bubbling with excitement as she replied to Craig who was confirming that the one-week briefing started the following Tuesday in Brisbane and giving her details of her hotel reservations. She chatted to him for a while, telling him how beautiful Dunk Island was and suggesting he come and visit some time.

When she put the receiver down she sank into a chair and stared out over her mother's bent head. 'He's a nice man,' she said finally, half to herself, then rose and walked out.

Ten minutes later her mother popped her head round the door. 'Phone for you ...'

Deep in thought, Kylie hadn't even heard it

ring. She stood up and took the cordless phone from her mother. It was probably Craig again, ringing with some small detail he'd forgotten. 'Dunk Island Resort, Kylie Harris speaking.'

'Kylie! Hello, it's Danno,' said a familiar voice

Kylie's heart turned over. 'Hello, Danno, how are you?' she said stiffly.

'Good, how's yourself? I hardly recognised you. You sound so ... official.'

'Really,' Kylie managed to stutter dry-mouthed. There was so much she wanted to say to him, so much she had gone over in her head a million times. Now she couldn't string three words together.

'How are you enjoying your leave?' asked Danno chattily, the merest hint of uncertainty in his tone. 'I just got off the plane in Brisbane. It's so good to hear your voice. I've missed you so much,' he said softly. 'The reason I'm ringing is that some mates and I are planning to go to Perisher for the weekend before we shoot off across the globe and I wondered if you felt like joining us?'

Kylie slid silently to the floor, her legs like jelly. Her fingers were clammy around the receiver pressed hard to her ear. What on earth did she do? Did she tell him to go to hell, or did she risk breaking her heart again?

'I just couldn't imagine screaming down the

slopes with you not there. Please say you'll come,' insisted Danno.

'Sounds great.' Kylie's voice was suddenly hoarse. She cleared her throat and walked through the French windows into the fresh air.

'Kylie, are you still there?'

'Sure I'm here. Why did you stop the notes?' she blurted.

'Can we talk about it down the snow?'

'I haven't said I'll come.'

'I thought you just did.'

Kylie couldn't help laughing at his sheer presumption. 'You stop all communication between us and then the weekend before I'm about to leave for six months you casually ask me to drop everything and rush off with you down the snow!'

'Something like that, but I can explain, I promise. Just tell me you'll come.'

'Hang on.' Kylie raced back inside to Susan's office. 'Danno's invited me down to the snow for the weekend. It'd mean tomorrow'd be my last night here. Would you mind?'

Susan took one look at Kylie's glowing face, the excitement and longing in her eyes, and said without hesitation: 'If you can get a flight, go!'

'You're lucky I've got such an understanding mum,' giggled Kylie into the receiver.

'Then it's settled!'

Kylie grinned at the obvious elation in Danno's voice. 'Just remember, we have to talk,' Kylie said firmly after she had scribbled down all the details.

'All day and all night for the whole weekend,' promised Danno.

Kylie replaced the phone in its cradle, not sure whether to clap her hands or burst into tears. She wondered if she had been foolish to agree to go. It was all so confusing, but at least she was going to have three whole days with him.

'But is it as his girlfriend or just a good mate?' she asked, gathering Tiger, who was chewing one of the straps on her rucksack, into her arms and burying her face in his soft fur, happily accepting all his licks.

Chapter Eighteen

The flight from Brisbane to Canberra seemed to last an eternity, though Kylie kept reminding herself how lucky she'd been to get a seat at such short notice. Searching the coaches waiting at the airport to take groups to the snow, she started to panic when she couldn't find Danno. Then she heard a cheery shout and Danno appeared from behind the line of buses, grinning from ear to ear. Grabbing her bag and skis, he stowed them in the baggage compartment, then they both climbed onto the bus. There Danno introduced her to the group, which was made up of seven men and women of mixed ages. They were all aid workers using up their last weekend before heading overseas, and they were all boasting about their expertise, or lack of it, on the ski slopes.

Kylie quickly joined in with the friendly banter, realising any private conversation with Danno was out of the question. Secretly she was relieved. It was disturbing enough just sitting next to him, feeling the little shockwaves of pleasure that ran through her when he accidentally brushed her arm or touched her shoulder. Added to that, she still felt very confused about where she stood with him, whether she was his girlfriend or just a buddy to bring along for the weekend.

Perisher Valley hadn't seen snow like this season in twelve years. The place was knee-deep in the stuff. Even the car park at midday had a light coating of snow, and there was another heavy overnight dump forecast. Everyone shouted and laughed with delight as they tumbled out of the bus, slipping and sliding as they grabbed their gear and crunched across packed snow to the lodge where they were staying.

Beautiful Highpeak Lodge was owned by friends of Danno's father. Set high on the hillside overlooking the resort, it had been modelled on an American-style chalet. It had an attractively terraced garden with an outdoor area complete with tables and chairs now covered in several inches of snow, and inside contained all mod cons, including a hot tub, sauna and billiard room. But what really made it so great was that it was almost always snowed in, which meant an easy three-minute ski run straight to the bottom of the first chairlift. Coming home, by staying high guests could ski right to the door instead of having to trudge uphill, skis on their shoulders.

Kylie gazed around her delightedly. Perisher was in top form. Even she hadn't seen conditions this good. Agreeing the snow was too good to waste, she hurriedly changed into her ski gear and within twenty minutes of their arrival was standing at the top of the quad chair.

'Race you to the bottom!' cried Danno.

'Done!' shouted Kylie, adjusting her sunglasses and pushing off.

By the end of the afternoon they had skied half the Perisher runs, Danno playful but slightly distant. Riding one of the flattest and easiest T-bars, Kylie lost concentration and fell off, tangling her skis hopelessly under her. Danno immediately jumped off and raced down to join her at the bottom, joking about her fall and making her feel far less of an idiot.

'I hope it really does dump tonight,' said Kylie as they ambled back to Highpeak a couple of hours later. She had decided to wait for a quiet moment later in the evening to ask the questions that still burned inside her. She felt pleasantly tired now. It had been a good beginning and she was unwilling to spoil things.

After everyone was fortified by mountains of delicious homemade pasta and several glasses of cold lager, the evening was spent playing pool, creating hoots of laughter. Kylie found herself having too much fun to confront Danno. When the conversation came round to stories of their time together overseas, he slipped his arm lightly around her waist, for a moment waiting his turn in the game. Then he accepted the cue and sank the black ball, exclaiming light-heartedly that he'd lost them the game.

By the time they all finally turned in for the night, Kylie felt thoroughly confused. Peeping through the heavy curtains drawn across her window, she watched the great snowcats hard at work flattening the pistes, their yellow headlights shining across the darkened hillside. Wondering what the next day would bring, she climbed into her pyjamas and fell asleep trying to work out the best way to approach Danno without totally ruining the weekend.

The morning broke brilliant and sunny. Huge icicles hung from the snow-laden eaves. Two sets of tiny animal tracks broke the pristine snow just below the bedroom window. Hurrying down to breakfast, Kylie looked around for Danno, who was nowhere to be seen.

'He's been gone for hours,' exclaimed Cindy, one of the other girls in the group, as she helped herself to cereal.

Crestfallen, Kylie walked to the French

windows and stood looking out at the beautiful white world beyond. The snow gums were waving in the breeze, some still holding their delicate layer of snow. Then she spied Danno waving and beckoning and her heart lurched. She tried the door and found it was unlocked. Forgetting she was wearing thoroughly unsuitable shoes, she slipped outside and raced towards him, slowed maddeningly as she sank into the snow, her toes freezing by the moment. Danno came hurrying over, grinning at her.

'So you finally got out of bed, lazybones!' he shouted as she hopped up and down to keep her feet warm. 'I've got a surprise for you.' Then he swept her up in his arms and carried her round the corner of the lodge where he slid her gently to the ground.

Kylie stared around then gave a squeal of amazement. In the lee of the building, out of the morning sun, stood an exquisitely carved snowhorse standing on its hind legs. Forgetting her freezing feet, Kylie stepped closer to examine the intricate detail of the animal's mane, its hooves, its eyes. Then she saw the horn coming out of its forehead and gave another cry of delight. It was a unicorn. The mythical beast had caused several heated arguments between them on hot sticky nights in PNG. Kylie swore the creature watched over you and kept you safe, while Danno teased that it was a whole lot of rubbish that came from reading too many fairytales as a kid. Their arguments had invariably ended in a friendly punch-up, or a long tender kiss if they were alone.

'It's a unicorn to keep you safe,' said Danno quietly. Then he gasped as he was almost bowled over by Kylie hurling herself at him.

'I love it! It's amazing! Did you really do it for me?' One hand in his, she reached out to the unicorn, her fingers just brushing the beautiful sculpture. 'Whatever time do you get up?'

'Early. But you're worth it.' Abruptly Danno kissed her and she thought she would melt in his arms despite the cold. 'Let's go and have breakfast, I'm famished.' And he let her go just as suddenly.

Breakfast over, they decided to start the day by doing all the runs from Perisher to Smiggins, then across to Blue Cow and Guthega. Bursting with energy, Kylie was first out of the lodge and raced Danno and the others to the lift queue. Squashed between Cindy and Danno on the packed quad chair, with Ben, another member of their party, on the far side, Kylie kept thinking about the unicorn, that Danno would go to all that trouble for her. She stared across the slopes, her lips still tingling from his abrupt kiss, and her spirits soared. Conditions were perfect. The sun glinted across the white world, sparkling on newly made tracks and on top of the stunted gumtrees that swayed beneath the chair as it sped up the mountainside.

'They look as though they're dancing!' cried Kylie, pointing as a sharp breeze sent a flurry of snow from the treetops as they bent and swayed.

'They do, don't they!' Cindy exclaimed. Danno was silent.

Once at the top, Cindy and Ben headed straight over to the runs at Blue Cow. Kylie and Danno decided to have another go at the Perisher runs.

'What d'you reckon first?' he asked, skiing over to Kylie who was adjusting her ski boots. He pulled out the map and looked at her. 'I'm glad you decided to come,' he said quietly, watching Kylie tuck back a wisp of flaming hair. She was so beautiful, so desirable, yet detached somehow. God, how lonely he had felt those last two weeks in PNG without her. It had been worth getting up before light this morning to build the unicorn for her.

He tucked away the map, a brief frown flitting across his face. She had made no more mention of his sudden lack of communication. Perhaps he was putting too much importance on it. Perhaps she hadn't even missed the notes.

He wanted desperately to talk openly with her, yet he was afraid of what she might say.

'Why don't we do this run, then take this chair across to Sun Valley? There's a beaut run through the trees here.' He stood close to her, breathing in the soft scent of her hair. He must talk to her. He must explain.

His smile washed over Kylie, making her suddenly feel weak. First things first, she told herself firmly. A couple of runs and then she'd tackle him. 'Sounds good to me,' she smiled back, pushing off.

Together they raced downhill, twisting and turning, the wind rushing in their faces, the sun blazing down on them. They schussed to a stop at the bottom of the chairlift, snow spraying out behind their skis, then clambered off the T-bars further along the mountain. The whole white world was theirs to enjoy.

Taking a sharp turn halfway down a wide piste, Kylie shot between the gumtrees, ducking and weaving. One ski sank into soft snow. Losing control she charged forwards and landed in a giggling heap at the bottom of a huge gnarled tree, whose trunk was painted vibrant colours she knew so well. Her skis were firmly embedded in the snow up to her boots. Floundering around, no matter how she struggled she couldn't reach to release them. Her only choice was to wait helplessly for Danno. Seconds later he charged through the trees and did a perfect stop beside her.

'I hate you!' she laughed, feeling foolish.

'That really makes a man want to rescue a maiden in distress!' he teased.

'Please help, Danno!' she cried, struggling uselessly.

Quickly Danno stepped out of his skis. He scraped away the loose snow, released her skis from her boots and helped her stand up then pulled the skis free.

'Thanks. I'm supposed to be the skier around here,' she laughed, still embarrassed. Her words petered out as Danno drew her to him.

'You are,' he whispered. Then he kissed her. Not like the earlier abrupt kiss, but long and lingering, sending fire through her veins, stopping all thought save that he was kissing her and she was in his arms. She could feel him trembling against her. She gave in to her longing, lost in the deliciously sweet sensations that rippled through her being.

Finally Danno lifted his lips from hers. 'I've wanted to do that ever since you poked your head in my truck and asked me to keep writing those silly notes,' he murmured hoarsely.

Kylie gazed into the depths of his blue eyes, her love for him washing over her in waves.

Whatever he had done, for whatever reason, she no longer cared. No one could take this moment from her — ever. A flurry of snow showered around them as the breeze caught at the branches. She glanced up, her face glowing with joy. 'Look! The snow gums are dancing.'

'Dancing for us,' he whispered and covered her mouth with his. This time she slid her arms around his neck and abandoned herself to his embrace, their bodies trembling together.

'Why did you stop writing those silly notes?' she asked finally, her voice husky.

'I wanted to write ...' he started. His fingers traced the soft outline of her cheeks.

'Thought you'd be over at Guthega by now,' shouted a voice.

Bugger! thought Kylie as she quickly bent and reached for her skis.

'Have a bit of a prang, did you?' laughed another of the blokes from their group.

'You can talk!' grinned Kylie, cheeks burning, to the shorter of the two who had never skied before this weekend. He had done a superb wipe-out the day before on an easy slope, losing both skies and sending his stocks and beanie flying across the snow. Undaunted, today he had continued to crash and plunge his way down most of the intermediate and even some of the black runs.

'You should try the Olympic run. It's phenomenal. Never come down so fast before in my life! Scared myself stupid!' said the bloke.

'You are crazy!' cried Kylie, fumbling with her gloves, fingers trembling.

'You didn't expect sanity this weekend, did you?' smiled Danno, inwardly cursing his mates for their incredibly bad timing.

'Silly me! I'm starved, what say we head over to Blue Cow now?' called Kylie, starting to ski through the trees back to the open piste.

There was no further opportunity for the two to talk privately as they skied across to Blue Cow for lunch, then spent the afternoon skiing across to Guthega and back to Perisher. By the time she climbed the last T-bar home, Kylie was aching all over.

'A dip in the hot tub sounds the go,' she shouted.

'See you there!' called one of the others as they all shot off down the slope towards Highpeak.

Kylie made it to the hot tub first. She lay back in the water, the heavily chlorinated steam rising around her. Her body gradually relaxed, the tingling heat from the bubble jets pleasantly hitting her back and easing her stiff limbs. She started to daydream. Closing her eyes she relived Danno's kisses, felt his mouth on hers, his body trembling against hers ... Her mind flashed briefly back to Aspen when she had lain in the hot tub wishing Mr Right would walk through the door. Now Mr Right was about to do just that, only she wasn't sure he knew he was Mr Right and he was coming with an army of his mates. She gave a huge sigh and plunged further into the water, swimming around, letting her legs float over the stream of bubbles.

The door opened and Danno walked in, clad in a neat pair of bathers, a towel over one broad tanned shoulder. 'How is it?' he asked as he tossed his towel on the bench and strode towards the shower.

'Great! Hot!' called Kylie above the noise of the shower water. Her pulse was racing as she tried to get her thoughts into some semblance of order. Two minutes later Danno reappeared, walked to the door and turned the lock. 'What are you doing?' she asked.

'Carrying on where we left off,' he announced. 'Ooh! Ouch! Hot!' he grinned as he carefully lowered himself into the steaming water. Taking a deep breath he plunged in up to his neck and swam over to Kylie. 'I decided we needed — I wanted some privacy. Come here!' Before she could think he drew her into his arms and kissed her long and hard.

'I've missed you so much,' he said, gazing into

her eyes. He pulled her gently so she was sitting on his knees, one hand still around her waist, the other slowly stroking her shoulders, tracing the top of her bikini. 'You're stunning,' he murmured, then bent and kissed the warm flesh and slid one strap off her shoulder.

Kylie pulled the strap back on her shoulder and kissed him hard. 'We have to talk,' she said firmly, knowing there was no hope for her if she didn't stop him now.

Danno kissed her shoulder again. 'I know we do and I'm not trying to avoid talking ... just maybe postponing it a little.' He raised his face, his lips perilously close to hers.

Kylie ran her fingers through his hair then traced one trembling finger along his cheek, his strong jawline, his mouth. 'Why did you stop writing me those notes?' she asked matter-of-factly, placing her hands on his shoulders. She was in control. She could handle this. Her lower lip started trembling. Quickly she slid off his knee as tears sprang to her eyes and slid down her cheeks.

'Hey! Where d'you think you're going?' demanded Danno, reaching for her.

'You just stopped ... everything ...' She was crying now, ashamed of her weakness.

Danno dropped his arms, suddenly feeling trapped. He'd had no choice. If he told her the truth, would she believe him? 'I couldn't! I wanted to, but I couldn't.'

'Why not?' demanded Kylie.

'Your boss!' replied Danno, an edge to his voice. He explained how Craig had told him to stop the notes and had accused him of being on the take. His heart sank at the increasingly frozen expression on her face.

Kylie folded her arms. 'No, that can't be right! Craig knew all about the notes. We laughed about them that evening, and he'd never accuse you of being on the take. You must be mistaken. He knows you.'

'He also has the hots for you!'

'That's ridiculous!' Kylie laughed at the absurdity of the idea. She swam across to Danno. 'Are you saying you were jealous?' she teased.

'I might be,' replied Danno, realising she wasn't ready to hear the truth about Craig. He pulled her back onto his knee, no longer interested in talking or even thinking about that double-crosser.

Kylie slid her arms around Danno, hooking her legs around his back. 'You really were jealous of Craig. That's so funny!'

'He had the hots for you, let me assure you. Men know these things.'

'Oh I'm sure they do,' replied Kylie, eyes

twinkling, 'but you still haven't told me the reason for stopping the notes.' She was determined not to let him escape.

'Maybe I got it wrong, but I was worried that if I kept writing them Craig'd have a go at you. I didn't dare take the risk. The last thing on earth I wanted to do was to hurt you. Kylie, I was scared for you ...'

'I think that's so sweet,' murmured Kylie, deliciously disturbed by the hardness of his groin. She gazed up into his eyes and was shocked at the intensity of emotion there. 'Did you really miss me ...?'

'They were the longest, loneliest weeks of my life,' rasped Danno, kissing her gently. Satisfied, Kylie abandoned herself to his advances.

Danno ran the tips of his fingers down her cheek and across her mouth, passion spilling from his eyes. 'I love you, Kylie. I think I have loved you from the moment I met you when you were a giggly schoolgirl,' he rasped.

'And I love you.' Kylie gave a little gasp as Danno undid her bikini top and cupped one hand around her breast. Deciding it was too hard to make any more decisions, Kylie sank into a glorious confusion of sensations as Danno's hands wandered over her body, his fingers stroking the curve of her waist, her hips, her thighs, her breasts. He kissed her again, setting the tiny pulse throbbing between her legs, and the sensations he aroused were like nothing she had ever experienced before. Although she had lost her virginity at sixteen, in one of the bushmen's huts at Lyrebird Falls, she was inexperienced sexually.

She gasped as his fingers, then his mouth, found her hardened nipples. She pressed herself against him, trying to take in that Danno, whom she had loved since she could remember, was finally making love to her, wanting her as much as she wanted him. The thought made her body respond more urgently to his kisses and she kissed him back with greater passion as his tongue explored her mouth, the urgent throbbing between her legs increasing as his fingers gently brushed her soft bush then slid between her legs.

Suddenly he straightened. 'I'm getting too hot, why don't we get out of here?' he said, running his fingers through his hair. Clasping her hand he helped her out of the tub. They cooled off in the shower, then she gave a little cry of delight as he wrapped her towel around her and then swept her up in his arms and carried her to his room.

'What happened to the others, I thought they were joining us?' giggled Kylie as he kicked the door shut behind them.

'You ask too many questions.' He kissed her again and set her down.

The room was in darkness, illuminated only by the fading light from the wide picture window. A thick sheepskin lay in front of the fireplace with its fake log fire. Beyond faint shadows dotted the mountain. Lights from the huge machines already working to flatten the piste shed familiar pools of yellow on the slopes. A solitary skier made their way downhill. Danno flicked the switch to light the gas, and flames licked up behind the artificial logs.

Gently he pulled her back into his arms and they sank down onto the soft creamy wool, the gentle heat warming them, the flickering light dancing across their bodies.

'You are so lovely,' Danno murmured again, running his fingers over her body.

Suddenly Kylie felt hopelessly inadequate in this man's arms as his fingers roamed over her silken skin, igniting sensations she had only ever wondered about. Sensing her uncertainty, Danno continued to caress her until she relaxed. Gradually he aroused her, kissing her, whispering his love, until she clung to him, her whole body throbbing with desire. His fingers were between her legs again, probing, insisting, her secret place wet, inviting. She was floating, lost. Her legs started to tremble violently. She clung to him, unable to resist, then froze suddenly.

'What about …?'

'It's here somewhere,' rasped Danno, fumbling in his wallet for a condom. Then the awkward moment was past and he was kissing her again. With every stroke Kylie's senses heightened, more acute than she had ever known.

He kept kissing her, playing with her nipples, stroking her, then he was on top of her, sliding inside her, hard, throbbing. She felt herself close around him, her soft wet warmth so ready for him, more ready than she could ever have imagined. Her fingers clutched his smooth back and she thrust against him, arching herself closer, giving herself up to this man, this energy, this love that seemed to fill her entirely. She was conscious only of the sensations that swirled through her body. Her fingers clawed at him, her mouth sought his over and over. Her breaths were coming in short hard gasps; she could feel the heat growing between them, she was arching further, grabbing at him, almost biting him, desperate to reach that peak she knew was almost there, she could feel it, she was there, she was ... She held her breath, then felt him come, and their bodies relaxed together.

Danno gave a huge sigh, kissed her, then gazed down at her, shifting his weight so he didn't crush her. 'You are so beautiful,' he smiled gently. Then he rolled off her and snuggled her close, wrapping his strong arms around her.

'Am I?' murmured Kylie as she ran her finger along the scar on his arm where the pig had gored him. She basked in the sense of security and protection he gave her, and wondered briefly if she should have let him go so far so quickly. It was too late. Besides, he had been wonderful. She kissed him again, firmly, demanding.

'Hey! Give me a second to recover, you tigress. What do they feed you on that island of yours?' laughed Danno. Then he kissed her again and they made love again with equal passion. She lay back afterwards, smiling, floating in a wonderful cloud of sensations. There didn't seem to be one corner of her being that he hadn't reached.

Danno stood up. 'Time to celebrate!' He strode over to the small bar fridge and pulled out a bottle of Krug. Popping the cork so it bounced off the ceiling, he filled two glasses, the white froth bubbling over the top and sliding down the sides onto his fingers. He handed a glass to Kylie. Sitting down beside her, he traced his champagne-soaked finger along the line of her body. 'You are the perfect reason to celebrate,' he grinned and downed a large gulp.

Kylie sipped her drink more slowly, feeling it mingle with the fire already pulsing through her veins. She felt more content and more aware than ever before, and at the same time she felt a sense of awe that the love she had longed for for so long had finally become real. 'Have you really wanted me that long ... I mean, since I was at school?'

Danno nodded, watching her beautiful glowing face.

'How shocking!' teased Kylie. She rolled over and stared at the ceiling, digesting the thought. Then she rolled back on her elbow, resting her head on one hand. 'Why didn't you ever ask me out?' she asked hesitantly.

'I didn't think you were interested. I certainly didn't think you thought of me as a prospective boyfriend. Even when we were working together in PNG you had me guessing.' Danno reached for the Krug. She watched him refill their glasses, running her eyes over his body, noting its angularity, the broad shoulders and narrow hips, the strong legs. Just looking she wanted him all over again.

'You didn't think I was interested? That's so crazy! You didn't even know I existed, not as a girlfriend or anything,' exclaimed Kylie. 'You went out with my sister, for God's sake! All those years, both thinking neither of us was interested in the other — that's such a waste.'

'Nothing like the present to start making up for it,' laughed Danno, removing her champagne glass and pinning her gently down with his body.

'I don't have any objection to that,' replied Kylie cheekily. Between sips of Krug, laughter and playful romps, they made love again, finally lying quietly in each other's arms in front of the fire.

'What happened with Gwyn?' asked Danno after a long while.

Kylie lay silent for a moment, suddenly afraid of spoiling the magic between them. 'She died of an overdose,' she said, looking straight at him. If it was going to work between them, he had to know everything. 'We were in Aspen and she ...' Her eyes filled with tears. Suddenly it all came pouring out — how she had pushed her sister to stay, how if she hadn't been so selfish Gwyn would probably have been alive now, how helpless she'd felt that final dreadful day Gwyn had died.

'How I hate that man. Michael didn't give a shit about anything except his precious reputation. He even tried to bribe me to keep my mouth shut about the whole sordid little affair. His bloody tart of a wife must have known he regularly had it off with anything good-looking under thirty-five. How come I was so blind?' She stopped, choked with the memories. 'It was so awful. I didn't know how to stop it. There must have been something I could have done, some way I could have saved her ... I'm sorry, I'm such a cry-baby.' The tears were streaming down her face, and her body was racked with sobs as she finally released all the anguish she had hidden deep inside herself for so long.

Shocked, Danno wrapped her in his arms and held her close, stroking her until her body stopped shaking and she relaxed. He kept stroking her, wishing he could wipe away all the pain and suffering he saw in her tear-stained face. 'I'm so sorry. I had no idea,' he said softly, his eyes filled with tenderness.

Kylie gave a shuddering sigh. 'I'm glad you asked.' She reached up and stroked his cheek. 'I love you so much. Make love to me again.'

This time their lovemaking was filled with tenderness and compassion, and when they lay together afterwards, drifting off to sleep, Kylie wasn't sure where her body stopped and his started.

Kylie woke to find a warm blanket over her and Danno fully dressed, sitting in a chair watching her. She opened one bleary eye and peered at the clock. It was nine-twenty. She sat up abruptly. 'I'm sorry, I must have been tireder than I thought.'

'Sorry! For what, the most amazing experience of my life?'

She smiled up at him. Somehow she felt lighter since talking about Gwyn. She propped herself up on one elbow, the blanket tucked around her breasts, her hair cascading around her shoulders. 'You're dangerous! I could want more of you,' she grinned wickedly. Then she gave a little shriek and clutched at the blanket as he threatened to rip it off her. 'Later,' she pleaded, flopping back and feigning exhaustion.

'Time to get up!' ordered Danno. 'The others'll think we drowned in the hot tub.'

Kylie stood up, only to have Danno grab her and start kissing her all over again. 'Hey! You're dressed. You've got an unfair advantage,' she cried, unresisting.

'You've got twenty minutes. I don't know why you're taking so long to get ready for dinner,' he teased, finally letting her go with a gentle pat on her firm bottom.

'I'm going — now!' Grabbing her towel, she wrapped it around herself and headed for the door.

'Don't be long, I'm scared you might vanish,' Danno called after her.

'Not a chance!' grinned Kylie, popping her head back round the door.

Half an hour later they were sitting in the cosy restaurant of Highpeak Lodge, sipping mulled wine and eating freshly cooked seafood.

A real log fire crackled in the grate, whilst the rest of the group dissected every run, boasting of their achievements and vying to do better the next day.

Kylie smiled radiantly across at Danno, her heart spilling over with love for this man, so grateful he patently loved her as much in return. She thought back to the kiss under the dancing snow gums. She would never be able to look at snow gums again without thinking of him or smiling at their happiness.

Chapter Nineteen

Sunday was tantalisingly short. Kylie and Danno escaped from the others again and spent the morning skiing the Perisher slopes, only too aware that in a few hours they would be heading back to Brisbane and their separate lives.

'I'll write to you,' promised Danno at the top of a triple chair, their final lift for the weekend.

'Don't make promises you can't keep,' said Kylie, struggling not to cry at the thought of their parting.

'I don't want to lose you again.' Danno held her tight, locking her skis between his.

Kylie squared her shoulders. 'Look, I'm not going to do this aid work for the rest of my life. I want to settle down in a couple of years and live happily ever after with a brood of kids — so watch out.' She grinned up at him, her gloved hands flat against his chest. 'Let's be practical about this. At the moment we both want to keep on with our aid work, yes? We'll both be away for about four to six months on our next contract. I don't like the thought of being away from you for that long, but it's not the end of the world. Maybe we could even get ourselves on the same contract. You've been in this game longer than me, you must have a few tricks up your sleeve.'

'I wish,' Danno sighed and kissed her, his eyes thoughtful. 'I'm sure between us we can come up with something,' he shouted as they skied back to the lodge.

The journey to Canberra was uneventful, the parting excruciating. They both fought back tears as they hovered around the departure gate.

'Just remember, whatever happens, you're my girl,' choked Danno, oblivious to everything except her luminous face.

Kylie nodded, unable to speak. She reached for him one final time and kissed him, tears rolling down her cheeks. 'Take care, I love you,' she mouthed, then disappeared through the gate.

Buoyed up by the discovery that Danno really cared for her, Kylie bounced into the briefing room in Brisbane and discovered to her delight that both Beth and Dr Chung Li were included on her new team. She was quickly sobered when she learned they were going into the midnorthwest coast of Sri Lanka, which was in danger of being cut off by Tamil separatists in the ongoing civil war. Already the Tamil Tigers, as they were called, had stopped several relief trucks getting through to the north, leaving civilians trapped there desperate for food and basic supplies. The immediate disaster Craig's team was involved in was helping clean up after extensive flooding from weeks of thunderstorms and torrential rain. Villages and roads had been swept away and all power and communication lost. Thousands, it was reported, had abandoned their homes and taken refuge in the local churches and schools.

The training was intense, this time with more emphasis on personal safety. The team needed to know how to reduce the risk of being blown up by landmines or being caught in sniper attacks, as well as how to interact with local customs and avoid the dangers presented by indigenous fauna and flora.

Three days into the briefing, engrossed in a heated discussion with one of her team, Kylie's concentration was suddenly broken by the sound of a familiar voice. Heart starting to race, she turned and stared in disbelief as Danno walked into the room, deep in conversation with Craig.

'Guys, I'd like your attention for a second,' announced Craig slightly pompously. 'Meet your new team member, whom some of you know already, Danno O'Keefe. Danno has had a lot of experience in Sri Lanka. As you know, I have not! After a lot of persuasion I managed to extract Danno from his original assignment so he could assist us.' That wasn't quite the truth but Craig wasn't about to admit that O'Keefe had been foisted on him after his first choice of expert had been called away to a family emergency.

'Did you have any idea?' gasped Kylie during a quiet break.

'Not a clue. First I heard was a phone call from head office two days ago. I'm not unhappy about it though,' he finished, giving Kylie a gentle nudge.

'How's it all coming together?' asked Craig, walking up and clapping Danno and Kylie both on the back. 'This is going to be quite a different situation, Kylie, with a lot more tension. You comfortable with everything?'

'Sure. Bit nervous, but nothing I can't handle.' Kylie had appreciated Craig's considerateness over the last few days and the trouble he had gone to to reassure her.

'Well then, I'll let you finish your coffee break.'

Danno smiled back slightly stiffly.

'You're still jealous,' Kylie whispered when Craig was out of earshot.

'With you looking so appetising, what d'you think?' Danno grinned but his eyes were serious. 'You know that once we're on site it's better we're just "good mates",' he said, recalling the uncomfortable meeting he'd had with Craig earlier. It was clear the man didn't want him on board, and he wouldn't put it past Craig to try and get him sacked. Then he smiled and his whole face lit up. 'I'll make it up to you, I promise!' he murmured mischievously.

'Before we go?' asked Kylie, equally flirtatious.

'Before we go and when we get back!' nodded Danno, his eyes wandering lingeringly over her.

'Now there's a thought I can handle!' Kylie grinned back, his glance sending delicious ripples of anticipation through her.

Sri Lanka was very different from Papua New Guinea. While the disaster situations had similarities, Sri Lankan customs and the threat of attack from the opposing factions made everyone a lot edgier. Army troops mingled obviously with rescue aid workers, giving them an uneasy sense of security. Kylie's job was similar to her previous one, but this time Craig insisted on much greater security for her. She was assigned two guards who were ordered to go everywhere with her.

She had braced herself for the fact that Danno might be sent to a different area, and in a way felt it might be easier; however, she was overjoyed to find that on this assignment Craig was adamant his team stay close together. Having known more or less what to expect this time, Kylie felt more able to deal with the desperate, traumatised people who had lost their homes or were searching for their families. She also found there was almost no time to think of her personal life as she helped Beth and Chung, both run off their feet trying to cope with the enormous number of sick and injured. Far more confident, Kylie initiated activities for the women and children, in between fighting to get a reliable system into place for the transport of supplies.

Getting on with her day-to-day routine, despite the tragedy around her, Kylie felt amazingly content. Sometimes she felt quite wicked about feeling this way, but just to be able to grin across the table at Danno or to see his back as he climbed into one of the trucks made her insides melt with pleasure. With each day her love for him increased, and while they maintained their 'mateship', few of the others in the team were fooled.

'You're like some bleedin' lighthouse beacon, the pair of you!' exclaimed one of the team, a cockney who had lived in Australia for years.

Beth grinned at her and nodded. 'He's right, you know.'

Kylie blushed scarlet and laughed. The only time she got really nervous was when Danno drove up north where all the trouble was centred. Tales of villages decimated and people tortured and killed filtered back to the camp, and recently an army truck had been blown up nearby. Although the safety crew checked the roads for landmines every time the trucks left the base, there was always the fear they might have missed one.

Used to the constant dangers of his work, and with more experience than the others of life in Sri Lanka, Danno had rather different concerns. Still highly distrustful of Craig, he almost ran in on him one day in the supply depot as Craig was handing over a box of medical supplies to one of the guards. At first thinking nothing of it, Danno's deep mistrust of the man made him step back into the shadows and watch.

The two men talked for a short while. Bored, and deciding he was getting paranoid, Danno was just about to leave when the guard handed Craig a large wad of what was unmistakably crumpled American currency, which he shoved into his pocket.

Danno sucked in his breath. 'Well I'll be damned!' After all that claptrap about him being on the take in PNG ... and right under everyone's noses. His suspicions about the lying, conniving bastard had been right all along.

Two days later he saw Craig repeat the process. However, with no proof except his word against Craig's, and knowing the trouble the man could cause, Danno knew that to confront Craig would merely get himself fired. That, he wasn't willing to risk as long as Kylie was working on the team.

That evening, for the first time, Danno and Kylie had an argument over a new rule Craig had insisted be implemented in the camp. In Danno's view it was trivial and unnecessary, typical of the man's small-mindedness. He made several derogatory comments about Craig.

Kylie was tired and irritable and she couldn't understand Danno's persistent antagonism towards their boss.

'Not all that stuff again! Now you're just being downright unfair. He's just uptight like the rest of us.'

Both of them had entirely missed the fact that some of the grisly things Danno had seen on his travels to the northern blockade were starting to get to him.

The argument quickly escalated out of all

proportion, the two throwing accusations at one another. Kylie insisted Danno was being grossly unfair and ignoring Craig's good points, while Danno demanded Kylie open her eyes and realise that not everyone was as nice as she was. Frustrated, tired and miserable that she and Danno were fighting, Kylie stood up blinking back tears and about to storm off.

Danno immediately backed down. 'I'm sorry, I never meant to say anything to upset you. If you get on well with Craig, that's fine with me. I am sure he tries to do the right thing with everybody. It's not easy being in charge with all the stuff we have to cope with.' He drew her into the shadows and kissed her. It was a long, lingering kiss that left them both satisfied and at the same time hungry for each other.

'I love you so much,' Kylie murmured. Then she reached into her pocket and pulled out her precious carved pig. 'Here, take this. I want to know there is a part of me always with you. He's not a unicorn, but he's my very precious talisman and the start of our love.' Her smile was tight and brief.

Wordlessly Danno slipped the carving into his pocket and pulled her back into his arms.

❄ ❄ ❄

One day in mid-October Kylie stood by the latest convoy of trucks, checking supplies, while Danno did a final check on his motor. Everything worked, unlike the old rubbish heaps they'd had to drive in PNG. He joked about it to Kylie, partly to allay his own nervousness. He disliked going up north as much as the other men.

Slapping the side of the truck with its huge red cross blazoned on the side, he opened the door and pulled Kylie quickly to him. 'I'm counting the days till I can rip your clothes off and make passionate love to you,' he whispered. Then he kissed her hard on the mouth. 'That'll have to do for now. Remember, whatever happens you're my girl!' He climbed into the truck and slammed the door.

'And don't you go talking to strange women!' Kylie ordered with a laugh. It had become a little ritual they went through whenever he went on one of the deliveries.

Danno leaned out of the cabin window. 'By the way, there's something I've been meaning to tell you in case you've forgotten.' He paused, his eyes soft on her face. 'I love you.'

His words sang in her heart as she watched him drive off, the last in the convoy of five trucks.

Five hours later a grim-faced Craig gathered

his team together. 'I've got some bad news I'm afraid. Danno's truck has hit a landmine. I'm afraid he didn't make it.'

Kylie reached for something to lean on, the colour draining from her cheeks. Beth caught her before she fell. She couldn't take in the words that were coming from Craig's lips. Only a short while ago Danno had been laughing and joking with her. He'd kissed her. He'd said, 'Whatever happens ...' Had he known? She felt choked. She couldn't breathe. She could feel the hysteria rising inside her.

'How could this happen? They were in convoy, for heaven's sake! Didn't anyone check for mines?' she shouted.

'Kylie, calm down. I knew you'd take this hardest. Danno radioed to say he had a flat tyre and he'd catch the others up,' Craig explained. 'We had no way of knowing he was going to take a short cut. He was unlucky,' he finished lamely.

'I have to see ... I have to see! He could be lying by the roadside hurt ...' She knew as she spoke that they would have combed the area, but she was desperate.

Craig was at her side, his arm around her. 'Take it easy, Kylie. They found the body. This is a dreadful shock for all of us.' He felt the tears start in his own eyes. No matter how much he had hated the bloke, he wouldn't have wished this on anyone, and he had lost one of his most valuable team members. Yet somewhere deep down, as he glanced at Kylie, he felt something he didn't want to confront — excitement.

Kylie wasn't about to give up. She insisted on seeing for herself where Danno had died, and after much argument and a thorough check for mines, Craig drove her the five kilometres to the accident site. The mine had blown a massive hole in the dusty road, destroying a small bridge. The truck lay on its side down in the creek, a burnt-out hulk. The rescue team had reported that the body was burned beyond recognition.

Kylie walked up to the edge of the bridge and stared at the truck in blank disbelief. The creek sparkling in the sunlight mocked her with its beauty as it bubbled and gurgled its way downstream through the encroaching jungle. It felt surreal.

Craig came over to her. 'There's nothing more we can do here,' he said softly.

Kylie turned on him, anger and misery pouring from her. 'What was the hurry? If he hadn't had to hurry, he'd still be alive. Why couldn't the others have waited? Why did you let it happen?' Her voice rose hysterically. She rushed at Craig, beating her fists against his chest, accusations pouring from her lips. He was in charge, he should have made sure they were safe, he could have radioed through, given orders ... It was his fault ... She fought him as he tried to catch her flailing fists, then she suddenly collapsed against his chest, her whole body shuddering violently.

Craig held her tightly to him, letting her sob. He had to stop himself from silencing her suffering with his kisses. Instead he held her close until she calmed.

'I'm sorry, I didn't mean any of that stuff,' she said, wiping her nose on her shirt sleeve. 'Danno made a choice ...'

'Shh!' replied Craig softly. 'Let's get you back to the camp. I think it's time the whole team had a debriefing.'

The next day they held a short memorial service for Danno. Afterwards, Craig gathered up Danno's belongings and asked Kylie if she wanted to write to his folks. Kylie stared at him hollow-eyed and shook her head. She knew she should, but she couldn't bring herself to put the words down on paper, not now, not when the pain was all so new. She hardly spoke for the next two weeks. Instead she poured her energy into her work as she tried to shut out the horror of Danno's death. Still, she couldn't help jumping whenever someone spoke to her, hearing his voice instead, unable to stop herself from imagining him striding through the camp to greet her.

Finally Craig took her aside. 'Look, maybe it would be best if I organised for you to fly home. I understand what you're going through. The whole team understands.'

Kylie started back, her eyes like granite. How could he possibly understand the depth of misery and loss she felt? Finally she gave Craig a watery smile. 'I'll be okay, really. I don't want to go home,' she hesitated. 'I couldn't cope going home.'

Craig nodded and patted her on the shoulder sympathetically, then walked off. Kylie returned to her work, determined never to give him another excuse to offer her that option again. Within a few days she was putting on a good front, but a sadness hung over her which she couldn't shake off.

As Kylie continued to help people rebuild their lives, the pain of losing Danno gradually became a dull ache. The work sustained her, and whenever she hit a really low point, Craig was somehow always there to listen, and gradually their friendship grew.

The months passed. Kylie began to work more closely with the Sri Lankan women and children, and something in the strength of the love she saw in the mothers' eyes enabled her to put aside her own suffering. Kylie persuaded Craig to allow her to spend a few days working with some women in a small town to the southeast, helping set up the local school. While Craig hated for her to go, he knew the change of location would do her good.

He thought about her all morning after he'd waved her off, imagining how it would feel to run his hands down her body, cup his hands around her pert young breasts. He didn't know how much longer he could stand being so close to her yet so far away. The camp was deserted; Beth and Chung were off helping at another clinic for a couple of days. The wooden hut he used as an office suddenly felt stifling. He needed to get away, to breathe different air. Even his little venture capital deal with the guard had lost its edge.

He continued to stare at the mounting paperwork, suddenly remembering an offer from one of the wealthy landowners to stay at his place if he needed a break. The man lived several hours from camp and had offered his house as a haven. Craig had already sent a couple of his team there to recuperate. It was just what he needed. Maybe the landowner's beautiful wife would help him to stop thinking about Kylie for a few hours.

Calling up Bill Meadows, his second-in-command, Craig informed him he would be taking a three-day break. Things were pretty quiet at the moment so he was not concerned that he would be placing his team in jeopardy; besides, he had every faith in Bill's ability to handle things. Throwing a few clothes in a bag, he grabbed his keys and strode from the hut.

Two hours later, deciding to take a short break from driving, he stepped out of the truck and stared across the lush green countryside to the distant mountains. Around him the jungle teemed with invisible life. He breathed deeply and stood drinking in the beauty, knowing he was well away from any trouble spots. Birds called from the trees, the breeze ruffled the leaves, branches dipped in the creek. He sat down, resting his back against a rock, and shut his eyes, listening to the sounds around him. God he was tired. He'd be glad when they were out of this place. He laid the rifle he always carried across his knee and lifted his face to the sun, letting its warmth seep into his weary body. Maybe he and Kylie could take some leave together. The ache in his groin was a constant reminder of how much he wanted her.

He could feel her hands pressing lightly on his chest, her fingers at his shirt buttons. He reached out for her. Her fingers were stroking his face, his eyes, her mouth almost touching his ... His head jerked forward and he woke with a start and a huge erection. Heart racing, he grabbed his rifle, only relaxing after he'd taken in the empty road. With a sigh he rubbed his eyes, then stared absently at a log wedged at the creek bank. He watched the current push at the log, playing with it. It hadn't been there earlier. It was a strange shape, almost like a body. Suddenly Craig was fully awake. It was a body!

Leaping up, he raced across to the water's edge and grabbed onto the sodden figure. A deadweight, it took Craig several minutes of sweating and panting before he managed to heave the body out of the water and onto the bank. The man was still alive, but only just. Craig started mouth-to-mouth. The man gave a moan, then threw up and started coughing. Craig sat back on his haunches, taking in the stranger as he vomited again. Burned black by the sun, his face was caked with dirt and dried blood; a shaggy beard hid a face drawn and lined with suffering; the body was wasted under the clothes. The man was filthy and stinking, with what looked like a new bloody wound on his forehead, and Craig had to look twice before he could believe his own eyes.

'Danno?' he whispered, wondering if his mind was playing tricks. Danno was dead! He pulled out a grubby handkerchief and shakily stemmed the head wound.

'It's okay, mate,' rasped Craig in shock. He heaved the injured man to his feet and half dragged, half carried him back to the truck. The man slumped down in the passenger seat, barely conscious. Cautiously Craig searched through his pockets for identification. All he found was a penknife and a broken wooden carving. Craig's heart gave a horrible lurch. The last time he had seen this carving it had been in Kylie's hands. How the hell had Danno managed to turn up here? What if Craig hadn't been the one to find him, what if local villagers had found, him, or worse, one of his team? It was pure fluke that he had decided to come up here today. For a moment he thought he was going to throw up too.

'You'll be right, mate,' he said, shutting the door on Danno. He stopped a moment, cursing to himself across the peaceful scene, then he hurled the carving as far as he could into the undergrowth.

He raced around to the driver's seat, ground the truck into life and raced back to the camp. Parking a small distance from the clinic, he ran inside and grabbed one of the local male nurses. Between them they cleaned Danno up as best they could and tried to calm him — he was raving now, making no sense at all. Nervous as hell that some of his team would turn up and recognise the man before he could get him away, Craig grabbed Danno's passport and the belongings that he had been meaning to ship out, then drove him straight to the airport. Craig stayed with Danno for the next two days until the plane arrived, briefing the paramedics on the importance of complete secrecy.

'Listen, if he really is O'Keefe, and even that's debatable, he needs rest and time, not a media circus,' stressed Craig. 'I want to make certain of his identity before we notify his family, and I don't want to give any of my team here on the ground false hopes.'

The men nodded sympathetically, and Craig heaved a sigh of relief when the plane finally took off. The airport officials had all the documentation regarding Danno's case, and if on the slim chance the authorities, either here or back in Australia, needed to follow up, they would contact Craig. He felt sure he could keep the whole affair from the rest of his team.

Two days later Kylie walked back into his office, her face wreathed in smiles.

'That's another group of happy mums and kids,' she grinned.

Spontaneously Craig pulled her into his arms and kissed her on the mouth. Kylie froze and

Craig quickly released her. For a few moments they stood facing each other awkwardly.

'So. Everything went well? Good to hear,' said Craig, clearing his throat, trying to sound normal.

'Yes, it all went really well.' Kylie hovered by the door, not sure whether to leave or stay. She lifted her arms and let them fall again, smiling across at Craig. 'Well. I'd better get on now I'm back.' She turned to go.

Two strides and Craig was at her side. 'I'm sorry if my kiss upset you. I'm just so relieved to see you safely back. You know how paranoid I get when any of my team —'

'I didn't mind, really,' replied Kylie quickly. She kissed him on the cheek. 'You've been so good to me about everything.'

Craig shoved his hands deep in his pockets. 'Kylie, there's something I need to tell you. I ...' He looked straight into her eyes. 'I'm in love with you.' He held up his hand as he saw Kylie's startled reaction. 'I know you aren't ready for any of this yet, but I can't hide it any longer. I can't pretend I'm just your boss anymore ...'

Kylie took his hand, unable to meet his gaze. 'You've been far more than just a boss to me,' she said finally. 'You've been so loyal and understanding. I don't think I'd have got through it all without you.' She lifted his hand

and laid it against her cheek. It felt warm and comforting. Slowly Craig tilted her chin to him and kissed her again. This time she didn't draw away. It felt good, gentle. No, she wasn't ready for any real involvement now, but Danno was gone forever and maybe with time …

Bill Meadows coughed and walked in. 'Sorry Boss. I'll come back when you're free,' he said to Craig, who had busied himself searching through a pile of papers.

'What's up?'

'Nothing that can't keep,' replied Bill, nodding at Kylie.

'Whatever you like, mate,' replied Craig to Bill's retreating back and grinned across at Kylie.

Over the next two months as they worked the remainder of their assignment together, Kylie grew used to Craig being there for her, though she was glad he had made no attempt to kiss her again. His understanding and availability softened some of the anger and anguish she felt about the place and he was at pains to point out her contribution to the team's efforts. As their time in Sri Lanka drew to a close she felt genuine sadness at leaving the women and children she had worked with and grown close to.

The week they were due to fly back to Australia, she invited Craig to stay at Dunk Island and he accepted.

The weather was perfect back home, the sea deep turquoise. They strolled along the resort's dazzling white beach, the foam-edged water lapping at their toes.

'Would you ever consider marrying me?' Craig asked, casually throwing a stick for Tiger, who had grown to almost twice his previous size.

Kylie gave a long sigh. She knew she could never ever love anyone the way she had loved Danno, and nothing would ever eradicate the memory of that love, but she had the rest of her life to live, and while she didn't feel passionate about Craig, he did make her feel comfortable and safe. Kylie glanced up at him and then slipped her hand in his. 'Yes,' she said simply and let him draw her into his arms. She felt no passion when he kissed her, only gentleness and warmth. She hoped one day the passion might come too. For now, what she felt was enough.

After Craig left the island, Kylie sat down and put all her thoughts onto paper. She sat chewing her pen, the tears streaming down her cheeks, knowing she had to let go of Danno. When she'd finally finished writing, she rummaged around in a drawer and pulled out a battered flat box. Lifting the lid, she carefully spread apart the yellowing tissue paper to reveal the lock of hair she had kept after cutting Danno's hair that evening in PNG. Carefully she picked up the lock and stroked it, her vision blurred as she remembered every single precious second with Danno. It was all she had left of him.

She walked to the window and gazed out at the sea, the pain in her heart almost too much to bear. Gently she pressed the lock of hair to her lips. 'Goodbye, my darling,' she whispered.

Very carefully she replaced the lock in its wrapping, closed the lid and slid the box back into its hiding place. For a while she stood staring out at the sea, anguish descending over her. She stared blankly down at the words she'd written, knowing she had to find a way to move forwards in her life with Craig. But there was one more thing she had to do first.

Chapter Twenty

Kylie drove up in her hire car to the O'Keefes' house in Lyrebird Falls and parked on the opposite side of the road. She had gone over her speech a thousand times, how she was going to tell his parents how brave he had been, how lucky she had been to love him and have his love in return, how proud they should be of Danno and his work ... The more she stared at the house, the more she decided coming here was a very bad idea.

She felt deeply ashamed that she had not had the courage to write when Danno was killed. She twiddled the friendship ring Craig had given her, seriously thinking of driving off. The ring was stuck. She wriggled it and sucked her finger, finally yanking it off and placing it in the ashtray along with some spare coins. Her pulse quickening, she opened the car door, wiped her sweating palms down her cotton skirt and walked across the road.

It was a pleasant autumn day. A cool breeze ruffled her hair. It was always cool in Lyrebird Falls, she thought fleetingly. Her legs started to shake as she walked up the steps to the house. There was nothing she could say that would make Norman and Molly O'Keefe feel better about their son's death, but she hoped her visit might help a fraction and she needed to close the chapter. Heart thumping, she reached up and knocked twice on the big brass lion's head.

The wait seemed interminable. Finally Kylie heard footsteps. Her mouth dry, she watched as a shadowy figure appeared behind the frosted glass to the side of the door. The latch clicked and the door opened to reveal Molly O'Keefe.

A good-looking woman in her late fifties with short, tinted brown hair framing bright eyes and strong cheekbones, she was dressed in a smart fawn jersey dress that reached to her ankles; neat gold earrings and a thick gold chain with an embossed cross completed her attire.

'Hello, Mrs O'Keefe,' Kylie began, agitated.

Molly's face split into a delighted smile. 'Kylie! What a lovely surprise. Of course I remember you. How are you all? How is Dunk Island? I have heard great reports of the resort. You left a big hole in Lyrebird Falls when you moved. Come in. Are your parents with you?' She looked eagerly over Kylie's shoulder.

Taken aback by the effusive welcome, Kylie blushed then started again. 'I came on my own. I really didn't want to bother you, Mrs O'Keefe, but I wanted to offer my condolences about Danno ...'

Molly O'Keefe looked confused for a moment, then she exclaimed, 'Oh no, but Daniel's alive! It's a miracle really, after all he went through. Now I come to think of it, he mentioned in one of his letters that the two of you had caught up somewhere overseas. PNG, wasn't it? I guess it must have been. After that terrible tidal wave? I'm most terribly sorry. We tried to contact everyone. Come in, do please.'

Kylie gaped at Molly, not daring to believe her ears. 'Alive?' she whispered. Surely not — somebody would have told her, wouldn't they?

Smiling reassuringly, Molly put her arm around the trembling girl's shoulders and ushered her into the house. There was the sound of loud music playing inside somewhere. 'Come and see for yourself. Daniel's in the sitting room listening to some of that dreadful pop music he insists on having up far too loud. Listen to it! I don't have the heart to ask him to turn it down!' She stopped for a moment. 'I must warn you, dear, he's been very, very sick. He has been through so much. Don't get upset if he doesn't remember things. The doctors said it would be several more weeks before he regains his memory fully. How he survived all those weeks in the jungle, I'll never know.' She hesitated. 'Also, Kylie …'

But Kylie wasn't listening any longer. She had caught sight of Danno sitting at the far end of the sitting room, his chair turned to the window. Heart thumping against her ribs, she tore across the room, crying out his name, aware only that Danno, her Danno, was alive. She flung her arms around him, crying and laughing at the same time, then jumped back in fright as he fought her off with a blood-curdling shout.

'Danno, it's me, Kylie!' She stared back at the man she loved more than anyone else in the world, shocked at his haggard features and emaciated body, but even more shocked at his reaction.

'It's okay, Daniel, she's a friend of yours — Kylie,' Molly said firmly, quickly stepping beside him and stroking his arm. 'You remember Kylie. You told me you worked together.'

Danno turned his face towards his mother and Kylie realised with a sickening thud that he was blind.

'Well stand up and say hello,' insisted Molly, one hand under his armpit.

Danno stood up uncertainly and stretched his hand out in the direction of Molly's voice. 'Kylie?' he whispered after an agonising pause.

Kylie almost burst into tears. 'Hello, Danno. I hear you've had a pretty rough time,' she said shakily. She wanted to throw her arms around him, to stroke his poor, dear face and kiss his unshaven cheeks, but something in him stopped her, a reticence, a withdrawal. It made her go cold inside.

'It was interesting,' he replied in an attempt at a joke, still standing stock-still. 'Where were we working together? I'm not too good at remembering things.' He paused. 'Maybe that's a positive,' he went on with a half-smile. Suddenly he pressed his thumb and forefingers to his eyes, which had become all misty.

Kylie didn't know where to look.

'There you go, Daniel,' interrupted Molly briskly, stepping between them and guiding her son back into his chair. 'He gets very emotional. The doctors say that will pass too,' she explained to Kylie. 'I'm going to fix us all some lunch. My dear, why don't you stay and join us? It would be good for us both. Then when Daniel's having his afternoon nap, you and I can have a bit of a chat.'

'I'd like that,' replied Kylie numbly.

'Daniel, talk to Kylie!' Molly instructed, then left the room.

Kylie sat down close to Danno, the cold hand clutching tighter at her heart. He was just staring in front of him through those sightless eyes. All those months she had believed him dead. Now she didn't even know if he knew who she was. She daren't even touch him for fear of another outburst. She looked around her at the bright sunny room with its cheerful bowls of flowers and big picture windows and wanted to weep with misery for them both.

Beside Danno was a pile of books, the title on top screaming out at Kylie — *Beginner's Book of Braille*. She picked it up and opened it, running her fingers across the tiny raised dots.

'Heaven knows how you learn that stuff,' said Danno, sensing her movements, making her jump. He reached over to check she was holding the braille book. Their hands brushed for an instant and Kylie felt an electric shock run through her body. She turned her head to him, heart leaping, convinced he must have felt it too, but he gave no indication that anything unusual had happened between them.

'Do you remember us working together in PNG?' she started, trying to sound normal.

'Where's PNG?

'Papua New Guinea. Don't you remember the ride up the hillside to rescue that mad Dane, Fred, and walking along the beach in the moonlight? And the stench? I'll never forget the stench.' She searched for something to jog his memory, something to connect them, not daring to mention his disappearance in Sri Lanka for fear of upsetting him.

'Sounds pretty unappetising. Hey, I can read my first name in this stuff. Let me show you.' He went to take the book, misjudged the distance and knocked the pile of books onto the floor. He then started fumbling around and apologising, making things worse.

'It doesn't matter,' cried Kylie, quickly kneeling and picking the books up through a blur of welling tears. She couldn't reach him. He hadn't a clue who she was. She piled the books back on the table with shaking fingers. The titles shocked her. Most of them were about dealing with trauma and blindness — they must be for Molly, or perhaps she read them to Danno.

Molly walked back into the room, cheerfully announcing she hoped they were hungry as horses because she'd thrown together a rare feast. Kylie put on her brightest smile, shocked that she felt relief at the arrival of an intermediary.

Lunch was stilted and tense. Molly asked

again about Kylie's parents and her work, helping Danno with his food when he needed it. Danno politely asked Kylie what she was doing, unable to recall any of the team, hesitating over names and places. Misery clutched at her when he showed only polite interest in her descriptions of the activities they had shared. Dry-mouthed she struggled through her gourmet salmon and avocado sandwich, terrified she would start crying; afterwards she toyed with a freshly made Danish pastry, only politeness keeping her from fleeing the room.

Finally, having made Danno comfortable after the meal — explaining the doctors had ordered him to have plenty of rest — Molly suggested she and Kylie take their coffee out onto the back verandah. Kylie glanced back wistfully at Danno. He was almost asleep.

'Your mother always kept Sunburst Lodge so neat. Is she still happy running the resort?' Molly asked as she sat pouring freshly percolated coffee into white china cups, trying to keep the conversation light. Kylie gave a shaky smile.

The tree-clad mountains rose up splendidly beyond the chalet rooftops; the soft mountain breeze stroked their cheeks.

'I know it's a shock, dear,' said Molly gently, as she saw Kylie struggling not to cry, 'but it's not all hopeless. We're getting there slowly ...' She paused momentarily, her own emotions still raw from Danno's return. 'The doctors say that, given time and a good diet, he should completely regain his memory. He's much better than he was.'

Molly started rearranging the milk jug and sugar basin. The doctors. They were so dismal, always erring on the side of caution with their prognosis. She knew she was hanging onto straws, but they hadn't actually said he would never see again.

'The brain is an amazing organ, you know, able to reroute information and heal itself over time,' she said slightly too loudly, her eyes too bright. 'Goodness knows the poor boy's been through enough ... But tell me all about yourself.' She picked up her cup.

'Did the doctors say whether he would see again?' Kylie asked falteringly, terrified of the answer yet unable to bear the suspense of not knowing.

Molly's cup hovered near her lips, her face suddenly closed. She took a quick sip of coffee then carefully replaced the cup in its saucer on the table beside her. 'The doctors are being cautiously optimistic,' she replied. 'More coffee?'

Kylie shook her head. 'I thought he was

dead,' she whispered, tears spilling down her cheeks. She fumbled in her pocket and fished out a tissue, feeling as though her whole world was shattering around her.

Molly reached over and gave Kylie's hand a quick squeeze. 'I know, my dear, we all did.' She paused, staring at nothing, playing with her gold chain, remembering the day she and Norman had received the news of Daniel's death, their disbelief, the nights of torment at the knowledge of him dying in such a shocking way, their anger and grief. The simple memorial service had enabled them finally to let go and start picking up the threads of their ruined life, only to be turned upside down all over again by the call informing them that Daniel was in a Colombo hospital fighting for his life. When they flew out to Sri Lanka it was to find a Daniel who was so thin he was almost unrecognisable. Then they were told he was suffering from amnesia and was blind.

Back home, where he had to be attended around the clock, the doctors were amazed he had lived at all. They had diagnosed profound malnutrition and physical and psychological trauma, and they estimated that his shoulder had been dislocated for over a month. The nightmares, thank goodness, were becoming less frequent. A blow to the head had apparently caused his blindness. Amazingly, only the sight area of the brain had been affected. The doctors had seen this as a blessing. They had said they would have to wait until the swelling and bruising had healed before they could make any further prognosis. Although they hadn't actually said he might see again, Molly had clung desperately to that hope.

For the first month after he was discharged from hospital Danno had hardly spoken as he gradually learned to feel his way around his home. Then he became angry. It had been the start of a whole new dark part of their lives, brightened only by their love for their boy who had miraculously been returned to them alive. Recently Molly had brought home a set of talking books and a course in braille and announced to Daniel he would learn it.

'We are getting there slowly,' she repeated.

Kylie wiped her eyes and quickly stuffed the tissue in her purse, ashamed of her weakness in front of this woman who was so emotionally strong. 'It was such an amazing coincidence him showing up in PNG,' she said, smiling stiffly.

'I think sometimes things happen because they are meant to,' said Molly. She didn't know what the relationship between her son and this girl had been — and she was too discreet to ask — but she could sense the love Kylie felt for her boy and she was grateful for it. She found herself telling Kylie about the weekly therapy session, Daniel was having in Melbourne.

'The psychologist is very gentle and understanding and has dealt with hundreds of trauma cases. She says he is surprisingly together considering his ordeal.' She looked across at Kylie, wondering why she was revealing so much to this young woman whom she had never really got to know. Maybe it was like divulging your life history to a stranger on a train.

'You learn to notice every tiny change.' She sounded almost excited. 'Today was the first time Daniel actually felt confident to walk down to the post office with me. We've been working on trying to get him out of the house more. He knows his way around inside pretty well now.' She shook her head, thinking of the struggle she had even to get him to take his vitamin supplements, the fights over braille, his misery at having to be guided everywhere. 'Anyway enough of all of that,' she finished finally.

They chatted for a while longer about Susan and Geoff, Kylie's work; and they even laughed from time to time. As they talked, Kylie saw flashes of Danno's vibrancy in his mother and the reminders pierced her heart.

'How long are you staying in Lyrebird Falls?' Molly asked.

The question caught Kylie off balance. Falteringly, she explained she was planning to get married and had needed to close this chapter of her life, to say her final goodbyes to Danno. 'He and I got really fond of each other at one point, and when I thought he was dead ...' she stumbled, unable to stop the tears.

'I understand, my dear. It was a sweet and lovely thing for you to make the effort to come and see us. Molly patted Kylie's hand. Now you run along and have a wonderful life with your young man.' She stood up, once more in control, the businesslike woman who had made all her and Norman's endeavours so successful.

Kylie stood up with her, noticing for the first time the dark shadows under Molly's eyes. Her face was tired and drawn, the smile determinedly cheerful. She felt suddenly drained and shut out. 'Can I say goodbye to Danno?' she asked hesitantly.

'Of course, my dear,' replied Molly.

Danno had woken and was listening to his music, his hands playing with a smooth round pebble. Kylie felt a sharp stab of misery as Molly put her arm gently on his shoulder. 'Kylie wants to say goodbye, Daniel. Remember Kylie who worked with you in Papua New Guinea?' she repeated hopefully. 'He has memory lapses,' she said, wishing she didn't always feel the need to explain.

'Goodbye, Kylie. It was really kind of you to visit,' said Danno politely.

Kylie cringed. 'Goodbye, Danno.' Heart racing, she ignored his outstretched hand and instead hugged him, feeling him flinch as she kissed his cheek. 'I love you,' she whispered, hoping, praying for some flicker of recollection. Clumsily he kissed her back.

'Goodbye,' Kylie repeated hoarsely, cheeks flaming as she stepped out of his arms. Her vision blurred as she let Molly usher her from the room. 'Thank you for lunch and the chat, Mrs O'Keefe. If there is anything I can do ...' she choked.

'It was a pleasure, my dear. We'll be fine, thank you,' Molly said firmly.

Kylie fled from the house. Tense with misery, she drove off down the street, turned into the familiar main street and parked next to the public phone outside the bus station.

'He's alive, Mum, Danno's alive!' she cried when she finally got through to Dunk Island. Then she burst into tears. Through her sobs she explained Danno was blind and had amnesia, and that she had decided to go straight on to see Craig at his home in Wagga Wagga.

Susan's heart went out to her daughter. 'Are

you sure you'll be all right, darling? D'you want me or Daddy to fly down and join you?'

'No thanks, Mum. I'll be fine, really.'

'Love you,' said Susan, wishing her daughter's life didn't always have to be so hard.

'You too,' replied Kylie, feeling suddenly lonely.

The drive from Lyrebird Falls to Wagga Wagga took Kylie just over four hours and gave her plenty of time to think. With each hour she felt surer that she was making the right choice. By the time she turned onto the long dusty track that led to the beautiful, rambling old property that had been in Craig's family for four generations, Kylie had worked out exactly what she was going to say to him. He would be unhappy, of course, and she felt wretched at letting him down, but neither of them would want to be in a marriage that was doomed from the outset.

A flock of pink galahs flew up from the roadside, their loud screeches echoing across the countryside. Anyway, she comforted herself as tiny doubts crept in, he had always sworn he had her interests at heart and he would understand, he always had, that was his big strength. She sped up along the track, bouncing over potholes and ruts, and swung into the driveway. Stepping out she stretched, relaxed and smiled. It was a beautiful day. The house was beautiful too, flowers blooming in the garden beds just as he had described. She hurried across the wide verandah and slipped inside, calling for him.

Craig came hurrying in from the back in his overalls, delighted surprise splashed all over his face. 'Where the heck did you spring from?' he cried. 'I wasn't expecting to see you again so soon. Not that I mind of course.' He grabbed her, swung her into his arms and kissed her.

Kylie kissed him back briefly, her stomach tightening at the knowledge that she was about to shatter his happiness. 'Craig, we have to talk,' she said, her hand tapping anxiously against his shoulder.

'Uh-oh! Sounds ominous, but for you, my darling ...' He tried to kiss her again.

Kylie pressed both hands flat on his chest, holding him off. 'No, I mean really talk. I just drove down to Lyrebird Falls.'

Craig stiffened and released her. 'Oh yes? Beer, wine or a soft drink?' he asked, fear gripping at him. Casually he turned from her and headed for the kitchen fridge. She wasn't wearing his ring.

'A beer'd be good.' Kylie followed him into the kitchen. Craig twisted the top off two bottles of lager and handed one to Kylie. She took a quick slug, suddenly noticing his pallor. 'Are you okay?'

'Never better, especially now you're here.' He drank deep.

Kylie took a deep breath. 'I've just driven from Lyrebird Falls. Danno's alive.'

Craig didn't move a muscle. He just stared at her, mouth tight shut.

Kylie let out a great rush of air, realising with a start that she had been holding her breath. 'He's alive, Craig, alive! she repeated. Isn't that amazing and wonderful?' Then she told him the whole story, tears spilling unashamedly down her cheeks.

Craig felt as though he'd been slugged in the guts. Somehow he'd just kept on hoping she'd never find out. Stiffly he stepped towards her and wiped away a tear, his fingers shaking. 'Darling Kylie,' he said very quietly, his eyes never leaving her face. He relaxed fractionally. She didn't know the truth.

Kylie grabbed his hand and kissed it, loving him for being so emotional with her. 'I know this all makes everything different for us, but I knew you'd understand, I knew you'd be happy for me ... for us. You're such a good man.'

'Different? How does it make things different?' asked Craig. His voice was clipped now.

Kylie looked startled. 'Well, you know, I mean, you've always known how I felt about Danno ...'

'Sure, and that's lovely, and I wish him all the best. I'm not sure that it'd be appropriate to ask him to our wedding, if that's what you were thinking.' He forced himself to smile at her again, forced himself to stay calm. He went to try and kiss her.

Kylie stopped him. 'Look, we need to talk about this.' The knots in her stomach were tightening. 'You see, I have to help him ...'

Something snapped in Craig. 'You're not suggesting to me we throw away everything we have together so you can martyr yourself to some blind cripple who doesn't have the faintest clue who you are?' he shouted.

Kylie looked at him in horror. She had never heard Craig sound so vitriolic. 'You don't have to shout,' she cried, tears starting in her eyes.

'I'm sorry! I'm sorry, darling. Maybe I was a bit harsh. I feel just as stunned as you. It's such a shock. Blind! You've had a terrible few days. I understand, but you and I, we have a life, we have plans.' Craig was struggling to control his rage and burning hatred for a man who even half alive had managed to confound his plans. 'Jesus! I should have left the bastard die,' he muttered, turning away. He shouldn't have lost it with

Kylie. Darn it, where was his self-control? He was losing her. He couldn't, not now.

'Plans can change ...' Kylie froze. 'What did you say?'

'I need another beer.' He stormed over to the fridge and grabbed another bottle, twisted the top off and hurled it at the sink. 'Are you trying to tell me it's all over between us? You're going to finish it just like that?' He couldn't think straight. Even after all his efforts the lousy creep was going to steal her away.

'You knew? You knew? All this time you knew Danno was alive?' Kylie screamed, eyes blazing.

He grabbed her by the shoulders, staring at her with what seemed like hatred. 'Yes I knew, and I knew that if I told you, it would do nothing except destroy what we had. It wouldn't give you back the person you thought you once loved. He's gone, Kylie. He doesn't exist any longer. I did it for you, Kylie, for us. I love you, I need you and you need me.' His voice was back to normal. He slackened his grip and tried to draw her to him.

Kylie backed away. 'You knew all along!' she whispered. All those intimate moments they had shared, the tender words of comfort he had given her, the tearing misery he had let her go through when a single tiny sentence would have given her hope ... She went at him, fighting him, wanting to hurt him; her nails bit into his cheeks, her fingers tore at his shirt as she screamed out her anger and hurt, her humiliation that she could have let herself be so deceived.

'How could you do that? How could you say you loved me and not tell me? Why? Why?' Suddenly she didn't want to be near this man, be in the same room, the same house. All she wanted was to get as far away from Craig as possible, never to set eyes on him again. She held her hands in front of her face, fighting him off as he tried to wrap her in his arms, calm her, tell her that they still loved one another, they still had something worth saving. She fought free and made a bolt for the door.

Craig was too quick and he blocked her exit. 'You want to know why? I'll tell you!' he shouted. 'The fucker was always around, hanging off you, mauling at you, writing sentimental crap. D'you honestly think I enjoyed seeing all that?' As he raged on Kylie found herself becoming more and more calm. Quietly she waited as Craig ranted, red in the face, pouring out his vile abuse for the man she loved.

Finally he drew breath. 'Now you know the truth. I hope you are satisfied. You can get out now! Get out!'

It was the venom in Craig's eyes that finally

rocked Kylie's outward calm. She started trembling with fear. 'Well I guess now I know,' she said quietly. She slipped past Craig as he wiped his eyes, letting down his guard for an instant, snatched her purse from just inside the main room and raced from the house. Flying across the verandah, she leaped into the car and locked the doors.

He came after her, begging her forgiveness as she fumbled with the key in the ignition. He beat his fists on the window, wrenching at the door handle, begging her to wait, to listen, pleading that he could explain everything, that it could still work.

The engine burst into life. Kylie spun the wheels and raced away from Craig and the nightmare she had been part of. An ochre dust trail billowed in her wake.

She was shaking so violently she had to pull over once she reached the open road. Choked with misery and disgust, she kept wiping away tears that streamed down her face. She felt dirty and used. And it was not until she had put thirty kilometres between her and Wagga Wagga that she finally convinced herself she was safe.

Chapter Twenty-One

Back on Dunk Island, Kylie did little else but eat and sleep for the first few days. By the end of the week she had revived enough to escape to the bay and sail around with the turtles. Sometimes she took Tiger with her, but she hardly uttered a word to her parents. Finally, with the colour returning to her daughter's cheeks, Susan decided it was time to break through Kylie's wall of silence.

'You can't sit around here forever, you have to make a decision about what you are going to do,' she said one morning as they sat in the sitting room, Kylie still in her pyjamas. 'Bottling everything up is simply making things worse.'

Kylie dragged her gaze away from the view out of the French windows. 'I'm not bottling things up, Mum. I'm so exhausted I don't know what I want.' She had lain awake in bed for the last few nights, churning everything over and over in her mind, driving herself mad. Seeing Danno again had made her realise just how much she loved him. His memory was coming back, Molly had said so, and his blindness, well, they'd cope with it together. It was just that Molly had been so contained, so in control, there didn't seem to be any room for another person in their lives. And Danno ... If only he had remembered something about their love and not treated her like a polite friend.

'Indecision can be exhausting,' said Susan, trying to sound positive. 'Once you put some purpose back in your life you'll start feeling better. Are you going to continue on with your aid work?' While she hated the idea of Kylie setting off for foreign and potentially dangerous parts again, she had seen the joy her daughter's work overseas had brought her. Getting involved again would force her to focus on something other than this whole ghastly tragedy. 'You don't have to go overseas straightaway. You could always do something in Australia with the Red Cross or one of the other emergency services. They're always looking for people.'

Kylie shook her head. 'If I'm going back to it, I'll do it properly.' She picked at the arm of the chair. 'I've sort of got a contract later in the year if it comes off. It's not in immediate crisis work but something more ongoing, rebuilding communities, working with displaced children.' She gave a long sigh. 'I dunno, Mum! I just don't seem to be able to get enthusiastic about anything.'

Susan looked closely at her daughter. 'What do you really want to do, darling?'

Kylie's eyes filled with tears. Finally she said, 'I want to be with Danno.' She swallowed. 'It's just that I don't know how.' She gave a shuddering sigh, her green eyes huge in her tired face. 'Molly was very nice and everything but she's so ... so self-contained ... as if she can manage and anyone else would just be in the way ...' Her voice trailed off.

'Don't be too hard on the woman. She's going through her own private hell,' said Susan quickly. 'She and Norman went through the whole grieving process, then tried to get back to their lives. Then the son they thought was dead turns up without warning, terribly ill, blind and not even knowing who he is.' Susan shook her head. 'Darling, she's got to come to terms with a whole new set of conditions. She's not coping. She's doing what she's done for every person that's walked into that resort for as long as I've known her, putting on a show — my guess is she's struggling badly, and so is Norman. She's a strong woman but a very private one. I've always admired her ability to cope, but

Norman's a handful on his own, let alone all this other stuff she's got to deal with. We were never close. Molly wasn't that sort of woman but a couple of times she confided in me when things got a bit hard. I think we both helped each other.'

Kylie looked contrite. She remembered the weariness she'd seen in Molly's face. Maybe the woman wasn't as together as she appeared. Mother and daughter sat in silence for a while, lost in thought.

Finally Kylie said, 'S'pose I rang her and said I wanted to come down and help, d'you think she'd let me?' She felt scared at the thought, not knowing how she would cope with Danno's blindness, but she couldn't bear just to sit and do nothing. 'I mean, I could offer to help with the shopping, go for walks with Danno, maybe sit and talk. Be company. It couldn't hurt. Molly was saying he gets around the house really well already. I miss him so much, Mum.' Her throat constricted. 'You don't know till you've tried, that's what you and Dad always taught us,' she finished with a gulp.

Susan's heart turned over as saw the tiny spark of hope in Kylie's eyes. 'Darling, Danno may be blind for the rest of his life. He may never fully recover his memory, and you don't know what other damage might have been caused ...'

'Don't, Mum, please!'

'I'm just putting the worst-case scenario so you think before you walk into all of this,' said her mother gently. It wasn't only Danno who had been damaged. The girl had been through so much. Susan couldn't bear to stand by and see her be completely crushed. Every instinct in her screamed out to dissuade Kylie from going back to Lyrebird Falls, to protect her, to get her to make a new life without Danno. Yet in doing so she knew she might become yet another person hurting her. Kylie had to find her own way. 'I can't make this decision for you, darling, and it would be wrong of me to try. You have to decide how you want to live your life. Go with what feels right for you. All I ask is that you take a long hard look at the realities of the situation before you make up your mind.'

Tiger was scratching and whining at the French windows. 'I guess I've known the answer deep down ever since I saw him again,' Kylie faltered. 'I want to go back to Lyrebird Falls and be with him, Mum, whatever happens. I love him so much ...'

'Then if that is what you want, do it. Just don't burn all your bridges yet, hey?' Susan put her arms around Kylie and hugged her close. 'You are so precious to me, my darling girl. I love you so much. I can't bear to see you hurt any more.' She kissed her daughter's soft cheeks, blinking back her own tears, remembering how it had been when Kylie and Gwyn were little girls, how they had laughed and romped together. She missed the sound of laughter around the place. Maybe one day it would return.

'Oh Mum, thank you for understanding,' said Kylie. 'I've worked it all out.' There was a new energy in her voice. 'I'll get a part-time job with Parks and Wildlife at Lyrebird Falls, there are still heaps of people there I know, so it shouldn't be too hard. But I won't burn all my bridges — I'll leave things with the aid work as they are till the last possible moment.' As she spelled out her plans she sounded more and more confident, and Susan thought that the bright, energetic Kylie they all knew so well was starting to re-emerge, to take charge of her life.

Her heart swelled with pride at her daughter's courage. 'Fine, darling, no burned bridges, no shut doors,' she repeated, hugging her again.

Opening the French windows, Kylie called to Tiger who ran to her, his whole body wagging with pleasure. There was a new spring in her step as she walked out of the room, Tiger trotting behind. Susan watched her go, hoping she was doing the right thing in encouraging her to go back to Danno. She turned into her office, trying to get her head around the day's activities. No, she thought, gathering up some papers with a sigh, Kylie was a mature adult and this was a decision she had to make for herself.

Three weeks later, having talked her way into a part-time job with the Lyrebird Falls Parks and Wildlife, Kylie walked back up the steps of Danno's house, her legs shaking like jelly, and knocked on the door. This time Molly O'Keefe was expecting her. Kylie had rung to say she planned to work at Lyrebird Falls for the next few months and asked if it would be agreeable if she visited Danno on a regular basis. She had offered to do anything she possibly could to help his recovery and went on to explain how close she and Danno had become and how much she loved him and she believed he had loved her.

After Kylie had hung up, Molly had carefully replaced the receiver and then, for the first time since Danno's return, walked over to Norman, pushed aside the paper he was reading, sat on his knee and burst into tears. Today she opened the door bright and cheerful, every shred of the inner turmoil that was now part of her daily life concealed.

'Come in, Kylie, my dear. We've all been so looking forward to you coming. Daniel's memory is greatly improved. He's just been telling me some of the things you got up to in Papua New Guinea. My, you did have a few adventures.'

'That's fantastic!' exclaimed Kylie. Putting aside all her reservations, she hugged Molly, who suddenly had to turn away, complaining of something in her eye. Mum's right, Kylie thought with relief, there's more to this woman than she lets the world see.

'Who is it, Mum?' called a voice. Kylie's heart turned over.

'It's Kylie, dear. Let's go inside,' said Molly, ushering Kylie through the door. Danno stepped into the hallway and Kylie's heart turned over again. Silhouetted against the light, she could almost forget there was anything different about him. His was wearing the aftershave he always wore, and the smell took her back to PNG and Perisher and Sri Lanka.

'Danno! How are you?' she asked, not sure of her reception.

'I'm good, and yourself?' replied Danno. Then he started apologising for not having known who she was when she visited before.

Kylie cut him off, telling him that she was now working in Lyrebird Falls and asking if it was all right with him if she came up on her days off.

'That will be very nice for you both,' said Molly, a fraction more relaxed. 'Daniel's memory is almost back to normal. There are gaps and we're still going to therapy, but every day he is progressing.' Kylie wished she wouldn't talk about him as if he wasn't there. They were all still standing awkwardly in the sitting room. 'Well, I might get back to my garden,' said Molly abruptly, feeling the two needed time alone. She hurried out of the room.

Kylie fiddled with her bag. 'I hear you've been telling tales of our adventures to your mother,' she said, grinning, slightly uncertain.

Danno reached out and found her hand. 'Nothing too private,' he said gently. 'Kylie, I thought …' His voice cracked. Still very emotional, he struggled to gain composure. 'I thought I'd never see you again. When Mum started telling me about your visit, I was horrified at my behaviour. I don't even remember it. Then bits started coming back. I hope I didn't say anything too crass.'

'Only that it was really nice of me to visit and that you had no idea how people learned braille.' Kylie bit her tongue at her clumsiness in referring to his blindness almost before they had said hello.

'I still don't, but I am getting better. Mum's a real dragon over it.' He was still holding her hand. 'There are still heaps of bits you're going to have to fill in for me, but what I do remember is how much I love you.' He reached out and felt for her face, then kissed her slightly hesitantly on the mouth.

Kylie felt an enormous weight roll off her back. A great rush of joy swept through her. She melted into his arms, kissing him back, tears of relief seeping from under her closed eyelids, running down her cheeks and splashing onto Danno's hands.

'Hey! This is supposed to make you happy!' murmured Danno. Cupping her face in his hands, he gently ran his thumbs down her cheeks and brushed away her tears. 'My beautiful sweet Kylie,' he whispered. Then he kissed her again, this time more confidently. Her perfume enveloped him and for a few seconds he forgot he was blind as he held her trembling body next to his. Then he drew away. 'Perhaps I ought to let you take off your jacket and offer you a cool drink,' he said, feeling his way to the table where Molly had left drinks in preparation for Kylie's arrival.

Kylie laughed shakily, quickly reaching for the jug. Their hands touched and Kylie halted, annoyed at herself, suddenly remembering how Molly had specifically asked her not to try and help too much. 'It sounds heartless, but it's all part of him getting used to his condition,' she had explained.

'I can manage, it's okay,' said Danno, feeling for the glasses. Laboriously he spooned in ice then poured them both a glass of orange juice. Kylie watched in an agony of anticipation. 'There you go,' he said finally, holding out her drink in slightly the wrong direction.

'Oh I'm sorry, Danno, I didn't mean to try and take over!' apologised Kylie.

'Forget it. I'm used to people thinking I'm totally incompetent. That's why I'm perfectly happy for you to be my personal nurse. That is why you've come, isn't it?'

The words hung in the air. Kylie wasn't sure how to respond.

'Kylie! I'm joking! What happened to your sense of humour? Actually I'm not. I'm deadly serious. When Mum told me you were coming around, I was hoping you'd wait on me hand on foot. I'm much better at getting around the house but the furniture keeps moving and I really am sick of bashing my shins,' he finished with a cheeky grin.

Kylie laughed and gave him a good-natured punch, but she had not missed the anger and lack of confidence that lay beneath his flippant comments.

She drank down her orange juice, removed his glass and walked back into his arms. There were adjustments to be made and it was no good being too sensitive about everything. 'You have no idea how good it feels to be hugged by you,' she whispered after a long time.

'Oh yes I do!' retorted Danno, kissing her all over again.

Kylie visited Danno as often as she could. She and Molly had decided at the outset it would be less strain for everyone if Kylie stayed in lodgings elsewhere. Realising they both needed time to adjust, Kylie had agreed. Each night she went back to her lodgings planning what they might do, where they might go next time they were together. Before Danno lost his sight he had known the district so well. She decided it shouldn't be too difficult to get him learning his way around again. She also realised that while everything seemed the same on the surface, emotionally they were light years away from where they had been in Sri Lanka. Yes, he had kissed her and declared his love for her, but she felt an invisible barrier between them. Determined to be patient, she said nothing. Instead she ploughed her energy into helping Danno readjust to the outside world and into filling in bits of the missing jigsaw in his memory.

'Do you still have our little talisman?' she asked one morning when they were sitting in the local coffee shop drinking cappuccinos. She stared out at the pretty village street lined with trees wearing their rich autumn colours, aware that Danno could see none of it. He turned to her with a puzzled expression.

'Don't you remember? You carved all those wonderful toys for the kids, and you sent me a little carved pig.' Kylie reached over and took his hand. 'It was the last thing I gave you before … well, before. It nearly broke my heart seeing the children waving their little toys as they ran about laughing and shouting, me believing you were dead.'

Danno's face lit up as another part of the jigsaw slotted into place 'I remember. We had this D & M about me and my "seeing" my carvings. You must have thought me such a wanker. You insisted I took the pig with me before I set out on —.' He stopped. 'It must have got lost in the jungle,' he said abruptly.

It was on the tip of Kylie's tongue to ask him about what had happened, but something in his face made her decide against it. Instead she jumped up and suggested they go for a walk by the creek that had become one of their favourite visiting places. Gradually they had been taking walks further afield, relearning the local terrain as Danno got more confident using his white stick. The village had been easy, and this particular spot was one of the prettiest, with its tiny creek and huge boulders that in the wintertime were covered with snow.

'Why don't we go skiing again when the snow comes?' suggested Kylie, leaning against the small bridge, the creek bubbling merrily beneath them.

'Are you crazy? I'm blind, in case you've forgotten.' A shiver ran through Kylie. It was the first time she had heard him say that word in all the weeks she had been with him.

'So?'

'So I'd be a total liability on the slopes. Apart from having to avoid killing myself, I'd probably wipe out most of the population of Lyrebird Falls.' He started to laugh at the picture.

Kylie started laughing too. 'Well, the populations always was too big in my opinion!' She drew him to her and kissed his warm lips. At this moment she felt closer to him than she had since deciding to return.

On an unseasonably warm late autumn day, Kylie suggested they go on a picnic up into the mountains. Agreeing on the spot, which had been one of Kylie's favourite places as a little girl, she drove them along the steep mountain track off-road from Kosciuzko Pass and away from the usual tourist routes. The first snow had fallen up here and the surrounding countryside was painted with a light dusting of white. As they wound their way up the hillside she started describing where they were, what the valley looked like, and to her delight Danno interrupted her, describing every bend in the road, telling her when they were approaching a particularly steep hairpin and when they were almost at the top of the secret lookout she had escaped to many times as a kid.

'There's not much wrong with your memory. If it was your favourite spot, why didn't we bump into one another up here?' She explained exactly where they had parked, then helped Danno out of the car. She handed him his white stick and, slipping her hand in his free hand, led him up to the big rock that overlooked the valley and the mountains beyond. The sun shone brilliant in a clear cobalt sky, the eucalyptus trees enveloped in their familiar misty blue, their distinctive perfume wafting around.

'It's like sitting on the top of the world,' sighed Kylie, drinking in the fresh crisp beauty.

Danno sniffed the pungent eucalyptus and listened to the myriad sounds around them, his fingers playing with a dried gum leaf as he absorbed the peace that invaded the surrounding bush.

Happily they spread out their picnic in a sunny sheltered spot and tucked into the delicious food Kylie had gone to extra trouble to prepare. She popped the cork of the champagne, trying not to think too much of the time they had made love at Highpeak Lodge in Perisher Valley, then they sat chatting quietly, birds calling through the trees.

Danno turned his face to the wind and felt the lichen on the rocks, enjoying its dry roughness. He stroked the tiny alpine flowers, guessing at their brilliant colours.

'D'you remember this? It's one of my favourites.' Kylie guided his hands over the velvet of a deep purple flower, describing the colour as closely as she could, saying it was somehow dark and mysterious.

'Like your eyes. Only yours are dark green,' smiled Danno as he fingered the delicate petals. He turned to Kylie. She held her breath, feeling the atmosphere suddenly charged between them. Neither of them said it, but they were both thinking that he would never again look into her dark green eyes.

'What happened in the jungle?' asked Kylie gently.

Danno closed his fingers on the flower and

accidentally snapped off the head. Feeling around, he picked up the flower head and twiddled it around in his fingers. Then he started talking.

'It all started out pretty ordinarily. We were driving in convoy, with me at the back, and then a tyre blew. A local bloke came up looking for a lift and offered to help in return for being dropped off at one of the villages along the way. I was really grateful to the poor beggar. Those wheel nuts can be really tough to shift, especially on those old tanks. I, in my wisdom, thought the short cut was the only way to catch up and that it was clear of landmines. We would have never gone a different way from the others if we hadn't had to spend so much time changing the wheel. When we hit the mine it was that poor beggar that copped it, while I was thrown clear. His was the body they found.'

The awful irony of it was that Danno had lain hidden and semiconscious for several hours not far from the track. But no one was looking for another body. Danno didn't remember all the details of what happened directly after the explosion. His next recollection was waking up in a village hut with a throbbing headache and a shooting pain in his right arm. Some of the women in the village looked after him and nursed him back to health. Just as he was starting to regain some strength, work out who he was, and plan to get back to camp, the village was attacked. Still weak, Danno was asleep in his hut. He remembered choking smoke, flames licking the grass and crackling through the coconut-frond roofs, gunshots, terrified screams, people fleeing in all directions. Then being dragged clear of the burning hut by the woman who had been caring for him. He was set upon by a group of men who repeatedly beat him with their rifle butts and kicked and spat on him; they finally left him for dead and Danno crawled into the jungle, struggled to a creek and collapsed into unconsciousness.

When he awoke he had no idea where he was or how he had got there. He estimated it had taken him a week before he had had the strength to do more than struggle to the creek, sip water and pick at a few berries close by, hoping they weren't poisonous. He tried to wash his blood-encrusted wounds, but excruciating pain shot through him at the slightest movement, and he realised he had dislocated his shoulder. He remembered laboriously feeling for the leeches and picking them off his body, and wondering why the snakes that slithered across his legs hadn't bitten him. At one point he had almost given up.

'I kept focusing on your eyes. I kept thinking

of the love in them, of your lovely face. Thinking of you saved my life.' Danno stopped a moment, unable to continue. Kylie was clutching his hand, weeping openly. He started talking again, more slowly now, telling how one day had blurred into the next as he had become progressively weaker from loss of blood, lack of food and constant pain. Too sick to make it to the creek, he had sucked the moisture from leaves and used larger leaves to trap water. For once he had been thankful for the tropical rains. At one point his hopes soared when he smelt smoke and cooking aromas drifting invitingly across the still air. Somehow he had got up and stumbled to a clearing at the edge of a shallow ravine. He thought he could hear voices. Convinced he was finally on his way out of his misery, he started climbing down. Losing his footing he slipped, bashed his head and fell into a creek, where the current swept him downstream.

'That's the last I remember until I came to in the hospital. That was when I realised I was blind. Then Mum and Dad brought me home.' He lay down, propping himself up on one elbow, feeling the sun on his face. A kookaburra shouted in the treetops, one of the familiar friendly sounds he had longed for when he had felt so alone and desperate, a sound that helped block out those terrible memories that still haunted him.

'Kylie?' he said, alarmed, realising she had been silent and still for too long.

'I'm here, Danno.' Kylie went to him, shocked to the core.

Danno folded her in his arms. 'It was you who saved my life,' he repeated. Then he crushed her to him, kissing her passionately. He buried his face in her hair. 'I could drown in the smell of you,' he murmured. His hands stroked her face, her eyes, her lips, and then he kissed her again with such tenderness that Kylie felt her whole being opening up to him.

'Make love to me, Danno,' she whispered.

Slowly and gently Danno undressed her, kissing her soft warm flesh, revelling in her closeness, knowing her beauty as plainly as if he could see. His fingers trembled as his longing mounted. Kylie closed her eyes and gave herself to him, tears of happiness spilling over and trickling down her cheeks. Aching for him, she gasped with desire as he slid into her and she was lost in the wonderful whirlpool of sensations that sucked her down then spiralled her up until she thought she would burst with love. She felt his release and she was overcome with a great rush of joy and then contentment as their bodies relaxed together.

She marvelled that she could love and be loved so deeply.

'I didn't believe love could be like this,' whispered Kylie after a long time. She rolled over and snuggled close. The sun was starting to lose its heat now. Danno didn't reply. 'Are you awake?' she nudged. She reached over for her T-shirt, pulled it quickly over her head, and handed Danno his. 'You're very quiet. Couldn't you handle it? Have I exhausted you completely?' she joked, less certain. 'I think that deserves another celebration. Is there any champagne left, or did we scoff the lot?'

Danno felt for the bottle, misjudged the distance and knocked it over. The pale amber liquid spread across the rug. 'Damn,' he said, making a big deal of trying to mop it up.

Kylie laughed, snatching a tea towel from the picnic basket and dabbing at the wine. 'Here, let me! You're making it worse!' Their fingers touched and she was still. 'Danno, I love you so much. I don't care that you're blind. It doesn't matter. We can still have all the things we dreamed of, I'll be your eyes.' She wanted to recapture the wonderful intimacy and was confused at his sudden emotional withdrawal.

Damn it! She had taken over again and now he was upset with her, she thought angrily to herself as Danno fumbled for the champagne bottle and tried to fill her glass. It was always the little things. 'It's empty, Danno,' she said softly.

'I know. I'm not a complete imbecile,' snapped Danno, pulling on his T-shirt. Immediately he started apologising for his rudeness.

'What did I do wrong, Danno?' she asked, watching him finish dressing, resisting the temptation to help him.

'Nothing. Forgive me. My behaviour was inexcusable. You are the most beautiful woman I've ever known, and the most loving,' he said softly, but the intimacy was gone. He stood up unsteadily. 'Let's go home. It's been a great day but I'm really tired.'

Their relationship deteriorated after that. Kylie was confused by Danno's sudden emotional withdrawal and his refusal to discuss his strange behaviour on the mountain. She put it down to the fact he was still trying to come to terms with his blindness, which, she had to remind herself, was still very recent. She decided to ignore it and instead ploughed on, pretending everything was as normal, accepting his fluctuating moods.

Autumn faded and the poplars and liquidambars shed their bright yellow and orange leaves, exposing their bare branches. Kylie remembered she had to contact the aid agency about her next posting. Unable to bear the thought of leaving Danno with things as they were, she made a snap decision and told the agency she would have to let this one go and would make contact as soon as she was ready to take on another assignment. She felt marginally better having made a decision.

The next day they went for a walk down to their favourite spot. The weather was crisp and sunny, but the wind had an added bite. Kylie walked with Danno to the edge of the creek and trailed her fingers in the water. It was icy cold.

'Have you ever thought of becoming a potter?' she asked out of the blue. Her excitement increased the more she thought about it. Danno was so good with his hands, and he had always been so happy when he was working at his carvings. 'There's quite a contingent of potters around here and the clay's supposed to be pretty special in some areas. If you get into the whole commercial thing, potters can make quite a decent living …'

'A bit like basket-weaving for poor pathetic cripples,' snapped Danno. 'I'm not some lame dog you need to find a way to entertain, you know.'

'I never said you were. It was just a thought.'
'Well drop it.'
'No, I damn well won't.'

The whole thing escalated into a huge argument, ending with Kylie refusing to speak to him, wondering if there was any point in staying at Lyrebird Falls much longer, and starting to regret her decision not to take up the aid position. Finally, a week later, Danno rang her at work and apologised, saying he was being quite unreasonable, that he missed her dreadfully and could they be friends? Kylie put down the phone and burst into tears.

It was snowing — the first real dump of the year. Overnight the world turned white and the temperature plummeted. The ski season had just started and this was exactly what the resort managers had been praying for. It also jerked Danno out of his moodiness. Arriving at the O'Keefes' Kylie was surprised to see him standing on the front lawn, covered with a layer of snow. His arms were outstretched, his face turned to the heavens; snowflakes landed on his cheeks and whitened his sleeves.

'What are you doing?' exclaimed Kylie, bounding up to him.

'Catching snowflakes!' he replied with child-like excitement.

'You're completely mad!' cried Kylie, joining him, face to the sky, blinking as snowflakes splashed onto her eyes, delighted to find him so happy.

'Yes! But does anyone care?'

'Will you let me take you skiing?' Kylie asked, her heart giving a little lurch of fear that she might shatter this cheery mood.

'Who said it'd be you taking me? Have you forgotten I'm a bloody good skier?' laughed Danno. He followed her laughter as she made him run around the lawn. When he caught her he wrapped her in a hug.

'I don't care who takes who. Let's just get up there and murder those slopes!' retorted Kylie, beating at Danno in playful frustration.

'I'm sorry I've been such a beast,' apologised Danno softly.

Kylie kissed the tip of his nose, then, linking arms, they went in search of skis and ski gear. Afterwards they spent half an hour allaying Molly's fears, Kylie reassuring her that all he had to do was to remember what it was like in a whiteout where sighted people had to ski by feel.

By the time they were dressed and ready to go, it had stopped snowing and the sun was out. Danno was looking tense and slightly white around the mouth as they lined up for the quad chair with the small queue of early season skiers but he relaxed when the chair slowed almost to a stop so they could climb aboard. Holding onto his poles as well as hers, Kylie helped Danno into the seat and quickly pulled the safety bar down as the chair moved up the slope. She described where they were as they sped up the mountainside, the slopes beneath sprinkled with skiers and ski-boarders.

Alighting at the other end proved not quite as easy as Kylie had hoped. In fact, it turned into a bit of a disaster when Danno lost his balance coming down the ramp and fell in a heap. He had to half shuffle, half be dragged sideways out of the way of other skiers getting off the chair, which badly bruised his pride and his confidence. Once back upright, Kylie talked him towards the slope, which he remembered from his years on the mountain, then she grabbed the end of one of his poles.

'Think white-out. Relax your legs, lean away from the hill and keep hold of this pole. If instructors can do this teaching kids, why not us?' she said brightly. 'I'll tell you to go left or right or if anyone's in your way. All you need is to get your balance back.'

Inching a very underconfident Danno to the edge of the gentle slope, she waited till he was ready then pushed off. Their first few attempts led to more disasters, partly through lack of confidence, partly because Danno's hearing had become so acute since his accident that he flinched and pulled up at every sound. Feeling like a rank beginner, he gripped the pole between them too tightly and kept swinging round onto her. Several times he knocked them both to the ground, Danno not at all comforted by her giggles and kisses as she pulled him to his feet. When he fell on top of her for the fourth time, he swore roundly and started to take off his skis.

'What are you doing?' cried Kylie, trying to stop him.

Danno pushed her off. 'Can't you see this is a complete waste of time? All I'm doing is spoiling a lovely day you could be having on the slopes.'

'Oh, right! Mr Poor-Me-I-Can't-Do-Anything. Dig yourself into a hole and bury yourself, see if I care!' Kylie was angry now, partly at herself because she hadn't been able to guide him better.

'That's not fair! Kylie, face reality. Blind people don't ski!'

'Sighted people ski when they can't see five centimetres in front of them, so what's the difference?' shot back Kylie, determined to jerk Danno out of his defeatist thinking. 'Anyway do you really think I want to be up on this mountain without you? Daniel O'Keefe, you are such an arrogant fool, don't you understand anything?' She glared at him. 'What happened to the gung-ho skier who swore he could beat me down Murphy's Run blindfold? Well now's your chance.'

Danno had the grace to look sheepish. He jammed his boots into his skis and snapped the binding. He shoved away the guiding pole she held out to him. 'Blindfold it is!' he shouted. 'Just be sure you yell loudly enough.' Then he pushed off.

Heart in her mouth, Kylie raced beside him, warning him of bends in the run, shouting for him to swerve round a snow boulder, lean left or right, dodge other skiers. They arrived at the bottom both laughing and shaking like leaves. Danno did a superb stop, snow shooting out from behind his skis. Kylie fell onto him with relief. 'Not sure I was quite ready for that,' she panted.

'May I come to your class tomorrow, please miss?' Danno asked cheekily.

'If you promise to behave,' Kylie shot back happily.

Over the next week they went skiing as often as they could and by the fourth day Danno's confidence had skyrocketed and they were skiing much faster, his black moods a thing of the past. Sometimes they went in tandem, with Danno behind Kylie, holding onto her waist; sometimes they skied side by side, Danno amazed at how easily his skill returned. The days were the happiest and freest for them both since Kylie's return to Lyrebird Falls, and she rejoiced in them.

Friday was one of those perfect days that skiers wish for at the start of the snow season. It had snowed all night, coating the mountainside. The stunted snow gums were still heavy with snow from the fall, which continued in soft flurries tossed in the air by the breeze, as they travelled up the chair.

Wending their way down their favourite slope, Kylie skied alongside Danno, telling him how proud she was of him and what fun she was having. He grinned in her direction and challenged her to a race. Dashing after him, she yelled at him to stop but he laughed and sped on, relying on her verbal instructions. Finally he stopped, panting and leaning on his ski poles, his face alight.

'Now we do it my way!' cried Kylie, ordering him to get behind her and hold her by the waist.

'You're getting too bossy by half, not that I really object to holding you like this,' shouted Danno, obeying and giving her an extra squeeze.

'This is only the beginning,' warned Kylie, then she shot them down the mountainside. Zigzagging across the slope, warning Danno in advance, she jumped over a couple of tiny moguls. Danno, feeling her body prepare to make the jumps, anticipated with her and they sailed over easily, falling into a natural rhythm together.

They took off towards the trees. Danno knew when they were in amongst them because he could feel the temperature change. And he had a strange sensation of lightness behind his eyelids. His heart gave a tiny lurch. It had happened once before. It was like a thinning of the blackness he had become accustomed to.

Kylie felt his heart thudding against her and her pulse quickened as they wove their way through the dappled shade. Snow still clung to the gumtrees; the sunlight flickered on their clothes and dazzled her as unexpected rays pierced the overhead canopy. Slowing down, she halted beneath two gnarled old gumtrees, their snow-laden branches entwined.

'We're in amongst the trees,' she whispered, carefully stepping around to face Danno.

'I know,' he murmured. 'Tell me what it's like. Does the sunlight stream through the trees? Does it catch in your gorgeous red hair? Is the wind shaking little flurries of snow around us?'

Kylie let her skis slide towards Danno. 'It does all those things. It's like the place you first kissed me. I love you so much,' she whispered, then she pulled his mouth gently onto hers and kissed him long and hungrily. She felt a tiny hint of resistance, then he kissed her back with all the passion and longing she had felt when they had made love on the mountainside, and she exalted in the sensations that flooded over her. There was something else, an energy that flowed between them that made her want to cry.

'It's the legend of the snow gums,' she said, her eyes searching the face of the man she loved so deeply. 'How does it go? "To be kissed beneath the snow gums, their gnarled branches twisted and ... something or other ... is to experience love at its most pure and its most devilish ..." That'd be right, Mr O'Keefe! "... only immeasurable sacrifice can bring peace to the lovers." I reckon we've had the immeasurable sacrifice bit, and I have never felt more peaceful than I do now.' She reached up to kiss him again, but he stopped her.

'What?' she laughed.

'I wish you hadn't said that,' he replied bluntly.

'What? About the legend? It's just a lot of words. Romantic, poetic words. I know you think it's a heap of —'

'My darling, beautiful Kylie. I love you as I have never loved anyone and I do not believe I will ever love anyone this way again.' It wasn't his words but his tone that made her shiver.

'Except for our kids, I should bloody well hope not!' interrupted Kylie. 'Let's get out of here. It's creepy,' she said, the magic suddenly evaporated, wishing she hadn't mentioned the stupid legend.

'Kylie, please ... you're making this even harder.'

'What?' Now she was genuinely afraid.

'Kylie. This isn't working ...'

'What isn't working?'

'You, me, us!'

'What have I done now? Go on, tell me! You're not getting away with all that silent treatment rubbish again!' she shouted, anger welling up inside.

Danno fiddled with his pole. 'I know I've been very difficult to be with over the last few weeks and I'm really sorry. I never meant to hurt you. I love you so much it hurts.'

'So what's all this about then?' asked Kylie with a sudden surge of hope.

'After we made love on that picnic ... that was when I realised that it would never work. Making love with you was so sweet, so utterly fulfilling, and then —'

'Then I said, "I can be your eyes",' said Kylie, wishing with all her being she could take back those words. 'But I can! What's wrong with that? People are supposed to support one another in a relationship.'

'No, that wasn't it. What I realised was that I couldn't do this to you. I couldn't ask you to give up your life for me.' She tried to interrupt but he rushed on, knowing he had to do this for them both. 'A relationship is just what you said — two people supporting one another. With us it would always be lopsided. You would always be having to support me. Whatever hopes Mum has filled your head with, forget them. I am blind. This is it for the rest of my life. This is reality. I can't do that to you, ask you to live with a cripple. You have so much to give, so much that you can do …'

'Are you trying to tell me you don't love me any longer?' asked Kylie.

'It's because I love you so much that I have selfishly let this drift on for so long, living only in the present, unwilling to look further into the future. Believe me, I cannot bear the thought of life without you, but neither can I bear to destroy what we have by asking you to stay. I've gone over and over this in my mind. This is the only way. We have to stop seeing each other. You have to get on with your life and let me get on with mine.'

'Ah, we're into heroics now. Poor blind man sacrifices all for his love. You can't be serious!' she spat. Then her anger deflated and a terrible realisation came over her. He was terrifyingly, deadly serious. 'Danno, please don't do this to us! Please, I beg you.' She clutched onto his jacket, shaking from head to toe. 'It will work, it can work if we want it to. We can work it out together, please, Danno, I can't bear the thought of life without you and if you feel the same it's so silly ...' She couldn't go on. This wasn't happening, this couldn't be happening.

Danno gently removed her gloved hands from his jacket and held them in his. They were both trembling, both struggling to control their tears. 'It would work for a while, my love, then it would tear us apart. You would resent me for being a burden and I would resent you because I had to lean on you.' He lifted her chin and gently kissed away her salt tears. 'It would be so much easier if I could hate you,' he whispered.

Kylie straightened. 'Well, there's not much more for me to say, is there?' She was suddenly furious that he could so completely ignore her feelings. 'We love one another, Danno! How can you be so cruel, so selfish? Don't you care how I feel?'

'Let's go back. There's nothing more to talk about,' said Danno, almost grateful for her anger.

Kylie raised her arms and let them fall again in despair. There was nothing she could do. He had told her he didn't want her around any more. She turned and led him through the trees out into the sunshine. The slopes were busier as holiday-makers took advantage of the warmth and great conditions.

'You'd better hold onto my pole. It's safer that way,' she said mechanically. Blinded by tears, she skied them to safety and then drove Danno home.

'Shall I bother to come and see you tomorrow?' she asked, feeling as if her heart would break.

'It's up to you. I'd understand if you didn't,' said Danno.

'Right, so that's it!' she said and drove off.

Danno stumbled up the stairs and fumbled at the lock, finally inserting the key and opening the front door. A hollow sensation settled around his heart. He had just said goodbye to the last piece of real happiness in his life.

Kylie parked the car in a spot outside her lodgings, switched off the motor, put her head in her hands and cried her heart out. Why was he doing this to them? Couldn't he see she loved him more than anyone or anything in the whole world? Why couldn't he understand she didn't care that he was blind, that it could work, that all she wanted was to be with him? Well obviously he didn't feel the same about her. It was over. She had better get used to the idea. She blew her nose and reached over into the back for her jacket and purse. She stepped out of the car and locked the door. One thing she knew for certain was that if she could not change his stubborn refusal to understand the depth of her love, she would not let losing him crush her completely. She had been through too much for that. She stopped a moment, staring up at the remains of the day, her mind back under the snow gums. 'Goodbye Danno, my darling,' she whispered then marched into the house. Somehow she would have to get on with the rest of her life.

Chapter Twenty-Two

Kylie shifted carefully in her plane seat so as not to disturb her sleeping neighbour. She glanced at her watch in the dimness. Five hours and she'd be landing in Brisbane, and with luck she'd be home on Dunk Island by midafternoon. She was exhausted after spending the past eight weeks helping flood victims. She stretched carefully, pulled her thin blanket around her shoulders and settled back with a sigh to watch the movie for the third time in the past few flights. It seemed to be the only movie the airlines had been showing for weeks. She thought of Dunk Island, the soft swish of the surf on the beaches, the cool breeze, anything but Danno. Thinking about him brought on anunbearable emptiness. She hoped the year's posting overseas she had just accepted would help her put it all behind her. She dozed off.

She woke cramped and chilled. Snuggling

further under her blanket, with one hand she lifted the window blind two centimetres. Sunlight came flooding in on top of clouds so thick and fluffy they looked as if you could walk on them. They reminded her of snow and Danno. Damn it, everything reminded her of Danno. It didn't matter that she worked herself into exhaustion, there was always this huge feeling of grief hanging over her. At least after Gwyn had died there wasn't always this crushing hope that things might work out, and that had somehow made it easier to move on from.

She removed her earphones, that had slipped down around her neck as she slept, and reached for the newspaper she had been given on boarding the plane. The flight attendants were coming round with orange juice, heralding that breakfast would not be long. She accepted her drink and started flipping through the newspaper. She'd definitely go out on one of the hobbycats when she got home, and she'd go horse riding up the back of the island to see the great old vine trees with their huge roots hanging above the ground and watch the guineafowl scuttle through the undergrowth.

Her eyes flipped down the page. Same boring stuff, same arrogant critics. Then a tiny paragraph buried between items about an exhibition of nude paintings and a bold new production from the Australian Ballet Company caught her eye. It read: 'The weekend saw the opening of a special exhibition of sculpture and pottery introducing young blind sculptor Daniel O'Keefe who captured the interest of not only the local galleries but national buyers as well with his outstanding work …'

Kylie's heart turned over. It couldn't be — not that quickly. The words blurred as she read how Danno's tragic loss of sight had been the linchpin in discovering his extraordinary talent. The exhibition was being held in conjunction with celebrations of the opening of a new wing of the O'Keefes' main resort hotel.

'Would you like breakfast, madam?'

Kylie looked bemused. The male flight attendant repeated the question. Nodding, she accepted her tray, suddenly back in Lyrebird Falls with Danno telling her that pottery was no more than basket-weaving for pathetic cripples. Well, he hadn't gone for the basket-weaving, she thought, feeling slightly hysterical. He hadn't wasted any time either. That was her Danno.

She felt a strange mixture of sadness and excitement bubble up inside her at the sudden thought that sprang into her mind. She would fly to Lyrebird Falls before she flew out to her next assignment. And she would make the trip for herself. She would make no attempt to meet with Danno. In fact he need never know that she had even been there — but she needed to go. She needed to see for herself the success he had made of his life so quickly and to say her own silent goodbyes to the man she loved, goodbyes that in her misery and anger had not been said when they had parted so abruptly.

He was blind. So as long as she kept out of his way and the way of people who knew her, her secret was safe and she would not run the risk of him thinking she had returned to blackmail him with her misery. No, that was not the purpose of her visit. In fact she felt a sense of release at learning of his achievements. All she wanted now was to take one last look at the man she loved and finally shut the door on this chapter of her life. Deep down she knew this was the only way she would find the inner peace and strength she had been searching for to make it possible to move forwards, and maybe even find happiness again. The more she thought about it, the more she knew she had made the right decision.

It was blowing a blizzard when Kylie arrived. She took a room in a small motel at the far end of town, then spent the best part of the next hour getting chains fitted to her wheels. Her nervousness was increasing with every minute. For once Danno's blindness was a blessing in disguise. If he was there, as long as she didn't speak and no one used her name, he need never know she'd been. Pulling on her gloves with shaking fingers, she drove up the long winding road to Lyrebird Falls Resort.

Norman had been busy and the new wing was looking very impressive with large floor-length windows and a modern angularity to the entrance hall. Bending against the wind, Kylie walked in, keeping her hood up to reduce the chance of being recognised as she bought a catalogue of the exhibition. Several people were milling around in the vestibule but they were all strangers.

Heart pounding, Kylie walked into the exhibition and looked around. There was a large, rather ugly mound of metal to one side and some local pottery. None of it was Danno's. She walked on. The place had the almost holy silence that exhibitions seem to attract, people speaking in low whispers. Kylie walked along, wondering if she had read the article correctly, then she stopped and her heart flew to her mouth. There was her unicorn. Carved from pure white stone it rose graceful and strong on its hind legs, its intricately carved horn raised to the sky, its gentle eyes watching the world. Kylie stared at it, feeling its energy, feeling the love that had gone into its making. Tears spilled over her cheeks and down her face. They were tears of sorrow for what might have been, and tears of joy for the beauty that Danno had created.

'Amazing workmanship,' muttered a short fat man next to her, and she realised she had been staring transfixed for some time. 'Got to have had some help. Can't see how a blind person could produce something as good as that.'

Kylie glanced at the man in scorn. 'I mean, it's not possible,' he continued. 'No, he had to have had some help. Must have been a publicity stunt that father of his dreamed up.'

Incensed, Kylie turned on him. 'How dare you spread such vile rumours! Of course it's genuine. The artist is a genius.' Her voice was loud now but she couldn't stop herself. 'Why did you bother to come here if you're just going to —'

'Kylie?'

She felt a hand on her shoulder and froze. The man scuttled away. Slowly Kylie turned as if in a trance. She had opened her big mouth and he had found her. Fear clutched at her stomach; fear of what, she wasn't quite sure — maybe of seeing the man she still loved and realising he no longer felt the same.

'How did you hear of the exhibition?' asked

Danno as if they had just parted yesterday. 'What do you think?'

Kylie went on staring, unable to utter a sound, wondering if she should run from the room. It felt so awful standing in front of him, caught like some truant child.

'I've been overseas. I read about it on the plane home,' she said, finally finding her voice. She gave an embarrassed laugh. 'Amazing coincidence, I know. There was this little column singing your praises. I was so excited when I read it. I'm about to fly overseas for a year so I thought I'd sneak in and see what they were on about. I wasn't going to worry you.'

Neither of them spoke. Then Kylie said, 'The unicorn is amazing, I'm so proud of you.' They stood facing one another, Kylie twisting the end of her tartan scarf.

'It's so good to hear you,' said Danno tentatively.

'Is it?' she replied, staring at him, glad he couldn't see the tears glistening in her eyes. Angrily she brushed them away.

'It was you and your damned basket-weaving,' he said. 'I was so angry with you I wanted to prove you were wrong. Then I realised I was "seeing" the shapes just like I always had and once I started Mum insisted on sticking a piece out the front of the resort, and then all this happened. It's all happened so fast. I've got all these orders. I got two from Japan yesterday. I can't believe it. I have to thank you for my new life.' He reached for her, his hand on her arm. She snatched it away, terrified if she let him touch her she'd break down completely.

'So now you have a life. Congratulations, I'm really happy for you.'

'Now I have a life,' he repeated. Neither moved, the tension between them holding them like magnets. 'Thank you for coming to see my work,' said Danno softly. It was like feeling heaven just out of reach having her standing so close. He didn't know what to do, he really didn't. How could he ever expect her to forgive him after what he had done to her? He had needed the space, that had been true. He had really believed that his blindness would tear them apart, that until he got back his self-respect nothing could work. Not a day went by that he didn't tell himself that if he could only have predicted that all this success would happen with such whirlwind speed, it would all have been so different. But now it was too late. The one woman who could make his life complete was standing in front of him but he had lost her.

The snow was still beating against the big windowpanes, the wind buffeting around. A giant fir tree shook violently, sending snow showering everywhere.

'That bloody legend did its stuff all right. Where does the peace bit come in, that's what I'd like to know,' said Kylie with a pitiful attempt at a laugh. She longed to go to Danno, to feel his strong arms holding her, to turn back the clock and make all this misery go away. She didn't think she could bear much more of this pain. She should never have come. She had to get out of here.

'I wish we could be together but I know you don't want that and I respect your decision, I really do. I never meant to come and bother you,' she explained. But suddenly words started tumbling from her lips, words that told the truth, words she couldn't control. 'That's a lie! This whole pretence is a lie. I hoped like hell I'd bump into you, that you'd change your mind and see reason. All I want is to be with you, Danno, that's all.' She was shouting now, out of control. People were staring at them but she no longer cared. She just wanted Danno to hear her, to believe her. But then she saw the pain on his face, saw the embarrassment.

'I'm sorry, Danno, I never meant to hurt ... I'm sorry,' she whispered and fled from the room. Outside she was grateful for the stinging pain as snow pelted against her face. The wind was blowing the snow almost horizontal; visibility was down to a few metres. She bent her head and stumbled across the snow-covered lawn, half sliding, half running down the icy steps towards her car. Tears were streaming down her face. She ran faster, stumbling and sliding, thinking that if she could just get away, the physical pain that seared through her would stop.

Danno stood frozen. He had been given one last chance and he'd blown it. What a fool he was! Why hadn't he shouted over the top of her, shoved his pride away and told her the truth, that without her his life was nothing. No sculpture, no big orders, nothing could replace the joy and fulfilment he felt when he was with her, and the emptiness when she was not. He was such a stubborn, pig-headed fool.

'That was quite a performance,' laughed one of the potters, clapping Danno on the back. It was all he needed. Maybe it wasn't too late.

He stumbled out of the building as fast as he dared, bumping into people, reeling back, apologising. Frantic, he started across the lawn, swishing at the air with his white stick, searching for the steps. He called out against the wind, desperate, hopeless.

Suddenly he felt a gentle hand under his

elbow. 'Can I help you, young man? You're Daniel the sculptor, aren't you? I really love your work …'

'You have to stop her! The girl who just ran down that way.' He pointed frantically in the direction of the road. 'She's about my height, slim, flaming red hair and she's wearing a …' Jesus, what was she wearing? It had felt like …

'Brown woollen coat and tartan scarf? I see her. Stay there. Hey, excuse me, miss.' The woman took off down the steps, shouting and waving her umbrella. Danno felt for the edge of the steps and found it. He knew this path so well, yet his legs just wouldn't work quickly enough. He heard a car start and his chest tightened in panic. He'd know that sound anywhere. It was the way she stabbed at the accelerator before putting it into gear.

A woman tapped imperiously on the car window. Kylie wound the window down and stared out aggressively.

'There's a very agitated young man looking for you,' shouted the woman, pointing back towards the resort.

'I know, thank you. Tell him I had to go.'

'He needs you,' insisted the woman equally firmly, her hand on the window Kylie was about to wind up. 'I think he loves you ... Oh my goodness.' She gave a gasp as Danno slipped on the steps and fell, slithering and sliding, banging his head.

Kylie leaped out of the car, heedless of the freezing wind that grabbed at her coat. 'Oh my God! What have I done?' she cried, racing towards him as fast as the icy road would let her. 'Danno!' He was half sitting, half lying on the steps, one hand to his head. He looked towards her voice and immediately scrambled shakily to his feet.

'Kylie! I've been so wrong ... I wanted to tell you inside ... I love you. I want to marry you.'

'Is this some kind of bad joke?' said Kylie, colour rushing to her cheeks.

'I've never been more serious in my life. After all I've put you through, I wouldn't blame you if you refused, but please, please say you'll marry me.' There was silence. 'Answer me,' he begged, the wait unbearable.

Kylie hesitated. With three strides Danno had swept her in his arms, wrapping her shivering body with his jacket. Ignoring her resistance he kissed her long and hard. And Kylie let him kiss her, the tears oozing from under her eyelids and trickling down her cheeks.

'You really have to stop all this crying. It makes for very soggy kisses,' teased Danno, his voice husky. Then he kissed her again, and this time it was with all the longing and passion and love that he had held in for so long.

'You are such a stubborn idiot,' murmured Kylie. Her whole body was tingling from his kiss, and she no longer wanted to fight him.

'My darling Kylie, will you marry me?' whispered Danno.

'My dear, sweet, impossible Danno, yes, yes, if that is what you want.'

'Then that's settled at last,' said Danno with a sigh. He traced his fingers down her face, her high cheekbones, the lips he loved so much. 'You're right about one thing, I am a stupid stubborn idiot.' Then he kissed her again and a great peace swept over her.

Above them a huge snowgum shivered and danced, showering them with more snow. They were so lost in each other, they didn't notice. But watching from a distance, alone, was the woman who had run to stop Kylie. She was huddled into her coat, thinking of the old legend. She dabbed at her eyes with a sigh and then turned and walked away.

Kylie slipped her arm through Danno's and they hurried back into the warmth. Just before they stepped inside, she suddenly realised something was different. He was striding with more confidence. He wasn't searching with his cane. It was so subtle she had almost missed it. Her heart gave an involuntary leap and she glanced quickly up at him, unsure whether to say something.

'I like your brown coat and tartan scarf,' he said.

Kylie hardly dared breathe. 'That lady who beat on my car window told you,' she cried.

'You're right. She did.' Danno paused. 'Actually, though, I thought the scarf was only one colour.' Then he told her about the strange flashes he had experienced, the sense of a lightening of the blackness around him. Lately it had been tiny flashes of light and today, after he had fallen, he had seen a faint shadowy shape hurrying towards him. It had made him wonder if his mind were playing tricks, but it had been there. It was still there.

Kylie listened, hardly daring to believe as he told her about the strange sensation he had had under the snow gums on the ski slopes that day he had said it was all over between them. He'd known then that he had been pinning his hopes on it too much and it had made him all the more determined to let her go.

'There still could be a chance — a very slim chance — that I might regain my sight ...'

Kylie silenced him with her fingertips. 'I love you, Danno, I love you so much. Of course that's great news and it would be wonderful, but I don't care that you're blind. All that matters, my darling, all I want is to spend the rest of my life with you.'

Wordlessly Danno wrapped her in his arms and kissed her once more, wondering what he had done to deserve such great love.

Outside, the snow gums nodded and danced in the wind.

Song of the Bellbirds
Anne Rennie

From the bestselling author of Reach for the Dream *comes a bittersweet tale of love and heartache, set against the vast wheatfields of Queensland and the glittering opera houses of Europe and America.*

All young Lizzy wants to do is sing, ride the boundaries of her family's Queensland property and dream of one day performing on stage. But when a freak storm hits the area, wreaking havoc and bringing tragedy, she swears never to sing another note.

Lizzy, however, has a voice as uplifting as the pure beauty of the song of the bellbirds, and others are not quite so willing to let her remarkable talent go to waste. There is the loving but ambitious Sister Angelica, a natural teacher; the vibrant and dangerously attractive Maestro Leonardo Rominski, whose charms Lizzy finds irresistible; and the irrepressible Gran, whose love sustains Lizzy through thrilling highs and crushing lows.

But it is Lizzy alone who will ultimately decide if the price she must pay to sing is too high ...

ISBN: 0 7318 1018 X

Messy Business
Jacqueline Ross

Sure. Motherhood has given Sue a gorgeous one-year-old, Sam but it has also given her saggy breasts, grotty responsibilities and a butt even a mother couldn't love. After two years in a sex-free zone, Sue wants to get out there and have fun. How hard can it be? All she needs to do is ditch the chocolate addiction, switch off the telly, suck in the stomach, wipe the baby puke off her shoulder and find a man made in heaven. Her disgustingly fit-and-sexy flatmate, Linda, suggests Sue take control, put an ad in the personal pages and say hello to a new life and great possibilities. No problem.

Messy Business is a romantic comedy about babies, playgroup politics, sex and relationships — and a girl's discovery that her best advertisement is appreciation and respect for herself. Jacqueline Ross hilariously rubs the gloss off all those motherhood myths and tells it like it is.

Jacqueline Ross is a mother who has managed to survive the babyhood of her two children — but only just. She has written two books for children and a novel, *The Third Room*, for young adults. This is her first 'grown-up' novel.

ISBN: 0 7318 1010 9

The Disciples
Andy Shea

This is my fantasy. My dream. I have made it come true. I enjoy what I do. I enjoy the terror ... This is the way I want to live. Nobody can stop this, only me. And I don't want to stop.

A brutal serial killer known as the East End Slasher is stalking the streets of London. Each victim is horribly mutilated and branded with the sign of a cross, a sign that another disciple has been claimed. As the bloody trail of violence and depravity continues, it is up to Detective Inspector Clive Johnson to solve the case — and save his career. In desperation, Johnson turns to an FBI criminal profiler for help.

Working closely with the press, through ambitious journalist Dan Hyde, the police tighten the net around the Slasher but the killer manages to stay one step ahead. Dan's photographer girlfriend, Tracey Preston, becomes caught up in the terror as the body count rises and the city becomes paralysed with fear.

Andy Shea, a former London policeman and journalist, writes with chilling realism. *The Disciples* is an intricately crafted thriller that will keep you guessing until the very end.

POCKET BOOKS

ISBN: 0 7318 1072 4